(Le...)

10·01·2012

Karam's Kismet

Sohan S. Koonar

This book is dedicated to

Ken Hunsberger

Chapter I

1938

Sant Baba was a tall man, his large head completely shaved and framed by wing-like ears with lobes stretched low by huge steel earrings. His eyebrows were mobile, going up and down collectively or individually as the hazel eyes they adorned fixed themselves on the supplicant before him, the usually mobile face relaxing into a mask-like inscrutability, questioning, probing, and seeking the truth. No one lied, boasted, beseeched, or bothered the monk. Such was his effect.

His left hand held the gnarled staff with a brass ring encircling the bottom end that made the staff ring like a bell as he struck it on the cobbled street, announcing his presence, and his right hand extended the begging bowl forward for alms. Housewives scurried into their homes or hovels and rushed forth with a roti, a cup of flour, or a rock of *jaggery*. Besides the flowing saffron robe he wore, two cotton pouches hung on either side of him, their belts crossed across his barrel chest like bandoliers. He threw the flour into one pouch and the *jaggery* into the other, allowing only the cooked roti into the bowl, and he bellowed a blessing.

The only other ornament the barefoot giant had was a string of worry beads, rubbed shiny by years of passing through his rough fingers. He walked the entire village, not missing a street, a turn, a gate, or a courtyard. He called everyone by name, even the children—particularly the children. If they answered his question properly and had it confirmed by the mother or father, he rewarded them with a piece of the *jaggery*, a treat for the child. As such, he was usually followed by a squadron of children as he made his way through the village. Even though a Hindu, he accepted alms from the Muslims and the lower castes, including the untouchables. He joked with and picked on his benefactors, occasionally berating an odious or rude one. His voice thundered and made the addicted, the drunk, or the wife beater cringe and shrink into himself. Sometimes he lectured a particularly harsh mother-in-law and comforted her victim with soothing blessings. He could quell a simmering or escalating feud by banging his staff onto the ground and growling a curse at the combatants. It had an instant effect, and he had done it for the forty-odd years that he had lived as a monk in the communal woods a few hundred yards from the village. There he had served his guru tirelessly and now taught the ways of the mendicant to a couple of novices. He rebuilt his frail hut after each monsoon and bolstered it with another layer of insulating mud to pass the cold of winter.

He made no claims to holiness or enlightenment. He preached even less, mediated disputes, and counseled the troubled. He practiced the ancient art of healing through herbs and potions, both for his fellow humans and their cattle.

He was venerated by the entire village—by the Sikhs, the Hindus, and the Muslims as well as the odd Buddhist or Christian. He embraced them all. He was a living icon, the glue that held the community together.

It came as a shock when he did not come to the village for alms for several days. Soon it was whispered that he was laying deathly sick in his hut. Speculation rose sky high since only his disciples were allowed in, and they said little.

A sort of panic spread through the village, and people began to perform short pilgrimages to his hut, desperate for a sight of him or news of his well being.

A group of monks arrived and camped outside the hut in a vigil. These monks were apparently fellow disciples of his guru and thus of a brotherhood with the stricken monk. Each morning they begged alms in the village. A sense of doom descended on the community, the monks represented a bereaving party, only prior to a death. The villagers asked them in hushed whispers of their beloved monk. They in turn smiled beatifically and pointed to the sky. "Only Rama knows," one said. The other invoked Shiva, and so on it continued for a month.

Others turned up for a day only to return to their *deras* by nightfall. Families in the village sent for relatives, daughters who now lived a married life in other villages, or cities to come for a final benediction of the dying *Guruji*. A committee was formed to consult with the clutch of visiting monks and gurus for advice on how to honor the man after his passing. Women sat watch in groups. Children played but were subdued. It was as if the laughter and joy had been stolen from the village. So great had the influence been of the gentle giant.

In the courtyard of the *Chura*, the *Charmen's* clan, a different sense of anticipation was rising. Punna, the prettiest of the clan's wives, was pregnant again after having given birth to two daughters. "Perhaps this one will be a boy," intoned her garrulous and domineering mother-in-law, starting to be defanged by age, and white circles beginning to line her irises, the first sign of impending cataracts and insidious blindness. She guarded the entrance to the street for they could not afford a gate, and the pariah dogs and ferial cats were ever vigilant to pounce on an unguarded basket of roti. The *peepal* tree that shaded the courtyard was also a residence to crows, a thieving airborne menace to the poverty-stricken clan.

"You should pray to the monk," advised another crone squatting next to her with her walking stick at the ready to strike at any stray animal or bird that dared sneak by.

"I do, I do," cried the grandmother. "Prayers alone cannot suffice. One also needs to be able to afford alms."

The crone nodded, aware that the monk had given more to the children of the courtyard than the adults had in return to him.

"Pledge a sacrifice, perhaps a fast."

"If the gods so wish, I pledge my life," raising her hands to the sky and sighing. She suddenly lashed out at a mangy dog trying to take a flying dodge past her into the courtyard. "Get out, you filthy cur!" both women now shouted, and a well-placed strike at the animal's hind sent him scurrying off down the street.

"No sister," the crone protested, "the gods give you a long life to enjoy many grandsons."

And they got back to the business at hand.

The novices begged for butter or ghee, oils and pieces of hard, dried wood, and baskets of cow patties. They were preparing for a cremation, and the village deluged them their generosity. Plans came together in whispered discussions. The villagers dug holes to build temporary cooking pits for the funeral was to be followed by prayers, a fire worship ceremony, and a feast of sweet rice cooked with dried fruits and sultanas in saffron-infused water and white sugar. The headman gave a kilo of cloves to make the rice fragrant, and another family gave a bag of cardamoms. All activity came to a halt except for the necessary tasks of feeding the cattle and milking them. Most women and girls of age started fasts after long baths of purification and wore white, the color of mourning. A pall settled over the area.

One night, the pariah dogs set off a wail of howling, a sure sign of impending death, sending shivers down every spine. When the next dawn broke, the sound of a conch blown by a novice announced the inevitable: The monk had entered the *SatSagar*, the sea of truth, and now his soul swam to its other shore for salvation.

For a while, chaos reigned as people came off their cots, threw on a chador or a shawl, splashed water on their faces, and stepped onto their streets. The line of mourners stretched from the ring road all the way over the round dunes past the village pond and onto the orchard part of the woods where the monks lived. Their chanting now filled the air, and soon it was fragrant from the butter tossed onto the fire in front of the hut. The *pooja* ceremony had begun. The villagers, hands folded in respect, bowed their heads and sat down wherever they could, the men separate from the women. When one started to keen, a senior monk shouted "Quiet!"

Sant Baba had long abandoned his ties to the worldly ways, and his death did not warrant weeping and wailing. A holy man was not bereaved in the usual manner a man of the world would be. A holy man was honored with prayer, ritualistic customs, and ceremonies of purification; and those too by his fellow monks, above all his disciples, both of whom were preparing his still warm body for a ritual bathing before being wrapped in his saffron robes to be placed on the funerary pier. By midmorning, the woods were alive with crowds, which had now arrived from nearby villages and hamlets, and the air was thick with the acrid smell of wood fires.

The body lay, tightly wrapped from top to toe, on a wooden frame in front of the hut. One by one the people walked by, hands folded and heads bowed, some silent, others whispering prayers but most moist eyed. When all the Brahmins, *Jats*, the middle castes, the Muslim *Gujjars*, and the *Chamars* (shoemakers) had filed past, the *Chura* clan was allowed to pay its respects to a man who had treated them as equals. They shuffled by in silence except for Punna, who gave out a visceral shriek at the sight of the suddenly diminished looking remains. Immediately hushed by her elders, she was helped away and collapsed at the foot of a mango tree and whimpered long into the day and long past the rites.

After satisfying himself that all the necessary rituals had been observed, the senior monk nodded and the novices lifted the frame, *arthi*, and gently set it down on the funerary pier constructed of carefully piled wood, cow patties, and kindling. Then they lathered the body with oil and tins of clarified butter, *ghee*. A ceremonial blowing of the conch shells was followed by incantations, and the older disciple performing the duties of a son lit the pier and bashed in the skull with the point of a stick to prevent it from exploding during the cremation. The flames quickly rose and soon engulfed the entire pier and the body. The air grew thick with the sickly smell of burning flesh and fat, the throaty incantations of the monks, and the whimpers of Punna and the odd, uncontrolled keen of a woman or two overcome by emotion. An attendant expertly tended the fire, making sure it burned hot and long so that it would leave no evidence except for teeth or very small bones of the expired monk.

Then the monks turned on the hut, taking it apart with

their hands and throwing any flammable portion or part of it onto the pier, assuring that no worldly evidence remained of Sant Baba.

The villagers all filed over to the fire pits where the sweet rice and tea had been made and sat down in rows to receive the funerary feast. By the next day's dawn, even the pile of ashes had been gathered, the base of the hut swept away. The monks began one final round for alms; going door-to-door they received generous amounts from the upper classes. Then they walked into the courtyard of the *Churas* and the *Chamars* and those of the less fortunate and distributed the flour, the *jaggery*, and pieces of cloth they had gathered. Keeping only a day's supply of cooked food, they filed out of the village and onto separate paths, not stopping to help the older disciple who was now busy building a shelter for the night in the same woods he had shared as home with Sant Baba for the last ten or more years. He would stay, but only if his mind settled and calmed. If not, he too would start on a journey.

One week later, the headman tallied the pledges of money and informed the village that enough had been raised to build a *Samadhi* in memory of Sant Baba. It would stand on the site of the hut. He gave the task of constructing it to the bricklayer clan. Soon after, bricks arrived on the backs of a line of mules and cement was delivered by cart from the town six miles away. Foundations were dug, and the noisy job of building the edifice started. Volunteers pitched in, and it was finished in five days. After allowing it to dry, workers applied several coats of whitewash. The disciple performed circumambulation around the *Samadhi*, purified it with incense, and blew his conch shell to let his deceased guru know of its completion. Then he fasted for three days and meditated, seeking guidance from the departed spirit.

On the fourth day, he entered the courtyard of the *Chura* clan and called out for Punna. She lay exhausted and delirious with happiness on her cot, holding her newborn son, and at the sound of her name, she lifted herself up. But she did not get up and step outside the door, afraid that bad spirits could attach themselves to the newborn. Her mother-in-law had already raced over to the monk and invoked a blessing. "I have come to give a gift from my guru to the newborn," the monk said as he smiled.

"A gift, and for my grandson!" The old woman was dumb with amazement. Nothing like this had ever happened before: a monk bearing a gift for a *Chura* baby.

"Yes," the monk explained patiently as the rest of the clan gathered around him. "It was given to my care by my guru and I must give it only to the mother."

They ushered him into Punna's one-room hovel, and he squatted beside her bed. He waved the following away from the doorway, as their huddling at it blocked the only source of light.

"May the blessings of the gods and all the goddesses be upon the child," he said placing his hand in benediction on its head. Then, seeing Punna's puzzled reaction, he continued.

"My Guru knew that you would be blessed with a boy, Punna, and he knew that the child will be special. So he gave me one of the beads from his *mala* as an amulet for the boy." He put the ancient and shiny bead onto her outstretched hand. "Make sure he always wears it around his neck so that the *Param Atma* will recognize him and always protect him."

Punna bowed her head as tears filled her eyes and began flowing down her drawn cheeks.

"Do not cry, oh lucky mother of this blessed baby," the

monk admonished. "All your dreams will be fulfilled by this child. Just make sure he turns to good deeds only."

And with that said, he rose, and without acknowledging anyone, he marched out of the hovel and the courtyard and onto a path leading away from the village, the woods, and the *Samadhi* honoring his Guru.

Chapter 2

*S*he named her son Karam. The father, Ruldu, and the extended clan deferred to her wishes. The Sant Baba had personally blessed the child with the gift of his only known and existing worldly possession, the prayer bead. It now rested on his tiny chest, necklaced by a strong, black thread.

After the requisite forty days of rest and recuperation indoors, Punna stepped out and let the boy be carried in the eager arms of his many kin, including some only a year or few older. He had large brown eyes and a mess of thick, wavy hair, his skin just like his mother's: fairer than most. His grandmother then guided the clan to pray and give thanksgiving at the Sant Baba Samadhi, and thus it became his parent's only place of reverence and worship. Ruldu took it upon himself to sweep the grounds around it and keep the main high tomb clean of bird droppings, leaves, and the other detritus of nature. Punna pledged a yearly coat of whitewash and a monthly distribution of sweet *Prasad* to the courtyard's children. As *Churas*, no other caste would accept food or drink from their hands or off their utensils. They were the lowest of the low of all castes. As the village *Charmen* and women, they swept the streets, cleared the open drains, cleaned the courtyards of the *Jats* of dung and dust, and carried it in baskets weaved with mulberry branches. Each family was indentured or contracted its services for an entire year or lifetimes to certain families and served them each and every day of the year, no matter the weather or occasion. Sunday, or a day of rest, was unknown, and the unlettered clan depended on the honesty and generosity of those they served.

They were paid in kind, rarely in coin. At the end of each harvest, they, along with other service castes including the carpenters and blacksmiths, collected their per diems in grain, *jaggery*, lentils, pulses, peanuts, and cotton. If the family enjoyed the ownership of a skeletal cow or buffalo in hay or straw, a share of the cow patties was also an inevitable reward for those who swept, removed, and thumped the dung into shape to be dried in the sun and stacked high in neat piles that encircled the village along with the manure piles. Additionally, they visited the homes of their employers each evening to collect leftovers that often included buttermilk, and on occasion, after some persuasion, some clarified butter, a glass of milk, or sweetmeats left over from a celebration.

Their diet was of grain, more grain, a dab of beans or lentils, and the occasional vegetable. Within the courtyard they had set aside a corner to raise some onions, garlic and herbs, and the occasional vine of bitter melon or green gourds. As untouchables, they were not expected to adhere to a vegetarian diet, and men of the clan hunted for wild boar, rabbits, and fowl in the public lands and *nullahs*. Sometimes they traveled to the swamplands of the Sutlej River to hunt deer, bringing along a bloodhound or two raised especially for this purpose. This high-quality protein supplemented their miserable diet—that is, if a *Jat* or person of means did not first buy or simply swat the kill from their hands. Their mighty protests sometimes resulted in the barter of oils or fresh vegetables, and sometimes moonshine.

They had secret and quiet romantic relations with

their benefactors. They were furtive and took place under the cloak of darkness or depths of a lush field of corn or sugarcane high enough to hide a man or a woman standing on tiptoe.

Punna had resisted all who pursued her, as many did for her fairness of skin and striking beauty and build, in particular when she had first come to the village as the young, nubile bride of a pimply faced teenager. That was when she had caught the attention and received the protection of Sant Baba. On one occasion, when she had hurried into the woods to relieve herself, she was set upon by a group of waiting louts, and her screams had attracted the holy man to the location of her misfortune. Before any damage was done, Sant Baba had driven off the men with several swings of his stout staff. He had accompanied her back to the courtyard and berated her mother-in-law, then proceeded to shame the attackers individually in their homes. Since then she had been shunned by the men of the village, at least for the purpose of satisfying a primal urge. Ruldu was faint with relief. He had little resources to protect his attractive wife, as did the clan at large, short of abandoning the village of their ancestors and stepping into the unknown and even less protection.

Now Punna and her son were doubly blessed, and she prayed, scraping her forehead to the gods for the soul of her benefactor and protector. She made pledges of undying devotion and worship.

In 1938, the year of Karam's birth, the village of Noorian was one of a thousand like it in the state of greater Punjab in British-ruled India. Settled centuries earlier, the village fanned out from a central, ancient well and common circle via five main streets into a crow's nest of jumbled side streets, crowded on either side by high mud walls of large and small courtyards and abodes of extended clans of *Jat* Sikhs and

Muslim *Gujjars*, the landed castes. Sprinkled in were the much smaller and tighter courtyards of the subservient castes of the artisans: carpenters, blacksmiths, bricklayers, goldsmiths, and the subcastes of *jeurs*, *nais*, and *marasis*. The highborn Brahmins occupied the central plaza, their shops on the main floors and residences on the second. The untouchables, the *Chamars* and *Churas*, shared one long street that ended with the *Chura* courtyards. All streets had open drains on either side that collectively drained into the village pond that occupied an area of several acres surrounded by shade trees with what can be called a beach separating the water from the plant. It was on this piece of sandy soil that the young men gathered to play *kabbadi*, wrestle, or lift heavy, wooden clubs called *mughdars* to build muscles and endurance. Early morning and an hour or two before sundown the shepherds brought their collective herds of cattle, goats, and sheep for watering and would let the buffaloes wallow in the shallows to cool off.

Noorian boasted a landmass of 3,000 acres, and about a quarter was common land left fallow for shrub and grass to grow for the substantial number of livestock. A tenth of the common was a wood including an orchard of various fruit trees planted by Sant Baba and his predecessor monks. They had dug their own narrow well and tended the orchard and its many bushes of berries and herbs only they knew the uses of. The monks were known to grow some plants that they consumed or smoked to ease their bodies during long sessions of meditation or yogic asana or to help clear their minds of worldly thoughts and temptation. They were reluctant to share these secret potions with the general public and only made these available to fellow monks or mendicants who often visited to exchange ideas or wisdom. Among the villagers, the Muslim castes and some of the lesser ones smoked tobacco or chewed it in various forms. Mostly men indulged in this, but the women used snuff, and its use was tolerated among some of the Sikh families. The adventurous distilled, consumed, and sold moonshine despite its illegality and the threat of police raids and long sentences in jail.

The landowners planted wheat, pulses, and sugarcane for the winter and cotton, maize, millet, and peanuts as summer crops besides vegetables and the odd row of perennials like limes, lemons, and oranges. Mango trees were popular as was the *beri* tree, both for its fruit and wood. The land was mostly flat, allowing for irrigation from wells dug and owned by individual families or clans. The undulating acreage was only tilled during the monsoon season as the winter rains were often unpredictable and no one wasted precious seed. The families kept what they needed for themselves and their subservient castes per diems and took the surplus loaded on carts hauled by oxen or camel to the nearest market towns of Samrala or Jogpore. There they sold it at prices set by the merchants that were arbitrary and often outrageously low, but the farmers had little choice for they lacked the storage, skill, and resources to hoard the grain and wait for prices to rise. Often the driving force was their indebtedness to these very merchants and the criminally high interest rates they charged. Often the unlettered farmer paid a larger sum of interest than the borrowed amount. This kept the rural population poorer than the urban and less in control of its destiny. The finished goods like clothing came at exorbitant prices and most made do with homespun. Fashion was an unknown commodity and indulgences few and far between harvests. Most families bought the very barest of necessities of salt, spices, and medicine, and books for the boys who could afford school. Most girls were kept illiterate and married off at an early age to avoid any possibility of scandal. All these unions were arranged by the clan while the brides and grooms were barely toddlers. Once promised, the union rarely was not consummated—only in cases of death or disability or a natural calamity.

Yet such conservative and hidebound people were at heart the biggest romantics. Their literature and lore was full of songs and tales of requited and unrequited love often ending in pain and tragedy, mainly death by murder or vendetta.

Legendary love stories were written of lovers along the shores of each of the five major rivers of the Punjab, and wistful parents often named their children after the protagonists in these heroic tales. It was not unusual to have a Sikh wedding party employ a troupe of gifted Muslims for entertainment as they were regarded as better musicians, dancers, and storytellers and entertainers. Once or twice a year, an itinerant storyteller would stop at the village and regale the populace each evening with mythical tales via word and prose, and sometimes a troupe of acrobatic *bajigars* would perform their fantastic contortions, jumps, and athletic feats. At least twice a year the village was invaded by *ghadiwallahs* or gypsies who swept through like locusts, trading for scrap and offering repairs to metal or sharpening knives and scissors in return for a kilo of grain. Courtyards went into a state of caution lest the fast-talking and nimble-fingered visitors robbed them of anything. And surely tales were told of objects missing and never found, whether true or manufactured, to cover self-deception.

Noorian and one hundred and seven such villages and hamlets were governed by the first layer of officialdom, the *Tehsil* of Samrala. They sat in a round colonial building, the *Tehsildar,* both magistrate and administrator of the territory. The *Tehsil* had judicial as well as executive powers. It was also the seat of the superintendent of police, and the station was a walled warren of offices and jail cells opening into a large courtyard. The tall iron gate was guarded all day, every day by an armed sentry. The constables under the command of an inspector, several sub-inspectors, and sergeants patrolled the area, covering scores of square miles on foot, bicycles, and horseback. Only the *Tehsildar* and the superintendent of police had motorized conveyances that were frequently under repair. Both gentlemen were of Indian origin and college graduates, scions of prominent Punjabi families of wealth and privilege. Both had attended institutes in Lahore, the state capital, to learn the art of administration and the law and jurisprudence. Recipients of lavish gifts, money, and entertainment, they in turn passed a percentage of the take up the ladder to their superiors seated at the District of Ludhiana: the commissioner and the senior superintendent of police, and in turn the governor of the province and the inspector-general in the state capital of Lahore. The Indian bureaucrats had a careful system of letting their colonial and ostensibly pristine commanders and superiors of British lineage gain from their squeezing of the populace.

Graft, bribery, influence, and office all came together in the administration and policing of the vast province that was the breadbasket of India. Once the crown jewel of the sub-continent, it continued to supply both food to the country and fodder in the form of soldiers to the colonial masters' other colonies. *Jat* Sikhs and Muslims were much in demand as the Royal Indian Army's rank and file. These were the only fighters to have subdued Afghanistan for the British, and they were feared locally and abroad.

The village was administered by a headman, the *Sarpanch*, and *Lambardars* who collected the taxes from landowners and filed them at the *Tehsil*. These were positions of prestige and power. The *lambardai* was hereditary, and its origin lay in the old system of rajas and continued uninterrupted by the cunning British. These bureaucrats were the tentacles of the Raj: junior and full-time, administered by *Patwaris* and *Kanugos*, trained in the surveying of land and registration of deeds, wills, births and deaths and the issuance of documents attesting to same. They had notary powers to attest and affix official seals and swear testimony. Needy supplicants first sought out and pleaded with these minor officials and thus ever so slowly moved their cases and appeals up the ladder for final judgments that took years to get and exacted a cost that decimated a family's holdings and morale. Many proud and well-to-do families were thus impoverished by the system if they dared fall prey to it through the act of murder or some crime of passion, a simple challenge of authority, or nonpayment of taxes and tithes due.

The *Churas* were so lowly and so outside the system (as they were too poor to be squeezed) that they were left alone. No *Lanbardhars* came to their courtyard to collect seasonal taxes, and no *Patwari* or *Kanugo* came to be kowtowed to. *Churas* were in demand, though, for certain administrative tasks that only men of their ilk would perform, such as hangings and the secret slaughter of buffaloes for meat. The British loved their beef, and in the Punjab it was the water buffalo that provided the red meat; the *Churas* were the butchers.

Punna's father was such a *Chura*. She hailed from the city of Ludhiana, and he was the hangman at the District Jail. When not in demand for a hanging, he painted houses and mansions to support his family, and they lived within a growing community of Christians adjacent to the Brown Memorial Hospital. Although constantly invited and cajoled, the family had refrained from conversion, seeing little benefit from it. Many in the Christian community were from lower

castes and generally shunned by the other three major
religions, and they were often seen and treated as traitors,
toadies of the British and missionaries from Europe and
America. They were coddled until converted, then ignored.
Her father, a quiet and introverted man, shied away from the
pastors and the priests. His was a gruesome profession, and
he allowed it to eat away at him through drink and loneliness,
but it had one beneficial effect: no one bothered him or his
family.

People crossed the street to avoid him and rarely made
eye contact. Fewer ever spoke to him. Yet the families of the
condemned men sought him out and proffered gifts of liquor,
cloth, grain and sugar, even coin, urging him to make the
final moments of their loved ones swifter and painless; to tie
the noose in his special way that death came instantly and
there was no suffering and twitching of the body in spasms of
agony. He kept his promise, then drowned his sorrows in the
moonshine so amply supplied by the relatives, or the bottle
of rum traditionally given him by the superintendent of the
jail as part payment for the deed. He supplied the convict a
good-sized lump of opium to swallow a few hours before
the hanging, thus assuring a compliant and sedated subject.
He was fast and efficient and often applauded by the rest of
the prison population for his dispassionate undertaking. In
his later years, he would receive a pension of five rupees a
month, the same amount as veterans of the Second World
War: a pittance.

He had betrothed his only child to the *Chura* clan in
Noorian for no other family wanted him or his in the city.
Thus Punna, a city dweller, ended up in the hell of a hovel in
the village. But she had a caring and loving husband, in fact
an infatuated partner, eager as a rabbit to mate once or twice
a day, and it was this constant botheration that turned her off

from love, romance, and sex.

Cognizant of her father's work and the effect of karma, she was convinced he would reenter life as a lowly creature and begin the cycle thus punished, and a long cycle it would be. But convinced that if she did good deeds, she could earn enough positive karma to cancel his negative, she prayed and performed cleansing rituals and sacrifices of fasting and self denial. She gave up any form of jewelry and self-embellishment through tattoos or chewing nuts that colored her mouth and lips a seductive red or combing and oiling her hair into braids tied with ribbons or colorful strings, enhancing their sinuous sway as she would walk, swinging her hips for maximum effect. She knew all the wiles of women and the art of seduction but refused it all to benefit the man she loved the most: her father.

This made her different from her caste sisters. They had accepted their miserable lot and sought relief from it in secret affairs and the receipt of gifts and goods from their lovers. They would stuff themselves with sweetmeats during the rendezvous and squirrel away the treats for later consumption, occasionally sharing the booty as an innocent manna with their families. As much as Punna had been and was pursued, on occasion tempted by the masculinity of the few she felt attracted to, she never took that step into the inevitable. She never allowed her gaze to be held by the admirer, a sure sign of interest and assent. As such, her family suffered wants and shortages. They ate plain *roti* and pushed it down their gullets with copious amounts of water instead of extra servings of *dhal*, *saag*, or vegetables allowed to be picked out of the admirer's field, added, of course, to extra dollops of ghee or pickles or sweets.

The husband, though, had accepted the cuckolding and its rewards. It was everyone's dirty secret, unspoken and unacknowledged, but it was a reality just the same. The higher born worked the lower born in more ways than one.

Punna's parents finally made the trek to see their new grandson. At the sight of them she burst out in tears of joy and fell into their arms. The three of them hugged and wept, but because this was a happy occasion, the baby was soon cooing in his grandmother's lap. "Looks like you," she told Punna matter-of-factly, remembering her at the same age.

"He looks like his father," crowed the paternal grandmother, busy pawing through the gifts of cloth and sweetmeats they had brought, neatly dividing up the largesse for distribution to immediate kin. She particularly liked the fact that there was a five-yard length of sturdy cloth that was for her and a shawl for the colds of winter, but there was no jewelry, not even a silver trinket. But for their daughter there were three full suits, a silver locket and bangles, a bagful of knick knacks, and for Ruldu a suit and a turban. There was even a pair of the newfangled rubber sandals. She had suspected that the hangman, Bola, was better off than he let on, and who else did he have, except his daughter and her family, to shower gifts on? Even the girls got clothes and sandals. The grandmother's own husband had passed away recently from consumption and too much hookah smoking, coughing his lungs out in great gobs of foul-looking and smelling phlegm tinged with blood. Only Sant Baba's potions had given him respite from his spasms of coughing and the awful pain. In the end, they gave him tea laced with opium to ease his suffering and found him dead a few hours after peacefully falling asleep on a cot under the *peepal* tree. Bola and his wife had met their obligations of supporting their daughter and son-in-law with the expenses of the aftermath. Death extracted a severe bout of giving to assuage the gods and tradition. Births were cheaper to celebrate and more welcome.

The elders of the clan gathered around the visitors, and that evening, the young went to gather the daily evening meal from the homes of the *Jats*. Punna made fresh *roti* and cooked a stew of onions and bitter melons for her parents. They would be served the best available food and drink. As they separated into their own group, Bola pulled two bottles of 90 proof, double-distilled moonshine and a large can of pickled boar from a sack, and seeing this bounty, the men, their spirits lifted, fired up the hookah, lined up the glasses, and called for a bucket of cool water to be drawn from the well immediately. Younger ones, not yet called upon to join them in the feast, scrambled to obey and then lingered over the seated benefactors of the evening's main event. Before long, the elders were in various stages of inebriation and slapping each other's shoulders in great shows of camaraderie, congratulating Ruldu on his new son, Karam. The usually reticent grandfather had a broad smile on his pock-marked face and forgot the arduous twenty-mile bicycle ride with his wife on the back seat and the bundle somehow balanced over the handles.

The younger ones began helping themselves to the leftovers, and nary a drop of liquor escaped their eager lips. The pickled boar, cured with a mixture of at least forty herbs and spices, would remain as one of their most memorable tastes.

And later, as the courtyard hummed with sounds of celebration, laughter, and bonhomie, Punna told her mother, "I pledged that father would put a coat of whitewash on Sant Baba's *Samadhi*."

"It will benefit his karma if he does it," was the matter-of-fact reply.

Chapter 3

The world suffered a great spasm as Karam turned one year old. The Second Great War started in Europe and catastrophe of unimaginable suffering started to befall most of Southeast Asia as Japan began to exert its imperial ambitions. In Noorian, little changed except for the opportunities this offered the young men. They could be soldiers and embark on foreign adventures rather than do backbreaking field labor, and a few dozen enlisted at the recruitment office in Ludhiana. The primary benefit of this flight of eager young men from the village was the reward of an elementary school. It was donated to the village in recognition of having supplied the largest number of soldiers for the defense of the Empire.

Around the same time, the ailing watchman of the village passed away. This post was traditionally held by a *Chura*. Having no male issue to inherit the position allowed Bola to call in a favor of the jailor who had the ear of the *Tehsildar* in Samrala. Thus Ruldu escaped the fate of sweeping dust and dung for the rest of his life. Appointed the new watchman, he was sent to the district for a month of training, basically that of the village constable. He lived with his in-laws for a month and there developed a taste of city life. Relieved of the physical labor and poor diet, he put on several pounds and reappeared in Noorian almost unrecognizable to his very wife. He was well groomed; he essentially now bathed with real soap and therefore smelled better, and he cleaned his teeth daily, his breath freshened with a twig of the *neem* tree. He wore a government-issued *kurta/pyjama* and moccasins. A smartly tied white turban completed the image of a substantial man wielding some authority, especially projected by the shiny staff, studded with brass top to bottom, he held casually in the crook of his right arm. Watching him walk into the courtyard so regally caused Punna to almost swoon with pride while her mother-in-law put her arthritis to a lie, racing effortlessly to be the first to embrace her suddenly rather handsome son. She almost trampled her granddaughters underfoot, so eager she was. Soon the girls had climbed their father's sides, and he carried them with his mother hanging from his neck over to Punna to bend over and gaze into his grinning son's face.

"Thank you, Sant Baba, thank you," she intoned, tears of joy running down her cheeks. The appointment meant that she too did not have to do the work of a charwoman. Her husband would now enjoy a salary paid regularly at the *Tehsil* and additional payment from supplicants he would accompany there, seeking documents, registrations, favors, forgiveness, and release from fines and penalties. Plus being a member of the local government would entail some palm greasing.

When he told her, after a hectic bout of lovemaking, that her father had agreed to give them sufficient money to build a proper brick and cement house on their tiny plot of land currently occupied by the fetid, dark, and dingy hovel they inhabited, she almost passed out from joy. Gathering her family, she marched them for a thanksgiving at the Samadhi and was amazed to find the older disciple building a hut in the grove. They bent to touch his feet and receive benediction. "What brought you back, Babaji?" they asked.

"It is the first anniversary of Guruji's death, and I must

perform *pooja* for his soul," he replied. Then he gave them a list of requirements.

Thus as the first task of the watchman of the village, who also acted as the messenger of news akin to a town crier, Ruldu toured the streets announcing the ceremonies and calling for donations and volunteers. More to please him than in remembrance, a majority of the populace that had helped build the Samadhi pledged their support. So began a yearly ritual by the disciple to perform *pooja* in memory of Sant Baba to keep his legacy alive.

The world around them in turmoil, the villagers engaged with alacrity in the collective task of celebrating at the Samadhi. Families had lived cheek to jowl for centuries. Events beyond their control, invasions, forcible conversions, ancient customs, and faiths had insidiously cut and divided them into subcultures and clans with multi-tiered loyalties to beliefs and men who resided in faraway places and pulled strings that affected their simple lives. Lately, earnest men— in groups and individuals—had begun to visit the village, urging Muslims against Sikhs and vice versa. The Hindus aligned with the Sikhs. There were major decisions being made in London and New Delhi. Gandhi and the Congress party and the Muslim League were at odds over the future of a divided and diverse subcontinent, extracting promises of independence from a cynical colonial power now engaged in a super struggle for its own survival. Such forces were at play, and such innocents were to be sacrificed for the greater good.

The fear and foreboding began to bring some people together. But others were suspicious, and with minds poisoned by the retelling of past injustices, they started sharpening the tools of revenge. It was happening across the Punjab and right across the vastness of the Raj, particularly in the urban centers where literacy was becoming a tool of division and the newly read easy converts. They had yet to learn to decipher the propaganda and its falsehoods, and fundamentalists wedded to a particular cause ran amok. As the war progressed and Europe began to reveal the ugliness of man's injustice to man—the stories of the Japanese atrocities told by fearful and incoherently frothing survivors—the populace began to expect the inevitable, creating a sense of apocalypse.

Yet it brought out generosities of spirit and sisterhood in the women of the village. Her newly raised status got Punna the position of assistant midwife to a *Gujjar* woman who had delivered every child in the village for the last twenty years, including her son Karam. Initially all she did was clean the area and get rid of the soiled dressings and such, but slowly she was instructed in palpation, massage, and manipulation of the uterus and the life within, to ease a child's entry into the world with a mother still left capable of nourishing it. Knowing when to stop the exertion and effort and let nature take its toll, even though it happened only in rare cases, a still birth left her drained and depressed, having worked with and known the expectant mother, particularly if she left behind a brood. At these times Punna would find escape and solace in prayer and the ritualistic cleansings, incantations, and meditation. She had learned much from the celebration at the Samadhi. The disciple had a slower mannerism, easy to follow and understand if one paid attention.

Punna gained confidence and an aura of competence.

Soon she was sought out and invited and let into the homes and bedrooms of the highborn to attend to their womanly problems. Over the next two years she received basic training by the disciple of botanicals, poultices, and preparations concerning celestial order, the alignment of the stars, and the auspicious or inauspicious signs. Her mind was a sponge, absorbing knowledge, technique, and touch. She learned to control her words, expression, and mood, as well as her posture. She did all this in order to give comfort, to ease suffering, to enhance the occasion of childbirth and to increase the experience. In her soothing words, her gentle touch, and her reasoned acts, the women found succor. Soon she was allowed independence by her guru, the *Gujjar Dai*.

Each night before she put him to sleep, Punna rocked her son, sang to him, and hugged and kissed him. She made him stand out among his clan by dressing and grooming him with care while crooning encouragements, calling him her prince and a lion cub. The boy fixed her with patient and long looks and responded to her mothering and patience with growing intelligence. As their lot improved by the building of the new abode with a brick floor and abundant light, he seemed to mature beyond his years. The rest of the children, including her daughters, ran around in the dust and detritus of the courtyard. Yet Karam avoided being soiled and covered by a swarm of flies setting on the face to feast off the runny nose and giddy, unwashed eyes. He learnt to ask for a trip to a corner to be relieved, and he washed off and redressed properly. He gave no indications of his heritage as a *Chura*. He was uncomfortable and literally intolerant of the filth that lay beyond the doorstep of his home. He was as neat and clean as the house his mother kept.

The local school was now up to eight grades, having recently added three more classrooms. A new headmaster, by the name of Shrikant Sharma, arrived to run the school. He was accompanied by his wife, who was pregnant and toting another toddler. The headman assured them the rental of appropriate rooms. The classrooms soon filled with students from surrounding villages and hamlets who could afford the fee and books necessary for attendance. It also became the local post office, and Mr. Sharma served as the postmaster. There he handled the sale of stamps, the registration of special mail, and the delivery to individual households of their letters and information about money orders sent to them by someone in the army or those who had emigrated to serve British interests in Burma, Singapore, Hong Kong, and the East African colonies of Uganda, Kenya and Tanganyika, as well as Malaysia and the farther reaches of Canada and America. The village boasted emigrants in all those locales serving as constables, carpenters, shopkeepers, and civil servants enforcing the rules of the British Empire. Without these foot soldiers, Britain's reach and power would evaporate. For every Englishman serving his royalty in the colonies, he had the support of fifty or more so-called coolies from India.

One of the oldest such emigrants was Inder Singh Pardesi, who was a prominent, altruistic Sikh that had climbed the ladder to become an influential civil servant posted in Nairobi. He could issue a letter of guarantee, and anyone from his village would receive entry to these colonies. Once there, they prospered as civil servants, small businessmen, artisans, or policemen. They helped conquer and dominate the Dark Continent, cutting railway lines into the interior, building quarters for the rulers, and supplying the roles of a middle class between the rulers and the ruled, thus becoming the resented ones by the natives. They were the bridge between the populace and its standoffish aristocracy, and what an aristocracy it was, containing the crud of British society sentenced to serve the throne in the colonies. Only the most accomplished, trusted, and proven occupied the real posts of power. They were the governors and commissioners who doled out the largesse to the lesser of their breed and maintained the patina of power, exercised through the use of colonial soldiers and servants willing to lay their lives down for their masters.

Thus began the slow changes in awareness and awakening for those in the village interested beyond its borders. The majority were in the survival mode that the certainty and immediacy of natural need caused. If there was the lack of work or if there was not enough fuel for the cooking fire, then hunger was assured. They worried of disease or disability and unforeseen calamities: the needs of the cattle to be watered, grazed or fed grain or hay, water, if the rains failed or fell too torrentially, not only flooding the field but wrecking the flimsy homes of the poor, held together by sticks supporting layers of mud mixed with dung and straw. They were only moments away from disaster that could strike without notice or warning, and they could only fight with prayer or the help of the gods, thus the amulets around their necks, the holy tattoos, and the *toonas* that hung over the doors and the almost maniacal adherence to superstitions. It was a vast chiasm from this level of ignorance to any enlightenment that science and discovery was bringing to the outside world and only now slowly trickling into Noorian. The best and brightest were being drawn to lands far away. There was news of some Brahmins, who should know better, crossing oceans to travel to England, endangering their souls' salvation in the afterlife, having attained the highest status available to a human in this.

Headmaster Sharma, a Brahmin by birth but a socialist in belief, set to bring about the one revolution that would most benefit the populace: education. He began to harangue parents to start sending their children—including the daughters—to school, if only for a few grades, so they could acquire the basic skills of reading and arithmetic. In two years, the first and second grades were coeducational. Children of every caste were represented in them, and during the morning and early afternoon the courtyards and streets were empty of aimless urchins running or playing in the dust. Rather, they were seated in neat rows on grounds of a still-unfinished school, reciting the alphabets of Urdu and Punjabi and the basic tables. And when he secured the transfer to the village of two women teachers, the headman offered an empty *haveli* as the nascent primary school for girls, resulting in a sudden surge in the registration. Parents who were against the mixing of the sexes (at least in their sights and supervision) were content and tolerant of allowing their daughter a few years of study and were aware that at their age they were too tender to be put to work of any value. The village now had another educated man move to Noorian, the husband of a daughter of landowning parents with no other issue. This man could practice some modern medicine as he was trained in a dispensary and had an official certificate to prove it. He was also a great admirer of what Lenin had done in the vast land of Russia and how the peasants there now boasted an industrial empire, great military power, and above all, a rapidly literate public.

The first telegram informing a father of his son's death in the war was a rude awakening. Some of these fathers had fought in the First Great War, and one or two had been injured, but this was the only such death of one of their own. Soon the family was visited by a small party of dignitaries from the officialdoms in Samrala and Ludhiana, which included an older officer, a Sikh with a chest full of crests and medals. They gifted the widow a sewing machine, a framed portrait of the deceased, and a British flag, and then pledged to name one of the schools after him. She was also assured of support in the form of a pension for life: a guarantee of scholarships and support for her only child, a boy too small to know what the whole fuss was about. At a ceremony of *Sanskar* for the fallen Sikh, they returned to extol him as a martyr and urged others to enlist. Surprisingly, others did. Another dozen men went to serve.

Others served a different master now: the dream of an independent India. They followed two different paths: one invoked Gandhi and nonviolence in its protests and boycotts, and the other was a more urgent and violent movement led by fierce men like Lala Lajpat Rai, willingly throwing their bodies against the well-armed police and protectors of the Raj. No one from Noorian was captured or convicted or suffered a jail term, but a *Chura* of a neighboring village gained notoriety for his brave battles. He was often bloodied, beaten, and dragged off to jail to be tortured, but he was of a different make. He never spilled the names of his cohorts through teeth now loosened by the blows struck by interrogators long into the night. Even Punna's father was amazed at the punishment the man could endure and not bend. Chandu Das was quickly turning into a local legend. "Just make sure you do not put me in the position of having to hang you," said Bola to him while standing outside his cell. Bola was in charge of feeding the prisoner for they were of the same caste.

"I am not afraid of death," Chandu Das replied, "and I will not blame you for carrying out your duty."

"You are a brave man," Bola, the hangman said, duly impressed by the sincerity. If anybody could smell fear, he could, for he had seen big, blustery killers soil themselves at the sight of the gallows. "Try to stay alive."

He had already calculated that Chandu Das had the qualities of leadership, and his desperately trampled caste was going to need a bull like him if and when India got its independence. Although Gandhi already had come out in strong support of the untouchables, calling them the "children of God" and thus bestowing a moral status on their plight, it was going to take men of Chandu Das's ilk to carve something out of it. Bola decided to curry favor by having his wife cook meals for Chandu Das during his sojourns at the jail. This the politician truly appreciated for he was a huge man in height and heft and was famous for having brought down a *neelgai buch* weighing three hundred pounds, having latched onto its antlers and twisting and turning its neck until it snapped. Then he pulled the carcass out of the muddy swamp for a mile or so. "When the time comes, Bola, I want you in my camp," Chandu Das told him. "Men like you are going to be necessary for what we are going to have to do to get justice."

He had already seen the effect the mere appearance of the hangman in the hallway had on the rest of the prisoners; some actually trembled if he as much as looked at them. "Can you imagine having Bola beside me when I ask the bloody pundits for a legislative seat?" he thought with merriment. It eased the pain and bruising he had had to endure earlier from a particularly harsh interrogator. Chandu Das had already inquired of the man's background. He knew that one day he would repay the abuse in ways only he could devise, none of them pleasant or merciful.

And now the Sant Baba Samadhi had less visitors and support because the village Sikhs, mostly *Jats,* had decided to build a tomb in memory of their *Shaheed,* the soldier fallen in battle. Before long, donations started to arrive from the emigrants, other villages, and organizations, and instead of just a tomb, a temple rose for the first time in Noorian. The village until then had not had a place of worship for any of its faiths. The Muslims began to talk of the need for a mosque, as most men lost the day from work each Friday walking to one three miles away in a village largely inhabited by men of their faith and rich in land and cattle. Punna doubled her efforts to take care of the Samadhi, and it began to be known as the *Chura's* Samadhi, the village dividing into distinctive groups asserting fealty to their beliefs and faith. The Hindus, too few in numbers, gave for the temple and reluctantly for the modest mosque. Most of the Muslims had, like Sikhs, converted from Hinduism and continued the practice of honoring the Brahmin's position in the pantheon of castes.

Soon, the Great War ended with the defeat of the Germans and the Italians, the Japanese brought to their knees by the atomic bomb. Noorian remained largely ignorant of the Holocaust in Europe and the genocides in the rest of Asia. The soldiers returned on furloughs, and the village celebrated wedding after wedding and the festivities turned their attention away from the calamity coming their way: independence, division, and a rending apart of their village and their province, all done to satisfy the demands of men in positions of power unable to share the thought of a united country that gives its citizens a chance to enjoy its fruits together. In an all or nothing struggle, India was torn into three distinct and parochial entities: largely Hindu India in the middle, and a West and an East Pakistan flanking either side. Pakistan was of course for the Muslims.

Chapter 4

*A*s the village watchman, Ruldu was relied upon to inform his superiors at the *Tehsil* of any untoward happenings there, of the comings and goings of men suspected by the authorities of fomenting trouble, and, of course, of residents packing up and sending their families away. At nightfall he patrolled the streets, and now and then banged his staff on the cobbled streets to let the residents know that he was around and they were therefore safe. The Muslims were nervous as the borders were discussed and knew that the district of Ludhiana was to remain in India. Already Hindus and Sikhs had started sending their womenfolk and children to safety on the proposed Indian side, and well-connected and informed Muslim families sent theirs to areas around Lahore and *Gujjanwalla*. There was still agitation and demands for a Sikh state, independent of India and Pakistan, and ostensibly the British were keen to grant one in recognition of their service to the Raj.

At one of his visits to the *Tehsil*, Ruldu was asked to conduct a census of the Muslim families, and a minor official was dispatched to assist him. As they went door to door only calling upon the Muslims, an uproar started among that group, and people began to ask questions that Ruldu had no answers for. The two of them muddled through the task for the day, and that evening, several heads of Muslim families furtively came to his courtyard to ask specifically the reason for the census. "Is it the beginning of our end?" one elder asked plaintively, tears welling in his kohl-lined eyes.

Unable to embrace and thus reassure the man he had known all his life, Ruldu offered the best platitudes he could and began to hate his job. Yet the trust he had of the populace sustained him. His trust in the power of the British to conduct an orderly and bloodless division, if it came to that, was absolute, but he was privy to rumors of dire consequences. What if the British just up and left and left things to be worked out between Jinha and Nehru, the two apparent winners and decided future leaders. "What, oh, what?" he thought, and he was unable to even imagine the outcome.

He sought the council of elders—all elders—and sometimes late into the night they debated, speculated, planned, and prayed. He worried terribly for the safety of his own family and how to defend them if the violence that some feared came to pass. All he had was his staff, so he quietly assembled a small armory of axes and swords and divided them to be hidden in easily accessible places by his kin in the courtyard. If challenged, they had at least a dozen men of fighting age who were not frightened of a little blood. It came from the hunting and killing of animals they did so routinely. "One just closes his mind," he told them, "and swings." Straightening his arm and letting it fall in an arc, mimicking a strike with a sword.

His son, now eight and the best and brightest student in the school, as he was told by the respected headmaster, gazed at him. His small mouth was open and his eyes wide in fright, or amazement, he hoped. His wife was always telling Karam that he was a lion cub. "But is he a lion?" he wondered, and he suddenly felt his bowels grumble. He hurried off down the street and into the fields, needing solitude and solace.

* * *

Up and down the chains of command at the *Tehsils*, the districts, and the provinces, bureaucrats began advising and assisting the movement of their colleagues' families to safety. A month before the fateful days of independence, the connected, informed, privileged, and wealthy had mostly secured their loved ones and their possessions. Only the stubborn, the poor, and the ignorant stayed rooted to their homes and lands, their sources of day-to-day survival and sustenance. In Noorian, only three families had left, and Karam still played at school with his best friend, the grandson of the *Gujjar Dai,* his mother's guru. He even spent the afternoons doing homework under the shadiest tree in their courtyard, often rewarded with *jaggery* and treats by the indulgent old midwife. He was the only child of his caste who was growing up with some latitude in relations with the higher born. The others were put into place by a sharp rebuke or a kick to the backside. No one had done that to Karam, and it was a testament to his father's position and his mother's talents as a *dai*. It was probably a first in the history of the region for a charwoman to help deliver a *Jat* or other baby outside of her own caste. But in Noorian, it had become routine to race to her house breathlessly beseeching her immediate attention.

She even had the support of the Comrade, or Dr. Surjit Singh, as most called him, although he preferred the former. As a wealthy landowner, he could afford the altruistic giving of the odd medical service, but his training helped save a few lives of mothers and babies that Punna cared for. He taught her the principles of antisepsis, the boiling of water, the washing of hands, the sterilization of the scissors used to cut the umbilical cord, and the stemming of bleeding by applying the appropriate pressure. Women still resented the presence of males during such an event, and in a Muslim home, it was taboo. Karam accompanied Punna to the Comrade's home when she visited for supplies and instruction, and the kindly man took an unusual interest in the boy, probing his intelligence, linguistic skills, and cognitive behavior. He pronounced him ahead for his age and unusually intelligent for his caste. Then suddenly realizing the faux pas, he covered it with a generous gift of bandages and iodine for the mother and a bag of candy for the youngster. From then on, whenever their paths crossed, the Comrade always acknowledged Karam with a nod or smile. It gave the youngster a feeling of importance because the Comrade was now a very prominent citizen of Noorian. He was the only one who had newspapers and magazines delivered to his door, and he was the first owner of a radio. Many gathered in his courtyard to listen to the newfangled technology, disbelieving that live voices emitted out of an inanimate box. They called it a miracle, as they had the first motorized vehicle, the first train, and the first flying bird that carried humans. They had heard of the capturing of lightning, but it was not available in the villages yet. However, gas-lit lanterns were the rage for their blinding wattage in the village, particularly during weddings—they allowed celebrations into the night.

The Comrade listened to the news on the radio alone and read selectively from the newspapers to his growing audience. He was very aware of the coming storm, and as it approached, he grew fearful of its effect and consequences. He was, after all, a man who could afford that title out of choice rather than necessity. Even his beloved Soviet Union was now showing its muscle, fangs, and claws to its erstwhile allies, the British and the Americans. It particularly wanted them out of the Indian subcontinent so it could curry favor with its new leadership and eventually find what it sought: a warm water access to the Arab sea or the Indian Ocean. The British had ruthlessly denied it this ambition, but the British were now weak and vacillating.

And the British did what a weak and vacillating power does. It ran from its responsibility, from the mess resulting from the secret promises they had made in order to gain the support of the Sikh, Hindu, and Muslim alliances to serve their own purposes for the war against Hitler and as a bulwark against the imperialism of Japan. Having survived wounded but alive, they decided to let go prematurely of India, and they allowed it to be sectioned along religious lines at the insistence of rabid parochialisms, putting millions of lives, livelihoods, and lifestyles at the mercy of ancient animosities. Neither of the new nations or their leaderships were ready for such a cataclysmic uprooting of peoples from the lands of their ancestors; it started and ended badly, for both nascent nations.

For Karam, as a nine-year-old, grade-four student, the first inkling that life was about to do a 180 degree turn was the sudden disappearance of all his Muslim schoolmates. They were kept home by fearful and confused parents as an instinctive gesture of preservation. Their gates shut, awaiting the promised arrival of armed government personnel to help them cross the border into Pakistan. Unsure of the long and careful alliances built with the Sikhs and Hindus, they coalesced into a tight little communal group of just about three hundred souls of all ages. However, a few families ventured out and left with their possessions loaded onto carts or the backs of camels or carried on their heads, crying and weeping their hearts and souls out in rending screams, in the company and under the protection of their Sikh allies. Most such groups made it to the safety of government camps established for their safe removal under army or police protection.

But then news came of a train that had arrived in Amritsar, the Sikh holy city, containing the massacred and defiled bodies of Sikhs and Hindus by rampaging mobs of Muslims in Lahore and other more frightening rumors and reports of untold atrocities committed. Temples and *Gurudwaras* had been defiled; holy scriptures were burned; women and girls had been raped, and men and boys were decapitated. These stories told by the leaders of militias suddenly formed to seek revenge by unleashing similar terrors and atrocities on existing Muslims under their control started a blood lust of unimaginable proportions all over the territories stretching from one end of the continent to the other. The land descended into a virtual free-for-all of murder, looting, and rape by every one of the three religions that had existed side by side for centuries. They had gone through periodic upheavals but never at such a scale of inhumanity.

Punjabi citizens had kin spread all over Greater Punjab, and as the borders were defined, letters and messages became more urgent. The Muslims in Noorian sent and received letters and visitors urging them to pack and leave to join their relatives in the safety of the soon to be Pakistani section, while Sikhs and Hindus urged theirs to do likewise. Because of the riots and conflicts that erupted in urban centers encouraged greatly by agitators from the Muslim League and the *Akali Dal*, passions rose and tempers frayed. Suddenly the flight of people panicked and in fear of their lives started. The roads and pathways became crowded with long lines of carts loaded with household goods, entire family fortunes on the back of a camel or a bicycle. Some people dragged bamboo frames, and all kept huddled closer for safety of their own kind. The men carried rudimentary weapons for protection. Some groups were accompanied for safety by kind-hearted and concerned neighbors at least until they could hand their charges to the army or police, parting from lifelong friends with promises of future meetings.

Not everyone was that lucky. Out of the perimeter of their own village and often within it, they were set upon by bloodthirsty thugs, eager to kill, maim, rape, and loot, and each morning bodies would be found in the commons of villages or left floating in the ponds. Men, women, and children lay dead where they fell from awful wounds to their heads, torsos, or limbs, pools of congealed blood gluing them to the grass or ground. Girls and women would often have their underthings removed and had obvious signs of degradation visited upon them by men freed of any moral restraints in these times of communal madness. Some took great pleasure and pride in the opportunity to fall on the helpless and have their way with them and often traveled far and wide in small and large marauding parties. They either hid or hurried home under the cover of darkness to put away the loot of material and cattle. None of the bodies found had any precious items left on them. Bangles, amulets, nose rings, earrings, and so on were ripped off to be hoarded until it was safe to trade or use them. The marauders were a small minority of the general populace and had a history of crime, violence, or perversion; the insane had been let out of the asylum.

Many were disgusted by these gangs and formed their own militias to challenge them and defend the fleeing Muslims, and some were injured or died in their valiant efforts. The marauders had better weapons and a stronger bloodlust, but when captured, they would suddenly plead for brotherhood and forgiveness, loudly protesting that they were on a higher calling to "cleanse the lands of interlopers."

Some families simply sheltered Muslims too fearful of leaving who was willing to stay in the Indian Territory. Eight families chose this path and did not lose a family member, a goat or cow, a stick of furniture, or an inch of land, and they continued to live peacefully as full members of the community. But it would be decades before they could be visited by or visit those that had crossed over to Pakistan. In other parts of India, particularly the south and central regions, fewer left, and in some urban areas, entire Muslim communities stayed and thrived. At the end of it all, India had a larger population of Muslims than both sections of Pakistan, but Pakistan had cleansed itself of Hindus and Sikhs, allowing very few to live peacefully there. The Christian, Parsee, and Jewish citizens stayed in the lands where they were settled. There was little cross-border flight there.

Ruldu was in charge of securing the empty dwellings of those who had fled to be later assigned to new refugees arriving daily from the camps. They would receive deeds and almost equal lands as they had left in Pakistan. Only the urban Sikhs and Hindus took longer to settle. They could be found hawking family trinkets to survive, and the towns and cities were packed with these refugees, most of them speaking in Peshawar or Bari dialects. They proved to be an enterprising and hardy lot, for within a decade they had taken over most of the shops and daily commerce of the Punjab, formed enduring relationships with clients in the countryside, and earned lifelong fealties.

Thus Karam saw the worst of humanity and some of its best. The village and his school were stripped of their Muslims. His best friend was gone. The only courtyard he was welcome in was now occupied by a family of strangers—withdrawn, suspicious, and almost hostile with their strange accent. The new children admitted to the school had distant looks, almost trance-like. They acted strange and took a long time to warm to the children of the village. The headmaster hovered over them like a mother hen and tried ever so hard to push forward the curriculum for that year, but it was a lost year. The village was changed. The people were tense and tentative. A couple of families had been quietly ostracized as they had been found in possession of property looted from fleeing Muslims, their men suspected of having blood on their hands.

At home, Karam detected a conflict between his parents ever since his mother had found trinkets from the homes of the Muslims in the pockets of his father. His mother berated his father, who sat there with a defiant look on his face. "It's not like I stole them or looted them. They were just lying there. Anyone could have taken them," he justified.

But Punna would have none of it. She made her husband return them. He claimed he did, not quite meeting her gaze.

No one wanted to talk about the trauma of partition, now eager to move on. There existed the sense of guilt, of having been part of something ugly and sinful, even if they had not done anything wrong; a sense of collective burden too heavy to bear but too early to be lifted off the conscience. For Karam, it was confusion and questions. No one explained anything, so he turned to his books.

The Urdu language was removed from the curriculum. "One less language to study," Karam thought. But soon it was replaced by Hindi, the new national language, besides English, and English would be taught in grade six, two years hence.

* * *

Many years later, a Comrade in name only, Dr. Surjit Singh, would write the epitaph on the tragic events of 1947 after another communal riot caused by the hectoring of their congregations and followers by communal and religious leaders, resulting in many innocent deaths of both Hindus and Muslims.

"One day, humanity as a whole will have to decide on silencing the voices of hatred. How it will be done, I do not know. But I do believe it will involve cutting out the tongues of the mullahs, the priests, and the pundits, or lining them all up and swinging them from the gallows!" he wrote to Karam in a letter.

Chapter 5

*K*aram scored the highest marks in grade eight and won the provincial scholastic award. It made his parents beam with pride, and headmaster Sharma took it as the highlight of his teaching career. The village was suddenly in the news and received a visit from the local member of Provincial Parliament and a junior minister in the cabinet, Shree Chandu Das. Resplendent in his white congress hat and matching suit of homespun *kurta/pyjama* and a beige Nehru jacket, he arrived in his official Ambassador motor car accompanied by his personal assistant and a police escort in a jeep. He held court at the school, still closed for the spring break. The headman led the *panchayat* in greeting the junior minister as villagers gathered in the now walled grounds, the classrooms still lacking their first coat of paint, only the upper three classrooms boasting desks and the proposed privies still nonexistent. After winning his seat, the junior minister had found no time to even think of this community in his vast constituency of a 200 villages. He spent most of his time in the spacious manor he occupied in the capital, gathering a fortune while peddling influence unchecked.

But this occasion was of personal pride for him because a boy of his own humble beginnings and caste had proven to all that given the opportunity, a *Chura* could excel at anything. Just as he had in gaining elected office, a cabinet position, and the kowtowing of all castes and creeds needy of his stamp of approval in matters governed by his ministry. And the boy was the grandson of an old and trusted friend Bola. As a politician, he instinctively smelled an opportunity for self promotion and a push for his community. Once all the required greetings had been accomplished and he had the podium, Chandu Das, pointing to Karam and asking him to stand, led a lengthy applause for the youth, causing the boy to blush and lower his gaze as all eyes and attention was upon him. The villagers of Noorian, genuinely proud of his accomplishment, clapped thunderously and long.

"Today, my brothers and sisters, the aspiration of the father of our young nation, the revered and much grieved Mahatamaji," he paused, lowering his head for dramatic effect before continuing, "are being fulfilled by a son of the children of God. Our constitution, so carefully and wisely written, guarantees opportunities for all and particularly those who had none before. That is why this young man will attend high school in his own village!" Once again he had to allow for the thunderclap of appreciation as it occurred to the crowd that Karam's scholarship had won a high school for their community. And as the implication dawned on the young man, he had to sit down because his legs had started to tremble. His classmates crowded him, many openly hugging him even though he was a *Chura*. None of them would touch him under normal circumstances, tolerate sitting next to him, or even speak to him, but right now they were too giddy with joy to let that get in the way of showing their pride and appreciation. It did not escape the notice of the wily politician.

"Who knows," Chandu Das bellowed, "if he repeats it at matriculation." Then pausing for effect, he exclaimed "Perhaps Noorian will receive the grant of a college!"

The crowd was now almost uncontrollable in its glee.

He had them in the palm of his hand, from his own to the Brahmins, all hopping up and down and screaming his name.

"*Shree Chandu Das ki Jai,*" they screamed again and again.

"Remember that when the time comes to vote next year," he reminded them in his most charmingly humble but clear tone, so all could hear his message.

He motioned Karam to the podium and posed for a photograph while giving the youth the announced award of a full one hundred rupees, sending a gasp through the audience. It was a small fortune for any of them. "Better for my own than any of you," Chandu Das thought as he basked in the glory of the moment, all the old wounds real and perceived he had suffered to get to this position of power and influence now forgotten in the euphoria.

* * *

Long after the politician had left and the stream of congratulators had come and gone, Karam sat on one of the cots with his parents and counted out the notes to the wide-eyed stares of his grandmother and sisters. His mother immediately corralled 10 rupees for the Sant Baba *Samadhi* to pay for the coat of paint she had promised but not delivered because of the daily exigencies that had crowded their existence. Even though Ruldu received a monthly salary and she got paid in grain and kind for her midwife duties, her mother-in-law's painful and swollen joints and her rapidly growing in size, children, and her own need to look better than her caste ate all the income. This was a windfall, and before it disappeared to fill holes suddenly apparent and the litany of unfulfilled promises, she decided to grab it for her primary obligation: honoring the memory of a man who had not only saved her honor once but continued to have the gods bestow opportunity and honor on her family. When Ruldu raised an objection, she silenced him with a deathly stare he had become familiar with. Slowly but surely, the appointment as the village watchman had led to some opportunities of self-indulgence he could not have dreamed of before but which he enjoyed openly, and so he suffered the disdain and wrath of his wife. Particularly aggravating was the reward of a few coins pressed into his palm for a white lie that also served as an official testimony in minor matters of conflict and claims that were so common in the village now as a result of a wilder group of *Jat* refugees, men who had previously lived and grown up in less-governed territories, men quick to temper and violence. Their neighbors coped with this enforced cohabitation by simply keeping their distance, or if push came to shove, by ganging up on the newcomers. In the face of unfavorable odds, the *Jat* refugees backed off but took small and sneaky revenges with acts of vandalism. In some villages, open conflict and bloodshed had broken out.

Some of the older residents pined for their previous neighbors, the Muslims, and spoke fondly of the good old days, taking great pains to avoid mention of the partition and its calamities. Newborns in 1947–48 were given martial names by those who had suffered atrocities. Names like Jora and Jung were the most popular, and those who had turned inwards for answers gave their babies long and meaningful names unheard before like Paramjit, Swaranjit, and so on. After 1947, family names began to be popular and assertive, particularly among the land-owning *Jats*, army officers, government bureaucrats, politicians, and aspirants to power. A whole plethora of pseudonyms were also adopted by those that fancied themselves as poetic and sensitive: so and so Dukhi, Udass, Premi, and Arshi.

Families with emigrants in foreign lands and those who had served in exotic locales called themselves So-and-So *China*, *Americawale*, or *Waliati* if it was England. It was kind of a renaissance in literature as the opening of many independent presses gave aspiring and accomplished poets, authors, and storytellers a forum. Small and large fortunes were gained by novelists. Now the newsstands had a choice of dailies, magazines, and tabloids published in Punjabi, Hindi, and English as well as Urdu, as many of the literate had studied it and appreciated its "special sweetness" as a language of poetry and expression, and the film industry in Bombay continued to release opuses in this language of the Moguls.

As a quick learner, Karam had a good grasp of three languages: Punjabi, Hindi, and English. Thanks to the Comrade's open-door policy, he had access to an extensive library of magazines and books. It fed his insatiable demand for knowledge and reading. Thus when the Comrade sat on the cot and watched his ward disappear into the urgent and necessary needs of his family, he could not protest and take a share to spend on books. Karam got the school ones for free from the headmaster, who had recognized his intelligence long before anyone else recognized it or appreciated it.

Karam's maternal grandmother invited him to spend a few days in the city where his grandfather now tended the dead at the morgue. It was attached to the civic hospital built by the British and now the fiefdom of the state government. The job, a great relief for Bola, was his reward from Chandu Das, and it came with government quarters with two rooms in addition to a kitchen and a bathroom. The chief surgeon, who also lorded over the entire district's health service—including rural clinics—had magnanimously allowed Bola to pick sturdy furniture out of the storeroom for his home.

When the young man got there, he was surprised by the change in fortune of his grandparents, their substantial living space, and its fine furniture and furnishings. Here no one could guess their caste had they visited for the first time.

This was his first lengthy stay, two weeks in the bustling neighborhood dominated by the district jail, the civic hospital, and the internationally renowned Brown Hospital and its medical school. There were clean shops packed with goods he had not seen before and sweetmeats, sodas and the heavenly frozen concoction they called ice cream. His grandmother indulged his every wish and took him to a local clothier and had the tailor measure him for two suits of clothing. Then she bought him his first real pair of shoes— not moccasins but tie-on—and a pair of brown socks. His grandfather took him to a barber and had his unruly locks properly trimmed into a style he got to choose off the wall covered in pictures of well-coifed men and seductive women, obviously artist renderings to emphasize their doe-like eyes, massive hair-dos, and ample bosoms threatening to burst out of the flimsy blouses. For a youth just past puberty it was a heady place to be in. That afternoon he took a long and leisurely bath in the dark privacy of the bathroom, a luxury that was unknown to his clan in Noorian where the men bathed publicly at the newly installed hand pump in the courtyard and where the women bathed only after sending off the boys and men and constructing a temporary wall of cots lined on their sides.

His grandparents used real soap that lathered well and left his skin clean and slightly perfumed, and there was a mirror to gaze at. Once he had his new clothes on and his hair properly pomaded and combed, what looked back at him was a stranger, reed thin and brooding. Then his grandfather took him to a movie house in the center of town, and he was wide-eyed at its ornate and imposing presence dominating the long row of low buildings on either side. Directly opposite stood a similar structure, another cinema crowded with filmgoers. Seated on wooden slats at the very front rows, he spent three hours enthralled by the heroic epic of songs and dance, tears and laughter, fortune and tragedy, and the central figure, a woman he knew he would never fall out of love with. At night, his mind was filled with fantastic images of dreamscapes that can only be conjured by a newly awakened mind: the mind of a young virgin.

Suddenly his grandfather was his hero. Not the severe and dour man who had visited him twice a year in Noorian, but a giving man, the opener of doors to places and possibilities he could not have imagined. "You can live with us once you get to college," grandfather stated as he watched Karam's face light up like a gas lantern. The youth needed no other incentive or motivations. He was going to ace high school and escape forever the fetid courtyard of his clan, he promised himself. At the end of his holidays, he walked back into Noorian, and people did double-takes, for most did not recognize him, what with his suit of linen and shiny tie-on shoes, his hair styled like the film idol Raj Kapoor.

Back in school, grade nine was taught in another cavernous, abandoned *haveli*. It had been the home of a prosperous Muslim family and constructed of brick and mortar, its vast flat roof supported by great teak beams supported by tall pillars. It was airy and bright. The new teachers transferred in to start and teach at the high school were young, approachable, and idealistic men. Committed to their calling, they honed in on Karam and offered him encouragement, attention, and individual tutoring. They felt fortunate to have at least one student so bright and enthusiastic in his pursuit of learning, unlike the sons of

Jats, who were content to waste and wile their days away at school rather than wrestling with the soil. Most of them would go on to graduate with barely passable grades and onto entry-level positions in the police, the fast-expanding electricity board, the army, in offices as clerks, and at railway stations as bus conductors and ticket agents. The state and nation needed workers who could at least perform the tasks of reading and writing and basic arithmetic in the ever-expanding departments administering the vast reaches of India and help bring it into the modern world and its fast-changing technologies.

Some, like Karam, were fated for a higher education, the learning and honing of skills in the college campuses of the province's two universities: Punjab and Punjabi University. A new one called the Agricultural University was being built in Ludhiana, with campuses in Rohtak and Solan. Indian Punjab had two engineering colleges, four medical schools, and an expanding post-graduate campus in the new city of Chandigarh, beautifully laid out at the Shivalik foothills and housing its capital. Higher education remained an elusive dream for a majority of rural youth, its costs prohibitive even with scholarships for the scheduled castes and tribes. The parents and families needed extra hands to earn enough to survive and were unwilling or unable to support a deserving child. The villagers still tilled the land with oxen and cattle, a laborious task needing manual supplementing. Most had their physical strength as their only capital and sentenced themselves to a life of arduous labor, low wages, and the vagaries of nature, disease, and government neglect. Progress trickled slowly to the countryside, and it was decades before villagers would gain electricity, bus service, proper clinics (both medical and veterinary), well-managed schools with trained teachers, or radios and telephones. Television would be a longer time arriving or becoming affordable.

But progress of another sort was now well underfoot. The Consolidation of Land Holdings Act, initially resisted but quickly embraced, would pool in one larger plot a farmer's fractured fields, thus increasing investment in irrigation; define property lines to cut conflict and bloodshed; straighten ancient and winding pathways into wider, negotiable roads; make allowances for ditches to drain floodwaters and bring water from snowmelts to arid acres; give further allowances for common areas to build community centers, schools, and places of worship, clinics, and playgrounds; and make allotments, albeit small, for the landless to build permanent housing, giving the previously indentured their own economic stakes in their communities.

It forced large landowners to abandon their claims to whole villages and reduced the maximum acreage an individual could hold to one hundred, the rest divided among his sharecroppers. Proper deeds of ownership and registration of the same would now allow smoother inheritance and passage of land from generation to generation. It took several years of tedious surveying by *patwaris* and *kanugos*, but the act changed the geography for the better. The common woods near the village were quickly felled and plowed into productive fields, and pasture disappeared under the plow. The country began to grow more food to feed its growing masses. There was an increase in intensive farming, extracting more food and fodder per acre and putting more in the farmers' pockets; a sense of increasing prosperity pervaded the landed classes. With more money coming in as remittances from emigrants and expatriates, those receiving this largesse began building more durable housing of bricks and mortar, putting the artisan castes on a burst of employment in bricklaying and carpentry. Tall smokestacks rose over the countryside as kilns went up to supply this demand both in the cities and villages.

The new school was fully completed and opened its doors the year after Karam graduated as a matriculate. Karam was a provincial scholar once more, and the Government College in Ludhiana immediately invited him to obtain an FSc in sciences. His mother took him to give thanksgiving at the Sant Baba *Samadhi*, now standing naked of any surrounding shade or foliage in the middle of a field, a small bit of earth granted as its perimeter allowance and a narrow pathway from the road as access for its pilgrims. Punna lamented the loss of the peaceful grove it had been built in and carried a dream in her heart of one day restoring it to its original glory. As Karam bowed before it, she had an epiphany of her son being the instrument of the *Samadhi's* restoration, and watching his devotion for the edifice, she began to pray for it to be fulfilled, at least in her lifetime.

Chapter 6

*D*r. (Lt. Col., retired) Pratap Singh Grewal, Chief Surgeon of the civic hospital in Ludhiana, also served as the district chief medical officer. He held court in a round corner room of the colonial-era building with grand verandas, spacious wards, surgical suites, a residence for the female nurses and attendants, and a row of quarters for the nonmedical staff. It had a large pharmacy that stored and distributed medicines to the other government clinics and a central laboratory and public health department that sent out roving teams to stem breakouts of infectious diseases that constantly threatened the populace largely because of ignorance, neglect, and lack of sanitation. Six years after independence and self rule, the once shiny, well-funded hospital had seen its own sanitation decline along with all the standards of care and professionalism the British held so dear. It had a lot to do with spotty funding from a provincial government yet to get a good grasp on its cost, budgets, and collection of customs and duties. Everyone dodged taxes now. The thread of corruption and graft ran all the way from the peon guarding his office door to the minister in charge of health in Chandigarh and his federal superior in New Delhi. Service to the public was free in name only with the indigent receiving the diluted doses in reused bottles while the well-to-do paid and got the best available medicine. The payment, of course, disappeared into the pockets of the medical officers and doctors and supplemented the low wages. The rest of the staff did its best to extract baksheesh from the unfortunate relatives of the sick or injured, establishing a multi-tiered level of care. It could be seen in the assignment of beds, the provision of services and meals, right down to the changing of the bed sheets and emptying of commodes. Being the only free hospital in the city, it was crowded morning to night with outpatients vying for relief and inpatients for rudimentary care and attention. Those who could afford it enjoyed the privacy of a single room, surrounded by relatives, and they were tenderly attended to by the senior staff.

A legal task of the chief surgeon was the conducting of autopsies on bodies of murdered or suspected victims of a crime, brought or sent there by the police. As well, he had the task of examining those wounded in criminal acts of robbery or domestic violence (mostly acts of revenge or vendetta). All accident victims had to report there for medicals. The official morgue managed by Bola was there as well. It was a feared section of the hospital and also housed the autopsy room, large and well-lit, built thus so medical students and interns could attend as a class or group. Hushed relatives were allowed to wait under a *peepal* tree on stone benches. Bodies were released by the authority of the chief surgeon and delivered into the care of the grieving kin by a suitably somber Bola. He accepted their gratitude in coin and eased their exit by calling a *tonga* or rickshaw to a side gate opening up to an empty alley. Bola sometimes took in three times his salary, and anticipating a call for help with the impending weddings of his two grand-daughters and the task of supporting Karam, he banked every penny in his savings account at the post office.

As soon as the results of the matriculation were reported, he summoned his grandson for presentation to his boss,

Dr. Pratap Singh Grewal. The wily former hangman had a longstanding relationship and knowledge of the severe-looking Sikh. He knew that beneath that fearsome exterior and booming bluster, a deeply pained and kind man existed. The doctor was a man known for always keeping his word. "If the boy gets a first division in his marks," the doctor had promised Bola, "I will see to it he gets into medical school in some capacity."

Karam had not disappointed and now sat awaiting an interview with the great man, his grandfather tastefully attired in his best and crisply pressed white suit with nary a scuff on his shoes or a hair out of place on his grey mane. Just like his grandfather, Karam had given up wearing a turban or any sort of covering on his head. Neither enjoyed a second name, and his matriculation certificate stated:

Karam s/o Ruldu, Vill. & P.O.
Noorian, Teh. Samrala, Distt. Ludhiana.

It was the most significant document he would ever possess because in India, it was the evidence of birth, birth place, and lineage, and it was absolutely necessary for the issuance of passports by the Indian government and visas by the foreign ones.

The peon came to with a start, stuck his head inside the louvered door, and guided them in. Dr. Grewal stood up and stepped around the huge desk covered with stacks of file folders bursting with paper of a rainbow of colors. A clerk sat behind a smaller desk, his head buried purposely into a register. A large fan with wooden blades turned lazily from the domed ceiling. "Sahib," the elder grinned, presenting his charge. The unusually tall and absolutely erect officer dressed in the long, white coat of his profession proffered his right hand to be held. Karam took it instinctively and received a hearty shake and a resounding slap on his shoulder.

"*Bale, Bale, Beta!*" the doctor boomed, fixing Karam with his bespectacled eyes. "Well done, well done, son!"

Karam bent down to touch the great man's feet but was easily rebuffed "Old customs, my boy, old customs!" Dr. Grewal turned around to get back to his seat behind the desk. Pointing to the chairs arranged around his desk, he bade them to be seated. Once they had, he took a long, unblinking look at the fifteen-year-old aspiring scholar in front of him and finally smiled a kindly and indulgent grin without a sign of superiority. Instead, he studied him with curiosity as if examining a new and unknown specimen. The doctor was the scion of one of the district's most distinguished families, a family which counted officers, elected officials, judges, professors, and army greats, and he had a hint of royalty in his lineage. He was a *Jat* Sikh of substance, authority, and education, now seated before a subservient *Chura* and his bright descendant. "The future of India," he wondered. The boy looked clean cut and respectful and had arrived in his office already a minor celebrity in the province if not the country. Dr. Grewal felt his shoulders sag from the fatigue of a life lived to maintain and enhance a status. The youth seated before him had probably already accomplished more for his people than he had contributed to his in decades of education in the best schools in India and England, service in the Royal Indian Army, and now in his status as the district's chief of medicine. His people had emulated the British and lived and competed for a social standing and managed to emasculate themselves and breed out the brave in favor of "gentility." The scientist in him, not the socialist, was now in charge. He felt he was on the cusp of a discovery, a revolution of unimaginable consequences; the uplifting of the teeming masses, of the unwashed.

"You did well," he repeated after the lengthy pause that had occupied his inquisitive mind. Karam nodded eagerly, awaiting an award: the fulfillment of a promise of entry into medical school. He was acutely aware and informed of the Brown Memorial Hospital up the street and the Christian Medical College, an island of opportunity, prestige, and standards unlike the declining grace of the civic hospital, its slow decay already visible to his unadulterated eyes. Beside it, the foreign-run institution was thriving, growing, and shining.

As was customary, Karam lowered his gaze and shuffled his feet, a sign of humility that did not go unnoticed or unappreciated by the doctor. "I made a promise to your *Nanaji*, a promise you have earned young man. And I must keep it."

Karam looked up and met the determined gaze.

"I will support your education if we can get you into medical school young man."

"I am ready, Doctor Sahib," Karam blurted.

Dr. Grewal threw his head back and laughed. "I like your enthusiasm, young man, but before you get in, you have to decide into what."

Both visitors looked askance at him.

"Medical school can train you from an orderly, a nurse, technician, radiographer, or therapist to a doctor and eventually a surgeon or a specialist," he elaborated. "A pharmacy assistant to a pharmacologist."

They were silent now.

"So what do you want to be?" he asked, and then continued, "How many years are you willing to sacrifice before you can begin to earn a penny?"

A long silence followed. The clerk in the corner lifted his

head, a knowing smile creasing his face. He was familiar with the way of the doctor. He was methodical and dogged in all pursuits, looking at everything as if examining a diamond, every surface and facet, every fault and finish, every cause and effect. No wonder his autopsy reports were routinely accepted by judges and treasured by police detectives true to their calling. There was reasoning, an explanation. No wishing. No washing. He provided the facts and only the facts. No fantasy. The doctor was beyond those. Ever since his one and only beloved daughter had eloped with a Muslim army officer to Pakistan and did not return despite desperate pleas and offers from the distraught parents, he had been shamed to the bone by this display of filial disloyalty. The doctor, using his old connections, had visited her new home in Lahore. Finding her in her third trimester, he had accepted the inevitable and crossed back to India, shut himself in his ancient, musty manor, and drunk to the last drop his stocks of stored scotch and gin, rum and whiskey. He was finally lifted and transported by the strong grip of Bola to a sanatorium up in the hills, in Kasauli, where on long afternoons he had sat and contemplated life from 4,000 feet above the plains of Punjab.

The doctor was watched and waited over by his trusted clerk and Bola, the only ones privy to the family secret. His wife had passed away from grief or consumption or a secret addiction to opiates, so much had the loss of her only child consumed her. The good man was only a lonely shell of himself now but bravely carried forward, methodically and scientifically as he had been trained to do in the Middlesex Hospital in England.

Askance! The *Churas* before him were clueless.

His shoulders sagged in resignation. To buy time he called for a serving of tea and waited, collecting his thoughts while the peon brought in a silver tray laden with a teapot, cups, plates, and biscuits piled high on a porcelain plate. He watched the serving of the tea and biscuits and noticed with longing how Bola instructed his grandson in the custom of accepting such hospitality, making sure that Karam did not show his rural roots and caste by grabbing a handful of the fragrant offerings. In that moment, he adopted the youth. A visceral sense of proprietorship flooded him. Karam now had unwittingly earned another angel to watch over him.

After a lot of discussion between Karam and his grandfather, it was agreed that because he had the scholarship for two years at the Government College in Ludhiana, he would study for his FSc or a certificate from the Faculty of Sciences from Punjab University offered at one of its many campuses, the local one being the GC. Two other campuses competed against it for attention: the Parochial Sikh Khalsa College and the Hindu Arya College. But the faculty of professors and the number of prominent graduates from the Government College was a major consideration and applauded by Dr. Grewal, himself a member of its illustrious alumni. Its recent history in the struggle for independence and the involvement in that cause by its students were well-recorded. The GC was situated in the Civil Lines section of the city, a suburb that hosted among the district courts one of the oldest Catholic churches in northern India, the homes of its elite both businessmen and bureaucrats. It was a sprawling campus of greenery and grandeur in architecture and landscape. The principal, a consumptive Hindu, personally hosted the provincial scholar for tea at his residence, a gesture much appreciated by the grandfather and Dr. Grewal. For Karam, it was a head-spinning event.

He chose the subjects that would prepare him for studies in medicine: English, Physics, Chemistry, and Biology, with a

minor in mathematics. At Dr. Grewal's insistence, he joined
the National Cadet Corps, a collegiate version of boy scouts
elevated to twice-weekly military parading and training in
weaponry. The good doctor felt that if Karam faltered at
the institutes of higher learning, he had a fair chance of the
makings of an army officer now that it was hunting for good
candidates from the scheduled castes, a requirement because
of the constitutionally guaranteed quotas.

"Always pray to Sant Baba," his mother whispered
during deep sobs as she hugged him before finally letting
him go. His father and several of his kin accompanied him to
the ring road. He had returned to Noorian for the weekend
before college started. He had paid his respects by stopping
by the homes of the Comrade and headmaster Sharma, as
well as the school to thank the teachers who had devoted so
much energy and effort to him. To his surprise, Inder Singh
Pardesi had arrived from East Africa for a five-month visit
to the village, and the kindly, polite, and cerebral man had
thoughtfully purchased a bicycle for Karam. It was a reward
for his scholastic achievements. Karam was so thrilled that
he had spent most of his time giving rides to his sisters and
excited kin around the ring road, much to the chagrin of
some jealous highborn but to the amusement of many in
the village. His pure and simple joy at the receipt of this
gesture of charity from a highborn that had attained such
an exalted position to a lowborn like himself struggling to
succeed had even put a smile on the face of the donor: a
serious, unsmiling man whose kind eyes gave away the true
feelings he had.

With the rolls of *pinnis* his mother had cooked with so
much care and devotion and the meager collection of his
possessions still in Noorian tied securely to the handles of
his new conveyance, Karam bade goodbye and pedaled

vigorously away from the village to the city beckoning in the distance. His heart was no longer in Noorian but the vibrant city of Ludhiana. As he wound his way through the meandering trails cut across vast fields and a few village streets, he was surprised at the lack of emotion he felt as he put distance away from his place of birth that still housed his sisters and parents and most of his kin. He felt as if he was escaping from a toilet that had imprisoned him from birth to a much more fragrant place.

* * *

These emotions—or lack of them—as he passed through many more cities, counties, and countries in life would continue to haunt him. He was like a reptile shedding off a constricting skin as he slid from one field to a greener pasture of opportunity. Yet fate would bind him to Noorian in ways he could not imagine.

* * *

For a yet-to-be sixteen-year-old, college was a revelation, a new world and a sense of freedom Karam had never had before. He only had four classes a day and three laboratory sessions a week to attend. There were long stretches of time in between one and the other; time that he could spend in the spacious library, sauntering on the grounds, sitting under a tree, or going through the gate and onto the street to patronize a tea stall. His grandparents had seen to it that he did not lack for suitable dress or grooming. To anyone else, he was another well-dressed and quiet Hindu boy. Even his classmates, for he had not tried to stand out, made room for him beside them on a bench, shared a beaker or a microscope in the laboratories, or let him sit at the table with them in the library or the tea stalls. The English class had the highest attendance, almost a hundred or more boys. The physics and chemistry classes had about eighty each, but the biology class was smaller, with just fifty students. The lecturers focused on the material for the session and went through it in a methodical manner, leaving little time for individual questions or clarifications. The students were expected to spend hours in self study. There were few tutorials or personal attention by the lecturers, and the teachers were not easily located over the vast campus.

Karam struggled. Instruction and explanations were in English, it being the medium of instruction—not Punjabi or Hindi, languages that he had a much greater facility in. Even math, although a minor subject, still posed problems. It was being taught rapid-fire by the youthful instructor who, once he had taken roll call, never turned to look at the class, instead writing formulae after formulae on the long blackboard that virtually ran the width of the classroom. Only the laboratories were more intimate. Here, he had closer contact with his instructors, and these he took to with alacrity. He began to stand out from the rest of his fellow students and was noticed by the faculty.

The college also offered a large number of extracurricular activities in sports, the arts, and entertainment.

The established athletes, particularly cricket and field hockey players, were the popular ones. Always in the midst of an admiring throng of hangers-on, Karam maintained a solitary existence for fear of being found out as a *Chura*. Enough rough-housing among the obviously highborn groups resulted in verbal name calling. Some of it pained Karam, particularly when they singled each other out for ridicule by calling each other *Churas* or "Chura-like."

Karam hurried home on his bicycle each day as soon as classes were done, rather than linger behind and socialize with his college mates even though no untoward incident had occurred to point him or his caste out. A few had even reached out in friendship, inviting him to join them in the cafeteria or to skip classes to see the latest the cinemas had to offer. Instead, he arrived at the quarter and buried his head in his books. His grandparents watched him like two old hens constantly clucking about his welfare. His grandmother, finally having a child to fuss over, cooked a different dish of *dhal* or *subzi* for each meal they ate with *rotis*. Sometimes she made rice and bought a jar of fresh yogurt from the sweetmeat shop. Seasonal fruit was cheap and plentiful then, and a glass of boiled milk with a spoon of sugar was a suitable night cap. Nothing was too good or unattainable for her Karam.

Sometimes he would awaken to find her seated beside his bed fanning him, to cool him and not let flies sit on his peaceful and handsome face. "I want the most beautiful wife for you," she teased often.

"And I will probably get one cross-eyed and buck-toothed," he would snort playfully and receive a punch to his torso.

A month later, his mother and father traveled to Ludhiana to announce that matches had been selected for both his sisters; the proposed grooms were brothers from Jogpore. They stayed two days to negotiate the help they would receive from the grandfather and shop for materials they needed, and they returned to Noorian pleased with the results. The weddings were set to be performed jointly during Karam's holidays after the first semester of college. As a courtesy, they asked him to visit the home of his future sisters-in-law. He did that the following Sunday.

Jogpore was an old town on the Grand Trunk Road that ran to New Delhi from the north, once running through Lahore and passing through the major cities of Punjab, namely Amritsar, Jullundur, Ludhiana, Ambala, Karnal, and

Panipat, the site of the great battle between good and evil, the Mahabharata, as described in the Gita. Jogpore was like a lot of other market towns between these cities, and it straddled the Sirhind Canal. It also enjoyed a railway station on the line that ran parallel to the GT road. In fact, the body of the town ran from the railway station to the west to the GT Road to the east. It had a thriving grain market, a lumber exchange, and a bazaar providing merchandise of every kind. A couple of well-qualified doctors ran their busy offices. A little south of the railway station sat a row of low, brick homes that housed the *Chura* families and the domicile of Karam's new kin. A long, crumbling wall of ancient fortifications provided the outdoor privies for the locals. The waste from the privies was sustenance for a few dozen scrawny pigs the *Chura* kept supplementing their income. Karam soon discovered that these omnivores were the recyclers of general and human waste. They were fully grown and reproducing litters at the age of one year. His future brothers-in-law kept a herd of thirty, selling almost half of the herd for meat every year. They worked as coolies at the station, having inherited the positions from their grandfather and father, who now wiled their time sitting together under the shade of the veranda smoking a strong-smelling hookah.

The family and the clan in fact had just gotten up and occupied these homes once lived in by Muslims and had dared government officials to remove them by force. The homes with decent-sized courtyards and pens for animals were sturdy, although a century or more old. Built of small, fired brick and durable mortar, they were better than any habitat Karam had ever witnessed a *Chura* clan in, except for the quarter his grandparents enjoyed in Ludhiana. All other homes of his clan members in Noorian and relatives he had visited in other villages were all flimsy affairs on one-storied mud hovels. The *Churas* of Jogpore were living well, most employed by the municipality or the railways. Suitably arrogant of their superior status, they were humbled by the visit of the famous and fierce Bola. Every elder came over to shake his hand and pay respects. They exchanged minor gifts, refused the offer of food and drink, and as they took their leave, Bola had everyone's attention when he stated, "Take good care of my granddaughters, boys, and I will not have to visit you more than necessary."

"Absolutely!" intoned the entire clan, and Karam felt rather proud of his grandfather—proud and protected.

* * *

In the cool month of December, when the water drawn from wells sent a trail of white mist rising along the channels that flowed into the fields and a light dusting of frost on the ground greeted each dawn, the village of Noorian was the scene of a unique and historic event in rural India. A *Chura* double-wedding arranged to save expense suddenly put a lie to that assumption; it was a culmination of many events.

The brother of the brides was a top scholar in the province and now a student in premedicine at the eminent Government College in Ludhiana; the father was the village watchman and the mother the midwife; the grandfather was a well-known and feared figure, an ex-hangman now in charge of the morgue. The grooms were the sons of a *Chura* clan that had out defied the authorities in grabbing valuable residential property in a historic town and now proudly occupied it with its pigs and hunting hounds. Some said they controlled the opium and *doda* trade because of its penetration of the railway station, a central point in the province. The service and ceremonies would be attended by the local member of provincial parliament and the state minister of public works, Shree Chandu Das, the well-known freedom fighter, his exploits against the British already spoken in local history books and lore.

The headman of the village had granted the wedding party from Jogpore occupancy of the newly constructed *Serai*. The party would arrive in motorcars and *tongas*.

Most importantly, it would be led into the village by a band of uniformed men playing wind instruments, drums, and cymbals, just like those of the British era parades. The music stirred the martial blood of the populace and seeped in the legends of sacrifice and struggle.

Inder Singh Pardesi, the Comrade, headmaster Shreekant Sharma, and those highborn beholden or grateful to Ruldu and Punna in one way or another accepted invitations to be attendees if not participants or guests at the wedding. The gulf for some in the castes was too great to be bridged by a simple obligation. Few if any of the superior castes, as they considered themselves, were thinking of eating or drinking any of the offered or proffered treats or dishes and particularly not from utensils supplied for the occasion. Although the local Brahmin sweetmeat makers and the *jheurs* would prepare the dishes, they would be put out in trays supplied by the *Churas* and served by them. Payment in coin would be accepted and expected according to agreed upon terms: cash on the barrel.

Thus the day became a highly anticipated one in Noorian and the nearby villages and hamlet of the *Tehsil* of Samrala. Its *Tehsildar* and superintendant of police were expected to attend in person as instructed by the PA of the local MLA and the state minister of the PWD, the best and most lucrative ministry in the entire cabinet in Chandigarh. It built and repaired roads and bridges; purchased all government needs; and was in charge of all its property and publicly owned lands, causeways, hospitals, schools and colleges, not to mention bus stations, stops, and airports. With one of the largest percentages of the state budget and as a similar recipient of federal funds, it employed thousands and granted hundreds of private contracts a month.

In Ludhiana, Dr. Grewal had his old but trusty and still well-running Hillman motorcar cleaned and shined for the drive to Noorian. He was rather looking forward to the event. His guest, an old friend and senior correspondent for The Tribune, the only English daily in the province, was bringing along a photographer to record the event.

Chapter 7

The first day of the second semester was extremely stressful for Karam. His face had been plastered all over the newspapers after his sisters' wedding. The story and pictures occupied a full page of the four typically published by The Tribune to conserve paper. So much was its editorial significance; the other dailies picked it up. The last week of his holidays was spent in interviews and being photographed in the village beside his school; inside his parents one-room dwelling while on a cot; astride the bicycle donated by the altruistic Pardesiji, who was also made to stand beside the youth on the bike; with his parents, who insisted on carrying the tools of their trade, his father with his staff and his mother with her bundle of stuff needed for a delivery; at the quarter in the civic hospital grounds; standing between his proud grandparents, one a kind older woman, the other a man who made one cringe—the grandfather, Bola.

Now he was famous. He was just sixteen, and he was already in newspapers and journals.

At the college, everyone stared at him. Karam said little and acknowledged less. He was the most famous *Chura* in Punjab, bar none.

Troubled and fearful of exposure at first, then finding a reserve of strength he did not believe existed within him, he met their gaze, steady and smiling until they lowered theirs first. Before he knew it, he had friends, admirers in the ranks of not only the freshmen but the seniors. Most wanted to shake his hand and be introduced, to invite him into their circles.

He felt exotic, unique, and confident. He was not ashamed of his caste anymore but proud and assertive.

* * *

The disappointment came with the results of the first semester. His marks were middle of the pack, in English in particular. But his practicum marks were at or near the top. Dr. Grewal was neither surprised nor disappointed. "Not unusual," he remarked as Karam along with his grandfather looked anxiously at him. "University is different and takes some adjusting to, and I expect improvement." He passed back the single sheet listing his performance.

"Yes, Doctor Sahib," Karam promised.

However he skipped his first class that week to join his new friends in watching a matinee of a new film. Being in the company of his peers and equally dressed and treated was a different feeling, a new experience, and a new freedom. It was the freedom to decide to attend or miss the odd lecture, at once frightening and exhilarating. He felt alive and in a new universe during the screening, seated in the middle of the cinema on proper upholstered seats and in the midst of the rowdy row of young men. From then on to the end of the middle semester, he had gone at least once a week on these sojourns of juvenile abandon, of stretching his limits and exploring life where the oxygen was abundant and suffocation nonexistent. His circle of friends grew, and he was hailed as he traveled from one lecture hall to another. He smiled more. In this more enjoyable and relaxed environment, he found himself improving and growing in knowledge and not just from books, but from the discussions, opinions, jokes, and tall tales he was privy to now. However, his biweekly pedaling to Noorian depressed him, for the village remained a static and staid place, somehow locked away in its own time capsule. Things happened in Ludhiana, but life went on in Noorian in the same monotonous way as last month and the month before that. His parents and kin said and did the same things each visit.

He went to visit his sisters in Jogpore for three days during study week, taking with him three of his textbooks along with a change of clothing and a box of sweetmeats. He found them happy and comfortable, not doing any sweeping or cleaning for others. Their mother-in-law had kept them home for now. With few bills to pay and no real urgency for money, they lived off the sale of the piglets, the salaries of his two brothers-in-law, and the pension of the father and grandfather. The in-laws had an older daughter already wed and living in Ambala with her soldier husband, who visited every three months or so. Karam gave the box of sweetmeats to the woman of the house, received her blessing, and sat on a cot pulled down for him and covered with a clean, new sheet to signify his position as an honored guest of the family.

It took awhile, but Karam, now unused to the constant smell of manure and open sewers, was suddenly nauseous. He covered his nose with his handkerchief, and this did not go unnoticed by his older sister, who smiled sympathetically and made a face while holding her nose momentarily. Careful that her mother-in-law was not around, she confided, "It is a sewer, this Jogpore is," she hissed. "Noorian is a hundred times better."

"And Ludhiana a hundred better than Noorian," thought Karam. However, he slowly got used to the odor. His brothers-in-law went to great lengths to entertain him and make his stay enjoyable. They paraded him around their small town, its vast lumber and grain markets, the streets of the furniture makers, the new-fangled sawmill run with a noisy engine that could be heard almost over the whole territory, its oil mill, and its shops in the mile-long bazaar, with busy shopkeepers attending to customers seven days of the week. Everyone seemed to welcome them, including the Brahmins who owned the flourmill. Even the constable guarding the entrance to the police post nodded pleasantly. For the first time, he got a shave from a real barber under the canopy of a shade tree as he sat on a burlap sack, watching the traffic pass by: pedestrians, ox carts, cyclists, hand-pulled and bicycle rickshaws, horse-drawn *tongas*, the odd man on horseback or a kid riding a donkey, and the occasional bus or truck and the rare car. The wide, nonmetalled road was well-traveled.

"My brother is very intelligent," his younger sister was telling a wide-eyed girl, one of his substantial tomes opened before them. The girl, a couple of years younger than him, blushed when their eyes met and fled the room. His sister looked conspiratorially at him.

"What?" Karam asked.

"She might be your betrothed," was the reply, whispered loud enough for all to hear.

"I am never getting married," Karam stated matter-of-factly, but his insides now roiled because the visitor had been very attractive.

"Liar," his sisters laughed and set about feeding their brother a meal of curried pork, a luxury indeed. He soon forgot the incident as his younger brother-in-law poured him a stiff drink of moonshine.

Sure enough upon his return, his grandmother was agitated and kept looking at his face as if seeking an answer. "What, Naniji?" he had to ask.

"You saw the girl, no?"

"What girl?"

"The one with the curly brown hair and cat-like eyes," she explained.

Karam sat down hard on his cot, "Naniji, I will not get married until I have achieved something."

"She won't stop you," his grandmother said emphatically, closing the discussion.

Karam avoided the subject for the next week, but it got brought to a head by a visit from his older brother-in-law and his father. They had enjoyed the hospitality at the quarter and stuffed themselves with his grandmother's cooking and his grandfather's ample supply of rum. But on the morning after, having bathed luxuriantly and feasted on *parathas* and yogurt, they began the discussion of betrothing the curly haired girl called Billo to Karam. His grandfather listened attentively, taking furtive looks at his expressionless grandson.

They had good reasons. *Chura* boys and girls were married at an earlier age to avoid any accusations of mixing with and sexually defiling the upper castes, rendering the girls unmarriageable and thus extreme burdens on the parents. Girls of Billo's beauty would be soon pursued by the young louts of Jogpore and the surrounding villages. The caste was constantly under attack, sexually, by the predatorily higher born, who considered it a birthright to cajole and seduce or simply kidnap and rape girls and women of those born on a lower societal rung. It would take all the cunning of their clans in Jogpore to keep these Romeos at bay. What better for her than to be sent off as bride to another town, city, or village, thus shifting the burden to the in-laws?

"She is the prettiest," emphasized Sajjan, the brother-in-law, a little matter-of-factly. Bola gave him a long stare, which the man avoided immediately. "Perhaps Billo needs protection from her own," Bola thought. Then standing up and extending his substantial body to its full six feet and more, he declared, "I will consider the request and discuss it with my son-in-law." After telling Karam to get ready for a visit to Noorian that Saturday afternoon, he took his leave and marched off to his duties at the morgue. Karam did the same and pedaled off to the GC and spent most of the remainder of the day daydreaming, his thoughts going from a success in education and a position of power and prestige to the immediacy of intimacy with a girl whose cat-like eyes had seared a place in his conscious.

That evening they ate quietly. The elders and the youth retired early to lie on their cots, staring for answers at the darkened ceilings.

However, it was his grandmother in Noorian who put her foot down. "I want him to rise to a level no *Chura* has yet!" emphatically putting an end to the discussion.

A month later, Billo was betrothed to a youth recently recruited into the police under the strict quota for scheduled castes. A month after that she became a wife and the wisp of a dream in Karam's often agitated mind as it struggled with studies, socializing, and societal pressures. His marks in the middle semester were sinister in their factual brutality.

Dr. Grewal, still the optimist, cautioned him against angst and concern and losing heart.

"You will be fine," he told Karam. His confidence showing in his steady gaze, he took the grandfather aside.

* * *

Karam threw himself into his books and lectures and laboratory work. He paraded in the NCC uniform twice a week and avoided missing any further classes. Thankfully, there was electricity in the city now, and he could study late into the night, the closed windows keeping out the swarms of mosquitoes and insects. His grandmother fed him gruel of milk and almonds to help his brain. He stopped his biweekly trips to visit his parents as the forty-mile trip in two days left him exhausted now that the sun was getting hotter by the day. He pored over every page, every note, memorizing and understanding the diverse and difficult subjects he was learning, all this at a tortuous pace.

And it paid off.

He scored a first division in the finals and accolades from the Comrade, Shreekant Sharma, Dr. Grewal, the consumptive college principal, and Inder Singh Pardesi, from whom he received a long letter of congratulations and encouragement. He was sent to Noorian and later to Jogpore to spend a few weeks to relax and reconnect with his family. Of course, his mother once again dragged him to the Sant Baba Samadhi for prayer and benediction.

* * *

Dr. Grewal took part in an international health policy review in New Delhi attended by many foreign experts and health economists. It was sponsored by the United Nations. Once he had a few days to digest the knowledge he had gained, he began to think differently about the path Karam should take. Karam wanted to become a doctor, but being a *Chura* and the caste system being as strong now as ever, he was going to have to specialize in those areas requiring less direct patient contact. Even if he succeeded in getting all the *Churas* to be his patients, how would he make any money from such poor and bereft people? Also, Dr. Grewal had a feeling that the young man knew no better, that he did not have a true grasp of the years it would take, the expense of it all, and the toll it would take on his grandfather. Despite Dr. Grewal's offers, the proud man had not accepted a penny yet.

He invited Bola and the youth for a heart-to-heart at his home one evening.

After laying out as honestly as he could the mountain Karam would have to climb to become a doctor and the uncertain rewards that would await him, he recommended the position of medical technologist. "We have very few in Punjab, and only the Christian Medical College and the Medical College in Patiala train about ten a year each. Takes two years and you are gainfully employed. I understand that the opportunities to immigrate abroad with that certification are almost guaranteed. England, America ... Canada."

"And I can be admitted this year?" Karam asked. He had seen his grandfather's eyes light up at the mention of America.

"Yes," Dr. Grewal nodded. "In fact, I work closely with Dr. de Vries, the chief pathologist who runs the program here. I have already spoken to him about you. He thinks you make a good candidate."

"But I ..."

"I have told him about your scholastic achievements."

* * *

Instead of enrolling for his second year in the Faculty of Sciences, Karam was admitted to the two-year diploma program in medical technology at the CMC. Dr. Grewal personally paid the substantial annual fee upfront and bought the course books, two white coats, and a table lamp so Karam could study in better light. It was an intensive program, one year packed with theory and the second with clinical practicum. The classrooms were within easy walking distance of the quarter, and on the first day all, regrets and doubts about not pursuing the ultimate prize in medicine flew out of his mind as he walked to his orientation day. With his now tall frame and the mane of thick curls, the light-skinned youth with dark, smoldering eyes garnered second looks from all of the female students. And there were so many, a couple of hundred in nursing alone. Perhaps double that number, and then the medical students, radiotherapy and radiography, medical technology, not to count those working there. He had never imagined that the hospital and campus including the student hostels and the staff residences were almost as big as Noorian in area. It was a city within a city. The civic hospital was tiny by comparison, and dowdy. Even Government College could not hold a candle to the cleanliness and aristocracy of this institution. He was euphoric.

"*Naniji*, I am in heaven," he yelled, hugging the woman now a hand or so shorter than him while his grandfather sat with a broad grin on his face, watching his grandson wearing a white coat that represented education, authority, and a future.

* * *

Opened almost ninety years ago by an American missionary to administer to the poor of northern India, Miss Brown had chosen Ludhiana to set up the first training school for female nurses. Its educated and powerful merchant and landed families had supported her with land and acceptance. The generosity of Christian churches and communities, the dedication of medical missionaries from twenty-odd countries from Europe and the Americas, and the support of the British rulers had gone a long way in its growing into a full-blown medical institute of learning, specialization, research, and treatment. The year Karam was admitted as a student, it boasted twenty-seven different and specialist divisions, a number of community outreach clinics in other towns and cities, and a sanatorium in the hills of the Himalayas where the salubrious air attracted those with tuberculosis and the consumption. A large leperosium not only catered to the needs of the unfortunate sufferers but contributed through surgical advances, some first in the world in rehabilitation and reconstruction of the hand and feet. Its sister institute in Vellore in South India was larger and gaining ground in international attention and recognition. More than a half of their graduates had immigrated to foreign lands, and the alumni considered themselves a class apart from graduates of other medical schools in India.

Its financial support continued to be 50 percent foreign, with the provincial and central governments contributing the rest.

The Americans ran the medical school, but each department and specialization had a European head. The Dutch headed the pathology department, the Swiss gastroenterology, the British general medicine, and so on. Each country's main church donated money, material, and personnel. This assured that the technologies were up to date and world class. Proselytizing was prevalent both to the students and the staff as well as the patients and their visitors. Pastors in groups of two or three visited every ward daily, offering prayer and preaching while the patients and their visitors—mostly Hindus and Sikhs with a fair sprinkling of Muslims—were free to indulge openly in theirs. Five times a day, one would find a burqa-clad woman or a man in a fez kneeling on a prayer mat, performing duties in a corridor or hallway.

Fifty percent of the students admitted were of the Christian faith, and they came from all over India, particularly the state of Kerala, where Christianity had first taken root. Its patron saint was St. Thomas, the doubting Thomas, one of the twelve Disciples of Christ. Christians from that state continue to believe and perhaps correctly that they are one of the earliest continuous Christian communities in the world, like the Copts in Egypt. The rest of the students were from the Punjab and the adjoining states of Kashmir and Rajasthan, as well as the Union Territory of Delhi. Karam had the good fortune of admittance and acceptance into this cosmopolitan world.

It was a gift that would keep on giving long after he had traveled far and away in search of fame and fortune.

Just as he was finally adjusted to the prestige of belonging to the CMC as a student, its daily impact on his mind and thoughts, his enjoyment and savoring of the moments spent in the hallowed hall of learning, his eyes finally focusing in favor of the few in the crowds of female students, he got news that shook him to his core.

His grandmother in Noorian had suddenly passed away.

With his maternal grandparents in tow, Karam raced to the courtyard in Noorian where his one and only paternal ancestor now lay wrapped in the funerary cloth on the frame of an *arthi* as kin and relatives wept in shifts by her side. He had not had the opportunity to say goodbye or see her face a final time, and he had not received a last blessing, a hug, or, as she was famous for, a loud kiss on his cheek. Not even a mussing of his locks with her now claw-like hands and nails grown to curls under the pads. Garrulous, alert, and protective, she had guarded hers well. She was well-known and welcome in any home of any caste in the village. An oral historian of note, she had known who had wed whom and from where and why the relationship came to be; who were the matchmakers and what was or not served at the main wedding meal. Of the dowry, she could recount verbatim the entire contents of the hope chests of brides arrived and wed to the men in the village down to needlepoint designs of the pillow covers, who had got a mare and who a bicycle.

She lived her life serving her karma, never resentful of her low status, her "untouchability," an indifferent husband, or a string of lovers met in dark alleys or deep fields. She was not sure who Ruldu's father was, so busy was her sex life as a young *Chura* wife in a village rife with young men left unmarried for whatever reason and eager for relief of a primal urge, willing to share the luck of an unresisting partner as long as the price was honored in silence and substance. She appreciated the gentle. Roughness and horseplay resulted in long, fruitless waits in mosquito-infested hideouts with the object of affection ignoring the promise to meet. The crushing lack of satisfaction and the brutal sacrifice of silent suffering in the infested field was an unspoken lesson. A deal is a deal. No abuse.

She had spent her life, raised and protected her family, served her karma, owed nothing and owned nothing. Forty-eight years of life.

The biggest regret that would haunt Karam was that she never saw the best of what was to come. A glimpse, yes, a promise. She believed in him: witness her rejection of Billo. She had faith in him becoming the best of his caste, of uplifting them all, of escape. He would spend hours regretting the fact that she had not even seen him in his white coat as a medical technology student. She never heard of his potential, the chance to go to America.

Chapter 8

On his twenty-first birthday, Karam made the first of many remittances to his father in Noorian. It was a long walk from the St. Joseph's Hospital at the foot of Hamilton Mountain to the post office at King and James. He had all of thirty dollars to send, but there was lightness to his step. He took in a deep breath of the crisp fall air and stepped into the waiting area to line up for his turn. He had never before sent a money order, but he was confident that the person behind the counter would be helpful; once again he counted the bills and then the fifteen dollars in his wallet—all he would have for meals until the next pay check. He liked Canada, but he still had a lot of things to learn to fully integrate into society. The people had been so kind and welcoming: his bosses and coworkers at the hospital, his fellow residents at the YMCA, and even the sensei and students at the karate club. His first month had been a whirlwind of experiences: his first flight on an airplane, eating with a knife and fork, the different foods, the weather of early September, the total lack of mosquitoes and flies, the cleanliness of everything, the spaciousness of an American car, his first swim in a pool, his first hot shower, and learning to wash his clothes in a mechanical washer and then having them dried in a revolving drum that spewed them out hot.

Watching television was a totally new experience. He was so used to watching movies in India on huge screens that the 20-inch black-and-white floor model at the Y was quite a disappointment and took getting used to. The comedy programs ran a half hour, and he did not get the punch lines or understand the lyrics in a song, although the music moved him.

He had been allowed eight dollars of American currency to leave India with. Dr. de Vries had given him a parting gift of twenty dollars, a huge sum in India. Thankfully, Dr. Muriel King, his Canadian mentor at the CMC and his sponsor for the job offer from St. Joseph's that had allowed him to immigrate to Hamilton, had also warned him of the manner in which he would be paid and had advanced him fifty Canadian dollars. These offerings had saved him from embarrassment upon his arrival. Other than Dr. King, he knew no one, so she had picked him up at the airport, driven him to the YMCA, and paid for his first month of rent. He was thankful that the hospital was within easy walking distance. She was the one who had recommended he join a group activity or club, and one of the Jewish students who came to exercise at the YMCA had recommended the karate club. Karam had taken to this art form like fish to water, his body finally having an outlet for its genetic blessing of lean athleticism.

Because of the exaggerated stories about the Canadian cold by everybody at the CMC, including Dr. de Vries' delightful exhibition of a man freezing to death while "brrring," teeth chattering and body shaking violently, he had managed to arrive with a suitcase full of thick, woollen clothes, custom tailored from the Chaura Bazaar by the district's best known tailors. They were all inappropriate for Canada. He would soon discover all the worldwide misunderstandings about Canada. No one really froze to death here—only if one deliberately wanted this form of suicide or only from the most unfortunate of circumstances.

But he knew that happened in the Himalayas in India, where in the winter, hundreds froze to death in the snow, ice, and blizzards or from carbon monoxide poisoning from the coal heaters used to warm their dwellings.

Karam had learned a lot and had a lot more to learn. He was just too giddy with happiness that he had finally and truly become a man. He now could and would support his parents and family and be their protector. In his family, he included his grandparents, his sisters, members of his courtyard, and his clan in Noorian.

* * *

He had to be shown how to cash his pay check. One of his coworkers walked him to the nearby branch of the Royal Bank and helped him open an account and deposit his check. He would continue to use the hospital as his mailing address until he had a more permanent residence. Now on his own, he was learning for the first time the painful process of budgeting in a new country with a new currency. It was a painful experience that once or twice would leave him for a day or so without any cash to pay for meals. Then he would survive on potato chips, chocolate bars, and the odd small carton of milk that the small change accumulated since the last pay check would buy. Luckily, the Y supplied linens, the cafeteria the cutlery and crockery. He had yet to own a spoon, a plate or a fork, a pillow or a blanket. He was living off his suitcase and the only additions in the first month were some socks and underwear. In the evenings he spent long hours gazing at the large, glass windows of downtown shops displaying all kinds of nice goods that he felt he needed but could not yet afford.

Stefano, his new friend and an Italian Jew, was just as broke as he. The medical student from Italy on a one-year visa to Canada was an intern at the general hospital. Some evenings and almost every weekend they would meet at the Y and then walk around window-shopping together. At least Stefano was more adventurous and would drag him into the store, making him walk the aisles to assess the merchandise directly. Often he would stop to converse with a good-looking salesgirl while Karam stood about a foot taller, hovering and shuffling nervously. He still had difficulty approaching women he did not know or had not had a formal introduction to. He had yet to go on a date alone. At the CMC, he had gone to the cinema with his classmates, some of whom were girls, but never with one alone. He had been aware of a number of furtive romances and dalliances between some of the local Romeos what he thought of as harlots. He had, however, been content to exchange long looks with the ones who threw appreciative glances at him. He had secretly fallen in and out of love with at least a dozen girls and women at the CMC, never having the courage to boldly approach and speak to them.

There was no such problem for Stefano, who would actually leer at the prettier ones, and if he was blessed with a "come hither" look, attach himself to them like a bee to a pollinating flower. However, being a struggling and (as he himself muttered often) starving student, he rarely finished with a date. He lamented the lack of a car, an apartment, and mostly money. Karam had understood his point well. You needed all three for success with the girls. So the two exercised in the gym at the Y, swam in the Olympic-sized pool, worked with weights, and three nights a week, they tried to work out at the karate club. Karam was particularly captivated with the complexity of the *katas*. Even his sensei had commented on how perfectly and gracefully he performed them. "You keep it up, Carom, and you are going to win some medals!" the sensei exclaimed as he pronounced his name with a French-Canadian accent. Everyone else picked up on that and called him Carom, much to Stefano's delight for he, too, pronounced it that way. At times, his own Italian accent was impossible to decipher, especially if he became animated or agitated, and that could be quite often.

People had some difficulty understanding Karam, too. Dr. King noticed this and introduced Karam to the hospital speech therapist. All the Scottish woman did was make him read paragraphs from the Reader's Digest aloud, slowly and deliberately, and had him finish the sentences slower and louder. He practiced this for a month and suddenly realized that his accent had changed vastly. His entire department— even the nurses and doctors on the wards—his fellow residents at the Y, the sensei and students at the club were all amazed and commented on the difference. Stefano looked balefully at him, almost in pity.

"*Cultura, amico, cultura*! You have to maintain your culture!" Stefano exclaimed.

Karam had not the courage to explain to him just what a suffocating culture he had the good fortune to escape from, and he got busier becoming a Canadian.

* * *

After having safely arrived in Canada, Karam sent his parents a telegram to alleviate their worries, particularly his mother's. She had clung to him at the railway station in Ludhiana, where half the station was full of his well-wishers from Noorian, the CMC, and relatives from Jogpore and other villages. For them it was a matter of great pride, the first of their caste to travel to such a faraway place. His sisters had shed buckets of tears in the days preceding his departure. Punna made him his favourite dishes despite the expense and served generously all who came to say goodbye at the courtyard. She was especially proud of the Comrade, for he had graciously accepted an offer of tea and drank it out of a glass from her hearth. Karam's former teachers at the high school who were still there also visited and sat on the cots Ruldu had laid out in the thoroughly swept and painstakingly washed courtyard. For them, the watchman had bought bottles of soda from the Brahmin's shop. However, once he offered some rum, the soda was forgotten in favor of the hefty pegs he poured in cups made of glass he had bought on a trip to Samrala. The courtyard had a festive feel during those days. On the morning of the day of departure, Punna had made him bathe well and put on his best clothes and shoes. Followed by the whole clan and visiting relatives, he offered *Prasad* and prayers at the Sant Baba *Samadhi*. Dr. Grewal had sent his driver and the Hillman to transport Karam, his parents, and grandparents to the railway station where he too would come to see the youth off. Thus he had been put on the train to Delhi, accompanied only by his father and grandfather.

At Palam Airport, he boarded an Air India jet to London, England, where he boarded CP Air jet to Toronto.

In those days there were no telephones in the villages of the Punjab, but the telegrams and the postal system were reliable sources of communication. It had taken him almost a week to follow the telegram with a detailed letter. By the end of the month he had received a reply from his kin written in the unmistakable handwriting of the Comrade. His parents could not read or write. Plus, a letter had to be addressed in English if it had any chance of getting to him. After all the usual platitudes and wishes, the letter contained a firm request for money.

Thus he made a trip to the post office. The woman behind the counter charged him an extra two dollars for the money order. "Seven days, I guess," she smiled when he enquired about the approximate time it would take to get to its destination, "same as airmail."

He bought an international stamp and wrote to his father to tell him what the amount in rupees would be: almost five-months' worth of the watchman's salary. Every month after that he sent a larger amount that grew as his income increased. Karam turned to acquiring life's basics each pay check. Stefano had helped him make a list, and Dr. King gave it her blessing. The first one included a well-fitting parka, gloves, and snow boots. At the store, the snow boots took the longest to purchase because he kept asking for "snowshoes." Finally, the salesman understood. A little exasperated and harried by the honest misunderstanding, he fitted Karam with a sturdy pair of boots. The manager of the store, having watched the struggle over the term and greatly amused by the tall, handsome East Indian's puzzlement and then honest appreciation of having gained another bit of "Canadiana," threw in a free pair of socks and a water-proofing kit.

"Thank you, sirs." Karam bowed with his purchases in a bag now. "Thank you."

They walked him to the door and shook his hand, and Karam smiled and bowed deeper.

* * *

The accuracy, speed, and proficiency of his work in the medical laboratory at St. Joseph's did not go unnoticed or unappreciated. Dr. Charles Fletcher worked only as a part-time pathologist at the hospital and the rest of the time at the 300 James Street Medical Center that housed most of the specialists' offices as well as about twelve family physicians. The Doctor had a hell of a time getting all the community-based work done timely and proficiently by the high-turnover team of medical technicians. What lacked was a highly skilled technologist, and he offered Karam a part-time position for as many hours as he could work and on a per diem basis. After consulting with Dr. King, Karam started his part-time work Mondays to Saturdays and put in twenty-five to thirty hours and collected from it more in pay than his hospital job, thus doubling his income. With little else to look forward to during his idle time, this was a gainful way of passing time. By the end of his first year in Canada, Karam enjoyed a well-furnished bachelor apartment and a three-year-old Dodge that mostly sat six days of the week in the underground parking garage at Villa Marie, his new address. He had bought all the necessities of life: cutlery, crockery, pots and pans, a dinette table and chairs, a double bed and bedding, a sofa, a floor model black-and-white television set, and other sundries. His closet boasted a suit, an overcoat, a leather jacket, sweaters, shirts, and pants. His dresser was crammed with underwear, socks, pajama sets, and spare towels as well as a couple of blankets.

He now had two accounts, savings and checking, and a $50,000 insurance policy with his mother as the beneficiary, He stored his suitcase and in it the made-in-India attire. He replaced his MTI watch with a Timex, but he never even thought of getting a chain to replace the amulet from Sant Baba.

When it came time for Stefano to leave for Italy, Karam drove him to the airport, and they laughed at all the times the busy intern had snuck nurses into the apartment to have his way with them while Karam pored over a microscope in the laboratory. "You must go visit Roma, *amico*," insisted Stefano, "and visit my *famiglia*."

Karam promised that he would after he finally got a chance to go to India, and he promised to keep in touch. He watched as his friend disappeared behind the translucent glass at departures.

Driving back to Hamilton, it occurred to him that with Stefano gone, he had no real friend left in Hamilton. But the Italian had done him a great favour and introduced him to his uncle Moshe Berger and his family. Karam had bought all his furniture from Mr. Berger's store, been invited to eat at his table and spend time learning some valuable social skills by being around the large, garrulous, and argumentative but welcoming family. They had even taken him with them to attend the Holy Blossom Synagogue and to a few of the functions and get-togethers there. Karam particularly liked the son-in-law, Ben Roman, a cerebral and intense man who had earned two designations already, that of a chartered accountant and a lawyer.

And Karam always looked forward to meeting Ellie, the youngest daughter who had acted as his date and companion at these events. He wondered if there was more to this anticipation.

* * *

In Noorian, the first year her son was away also passed very quickly for Punna. The regularly increasing money orders, some unexpected in the middle of the month, had turned life around. They had received a total of almost seven thousand rupees from Karam. Ruldu had been able to purchase an acre of land on the ring road, and he constructed a brick wall around the property. He installed a massive iron entry gate between impressive pillars and employed the *gujjar's* mules to carry topsoil and raise the height of the property by three feet. He was allowing it to settle while fretting about what to build on it. In the meantime, he had a lean-to built that housed a *milch* buffalo. Not any *milch* buffalo, but a prize animal he fed the tenderest alfalfa and grasses to and nourished with feed made from cotton and mustard seed. He had even employed a cousin from the clan to graze it and its calf along the grassy stretches of the pathways leading away from the village. He had installed a hand pump, built a reservoir, and held court there. All this was done in cash. He had plans to build a *haveli* that would house his family and all the needed amenities, leaving enough space for a cattle yard for a dozen animals. Just days before, he had purchased a pure bred Alsatian pup to help guard his new abode.

His plan was to have his daughters move back to Noorian with their husbands and children, as well as his in-laws. So much had they contributed to his welfare that they now deserved a life of indulgent ease.

Furthering and consolidating his position, he had quietly and selectively loaned money to a few *Jat* families and had helped those in his clan who needed a hand up.

And with Punna, each day or at least every second one, he swept the Sant Baba *Samadhi*. For his own home still in the courtyard and the new property, his cousin was now the *Chura* who served them.

During the *Panchayat* elections that year, Ruldu was unanimously acclaimed as *Panch* to sit on the village council and represent the interests of the scheduled castes. He took it to be a great honor and knew that had it not been for many fortuitous events in his life, he would not have seen this day. He would still be like the rest of his clan and the other *Churas* sweeping the courtyards of the *Jats* and carrying their refuse in large, heavy baskets on his head and going each evening with a sense of trepidation to collect the leftovers from his employers, hoping that there would be enough to fill the bellies of his family.

Although now the villagers stopped in mid-sentence if they were spewing vitriol at his people when he came into view, he realized sadly that their lot would not change as quickly as his apparently had.

"We are blessed, Punna," he would intone every evening as he put his head on the pillow of his bed, a cot strung with *namar* that gave it a smooth and strong support, making the night pass quickly in a deeper sleep.

Chapter 9

Sunday was the one day of the week Karam looked forward to. It was his one day of sleeping in, cleaning his small apartment, and doing the laundry. For most of the week, he ate out. The hospital cafeteria was excellent and supplied the staff with plenty of choices, so he got in the habit of having breakfast and lunch there Monday through Friday, and for supper he patronized a Greek-run restaurant on Main Street. His refrigerator was generally bereft of any real food except for a carton of milk, another of orange juice, and a loaf of bread and some soft drinks. His pantry had teabags, a jar of coffee, a bag of sugar, a jar of jam, and a few bags of chips and cookies.

He was going insane craving Punjabi food, but none of the local families from India had yet befriended him, and he knew that because of his caste, he would not be welcome at their tables. Thus at least once a month he would travel to Toronto to sit on a bar stool at the Rice Factory and gorge on chicken curry and rice, lamb *korma* and *naan* or *saag* and *maize roti,* finishing his meal with a big bowl of *raas malai* or some other sweet dish. He would bring back with him a large take-out order and later polish it off out of the fridge cold. He had an oven that he rarely used, a toaster, and an electric kettle. Although he had invested in an iron and an ironing board, they never escaped his closet. He preferred to splurge on a drycleaner's services for his outer clothing and pants. His shirts, being of wash-and-wear brands, were quickly hung on hangers as soon as he pulled them out of the building's dryers. He did his sheets and pillow cases along with the towels, underwear, and socks, and he folded them properly as Stefano had shown him to do and placed them in their spots in the dresser. He wet-mopped the parquet of the main room and the linoleum in the kitchen and the washroom.

Every other Sunday, he spent most of his afternoon at the Bergers' home. They continued to welcome him even after Stefano was back in Italy months ago. It was as if they had adopted him, and he was ever so grateful for their kindness. One day, Ella announced that she was leaving to stay on a kibbutz in Israel. "Do my duty," she stated matter-of-factly, unable to meet Karam's baleful look. Then she added, "You know they need people, of any faith or background." She was right. Inspired by the valorous struggles of the nascent nation, all kinds of people, from Europeans to Latin Americans, were volunteering for life on a kibbutz.

"I need to work for money," Karam stated flatly, and she nodded in understanding. She was the one he spilled his guts to on lengthy walks or trips to the cinema.

"I would really like to meet your family," she had once told him in sincerity.

He did not have any pictures to show the Bergers. Except for his own graduation portraits from High School and the CMC, he had not one picture of his kin.

He wrote a stern letter to his sisters, and they finally arranged for pictures to be taken of Ruldu and Punna, his grandparents, and one of themselves with their husbands and children, all severe and unsmiling in their black and white glory. He received the registered mail packet a week after Ella had left for the kibbutz, so he had them framed, and they occupied one of the unadorned walls of his place.

He also had his color portrait done and sent several copies to his parents, asking them to distribute it to the family and kin. It was the first time in over a year that his mother had seen her son's face. Seeing him looking so handsome, dressed in a suit and tie and in color, made her ecstatic. She kept kissing it and had to be admonished by Ruldu. "Don't spoil it," he cautioned before he left on a tour of Samrala and Jogpore, not only to distribute the copies, but to have a couple of them framed. Back and sitting on his cot, he passed one to Punna. "Now you can kiss it all you like," he laughed. And in the frame, the photo took on an even better hue.

"How handsome, oh, how handsome," she cooed, rocking back and forth in joy.

But Ruldu, lost in his thoughts, was far away, dreaming of the strong family his daughter-in-law would come from, the humongous dowry she would bring and the wedding party he would assemble from Noorian and his kin to go get both.

* * *

Ben Roman helped Karam with his tax returns just as he had the first time Karam had filed them. He decided to have a long conversation with the youth for whom he had developed a lot of respect as there were not too many twenty-two-year-olds earning the kind of money he was; despite the fact that Hamilton was chock-full of steel workers in the two thriving world-class steel producers in the city. These industrial workers—partly because of the union at Stelco— were on the top rung of wage earners in North America in their category. Karam was not only matching but exceeding them by a good 200 percent from his part-time job; the man was a horse.

"Karam," he began, seated comfortably behind his ample

desk covered with neatly stacked file folders. It was past 10:00 p.m. on a blistery March night. His client, although having finished a 14-hour day, still looked fresh and eager. "Have you given any thought to the new changes expected in health care?"

"No." His reply was plain, simple, and emphatic. Karam had no time for newspapers or the news and politics, so he was oblivious of the passage of the Canada Health Act, mandating the provinces to provide universal health care for all residents. Free. The act's primary principles were "availability and accessibility" and the right to choose the practitioner. This was going to allow physicians the independence of private practice while payment of their fees and all medical expenses except dentistry and medicine became the responsibility of government.

Ben smiled, and not surprised at the response, continued, "How would you like to make me rich and yourself a very wealthy man?"

Instead of an excited response demanding further elaboration, he got a puzzled look, an absolutely innocent one.

"Whenever there are earthmoving changes in legislation like the Canada Health Act," he went on, the lawyer in him now taking over, "there are opportunities for those who get in on the ground floor."

He might as well have been talking to a wall.

"Would you be interested in obtaining a billing number for a private laboratory? Be your own boss?"

Karam nodded, not fully understanding the conversation. Be his own boss? How was that even possible? He would need a boatload of money to do that, but he could intuitively feel that this was a pivotal moment in his life. Ben was opening a door for him. He decided to listen. Sitting forward in his chair with the look of a disciple listening to his guru's revelations of some secret knowledge, he said, "Please explain. I am interested to learn what you have to teach."

They spoke long into the night.

The next day at the hospital, Sandy, the attractive ward clerk on the surgical floor looked at Karam as he greeted her and asked, "Boy, do you look beat!"

"Just tired and not sleeping well." He smiled, shuffling through the requests for tests. The ward was his favorite place as he got to do the urgent tests, and most surgeons respected his work and showed it. The staff was also accommodating and pleasant.

"Sit down, take a breather," Sandy insisted, and Karam sat down on the bench beside her. She quarterbacked the ward, booking and taking care of discharges; staff rostering; receiving and sending test results, referrals, reports; and all the sundry and important paperwork. She greeted the doctors, the patients, their visitors, and staff from other departments called to the floor to perform physiotherapy, laboratory tests, SPD, cleaning, and so on. Karam often sat with the male orderlies, a rambunctious group of large men with a cutting sense of humor and an eye and opinion on anything and everybody, and they had rated Sandy at the top of their fantasy lists. Her smile and flirting went only so far; married with two young children, she was an untouchable, apparently madly in love with her husband, whom Karam had never seen or met.

"You haven't been a bad boy," she teased.

"You know me, Sandy," Karam started, and before he could say anything more, she broke in.

"Yes, new immigrant, working hard and long to support your poor family in India." But she said this in a manner neither mocking nor condescending, and that was what he really liked about her. She was one of the few who really treated him as an equal and with respect. He looked at her, and she held his gaze. "So tell me, Karam, what is going on in your hectic life?"

"You really want to know?" he asked.

"Yes," she replied, gently squeezing his hand and sending electricity through him. She had never done it before.

"It will take hours." He had to swallow hard to wet his suddenly dry throat.

"You ever free to have a drink?" she asked, her eyes still clinging to his. It was like there were only the two of them, and the rest of the bustling ward did not exist.

"Saturday night," he uttered.

"I am free," she smiled.

"What about your husband?" he asked. "He can come, too."

"The son of a bitch is going to pick up the kids on Saturday morning and have them until Sunday evening," she said matter-of-factly. No bitterness. "I no longer have a husband, not for the last three months anyway."

The rest of day was a whirlwind of thought and action in the collection of samples from the various wards, drawing blood, and particularly in severe cases like burns from the femoral region, which required extreme concentration, a steady hand, and expertise he had developed at the CMC; and performing the tests, checking and rechecking the results, having them confirmed by the pathologists all within a set timeframe before reporting back to the wards. Some results were sent by internal mail, the urgent ones phoned in, and the stat performed on a priority basis and hand delivered. This required concentration and focus. One slip and it could cost a life or complicate one. Karam took his responsibilities seriously. Having lived as a monk to date had helped. His only objectives were to do his job well, work as many hours as possible, and earn as much as possible, and send as much savings as possible home to India biweekly. Rest, eat, and exercise, live, day in and day out. The only girl he had become fond of in Canada was now living in a kibbutz in Israel and having lots of sex with husky men. She had written it in her letters to him. He was disappointed but understanding. He could have pushed the envelope and slept with her, lost his virginity to her.

Now he had a date—his first—with someone he had least expected to ever have one with: a woman at thirty, married with children, and now separated—someone he had now known for almost two years, or had he? Who did he really know: Mr. Berger, Ben, Ella, Dr. King, his coworkers at the hospital at 300 James? The elderly couple who ran the restaurant he frequented so much: they knew him well enough to have his dinner on the table as they saw him cross the street. They knew what he would enjoy that evening. He knew people in the building he lived in; he saw them in the elevators, nodded and waved at them, and talked to them in the laundry room. They were his drycleaners, the car mechanic, the men who filled the gas tank, and the bank tellers. He knew a lot of people by sight or by being around. Acquaintances, all of them were. Other than the Berger clan, he had never socialized with any of them, been in their homes, or hosted them in his.

He was an alien to them, as they were to him. He knew their names and recognized their faces and their voices as they did his. Truthfully, he thought, Ella was the only one who had held his hand, hugged him, and kissed him often on the cheek. Well, Ella and Stefano. Stefano knew his soul. All of a sudden, his shoulders sagged, his eyes misted, and a lump rose to his throat. He suddenly missed his family, his clan, the courtyard, his grandparents, the Comrade, and Dr. de Vries. The test he was working on that should have taken ten minutes took twenty, and the one after that as well. It was Wednesday. He wished Saturday was today, right now, right this minute, so he could be with Sandy. Just with her. He needed intimacy of any kind, to touch or be touched.

Canada was a cold country and Canadians a cold people, not the emotional, touchy-feely people of India. He wondered if the long, cold winters made them that way.

He avoided the surgical ward on Thursday, and by 2:00 p.m., Sandy called for him at the lab.

"Just want to know if you want to pick me up or what?" she asked, her voice a little strange, huskier he thought.

After they told each other their addresses, they found out that they were actually neighbors. She lived just down the street in an apartment building, having moved there after the separation. Knowing that he worked at another job evenings and on Saturdays, she suggested, "I will get the liquor, and we can just order a pizza at your place. Be there at seven."

He sat for a long time, just open-mouthed and gazing at the phone. It was for real. He was going to have Sandy Robinson at his place, with a bottle of whiskey!

And then she was standing at his door, a bottle of whiskey in her hand.

He waved her in and shut and locked the door behind her. She was already in the middle of the room, beside the bed, arms spread outwards, the bottle in one hand, shrugging her shoulders and inviting him closer. Within five minutes they were on the bed, naked, the bottle sitting unopened on the side table. Sandy was moaning as he entered her, already moist and welcoming. Both were thrusting at each other, lips locked in a desperate attempt to find the back of their throats. Karam was amazed at the authority with which he had mounted and possessed her, she guiding and sliding under him, occasionally unlocking her lips to urge him on. She was making him push deeper and harder, her moans a guide, a serenade to his performance.

Neither let go after the orgasm, nor scurried to the bathroom. Instead they held onto each other in an embrace that spoke, more and more. He was like the Energizer Bunny, an advertisement he would watch on television in later years and think back to this moment, unable to recreate the urgency, the passion, the potency.

Sandy was a like a salve: his first and fulfilling. They were like two opposing magnets, tied together at each opportunity, inseparable. On days she was too sore, she took him in her soft mouth and introduced him to a delight he had never imagined and never would give up.

The affair lasted all of six weeks, she looking for more than sex and he a lack of time to spend knowing her, her children, and the support she needed to handle the task of being a single mother on a ward clerk's salary. This was the catalyst for him to listen more and more to Ben Roman and his plans to become rich through the Canada Health Act.

* * *

Karam filled in the forms for the application. Dr. King cosigned as the pathologist, a requirement of the Act. She was uninterested in owning a private billing number, and the CMC was expecting her back in India for a three-year tour. "I wish you the best," she informed Karam as she signed the transference of power of attorney to him, essentially giving him the ownership of the billing number. Ben made sure that everything was perfect and counted on a source within the newly formed Ministry of Health to approve the application.

The letter confirming a billing number in the name of Dr. King and Karam arrived the day after he saw her off at the airport in Toronto, back to India and the CMC. For three years he had the billing number and the power of attorney. Dr. Charles Fletcher was only too happy to step in as the pathologist for a better consideration than the community-based organization paid him at 300 James. He was particularly impressed with Ben Roman, believing him to be the owner and the power behind the enterprise. The billing number belonged to Karam now. All it lacked was a location and the capital to make it operational.

Ben showed his real colors then. He formed the corporation, and to give credit where it was deserved, he named his new enterprise King Laboratories, after Dr. Muriel King, the selfless pathologist, missionary, and humanitarian. He would spend millions in her honor, funding causes near and dear to her, particularly research in obstetrics, a subject of much concern; in birth control; onset of unpredictable labour; and maternal and child premature death.

He raised the funds, hundreds of thousands, to buy King Laboratories its own quarters, the equipment necessary all modern and up to date, the operating and marketing monies necessary to sustain a new enterprise in an unfamiliar social context. Ben gave up no equity, reserving 90 percent for Karam and 10 percent for himself as the CFO and in-house lawyer. Then he assisted Karam in approaching and recruiting the staff necessary to run and build the business. Within six months they had over 200 physicians collecting laboratory samples to be transported to their central location for overnight testing and reporting. In their first year, they crossed the $1 million mark and had a profit of over 30 percent putting Karam at twenty-four years old as one of the highest earners in all of Canada. His effective rate of taxation rose to almost 40 percent.

He sent over one hundred thousand rupees to his

father in Noorian, a sum that was unthinkable and mostly unmanageable by the family. Finally his father opened an account at the State Bank of India in Samrala and was soon its major depositor. Now the merchants came to the *Haveli* on the ring road, uninhibited by the caste that owned it, and made it their first stop to promote their wares. Inside the walls, his sisters struggled with their wayward and uneducated husbands, trying to control the brothers' proclivities, tolerable in a town like Jogpore but insufferable for a village like Noorian and its proud and jealous *Jats*.

A disaster was in the making, and it was only a matter of time.

Chapter 10

*L*ife was so filled with work and responsibility that Karam barely noticed the worldly events that had filled the news channels in those early years: China's takeover of Tibet and later invasion of India and the Cuban missile crisis, just to mention a couple. But it was the murder of President Kennedy that had given him pause. Just as his world was improving at a blinding pace, the world at large was lurching from one crisis to another, with some posing apocalyptic consequences. His role had also changed. No longer did he sit at a microscope but instead behind the massive desk of the President of King Laboratories, the fifth largest laboratory in Canada. Once the billing number had been issued and moratoriumed, a slow consolidation began as labs merged or got bought out by larger competitors. Some failed from sheer incompetence or lack of leadership and capital, and Ben negotiated the purchase of a couple in the neighborhood of the Hamilton region. They now had more than a hundred sample collection centers, and each evening a small fleet of cars and station wagons fanned out to empty the fridges in doctors' offices or medical centers. The sixty or so technicians set to work running the tests and recording the results, and the same fleet left in the morning to deliver the results and top up the supplies needed to collect the samples of blood, sputum, urine, and fecal matter. During the day, the team of marketing specialists worked the streets, visiting referring physicians and recruiting new ones, wining and dining and giving out rewards in the form of tickets to sporting or theatrical events, buying donuts and chocolates for their office staff, and documenting complaints. It was Ben's or Karam's job to intervene and solve problems on a priority basis, and it gave them a chance to meet the all-important doctors face to face and establish stronger bonds.

An administrative team took care of the billings, collection of receivables, and the proper maintenance of records. A full-time personnel manager kept the lab humming at capacity, hiring employees on a timely basis and constantly advertising positions, especially the technical ones, in the local papers and industry journals.

The universality of free health care soon began to see the utilization of services increase exponentially. Most people began to see the doctor for minor conditions, and doctors started referring more and more patients to specialists and other professionals like physiotherapy, audiology, and optometry. They began to prescribe more medicines and started a proliferation of pharmacies. Hospitals started expanding, and the number of beds increased by quite a margin. A shortage of qualified personnel began to be acute. Under pressure from the health industry and an impatient public, more and more qualified personnel and doctors immigrated to Canada. Thus began a serious brain drain from countries like India and Pakistan, their medium of instruction being in English and the adherence to British curriculum and practice standards. Suddenly Karam was employing technicians and two technologists trained at his alma mater, the CMC, and recruiting more and more Southeast Asian doctors. He had to socialize with them, too, but none were from the untouchable classes yet. It led to awkward moments where he would beg Ben to have lunch or dinner with the higher caste Hindus, but Karam would brave it with the Sikhs and Muslims, believing them to be less discriminating in matters of caste.

"You guys are worse than the Jews," Ben would complain, himself the object of derision by certain hidebound members of his own faith. He was more and more liberal and non-observant and began to thrive in the growing diversity of the medical professions. The Health Ministry was still in the control of the Anglo-Saxons, though. Only recently had they started to fill some positions with the non-Anglo-Saxon or French-Canadian candidates. However, if a British one was available and even though lesser qualified, just the fact that they were not of the minorities guaranteed the appointment. Those whose first or second language was not English had a very rough time. The licensing boards were like a wall, keeping them out and working at lesser or low-paying jobs, hoping and always hoping for the wonderful day of recognition and acceptance. A lot of Southern or Eastern Europeans were found fitting customers in shoe stores or driving taxis.

"Oh, no," he groaned, "not another one." His secretary had just poked her head in to announce the start of the business development meeting.

Ben was big on meetings, evaluations, statistics, performance parameters, projections, and quotas. Karam was amazed at the financial rewards of being part of a closed shop business entirely publicly funded with no real constraints on it. The doctor ordered the test, his lab performed it, and the government paid for it at the end or middle of the month. The more tests King Laboratories did, the more money it made. As soon as they crossed each incremental million per annum target, Ben raised the bar. The treasury account was now in excess of $1 million, all assets totaling a million-and-a-half and paid for. Karam was paid a personal salary after taxes of $100,000 a year. His personal living expenses were only about $1,000 a month, so the rest went to India or his savings accounts he had several, now. Because the company held many events per month where ample liquor and food was served and sent him on many out-of-town conferences or seminars, he rarely entertained or spent money out of pocket.

Left alone, he reverted to his old habits. He was still loyal to the same drycleaners, although now Mr. Ho picked it up and delivered it to his penthouse at the Villa Marie. He ate at the Papadopoulos' Steel City Grill; went for a drink to Gentleman Jim's, and sat at the bar to be served by Dusan, the Yugoslavian ex-boxer.

The cleaners at the lab sent a crew once a week to spic and span his place. They also did the laundry, ironed his sheets, and put them back neatly in his upgraded dressers. He had his clothes custom tailored at Mario's Tailoring and only bought the odd pair of jeans, underwear, and socks at the stores. A new restaurant in Toronto now sent him Punjabi meals via courier. A string of casual relationships kept him active and satisfied.

As a child in Noorian, he played handball alone in the courtyard because he was rarely invited to join the other youth of the village or school to participate in *kabaddi* or field hockey. A new employee, a Pakistani named Gul, now regularly partnered him at the squash courts at the YMCA. Karam had lavished a large sum on the building in gratitude for its welcoming him to Canada. He was also a patron of St Joseph's Hospital, and he gave annually to the Friends of Christian Medical College Society, reserving his monies for the laboratory services division in honor of Dr. Muriel King, who had extended her stay there and now looked to retire from her missionary work in India only upon her death. He kept in touch with all of his benefactors by letter and cards sent on occasion, or with postcards from his trips to America, Europe, and the rest of Canada.

Twice, now, he had helped settle immigrants to Canada from his village.

He had come out of his shell and could now speak to small groups without getting stage fright. Sitting at the head of the boardroom table at the meeting, he listened intently to the discussion. It was an extraordinary meeting. Other than Ben and himself, the attendees were their corporate lawyers and accountants and an investment banker from Toronto. Tim Davis, a partner in the firm of BTL & Co., passed around a folder marked "Confidential." It contained his expert analysis on King Laboratories and his current estimate of its net worth.

"I normalized your past quarterly statements. As you can see, there is continual growth, but it is starting to level off somewhat, a factor of reaching close to capacity in your current facility and marketplace," he explained.

"So the only way to maintain growth is to buy more licenses?" the senior counsellor, Ira Silver, asked.

"Right," Mr. Davis nodded. "Other options are mergers."

"Like ..." Karam leaned forward.

"Well." Mr. Davis took a deep breath before replying. "I value King at about seven million today based on a private 3.5 to 4 times earnings basis. You could value a couple of smaller ones and frankly absorb them for a combination of shares and cash."

Ben shook his head. "We are not going to issue more shares and take on minority partners."

"Then buy one on the table today for cash."

Ben looked at Karam and said, "That is a hefty price."

"That's what the market is paying today, and it gets you, in another year, to ten million in revenues and makes you a player."

Ben squinted, his signal that he had bought the argument. He knew that if they bought Stoney Creek's license, it covered the outlying town of Fruitland, Grimsby, and maybe Welland. They would almost control the Hamilton-Niagara region.

"I recommend that," Ira Silver said sagely, earning his hefty fee for the morning. Karam wondered why he brought the other two lawyers with him. They rarely spoke or contributed anything, and their auditor did the same.

"To fatten the bill," Ben snorted when he asked him back in the privacy of his office.

"And you let it happen!" Karam exclaimed and got a look back and a retort.

"Boy, somebody's starting to think!"

* * *

Ella was back from Israel, and they met at her parent's home. She looked so tanned—almost as brown as him—and healthy.

"All that digging and planting in the sun," she shrugged. "Hey, look at you, all rich and fat!"

Karam smiled. He felt like he was with kin. Ella had that effect on him. Ever since he had given up the hope of being someone more special in her life, their correspondence had settled into a comfort zone of friendly teasing and boasting. As much as she wrote about her conquests, he told her about his, and they caught up while looking at her albums that she had made of the kibbutz, Israel, her friends there, and places important to her. Moshe Berger was happy to have his baby daughter back, but Mrs. Berger frowned at most of what Ella had to show for her almost three years away.

She had expected Ella back, married to a nice Jewish boy, and maybe more observant.

"You should stop encouraging her," she growled at her husband, and the otherwise sage and kind man growled back.

"Stop your pestering."

It carried on like that until dinner. With his whole clan including Karam squeezed at the table, grandchildren at the smaller one in the kitchen, he looked at his daughter and formally welcomed her back. By the time he was finished with his speech, Ella and her mother had tears rolling down their cheeks. "You see what not behaving gets you," stated her sister, Mrs. Roman, weighed down already by her third child on the way.

"Yes, a great husband," Ben replied, "and a big home in Burlington."

"Don't forget the Cadillac," Ella chimed in, making a face at her sister but getting a smile back, one of pride tinged with envy.

Later, walking Karam to his car, Ella asked, "Is there anything I can help out with at your company?"

"Yes," Karam replied with a straight face. "You can water the plants. We have a lot of those now both inside and outside."

The punch on his shoulder stung. "Boy, you can hit."

"I also learned how to kill, and that is your fate if you don't find me something my mother will be proud of."

Therefore, much to Ben's chagrin, Karam offered her the position of assistant to the CFO, earning an earful from her brother-in-law.

The corporate offices occupied about 10 percent of the company's floor space but cost 25 percent of the leasehold budget. They were impressive and ornate, with lots of dark wood and special window treatments and all the furniture handmade by Mennonite artisans in Kitchener-Waterloo. The interior designer had given it a timeless look, expressing solidity and history, although the new occupants had barely been there three years. The separate entrance opened into a reception area tastefully decorated to put the visitor at ease with amenities like a washroom opening discreetly off it, a private cubicle to receive and make local calls, and in the main room, two sets of seating arrangements if they expected more than one group for appointments. Tastefully embroidered and framed scenes of country life decorated the walls. The receptionist, particularly chosen for her mannerisms and smile to greet and guide the guests into the inner sanctums, sat behind a two-tiered rounded desk both for privacy and unobtrusiveness.

A wall clock purposefully counted down the minutes and seconds.

Only four people—Karam, Ben, Dr. Fletcher, and Mrs. Cupido—occupied the spacious single offices; the assistants sat in the hall across from them. Behind the assistants were two separate boardrooms and a kitchenette and male and female facilities. A backdoor hidden from view by a short corridor led into the administrative offices and into the body of the lab itself. There were facilities for the comfort of the staff—mostly women working the night shift—that included a lunch room that catered hot meals and snacks, all at company expense as a holdover from Karam's view that the employer supplied his workers food during work hours. Thus nobody had to pack lunches or bring in bags carrying drinks. It also assured that the lab passed sanitation inspections. Controlling items like food that spoiled led to contamination and the place was kept above any recommended government guidelines and regulations. The health inspector pronounced King Laboratories as the best facility of its kind in Canada.

A suitably subdued Ella started work and began to prove her worth by organizing Ben and the considerable finance department with a military-like precision and soon had the moniker "Sergeant Major" or "the bitch" when the employees were out of earshot. Her take-no-prisoners approach had to be softened by several meetings, but she did more good than harm. She would walk right past Karam's assistant into his office and drive the grey-haired woman crazy by flopping onto her boss's lap. "Sir, you have to make her understand," the Englishwoman would hiss as politely as she could, and Karam pitied her: the fate of working for an Indian and now being aggravated by a Jewess. He was well-aware of the barriers faced by non–Anglo-Saxon immigrants to Canada, including their second generations. Some organizations and service clubs did not admit this kind yet.

So when Ella walked into his office one day and sat down heavily in one of the chairs and looked at him with sad eyes, he had a sudden premonition. Then she was followed by Ben, and he, too, had that hangdog look when he sat down. He was not catching Karam's eyes when he said, "I have bad news from India."

Suddenly Karam felt cold and clammy. He had not been back to India in eight years, preferring instead to work and now build the business. But he corresponded regularly and exchanged gifts and pictures. He sent money.

"Your brother-in-law has been badly injured in a fight and is holding on at the CMC," Ben said. "I just talked to Dr. King; she phoned thinking I should tell you."

Karam's face tightened. In a letter his grandfather had sent, he had warned of Sajjan's misbehavior and carousing, but he assured Karam that he was now under control. "Thankfully, he fears me," Bola had stated. "I am the only one he does." Now it occurred to him that in her letters, his sister had been quietly asking for his intervention.

"And that is not all," Ben continued. "Your grandmother has been at the CMC for two weeks now: colon cancer. She has weeks."

That hit Karam like a thunderbolt. His one and only surviving grandmother! Why hadn't anyone warned him?

"You have to go home, Karam," Ella said, coming into his arms as she saw him cry for the first time.

* * *

Returning to India after eight years, no matter the purpose of the visit, happy or sad, he was expected to bear gifts, at least for his family and those that had been kind and close to him and had made his life in Canada more pleasant through their letters. This would keep him occupied, as he had to wait two weeks despite his instinct to leave immediately. Dr. King had reassured him that his grandmother was in no imminent danger of passing away, not with knowing that her beloved grandson was racing back to see her. He made a list and thought deeply on the gifts appropriate for each recipient. For his parents and grandparents, he bought cloth appropriate for Indian-style clothing; he bought the same for his sisters but added a box of cosmetics for each of them. For his young nephews and nieces, he bought a rack of jeans, shirts, and sweaters. For his brothers-in-law, as much as he now despised them for their nefarious behaviour, he bought jackets and shirts; for Dr. Grewal, the Comrade, headmaster Sharma, and others, he bought high quality fountain pens, watches, and objects of art from Canada. All of these would take up one suitcase, and the second one he packed with weather-appropriate clothing and other necessities, from socks to shaving lotion.

Learning of his reason to leave at the earliest for India, one of the doctors benefiting from his largesse, a past resident of New Delhi, organized for his brother to be at Palam Airport to assist him in arranging for transportation to the village. The man, luckily involved in the tourist trade, was able to book him a driver and an American car for the three weeks he would be there. He would meet him and see him off, safe and sound. Ben worried about the circumstances, especially Karam's brother-in-law's injuries, and asked Dan for suggestions. The security specialist offered to go with him, but when Karam demurred, he suggested at least a trained bodyguard he could arrange with a private agency with offices in India. That was when Karam found out that the Pinkerton Group had a quiet presence in New Delhi, providing security for rich American and European business men with interests in the country. He agreed to accept the protection. An agent would meet him inside the airport as soon as he disembarked.

He had extensive meetings with Ben and his executives, and he informed and formally spoke to his key employees and as many of the referring doctors he could. Surprisingly, the referrals for tests spiked—out of sympathy or whatever— and Ben reported the best month the company had ever had, almost biting his lip to avoid saying, "You should have a dozen grandmas, Karam. We could make a killing." Instead, he called the spike an aberration he would have to study. Already any costs of going to India had been earned back dozens fold. Karam calculated the difference—almost a quarter-million dollars—and immediately pledged it for good causes in his grandmother's name. He would donate that money to the CMC and whatever other deserving situations he discovered.

Thus fortified with the support of his Canadian "family," he flew first-class to Rome, where he spent two days visiting with Stefano and his wife and four young children, only finding a few hours to visit the Vatican. Then he was off to New Delhi, arriving there at 3:00 a.m.

Chapter 11

India assaulted Karam's senses the moment the airplane's door opened to the early morning breeze of New Delhi. As he descended the steps to the dimly lit tarmac, the humidity and the heat hit him like a wave, and he immediately began pulling off the jacket he had worn to ward off the coldness of the plane's air conditioning. Added to the heat emanating from the engines, the tarmac smelt of burnt rubber, exhaust, and tar. Rather than becoming nauseous, he was strangely exhilarated, and he walked the 200 yards to the terminal. Upon entering the crumbling, old, and cavernous structure, he felt letdown. Nothing had changed! The coolies assaulted the passengers like a swarm of locusts as the luggage began arriving on push carts. The chaos was unnerving after eight years of being in some of the world's most efficient and modern airports. It was like a railway station except uniformed personnel stood behind folding tables to check documents, stamp passports, and rifle through the suitcases of the mostly Indian arrivals. There had been only five people in the first-class cabin: four Europeans and Karam. And now they stood as bewildered as him. He moved to the pile of luggage being assembled for identification and suddenly noticed a slight pull on his shirt sleeve.

"*Sahib, Pardesiji?*" the Sikh in the neat safari shirt and pants and a tightly tied blue turban asked.

"Yes."

"*Sat Sri Akal, Sahib*," he said, then folded his hands in greeting. "Please point out your suitcases and I will guide you out of here. I am security."

Karam focused to see the nametag. Jaswant Singh, Agent, Essential Services. "Not Pinkerton?"

"Yes, *Sahib*," the man replied hastily. "Here we have a different name, you see, *Sahib*."

Once he pointed to his suitcases, the man motioned to a coolie watching them who moved effortlessly to load the luggage on his cart. He stopped at an isolated desk, behind which stood a customs officer and a large Sikh wearing a well-decorated Delhi Police uniform. Both saluted him, and the customs officer stamped his passport and didn't even glance at his luggage. Behind and around him, his fellow passengers negotiated the maze of officialdom and delay as he was ushered out through the gates to a waiting long, black Buick driven by a uniformed and capped driver. There another man folded his hands in greeting.

"*Pardesi Sahib*," the man bent down to touch his knees in respect.

Karam shrunk back, not used to the gesture now, instead gathering himself and asking, "Dr. Vohra's ...?"

"Yes, *Sahib*," the youthful and well-groomed man smiled, "The same, *Sahib*."

In the meantime, Jaswant Singh stowed Karam's luggage in the trunk, and he firmly faced the youth. "Vohra *Sahib*, my instructions are to proceed immediately for Noorian. *Sahib* is anxious to see his grandmother."

Then remembering the relationship, Karam pulled out the 40 ounces of Chivas Regal he had bought as gifts for this encounter and added one of the cartons of Marlboro cigarettes. Making a show of reluctant acceptance, the young man touched his feet again, promising to come and

visit him in Noorian. "Good luck, *Sahib* and many, many
thank yous, *Sahib*."

Jaswant Singh opened the rear door of the idling car, and
Karam sank into the luxury of the bench seat. He would
lie down and sleep all the eight hours it would take to his
destination.

Sunlight streaming through the windows woke him up,
and he sat up from the curled position, looked out, and
smiled as they passed through a really green patch of the
Punjab. He could see pairs of oxen pulling ploughs in the
fields and camels walking in circles and drawing water for
irrigation from the artesian wells. Men in turbans or cloth
tied to their heads toiled while smoke rose in lazy plumes
from brick kilns and ovens of the *dhabas* sprinkled here and
there along the Grand Trunk Road. The vehicular traffic was
light, mostly buses and trucks, but he noticed more tractors
pulling large trolleys laden with all manner of goods and far
more scooters. Ox-drawn carts still fought for space in the
mishmash of modes of transports, two or three people on
a single bicycle weaving through the minor gridlocks that
developed occasionally. The driver of the car maneuvered
the attention-drawing vehicle by the judicious blowing of
the horn.

"We can stop at the new tourist garden in Karnal,"
Jaswant Singh suggested. "The food is very good, and it is
clean."

"Fine." Karam nodded, suddenly famished and looking
forward to a real Punjabi breakfast of *parathas* with spiced
eggs and yogurt washed down with sweet, milk-laced tea.
And that is what he ordered after they had muscled their
way into the overcrowded stop to a small table. The waiter
appeared almost instantly and came back a minute or so
later carrying the steaming *thalis* containing their orders.

Then he brought the tea, as well as glasses and a mug of water. Karam was surprised that it had a sliver of ice floating in it. Noticing his reaction, his companion explained, "International standards, Sahib." Every major district stop now has one of these. There was not a single non-Indian there. A lot of buses were arriving with people obviously arriving from abroad, Karam could tell from their dress and mannerisms.

The driver had opted to eat at the car, both to stay within his status of a servant and to guard his master's cherished property. A car of this caliber commanded a very high daily charge, and the *Sahib* from Canada had booked it for a whole three weeks. Few Indians arriving from foreign destinations paid the price. He mostly drove American or European guests on long-distance trips to Agra and the Taj Mahal or the palace cities in the desert state of Rajasthan, occasionally to the valley of Kashmir or on a daily rental basis to show sights around old and New Delhi.

* * *

They arrived in Noorian by noon and drove straight to the new courtyard of Ruldu Singh, as the prosperous watchman was now known, and until they crossed its iron gates, a small group of children and adults ran alongside the American car, seeing a vehicle of such grandeur for the first time. "It is Ruldu *Chura's* son from Canada," an urchin shouted, trying to hurry his brother toward the unexpected sight. Karam winced while Jaswant Singh and the driver looked ahead stolidly.

His family stood in a semicircle as he alighted from the car, stretched his frame to its full height, and went straight to his grandfather, bowing to touch his feet and receive a blessing and a long hug from the now slightly hunched but much meatier man. Bola took his grandson's face in his hands, and being of almost equal height, gazed at it with rheumy eyes crinkling with joy. Then he hugged him again. Once out of his grandfather's still iron-like grip, he proceeded to touch his parents' feet and receive their mushy kisses. Next, he was in the trembling arms of his sisters while their tears of joy at seeing their brother after eight long years streaked his shirt, and five children under the age of three reached and struggled to paw at him. He mussed their hair, pulled their cheeks, made faces, and gave them a little twirl by gathering them all in his arms, making them giggle and scream. Finally, one by one, he greeted the rest of his kin, including the younger brother-in-law.

"Let me look around," Karam said, and the crowd parted, finding places to sit down on the half-dozen cots laid out and covered in embroidered sheets. He surveyed the courtyard and noticed for the first time its size. It was big with robust walls around it, one-half devoted to a feed channel for the dozen or so cattle tied at it; further down was a long, rectangular building—a barn really—storing hay and sheltering the cows and buffaloes from the rain or cold winter nights.

The other half had a warren of rooms with doors opening directly onto the dirt-floored courtyard and the central half-wall sheltering the cooking pits and ovens. Smoke curled from the chimney-like structure that housed a triple-decker oven. A hand pump stood over a cemented reservoir, a channel running from it straight out to empty onto the street. It had been recently cleaned but still had evidence of dark and smelly water in places. The few trees had grown tall enough and had been trained to give ample shade from dense umbrellas covered in bright green, waxy leaves. In one small plot, someone was trying to grow vegetables and not succeeding, but it was a substantial and impressive courtyard for Noorian or any village in the Punjab, a courtyard that any landed family would be proud to call its own.

How different, thought Karam, just how different from the old one where he had grown up. His musings were interrupted by his mother's call to lunch. As he gestured for the driver and Jaswant Singh to join them, they both begged to be excused, "You enjoy, *Sahib*. Enjoy with your family. We are still burping from all that food we ate in Karnal."

It suddenly occurred to Karam that both the driver and the agent he employed were probably from a higher caste and could not be expected to eat at a *Chura's*, no matter how good the cutlery, how tasty the food, or how excellent the host.

"All right." He waved them away, and they retreated to the car and began talking to the now substantial knot of the curious gathered there.

In the late afternoon, having prayed at the Sant Baba *Samadhi,* he accompanied his grandfather and parents to the Brown Memorial Hospital attached to the CMC and spent a long time in the embrace of his emaciated grandmother, now in the terminal stage of a cancer discovered too late for any effective intervention and living on a saline and morphine drip. Why her? Karam could not fathom. She was the kindest of the kind, her affection for him untold, her devotion singular. He felt a great sense of guilt for not having visited for so long, and when he talked about it, he was shushed by his grandmother's simple act of putting her finger across his lips. The five of them cried together, sat in silence, and contemplated their lives and love for each other. In the presence of his own, loved without condition and selflessly, he asked if he had been the son they had expected. Had he been dutiful albeit absent? They showered him with praise and prayers, blessings and benedictions, his grandmother putting it in words. "Never had I dreamed of the days that I could stand proudly in my community and not bow my head to anyone."

"We are fortunate, my son, so very, very fortunate," his mother enjoined, "and may Sant Baba keep us always this way!"

The older men sat and looked at Karam with teary eyes glistening with pride. Karam felt truly rewarded for the eight years of exile from his family.

"Get married," his grandmother said, plaintively. "Let me die having seen my grandson's bride."

Suddenly animated, they began to tell him of the dozens of offers of marriage they had received for him. Ruldu was almost pleading; virtually on his knees so strong were his emotions on the subject.

"Wait until I show the jewels I have gathered for your bride," Punna promised, a hint of arrogant accumulation in her tone.

* * *

Sajjan had created a Gordian knot of a situation. Caught red-handed in the home of a *Jat* family in the village with the daughter-in-law, the husband away in Calcutta driving a truck, he had been thoroughly thrashed mercilessly by the cuckold's brothers and cousins, beaten to an inch of his life, and, some said, made to drink his own urine. Rescued by a squad of *Chura* and councilmen from the *panchayat*, Ruldu had to pledge to never let him come within the village's boundaries at the pain of death. It was a matter of great shame for the proud *Jats*. The woman had been beaten by her in-laws and sent to her parents to await her husband's arrival and a final judgment. By the time Karam arrived in Noorian, Sajjan, having recovered enough, was now living in Jogpore at his old clan's quarters with his elderly parents and their pigs. According to his younger brother, Bhola, he was planning murderous revenge on the Dial Singh family. Plus he had filed charges, and six of his attackers had been arrested and maltreated by the police in Samrala, some believing at the behest of Chandu Das, now a member of India's parliament and an influential mover and shaker in the central government so dependent on the votes of the scheduled casted for its continuing stranglehold on Indian politics despite the death of Jawaharlal Nehru, the Congress party's charismatic leader and a statesman on the world stage.

Karam decided to meet the problem head-on. At a gathering of the two families' elders called upon his request by the *panchayat* and attended by village elders, Dial Singh stood up and stated bluntly, "We have been tainted, our reputation turned into manure."

All agreed in collective silence.

"Since the fault can be laid at my door also, thanks to my whorish daughter-in-law, and in view of the charges faced in the courts by my sons and nephews, I would request a resolution. I cannot afford to be impoverished by the courts, corrupt as they are."

Karam had learned some conflict resolution skills in Canada thanks to Ben's artful negotiating tactics. "I am prepared to do anything possible in my power to facilitate a fair resolution to maintain our most respected Dial Singh's dignity and the reputation of his family. That is why I hurried home."

At this, the entire gathering showed its approval of his acts by nodding sagely in his direction. One of the *Panchs,* a relative of Dial Singh, then stood up and proposed, "Karam, buy my kin's property so that they can move to another region where this taint on their family is unknown. And make that devil of Jogpore withdraw the charges against his boys. If you can do that, I propose the matter settled."

Karam, without hesitation, stood up and accepted the proposed price of one hundred thousand rupees in cash. A gasp of disbelief went through the gathering. He had done it so casually that everyone in the village looked at him with wide-eyed wonder for the rest of his stay. Thus Karam came to own the Dial Singh courtyard and twenty-five acres of prime agricultural land. Fortuitously for Punna, it was the land on which stood the Sant Baba *Samadhi*.

"Everything has a reason, my son," she stated, hardly able to contain her glee at the unexpected outcome. To the rest of his clan and the villagers, he had paid a very heavy price for the actions of a loose woman and a randy brother-in-law. His sister asked for a divorce from her wayward and lecherous husband, and thus Sajjan would spend the rest of his life grazing his herd of pigs along the railway lines of Jogpore.

Karam visited Dr. King, the old classrooms and laboratories now populated by students who looked different in dress and mannerism. Dr. de Vries was back in his city of Maastricht in Holland, leaving the tireless woman in charge. From her, he learned of the centennial celebrations planned, including the construction of a new multi-storied building for private patients. He visited the new Mitchell Memorial Hostel and also got a tour of the new nurses' residence. The institution was on a march of expansion and growth. Karam, pumped up by his reception there and the honest efforts to bring modern medicine to the Punjab, pledged $100,000 toward the centennial building fund. This drew a deafening applause at the clinical conference, well-attended in the college theater by students, faculty, researchers, and administrative heads—even the Bishop of the Church of Northern India from his offices in Phagwara, a town forty miles northwest of Ludhiana.

Later he visited his old benefactor, Dr. Grewal, at his

manor, now slightly dated and a bit crumbling, in Civil Lines and presented the white-haired and retired man with a watch, a pen, and 40 ounces of Chivas Regal, a Canadian regimental tie, and a soapstone carving of an eagle with wings spread, ready to take flight. Dr. Grewal examined each one of his gifts, asking multiple questions of Karam and commenting on the quality of the gifts and his gratitude for receiving such largesse from a youth who he felt he had only helped because he deserved it. Karam could tell that the old man, dignified as ever, was touched by the gesture.

"Well, let us not waste the afternoon," he said, and he called his attendant for a tray, glasses, and some ice if there was some in the sputtering, kerosene-powered fridge.

"You look well, Karam, and here's to you, my boy!" He raised his glass and sipped delicately of the golden liquor, closing his eyes to savor the flavor. "So tell me everything, all that's happened to you in Canada. I have your letters, but I need to hear it all from you."

They talked for hours, well after dark and over the dinner served from ancient silver trays in the candlelit formal dining room of the British-era edifice. Dr. Grewal was in his element, proud to host his most successful prodigy, the grandson of one of his most loyal employees: one who had risen from nothing and "untouchability" to such heights of accomplishment as to put to shame those who still believed in a caste system in independent India. The constitution had guaranteed equality for all and the uplifting of the unfortunate, an ideal of the Mahatma!

But was it being carried out both in spirit and letter?

The good doctor, well-read and sensitive, was not so sure. In fact, he was sadly disappointed. India, in his opinion, had been hijacked by the socialist policies of the Congress Party, the ruling political force. It had made so many compromises, give and takes, and it had left so many doors open for the clever and the bold to step in and seize special licenses and monopolies, strangulating entrepreneurialism and innovation. It guaranteed these monopolies by closing the borders to limited and state-governed trade, reducing competition and flooding the country with cheap, unreliable, and low-quality consumer goods. Manufacturers thus protected from foreign competition saw no need to improve and upgrade or reinvest their profits in their industries, and India was awash in mediocrity. It was expected and accepted. Low standards prevailed, and this was in all kinds of essential goods, including medicines. A doctor of his experience could not be guaranteed that his patients could buy standardized and regulated goods in the pharmacies. Even the surgical instruments rusted, such poor steel used to make them, and no one cared—certainly not the underfunded ministries of health, the regulatory inspectors easily bribed to look the other way. The only safety was in the foreign-run hospitals and their imported instruments and pills.

Karam did not have the heart to tell the philosophic physician lamenting the declining values in his country of the excellent and enforced standards in Canada.

"Tell me an uplifting story," Dr. Grewal begged, having spit out his poison.

"My mother wants me to marry," he said in an effort to change the depressing subject. Dr. Grewal was well into the state of inebriation, and Karam was anxious to leave. The jet lag had begun to take its toll.

"I will raise my glass to that." The old man took one more sip, and his hand fell heavily onto the table. At a nod from Jaswant Singh, the attendant lifted his master and guided him into the darkened interior.

"*Sahib,* we go." Karam did not object. It had been a long day.

He awoke the next morning to watch a clutch of peacock hens led in the courtyard by their male escort fully in form, displaying his plumage in all its glory and dancing to a silent tune as the sun rose above the horizon and filled the courtyard with its early golden glow. Karam sat on the cot and pulled the cover around him and watched his mother's and sisters' morning ritual of cattle feeding and milking, the calves trying desperately to reach the teats now denied them. The steam was rising from the freshly laid dung in piles along the feeding channel. His indentured cousin carried baskets of chopped alfalfa mixed with straw to put before the restless buffaloes and the two brown cows. It was as ancient and established a scene as he had ever seen in any courtyard of his memory. The air was at once crisp and fetid. A niece brought him a mug of tea, and sipping the hot, sweet liquid, he watched the morning unfold.

The gates opened, and a family from his kin came in carrying dung-crusted baskets and brooms of sturdy mulberry stalks. They set upon the floor of the courtyard from one end, sweeping it in expansive circles and expertly collecting the detritus of dung, dust, and spilled feed into piles that they emptied into the baskets, which they helped each other lift onto their heads guarded by a discus-like hat made of rags tied together. Then they swayed under the weight out onto the street to dump them onto the massive manure pile owned by their master, the village watchman, Ruldu. He was kin and master. At least at his hearth they were welcome to sit and drink mightily from his hand pump, something they were forbidden from in the other courtyards they swept: the ones owned by the *Jats* or the odd *Brahmin* who owned a cow or two.

The indentured cousin, helped by another slight youth, then took the chains off the cattle and, one by one, led them to the reservoir that they filled pumping the water by hand for the insatiable beasts. This strenuous effort took an hour at the end of which they marched the milked, fed, and watered herd off onto the ring road and onto the grasslands along the now expansive pathways, thanks to the consolidation of landholdings.

Karam was mesmerized by the activity about him, his mother and sisters at the hearth cooking a breakfast of *parathas* and *subzi* after they had churned yesterday's yogurt into butter and buttermilk. He looked tolerantly at Bhola, who had worn one of his silk night suits and refused to take it off. In fact, he wore it the whole day, showing off his new attire around the village, not to mention his new watch and the one pack of Marlboros prominently displayed in one of the pockets. His sisters, among all the work they did, managed to bathe, dress, and feed their children, getting them ready for school. Once the kids were off, the adults gathered at the hearth to eat breakfast. Karam could not get over the aroma of *parathas* cooked with fresh butter and the yogurt almost tasting like a curd, somewhere between a curd and cream cheese. The tea was fragrant with cardamoms and cloves. He forgot about the fancy meals and champagne breakfasts of European five-star resorts. They could not hold a candle to a Punjabi breakfast cooked the old fashioned way in a village courtyard. There was no way to describe the feeling when he took the first bite and began to chew it slowly, savoring every explosion of taste and texture.

He decided to spend the middle week of his visit at the courtyard, relaxing in the bosom of his family.

Noorian had changed. Giving in to the fact that he was viewing his village with vastly different eyes than when he left it eight years ago, he felt he could be more discerning. There seemed to be more prosperity, better quality of habitat. A larger number of children attended school, which included all castes. More left for the main road and its bus stop to travel for higher education every morning, better dressed and groomed than they once were. A smaller percentage went for work outside of the village, and those who depended on their living in the village had a bit more help. The arrival of electric power, the availability of state loans to farmers, and the spread of newer seeds and chemical fertilizers had increased crop yields. Affordability and the ability to obtain diesel engines, electric motors, and loans to purchase the imported tractors from the Soviet bloc were changing *Jat* lives and fortunes. This was the dawn of the green revolution, and with the Food Corporation of India buying and setting fair prices for grain, the landowning caste was on the verge of a prosperous cycle. Remittances from family members who had emigrated to labor-short Britain and some on to Canada and the United States were building better, sturdier, airier, and more sanitary abodes. The veterinary evolution through artificial insemination was raising the quality of the livestock and milk production. There was more mechanization and more spending money, thus larger weddings that showcased a family's rise in financial status. More families had more children in service or school than in the fields.

However, that was not true of the untouchables, particularly his people, the *Chura*. Almost to a family they were still poor, living in the same if not worse hovels, the children and juveniles employed like the parents in servitude and indenture, the same degree of ignorance and belief in the Congress party to lift them up. Yet, nothing happened.

His visit to the school was more telling. No structural improvements, no additions, no upgrades in furniture or supplies. Teachers still held classes in the open air with the same curriculum and fewer teachers struggling to educate larger classes. The village had no playgrounds and lacked a community center, a public health facility, sewage, and governance of any kind. The headman and the *panchayat* were dependant on Block Development officers for state aid, meager as it was, and ran a cooperative bank to provide seasonal loans to landowners only, all other castes excluded. A *Chura* could not borrow a dime. If he did, he did so from the merchants or money lenders at atrociously high rates, further impoverishing his family and putting him at risk of default that often had criminal consequences.

Thus there was a chasm, and it was growing. The *Jats*, the merchants, and those with emigrants sending regular remittances were prospering; those without land sunk further. Part of the reason was their propensity to have as many children as possible as a bulwark against old age. In India, the sons cared for the parents. More sons meant better insurance.

The government had many plans: plans to spray DDT to reduce malaria, vaccinating the public against the scourge of small pox, polio, and so on, and offering vasectomies and tubal ligations to reduce family sizes, with monetary rewards for some. It was said that the bachelors in Noorian—especially those with no hope in hell of ever getting married—90 percent had taken advantage of the vasectomy service and its financial rewards (not to mention the fact that there could be no accusation of having fathered illegitimate children). Of the married men, only the middle-aged and grandfatherly answered the call to duty and visited the family planning clinics whenever they were held at the village.

The lucky set the standards of social behavior and trends. Bigger dowries were the norm, putting enormous stress on the poor to keep up with the Singhs and the Kumars.

The remittances—that is, easy money—flooding into selected hands led to increased demand in a tight market and a rise in prices: a double jeopardy for the poor.

* * *

Karam sought the Comrade's advice. Now grey-bearded and wearing spectacles, the father of three boys and still going strong in his practice of rural medicine, the doctor was all ears, learning of Karam's considerable affection for his clan and sympathy and a desire to benefit his own village. "Charity starts at home" was how the younger man had put it.

They traveled together to Samrala and met with the Block Development officer, an eager young man recently graduated from his courses and appointed. He promised to gather a list of priorities that the state and central governments were interested in promoting that could be accelerated if there were financial contributions from the village *panchayat* or on its behalf by a private benefactor.

Then they visited the teachers, the headmaster, and with the enthusiastic blessings of the former two, the office of the District Education officer. There the harried but determined woman struggling with a large district and its hundreds of underfunded schools was only too glad to accept the offer of financial aid as long as it first served the deficits in Noorian. She would provide a template and a budget and guarantee the money would go to the cause.

By the end of the week, a meeting of the *panchayat* and village elders was held at the front court of the Noorian Cooperative Bank, a one-room affair attached to a larger storage room packed with bags of fertilizers and sundry pesticides and herbicides as well as cattle feed. Seated on cots, collected for the occasion, for the first time in its history all castes and creeds were represented, and the Comrade chaired a productive meeting. They learned of Karam's desire to help, and realizing the benefits a metalled road to the main transport artery could provide for the village—proper cobbling and drainage for the streets, a proper playground for the children and youth, a community center that would also house a visiting rural health group, upgrading the local primary and high schools (especially the ones for girls), and the establishment of a scholarship fund to underwrite higher education for deserving students—left most attendees dumb with shock.

Calculating the cost of his promises at over 100,000 rupees, the Comrade wanted to clear the air lest some things not come to pass. "Can you afford this, Karam?"

A sum of $20,000 in Canadian funds represented exactly one week's profit for him from King Laboratories.

"Yes," he stated simply and humbly, his demeanour disarming all present.

The following week the grandmother passed away. Karam brought her home and held a fantastic funerary procession. Many dignitaries and some foreigners from CMC marched in the procession led by a uniformed band.

Punna was proud, as the grandmother of a boy like Karam deserved no less.

On the evening of the funeral, after the guests had left, Karam sat on his cot, his grandfather, parents, sister, and kin around him. He spoke of his deepest desires: to uplift his own. Not in a dramatic and magical way but a deliberate and determined plan.

"Helping them to learn fishing rather than giving them fish," he said.

Chapter 12

The District Commissioner of Ludhiana had recently been appointed to his post. A graduate of the Indian Administrative Services that prepared technocrats to administer regions covering a million plus citizens, he was also one of the few and early *Shudras*—a member of a scheduled caste—to make it to that exalted position in the civil services. He wanted to make a name for himself. Intelligent and a conceptualist and macro-thinker, Ajit Singh could hardly believe his ears. At a meeting of the district executive, the education officer talked at length of a new initiative she was proposing for the village of Noorian made possible by the generosity of a well-to-do man who was now residing in Canada. Apparently, he had also asked the Nilon Block officer to initiate projects benefiting the village too.

"How much is he contributing?" Ajit Singh asked.

"Sir, 100,000 rupees."

"What?" The commissioner leaned forward as if disbelieving the figure.

"One hundred thousand rupees, sir, and I believe he pledged five times as much to his alma mater, the CMC, for its centennial celebrations."

Ajit Singh sat back in his chair, stunned by the amounts. "Who is this man?" He turned to the senior superintendant of police.

"Karam Pardesi, sir. His grandfather was once the hangman at the district jail, and his father still serves as the village watchman in Noorian," implying without outright stating Karam's caste. The superintendent, a *Jat* Sikh, was starting to become sensitized to working with superiors of a lower caste. It still made him cringe that he had to address the youthful commissioner, fifteen years his junior in age, with the title "sir." The commissioner, having struggled with these kinds of prejudices, had developed a rather thick skin.

"How many men from Noorian are emigrants," the commissioner asked quietly.

"I guess at least thirty or forty."

"All from good families." The commissioner bared his teeth slightly, meaning from the highborn.

"I think so," replied the superintendent.

"And are any of them doing much for the village?"

"None, sir," conceded the superintendent, remembering to say "sir."

Ajit Singh had written a thesis for his IAS finals that had garnered a lot of discussion and debate, as well as excitement. His thesis recommended the creation of "Models," projects, communities, organizations, and institutions that would be designated as a Model Village, for example. A Model would be developed as a showpiece for others to emulate as an ideal. To fund these models, he had suggested private-public partnerships, getting a wealthy resident of India or an emigrant to agree to co-fund the project. He believed he had stumbled on a perfect storm called Noorian.

The next day, via executive decree, he declared the village of Noorian a Model Gram (village, in English). He authorized the maximum amount of money he was allowed under his authority to initiate all proposed projects: 20,000 rupees. It would make a hole in his budget, but he could not afford to not seize the opportunity to put his own idea into practice. A press release was duly issued.

* * *

At the offices of The Tribune in Chandigarh, the correspondent who had broken the first news story on Karam, now promoted to senior editor, immediately sprung to attention. He called in his best reporter and a cameraman and gave them instructions to do justice to the story. "I want a full page out of this one," he barked, fed up with a lack of spirit lifters lately. The paper came out every morning full of news of tragedies, thievery, more thuggery, and political spin. Most people bought the only English daily to keep abreast of the classifieds because they carried hopes of real opportunity: calls for construction tenders, job advertisements, and, best of all, matrimonial ads featuring foreign-based matches.

Surinder Kumar, along with the photographer, a *paan*-chewing old fellow with an ancient Leica camera hanging in a leather case of some years, boarded a bus from the sector 17 bus station. It took almost two hours because the Punjab Roadways bus stopped every mile or two to drop off or pick up passengers. It was autumn, and the cool breezes flowing through the half-opened windows kept Kumar cool and the stuffiness of the crowded bus at bay. They walked the mile of dirt path to Noorian as there was no rickshaw or rentable transport available at the stop, just a couple of *dhabas* serving tea and sweets and selling cigarettes and sundries. They asked their way to the massive iron gates of the watchman Ruldu's *haveli*, impressed by its size as judged from the ring road. An older man, grizzled and with a cold, steady, and scary gaze, greeted them and led them to the guestroom. It was furnished with tasteful armchairs, side tables, and a Kashmiri carpet on the floor, and the walls were decorated with framed color pictures of the *haveli's* famed son, Karam Pardesi. Soon their host appeared, hands folded and all smiles. That put them at ease as Bola, just by his presence, was putting the fear of God into them. As soon as the greetings were over, a young girl showed up with a tray of tea, fine china, and a box of Cadbury biscuits, unexpected luxuries in a rural home.

The correspondent got to the point, and Ruldu and Bola were soon engaged in the telling of Karam's exploits, both scholarly and in business, and of his generosity. The photographer got busy taking pictures.

* * *

The story was carried in the fifth page of the tribune with a lead on the front. SON OF SHUDRAS THE SAVIOR OF HIS VILLAGE it screamed, a picture of Karam proudly supplied by his mother in the center of the front page. On the day of issue, several thousand educated members of the scheduled castes read with pride a well-balanced article on the accomplishments of one of their own. In his office, District Commissioner Ajit Singh read it and his own interview in it with interest and intent. "Given the chance and a level playing field, people of all castes can reach great heights. *Sardar* Karam Pardesi is one of the first and deserves all the accolades this nation can award this true son of India," he had stated and was quoted verbatim.

Most of the newspapers in the Punjab picked up and reprinted the story, including the Hindustan Times and the Times of India. A picture of Karam and a lengthy article was devoted by the Illustrated India Weekly, a magazine almost as venerable for its editorial standards as Time and Life in America. It was also picked up by the BBC and Voice of America because of the CMC being known as the American Hospital and Reuters.

A week later, a reporter called Karam's office from the Toronto Star, and CHCH TV, the local TV station in

Hamilton, requested an interview.

Karam was momentarily stunned at the turn of events. Just back from India and busy since catching up on the performance figures, reports, and ranting of Ben Roman, he had not even had time to write to his parents, Dr. King, or any of his other friends in India, even to thank them for their kind condolences. He was still receiving visitors to his office as a grieving grandson. Few people, if anyone, had ever been or came to his home. He had the biggest gathering at the Bergers', where besides the warmth extended him, so were many "oohs" and "aahs" as he distributed gifts he had carefully picked for his adopted family in Canada. Mrs. Berger was especially proud of the hand-crocheted tablecloth, Ben by the marble carving of the Taj Mahal, and Ella by the yards of raw silk and other pure silk pieces. He had bought both sisters *Pashmina* shawls in differing designs and a white *Pashmina* scarf and gloves for the elder Moshe.

He called Ben and Ella to his office and told them of the breaking news.

"I am so proud of you," Ella stated.

"Puts you on the map, my friend," Ben added.

"But my background?"

"What about it?" Ben asked. "Karam, we are in a new age. Just watch."

He agreed to the interviews, and he was on the evening news at 6 and 11 p.m. on CHCH TV and on the eighth page of the Toronto Star.

Within the week, he had been invited to speak at several different service clubs. The Rotarians were particularly insistent, as were the Lions and Kinsmen. They had chapters in India and projects and some projects surprisingly similar to his: the uplifting of the poor of India.

It turned out to be better than Karam expected. He had

not exactly hidden his status as a *Shudra*, but in Canada, America, and Europe, where he had traveled outside of India, no one to date had asked or made an issue of it. His social contacts were largely limited to non-Indians. The TV reporter and the Toronto Star correspondent focused on his achievements in Canada, the prosperity he had gained, and the generosity he was now showing for his people in India. In fact, they highlighted his donation to the CMC.

However, Ben, the point man he had assigned to deal with most of the Indian doctors referring to King Laboratories, did come face to face with the caste-based prejudice among Indians and its immediacy. Visiting Dr. Vohra's office, he was called aside by the doctor's wife, a trained nurse from India, and told "If we had known this man's caste, my husband would have never asked his brother to be tainted by his gifts of scotch and cigarettes. My brother-in-law is blaming us now for putting him in that terrible situation."

As Ben stood open-mouthed in shock, she continued, "Please, no more gifts for us from your lab! Who knows if he touches them before sending them out?"

Rather than retorting, Ben had simply taken a deep breath, shaken his head, given their blonde secretary a nod, and left. Pledging never to give Dr. Vohra or his snarly little wife the time of day again, he chose not to tell Karam, as he knew it would upset the best friend and partner he had ever had. "Karam is way above this bullshit," he thought. After this incident, he urged on Karam's generosity to his motherland. He hired an attractive, young marketing graduate to handle the Indian doctors from then on; the doctors were increasing in numbers and now represented almost 10 percent of the physician roster; he did not want to lose their support. Much to his surprise, several of them actually came to the corporate headquarters, not only to offer condolences on Karam's grandmother's death, but also to tell him how much having one of them in the news and on Canadian TV had delighted them.

"It was great," Dr. Ram Sarup told both Ben and Karam as they had lunch in the boardroom. "Better than all those stories about the starving Indians!"

Ben uttered a silent thank you. "We need more like you, Dr. Ram Sarup," he thought. He knew that Dr. Sarup was not only a highborn Hindu but the scion of a prominent New Delhi family.

* * *

A month later, Ajit Singh chaired a meeting in the courtyard of Ruldu's *haveli*. The host had moved his cattle into the barn for the day and had the open space thoroughly swept and sprayed with lots of water to keep the dust down. He had even rented a substantial awning that was put up for shade and protection from rain. Underneath, on outdoor carpets rolled out generously, a stage-like setup had been laid out with armchairs for the honored guests, and facing them were folding chairs lined up carefully to seat the village council, the elders, and heads of clans. The district commissioner had arrived in an official Ambassador car, escorted by the police jeep of the superintendent of police. Also present were the education officer, the *Tehsildar*, the block development officer, the subdivisional magistrate, and the executive engineer from the state electricity board. Parliamentary representatives from both the MP and the MLA for the area were there, but Chandu Das was unable to attend because of urgent business elsewhere and had sent a message that was read as an opening remark. It congratulated Noorian for its good fortune and praised its good son, Karam Pardesi, singling out Ajit Singh for his initiative in declaring the village a Model Gram.

After the applause died down, Ajit Singh got down to the serious business of outlining his vision of what constituted a Model Gram.

He stressed the point that open drains, standing waters, manure piles too close to habitation, open defecation in fields, and drinking water drawn from ponds and used unboiled contributed to infectious disease like malaria, cholera, dengue fever, hepatitis, tuberculosis, and other afflictions. His plan was to drain two of the dirtiest ponds bordering the village, keeping the large, eight-acre pond to be planted with a variety of floating vegetation that would cleanse it naturally and introduce fish culture, allowing some of the village families to lease those rights and thus provide an income for the village council to spend on maintaining the pond and its adjacent land. He proposed building male and female outhouses with running water and septic tanks dug deep and lined. This brought giggles from the villagers, who thought it was the poor city folk who suffered mightily from squatting above a hole on their flush toilets. The Comrade had to harangue them into accepting this proposal.

The village streets would be cobbled, with proper drains constructed and connecting each home and courtyard. The ring road as well as the main path connecting the village to the Ludhiana-Chandigarh road would be metalled with stone and asphalt. This was necessary as it was a condition set by Punjab Roadways to provide direct bus service to the community. The applause could have raised the roof.

"This almost makes Noorian into a town," Bola leaned over and said into Ruldu's ears, the proud father too emotional to absorb the impact of the statement.

A Model Gram would have well-constructed and furnished schools. The high school would also house a library and an adult education center. The teachers could earn extra money in overtime if they participated in teaching reading, writing, and arithmetic to the majority of the village adults, who remained illiterate after almost twenty years of independence. They would need a playground large enough to accommodate field hockey and separate grounds for track and field. The schools would receive extra funding for properly trained coaches. A playground for the children would be on the grounds of the community center, which would have a rural health clinic, a well-baby nursing room, and a full-time MBBS physician and dispensary service.

Then the commissioner delivered the news that the peasants could truly appreciate.

There would be a government tube-well built, along with appropriate water channels to help irrigate Noorian's remaining nonirrigated land and no-cost loans given for leveling the land with bulldozers and heavy tractors, unaffordable by the ordinary *Jats*. This effort would bring those only getting one crop a year into the modern farming age and help exploit their land—their one income producing asset—and double its value and output. The meeting erupted into frenzied applause and shouts of "*Bale, Bale,*" and "*DCji ki Jai, DCji ki Jai!*"

Ajit Singh watched as the celebrations turned into a bit of a *Bhangra* match between clans, and once they were persuaded to sit down, announced, "At the special request and promised—actually delivered at a bank in Ludhiana—assistance of *Sardar* Karam Pardesi and a special dispensation of the Punjab and central governments, any family in Noorian of scheduled caste is eligible for a one-time forgivable grant in order to construct a *pucca* house. The supply of bricks and mortar and other building materials will be covered by Pardesiji while the district will pay the masons."

A subdued applause came from the *Shudra* elders and a muttering arose from the higher castes. "Sahib, extend this to us also," demanded Pyara Singh, for he still owned a mud brick house because he had no brothers, and his sons were too young to help in the fields or emigrate abroad. "Only last monsoons, part of the roof caved in."

"I am sorry," the commissioner replied. "You can apply for a loan from the cooperative."

Others stood up and began to form knots around the officials, each with a complaint of a need still not addressed, and thus ended the first Model Gram meeting in a melee of individual pleadings.

At the feast supplied by Ruldu, the other officials, all junior in rank, sat down at a long table to eat, trying hard to suppress their anxiety. Never, ever before had they dined at a *Chura's* house. However, the hosts, in their infinite humility, had ordered the food from the city, and it was served by waiters from the hotel it had been supplied by. The liquor was Solan whiskey and not the harsh rum sold in licensed *thekas* in the villages. As they left, the executive engineer took the time to thank the host on everyone's behalf. Surprisingly, most of the village council and some of the elders stayed behind because they had seen the earlier arrival and unloading of the large pots and the delivery from the English *theka* in Jogpore. They simply could not deny Ruldu's imploring to stay, eat, and drink to their hearts' content.

They would happily put up with the ridicule of their families later.

Chapter 13

*H*elene Boucher was a quintessential Quebecer, born on her father's farm outside of the city of Montreal on land that would in a few years be bulldozed under for the new Mirabel Airport. One of eight children, she counted in her ancestry an Irishman and a full-blooded Mohawk great-grandmother. Her father owned a milk license, and thanks to the monopoly enjoyed by the Milk Board of Canada, was saved from the savage competition of other farmers raising cows. His herd of seventy-five Herefords filled a tanker truck every two days to be transported to a dairy in a suburb of the big city. Guaranteed a steady price and timely payments, he had let his children select post-secondary education and helped out with their education as much as he could. Thus, Helene had a brother who became a doctor and a younger one who obtained a Master's in Political Science. Two brothers became professional hockey players, while the second oldest had the farming genes a little too strongly and stayed on the land. Her two sisters married their childhood sweethearts and lived within the county. Helene finished with an honor's degree in English from the University of Ottawa and became quite proficient in the language of the Anglos. It opened doors for the bilingual and outgoing young woman, and she became a marketing representative in the Toronto headquarters of Dow-Corning and worked in their laboratory glass division. In three years she had risen to an assistant director of marketing and had several key accounts, including King Laboratories of Hamilton.. She cultivated and maintained this account personally.

She requested a meeting with the principals, purposing a luncheon at the venerable Chedoke Golf Club. Because Ben was at Rebecca's side expecting the birth of their third child, Karam decided to accompany his director of services and Dr. Fletcher to the meeting. As a member of the golf club, Dr. Fletcher drove up the steep inclines of Hamilton to the graveled parking lot of the sprawling resort. Karam had never been there, having found golf to be a boring and hard-to-follow sport. Dr. Fletcher raved about the prime rib so much that Karam could hardly wait for lunch. He had spent a long and rather boozy night with his current squeeze, who had insisted they finish the bottle of whiskey before they crawled under the sheets. The hangover had lingered, and he still had a dull headache he felt the beef could help assuage.

Helene had reserved a private dining room, and accompanied by her boss, a Mr. Jones; the area representative, a rising star within Corning named Tony Nova; and a local and personal friend of the director of services, Syl Waxman. They played senior hockey together and talked about their beloved Toronto Maple Leafs for hours, often attending games at the Gardens together. Tony had nursed the account well and had made sure to brief his superiors well on their guests.

Once the introductions were over and everybody had been served their aperitifs, the two hockey enthusiasts began to break the ice with hockey as the main topic. "Two of my brothers play in the NHL," Helene said casually and without inflection. That got the men's attention, and as she spoke about her famous brothers and their athletic achievements, Karam had a strange feeling of being overwhelmed by the sheer presence of the woman. He had noticed her darker features but now studied the waist-length dark hair, the aquiline features, the expressive green eyes with a wealth of long eyelashes, and her well-shaped, thin nose? He speculated. Was it responsible for that unique accent? It fascinated him, and he focused on her lips: red, moist, and mobile over a set of perfect and strong white teeth. When she leaned forward to listen attentively, it was hard for him to keep his eyes off her bosom under the tasteful and severe blouse. She must have noticed him watching her silently with interest because she smiled. Their eyes held only for a second, moving away and back, giving away the immediate and powerful mutual attraction.

They started dating the same week they met. Thirty-year-old self-made millionaire, Karam and one of the rarest success stories in corporate Canada and a woman in a senior management position, albeit not with either an executive's title or responsibility. Her chances of becoming such depended on her continuity with her employment. If she took time off to have a family, she would be out of the game and forced to start again at a lower position. Helene was conscious of her predicament. Already twenty-eight and unmarried, she could end up an old spinster holding a high position. All of her old classmates had husbands, and most had children. Her parents worried, her sisters talked, and her brothers teased her. "All that studying, eh, Helene, and pas d'amour!"

Then she met the most unexpected man she could have dreamed of: a foreigner, neither Christian nor Catholic, rich, uncomplicated, and a philanthropist already and never before married.

And he made love like a bull. No long, romantic evenings, glasses of wine or champagne, chocolate, or roses. Just tear-her-clothes-off-and-mount-her kind of love. They were inseparable from Friday evening till Sunday afternoon, week in and week out. Each evening they talked of their day, the food they had eaten, the clothes they had worn, the people they had met, and the business they had done, but never in specifics because she respected her company's strict code of confidentiality, and he was not given to boasting about his.

She felt she got to know him well, and by Christmas, well enough to invite him to the family farm in Quebec. He accepted with alacrity. It was his first real Christmas holiday to be spent with a Canadian family. The Bergers had him over but not for their high holidays. He had spent three of the last Christmases in Acapulco.

They drove together in his latest Cadillac. The trunk was packed full of her gifts for her huge clan, their luggage, a silver cutlery set from him for her parents, and his gift to her: an eighteen-carat set of Italian jewelry studded with her birth stone, blood red rubies—a gift of promise.

He was enthusiastically received by the demonstrative, hugs-and-kisses Boucher clan. Karam liked her mother, her apron still warm from standing at the stove, cooking and baking. Her father walked into the kitchen and greeted him, apologizing for his hands being dusty and getting yelled at by Helene's mother while being assaulted by the toddlers and the crawlers. It was a scene so chaotic yet serene for Karam, familiar as he was to living in India in a courtyard with so many kin. He found himself yearning to be a part of a family again, to gain relatives and kin.

* * *

The letters from India, now almost two a day, kept him in touch with the progress being made in turning his village into a Model Gram. Punna had won her fight to reserve a good part of land around the Sant Baba *Samadhi* and had it planted with fruit and shade trees in an effort to restore the old ambiance of the hallowed space. She had put so much energy and soul into her dedication to the holy man's memory that it now began to develop lore: a legend. *Shudras* who prayed there and performed *pooja* began to talk of the minor miracles of some of their prayers being answered, and each month, quite a gathering took place at the *Samadhi*. Locally, it came to be called the *Samadhi* of the *Churas*. The name stuck. Mostly *Churas* worshipped there, and some *Chamars*, but *Jats* and other castes began to avoid it, preferring instead to visit the *Gurudwara*. The *Brahmins* went on pilgrimages to Hardwar, and most other castes went to the Naina Devi temple on a hilltop in the Shivalik hills near Anandpur Sahib.

The disciple returned to perform his duties and was amazed at the change within the year. He was now a guru in his own right and had a couple of novices as disciples. The novices were at first shocked but settled quickly in service of the Sant Baba, the first of the lineage that was now three generations deep. They quite liked the largesse of the rich *Chura* family. They were very generous, particularly the old woman, Punna. She had brought them new saffron robes, blankets, and bedding, and had promised to construct a proper ashram that met their every need as seekers of salvation. It would have a hand pump with a large concrete reservoir that doubled as a dipping bath and an expansive hut of the best reeds brought from the shores of the Sutlej River and properly supported by a sturdy frame of hand-cut lumber, buried deep enough and nailed strongly enough to withstand any known storm. Bedding of the finest cotton would be spread over properly dried layers of cotton bushes covered with finer reeds. The gathering area would be stomped by hundreds of feet into a stone-like consistency and layered with real sand.

The novices particularly enjoyed the evenings when the women and girls came to perform *pooja*. They ate well from the offerings of tasty food and sweets and reveled in the doe-like eyes of the devotees fixed upon the holy men.

There were rumors in the village spread by the upper castes that the Sant Baba *Samadhi* was turning into a sexual sect led by the older disciple and his novices, so women of the upper castes were forbidden by their elders from participating in the weekly rituals of *pooja* performed there. The village louts began to berate the *Chura* men for allowing their women the luxury of unsupervised forays to the place. Several even talked about burning the place down. The village could not tolerate such a den of inequity. Stung and offended by the rumors, Punna sought the counsel of her father. Bola, now retired from his duties as a hangman and caretaker of the dead at the district morgue, had been seeking peace from his demons, and it had come from the success of his grandson and his daughter's devotion to the Sant Baba. He decided to put an end to the rumors.

The next day, carrying a long-handled axe, he challenged the louts to a discussion of the *Samadhi*, loudly enough to attract a small crowd. The young men, seeing the rage in his eyes, almost lost control of their bowels and, muttering excuses, took off for the shelter of their courtyards. Then Bola went to the *Samadhi* and spoke at length with the guru and his disciples. He was amply rewarded, as things changed. The guru and the novices started collecting alms in the village just like the Sant Baba had, evoking memories of simpler times and winning over the women of the upper castes. Once they had accomplished that, the men fell behind their womenfolk and left the Sant Baba *Samadhi* to its true devotees: the *Shudras*.

Noorian now attracted a lot of attention. As work began

and progressed on the projects, a lot of local and other men suddenly found steady work, the artisan classes being the real benefactors. A family of *Jats* even invested in trucks to help haul the stone, sand, and cement needed. The *Shudras* took advantage of the offer to upgrade their homes from mud brick and fragile hovels to airy, brick abodes with light bulbs and fans on the ceilings. Students from surrounding villages now wanted to register to study at the newly upgraded and furnished schools in Noorian.

The roadwork finally completed, the entire village gathered to greet the first bus to begin serving their community, and Chandu Das did not disappoint. Alighting from the bus to a burst of applause and camera flashes, he made sure that he took credit for the progress being made. The death of Nehru had left a vacuum of power, and no clear leader had emerged to take over the statesman's position as leader of the ruling Congress Party. As a *Shudra* leader, he had sensed the opportunity to become a kingmaker, so fractured were the aspiring leaders. The communists had been hamstrung by the Chinese aggression toward India and their successful pursuit of nuclear power. Indians at large were now awaiting the emergence of a true and pragmatic figure to lead them, someone more in tune with global realities of the cold war that raged between the western powers led by America and the Soviet Union and its allies. Nehru had left India in the middle. Opting for a nonalignment policy and having taken some advantage of wooing by both of the power blocks, India was now adrift, both in policy and prosperity. With Nehru gone and its most powerful benefactor and much beloved Jack Kennedy assassinated and replaced by a nonpersonality in Lyndon B. Johnson, who was adrift in the war in Vietnam and in domestic issues of equality and civil rights, India sought a leader, not a stopgap replacement. With the help of the *Shudra* coalition, the party having elected one as its chairmen, they opted for the daughter of the great man Indira Gandhi.

Recognizing the cold-blooded Chandu Das as one just like herself, she appointed him to the exalted position of Minister of Agriculture, a particularly important position as the now tiny state of Punjab still supplied 40 percent of the country's staples and grain. Thus rewarded not only in title but power, the cunning politician moved into a substantial bungalow in New Delhi with ample greenery and gardens and authorized an official invitation for Karam to visit India and receive his first honor from his homeland.

The High Commissioner of India in Ottawa handled the delivery of the invitation by a liveried courier to King Laboratories. It caused quite a stir, as the invitation was contained in an envelope so ornate and official it was delivered on a silver platter. Mrs. Jennifer Hopkins, Karam's secretary, turned dumb at such pomp, but the ever jocular Ella had made light of the serious situation. "King of India," she had stated simply and turned around to get back behind her desk. Conscious of Karam's increasing involvement with Helene and declining interest in her and the Bergers, she had found herself suddenly melancholy and depressed. She missed his attention. It was as if she had lost her mirror.

* * *

Tim Davis returned with news. "The consolidation within the private laboratory industry is winding down," he said. "You are soon going to be faced with a dilemma. Stay independent, merge, or sell. Also, with all the new technologies, the ongoing investment in equipment upgrades, staff training, staff retention, and marketing battles are going to turn vicious. The big guys are going to try a new way. They are going to be the promoters of massive medical centers with physicians as equity partners on the real estate and buy themselves in-house exclusivity. They are already eyeing locations in Hamilton-Niagara."

Karam looked at Ben. They had bought Stoney Creek barely months ago, and their treasury account was at its lowest in that year. "How are they funding this?" he asked.

"By going into debt," Tim replied.

"Just like that, they can borrow that much money?"

"There is no shortage of capital, and with a combination of real estate and the EBITDAs in the lab business, it's not hard to raise money."

They reflected on that for some time. Then Ben spoke, "We have two options, Karam: sell or grow. I don't think either of us is interested in a share swap, losing control to operators we feel are inferior to us."

"I suggest you do an analysis, and I can help with that. Then whatever you decide, we execute." Tim started folding his papers.

Ben asked for two days to visit family in New York. Karam knew that he was not going there for that purpose alone. He had talked so much about opportunities south of the border, but Karam was hesitant. There was a lot going on in America that frightened him: first the assassination of Jack Kennedy, the passing of the Civil Rights Act, and the southern states' resistance to it and the painful integration process. He had great empathy with the blacks, almost like they were his own people. "But what about the crime rates?" he wondered. He had not been to some American cities like New York, Chicago, and Detroit because he had heard too many horror stories. Here in Canada, he walked home from downtown at midnight and never had a problem; no one had ever tried to mug him. He liked it in this country that manufactured crisis just to kill the sheer boredom of being peaceful and civilized. America was ablaze in conflict and confrontation. Also, he was thinking long-term now, as far as Helene was concerned, hoping to have a ring on her finger by her birthday. They were planning to go to India, and he wanted to go before the monsoons and before the cruel heat of May and June. Now was not an ideal time for major changes. He hoped Ben would not come back enthusiastic about the States and try to convince him to sell and move. He also knew that he trusted Ben's instincts. At the end of the day, he and his family were in this position of wealth and fame now because of Ben and his vision.

Karam spoke with Helene, and she enthusiastically agreed to accompany him to India. He had to go to collect his honor as the first *Shudra* to receive the title of Shere Punjab.

Ben returned from New York and locked himself in his office for the rest of the week. Finding that a bit odd, Karam asked Ella, "What is with him?'

She shrugged her shoulders. "The man has gone mum. He's not talking, not even with Rebecca."

"Well, tell him I am leaving for India in two weeks."

"With Helene?" Ella blurted, and then cursed herself for asking it in such a tone.

"Yes," Karam replied, still looking at Ben's closed door.

"I truly hope you have a great time and she enjoys meeting your family."

"Me, too," Karam replied and turned. He saw Mrs. Hopkins smile, a bit like the Cheshire cat. At his signal, she followed him into his office, and he began dictating letters that were piling up unanswered. Helene was occupying too much of his time, and worse still, his thoughts, and he was always hurried. He wondered if this was what falling in love was like. He hoped marriage would smooth life out.

Ben came to his office on Monday looking both tentative and excited, refusing to sit down, pacing in tight little circles. "Are you going to say anything?" Karam asked, exasperated at the weeklong silence. His partner paced some more.

Finally turning to him, he started, "I have been working behind the scenes, friend. I think we have a bridge."

"A bridge?"

It was at times like this that Ben wished that Karam understood high finance and its terminology. "A bridge, my friend, that helps us across the chasm to untold profits."

Karam leaned forward, a perplexed look on his face.

"Go to India. Enjoy your time there. Get your medal, and by the time you get back, everything will be more crystallized."

"Come on, Ben," Karam begged, "in plain English, please."

The Executive Vice-President of King Laboratories sat down, crossed his legs, folded his hands, and raising a confident face to his partner, he said, "A bridge, Karam is a financial term where we have the backing of a silent partner to go from point A to point B. Point A is the conundrum we face today. Sell, merge, or survive. The bridge allows us to survive but in a way that makes us a threat to the well-laid plans of our competitors. They have to pay our price."

Karam held his breath.

"The trick is to give the appearance of staying as we are but as an aggressive company, outbidding the competition on anything they start in our territory and then forcing them to give us a price-to-earnings ratio far greater than the rest got, maybe even six to eight times."

"That is almost double what Davis calls the norm."

"But we, Karam, are not the norm."

Chapter 14

The first hint that taking Helene on the trip to India was going to be a challenge came in the tone of the agent for Essential Services. "Sahib will be accompanied by a Canadian woman!" Surprise and shock mixed in the voice. Suddenly, Karam realized that Canada was a gentler, kinder, and increasingly more tolerant country. India had not changed, and an Indian traveling around with a white woman, particularly unmarried, was sure to raise eyebrows and invite attention and comment. What he did not realize was that if the Indian was a *Shudra* in this situation, it would invite double that. However, he pressed ahead, and Helene was so excited.

"I want to wear all those exotic clothes," she gushed. "I am going to shop til I drop." Karam resolved to make her visit memorable. He was going to make sure she was treated like royalty.

It started at the arrival. The Assistant Deputy Inspector-General of Delhi Police personally met them at the tarmac and guided them into a police jeep for the short drive to a side entrance that housed an obvious VIP area. There they waited for the luggage and had their passports respectfully checked and stamped by the senior customs officer. A uniformed attendant served tea and savory treats. The honorable Chandu Das, Minister of Agriculture, had assured this high-level greeting and attention. Karam was an official guest of the Indian government and here to receive an honor bestowed upon him for his services to his homeland. The airport officials were anxious that they receive no blowback from the tempestuous *Shudra* politician whose star was ascending. Any guest of his was to be given the VIP treatment. Mr. Pardesi was a gentleman and looked obviously pleased and grateful for their attention. The very beautiful woman accompanying him had told the senior customs officer during his gentle, polite, and routine questioning that she was indeed single but traveling with Mr. Pardesi. They thought him to be a very lucky man indeed.

"If she is indeed his lover," thought the assistant deputy, whose precinct included providing security for the main airport in the country, "what does he need a stupid medal from the politicians for? Karma has already met his best needs." He had always enjoyed his duties here particularly because of the interaction it allowed him with foreigners, especially the women. He was particularly fond of the tall, sinewy Russian girls that were sent in droves to work in the Soviet Union's embassy and many consular offices now spread over India. Lately, the quantity of females had increased from the western countries, but the quality had fallen tremendously thanks to the bloody hippies now showing up and overstaying their visas, drinking, doing drugs, and making themselves available to Indian louts. They had cheapened the image of the *Mem-Sahibs* as the British women were known and respected during the Raj. There were fewer and fewer of those arriving now, but this one was a definitely a *Mem-Sahib*, of that he had no doubt. His trained and cynical police brain told him that much. She was all class.

Karam Pardesi Sahib was a very lucky man. He would never address a *Shudra* by the title Sahib, but he would this man, all because he had a woman of such beauty and upbringing on his arm.

As they drove off in the big, long, American car accompanied by Jaswant Singh of Essential Services, he saluted them smartly.

At the guest house provided for their stay in New Delhi, the manager, an elderly Pathan with a regal bearing and a mustache to match, had Karam's luggage firmly placed in a spacious and well-furnished room with its own bathroom on the main floor. "And for you, madam," he courteously bowed to Helene, already yawning and tired of the twenty-two-hour-long journey, "I have reserved you a room upstairs."

When Karam tried to protest, the man looked at him severely, implying "you are in India and my domain. So shut up."

Cowed thus by the manager's demeanor and unable to argue further from fatigue, he watched as she was led upstairs to her quarters by the tall, elegant figure and his anxious entourage of coolies and attendants. Jaswant Singh, himself appalled and intrigued by Karam's behavior, bringing an unmarried white woman with him to India, said reassuringly, "She will be very well looked after, Sahib." Then he began settling him in, as light already showed through the wooden blinds in the early dawn of a spring morning.

* * *

Punna did not sleep; she could not, awaiting and preparing for the arrival of her son and a white woman. In his letter to his sister—for he only communicated such truths to her—he informed them of this truth. He had selected his own bride and wanted her to meet and be approved by his family. He was putting the onus on them: the poor, uneducated, and rural people. She had met white people at the CMC, and some had actually attended her mother's funeral last year, but none had come to live with them.

"Oh, Sant Baba," she prayed, looking for guidance, and then she turned to her father. Bola immediately left for Ludhiana to seek the guidance of Dr Grewal.

"Do not let her stay in the house," the wise doctor advised. "Tell him to bring her here; they can stay at my manor, or I will book them into the Gaylord Hotel. It has all the amenities."

"What about functions, visiting?" Bola asked.

"During the day, fine, spend all the time in public in Noorian, here and there. But in the evening and at night, stay in Ludhiana."

Thus informed, Bola returned and counseled his family. The sisters and their children wanted the white woman to live with them, spend days accompanying them on visits and trips, and in the evenings let them gather around her to soak in the experience of sleeping under the same roof as her. For them she was an exotic alien, an unattainable companion, and they did not want to be denied. For the elders, she was an unexpected conundrum, an unknown, a burden to be born for the sake of their son. After all, he had dug them out of the cesspool of servitude and "untouchability." But they still lived within the boundaries of Noorian and its centuries-old traditions. No man entered his parent's courtyard with an unmarried woman not accompanied by her parents or a chaperone.

* * *

They spent the first day sleeping in. Waking up in mid-afternoon and bathing to wash off the grime of travel, then dressing in light clothes. The dry heat, only bearable indoors, in the shade, and under the ceiling fans, hit them like a blast furnace as soon as they stepped outside. Helene wanted to stretch her legs and walk. Jaswant Singh guided them down the baking street and into a treed area where they walked in circles, trying to stay under the canopies of the huge mango trees interspersed with ornamental bushes and the odd *Bodhi* trees with roots dangling from branches, some having reached the ground, growing trunk-like features. Helene was fascinated by the flora and the foliage. She stopped under the tree and closed her eyes to listen to the song of the nightingales perched on its branches. "It is so beautiful!" she shouted in the tranquil island of shade and shadow.

In the evening they sat with the other guests, all foreigners, around the huge dining room table and on old upholstered chairs, and they were served an unforgettable meal of lamb *briyani, tandoori* chicken, and fresh baked *naans* with an array of chutneys and cooling cucumbers dipped in yogurt. For those with light stomachs, the chef served a *muntgawny* soup with fresh baked bread and various spreads. For drinks, they had mango juice, mango *lassi*—almost mango everything—and finished with aromatic *chai* tea, and finally, as some at the table agreed, the best cappuccino they had ever tasted. Afterward they played Carrom Board, Monopoly, Scrabble, and Snakes and Ladders, and Helene felt transported to a happier and more innocent time in her life. The manager saw to it that the women went to their rooms and the men to the rooms assigned to them. Only the confirmed married ones went to rooms with double beds.

The next day, Karam was taken alone to the offices of the Raj path. There he was instructed in the ceremony that would be conducted by the president of the country. He would receive a certificate of service honor only. His real reward would be held in Chandigarh by the Chief Minister of the Punjab.

The real India hit Helene like a brick to the head. In the late afternoon, they had driven to Connaught Place to indulge in some sightseeing and shopping, As soon as she got out of the car, a crowd of urchins surrounded her despite Jaswant Singh and the driver's best efforts to shoo them away. Once the initial shock had worn, she looked closely at some of the unfortunate vying for her attention. They were barefoot with matted and unwashed hair, snot-covered noses, and eyes with yellowish excretions. Some were lepers with no fingers, deformed and with sunken faces. Girls with tattered clothing and carrying naked babies on their hips extended their free hands, begging.

"*Bakshish Mem-Sahib, bakshish*," they cried in unison and rote.

"Ignore them," Jaswant Singh instructed, now in his security mode and roughly shoving the mob aside and clearing a path as they hurriedly escaped into the cool, dark confines of a clothier. The mob still milled outside, hoping.

Helene was breathless from the experience, and so was Karam. He had been away too long and was no longer unshaken by the phenomenon. "It's India," he stated flatly, unable to comfort her by taking her in his arms: just another taboo to observe in 1969 India. By now they had been swarmed by the shop's owner and his minions, drawing them deeper into the narrow, long, poorly lit and ventilated cavern of a structure. This was familiar and suited to the shoppers, locals who flocked to this mecca of merchandise and fashion, restaurants, and parks. Vendors and pickpockets, hawkers and touts, and crowers all flowed through it, blocking the vehicular traffic, the drivers responding with a cacophony of horn blowing, some sticking their heads out of the side windows to scream at the jaywalkers blissfully ignorant of their urgencies.

"Lady, please, please sit down," pleaded the owner with folded hands, and Helene did, onto a cushioned cane chair. One was proffered for Karam.

So began an experience she would remember for the rest of her life that she would talk and tell of to her enthralled audiences in Canada.

Suddenly, as if by magic, the young men, agile and quick, began rolling out sheets of brilliant hues of cloth of such amazing textures and colors, the designs and prints eye popping in detail and harmony.

Watching her reaction to the reams and reams of clothing arrayed before her, Karam had an idea. He began making a list of all his relatives in the village and beyond, friends and her family. Turning to Helene, he told her his plan to buy suit sets as gifts, right there and then. She was thrilled in helping select 3- to 5-meter pieces for people she had yet to meet but would now have real gifts for, as well as gifts to take back to Canada. Her mother, sisters, and sisters-in-law would be so pleased. Karam selected for her 7 different suits for Punjabi *Salwar/Kammezes* with matching *cholies*. The owner called for a whole phalanx of tailors, who promised to have the clothes stitched overnight and delivered the next day to the guest house. They measured her right in the middle of the shop, nodding in admiration at her height and beauty.

"*Mem-Sahib*, oh, you will look like a *Maharani*," the owners cooed, having sold over two thousand rupees of cloth and stitching in two hours. The owner called for cold drinks and cappuccinos on the rush to toast this unexpected event.

Helene watched fascinated as the sales men refolded and rearranged the hundred or so rolls of fabric with flying fingers and limbs and returned the shop for viewing by new customers who were standing around watching, fascinated by the western woman. As the driver finally rolled to the door of the shop, everyone folded their hands and bowed farewell, urging her to come back again. "Thank you, thank you," the shop owner folded the notes Karam settled with and shook his hand vigorously. Jaswant Singh had them seated in safety, windows up, before the crowd of urchins had a clue of their departure from Connaught Place. Turning to look at her, Jaswant Singh said, "Tomorrow, madam, the Red Fort and sightseeing."

Forgetting to mention that most of the sightseeing would be from the comfort of the car, to keep Helene happy and engaged, Karam and the driver devised a clever route through the main thoroughfares and major sights and stops.

* * *

As the Jewel in the Crown, the British built the seats of their power in India well. Victoria House and Gardens, Calcutta, in the first seat of colonial power for the East India Company, stands as evidence of the opulence they created to project that power, all of it from the wealth they looted from India. Only two hundred years earlier, India and China had produced half of the world's wealth annually. By independence, both had been impoverished to feed the industrial revolution that lifted Britain and Europe out of the medieval age; the Indians suffered the same fate as the Incas, the Zulus, the Malayans, and so many other economies.

They built the government building well, architecturally exquisite and spread out to be laid along a very broad boulevard landscaped with open greens and orderly beds of foliage and flowers. In those cleaner air days of 1969, the presidential palace, Raj Bhavan, took the prize, and in one of its massive halls, the ceremony was conducted with rigid protocol and pomp. Seated in the invited guest section, Helene was duly impressed by the tall, exotically uniformed soldiers, attendants, and bearers. The frail, bespectacled President of the Republic sat in an ornate, oversized, throne of a chair attended on either side by men in Nehru jackets and identically trimmed scalps and moustaches. She was amazed at the size and shape of the facial treatments.

The recipients rose one by one and strode to stand in front of the dignitary while a woman behind a lectern read their accomplishments and the name of the reward or recognition. The highest were announced first, and Karam's name was third to the last to be called. As the ceremony was held entirely in Hindi, she had no idea until translated later about what was said about Karam and the quick conversation between him and the president. She did note that in his case the president folded his hands in acknowledgment rather than shake Karam's hand, proffered as it had been. She also noted that Karam was the only recipient dressed in a western suit. All others, being Indian, were dressed in the fashions of their regions.

In his seat among the cabinet of the country, the honorable Chandu Das seethed at this insult to his nominee by the stupid, old hack, the Brahmin who occupied the most august and unelected office in the country: his refusal to shake hands with a *Shudra*. He exchanged knowing looks with certain members of his clique and vowed revenge; the nomination to the office was due only in months. They would work day and night to have the arrogant usurper of Ghandian ideals chased out and replaced by one of their own. The current chairman of the party was a *Shudra* and the longest-serving member of the shadow cabinet prior to independence, since heading various ministries under Nehru and the two or three short-serving ones since 1965.

After the ceremony, Chandu Das and the other *Shudra* politicians and office holders gathered around the young man and his beautiful white escort. As a couple, they looked so elegant and attractive, radiant and confident, humble yet competent. Karam, truly a model of the best a *Shudra* could be and achieve on a level playing field, was Chandu Das's mantra now. Chandu Das was determined to populate India with hundreds of thousands of them within his living days, the gods willing.

* * *

The next morning they left for Noorian, making sure to tip the guest house manager and servers. Most of the morning staff saw them off at the entrance, and Helene folded her hands and bowed her head in return to theirs. She had picked up a few essential words like *Namaste* and *Shukria, pani* for water and *chai* for tea. As they drove out of New Delhi and headed north on the Grand Trunk Road, she could not help but be amazed at the contrasts of this ancient country. Stuck to the walls of the courtyards of elegant and huge mansions like mushrooms were the straw huts of the poor. Only the gate and sentry standing guard separated wealth from want. There appeared to be a sense or semblance of order, but chaos ruled on the roads. Meant for vehicular traffic, these arteries of transportation carried waves of people on every imaginable mode of transport. Not much of a photographer, she looked wide out at the scenes unfolding in front of her eyes.

The landscape was a golden hue from the vast fields of ripening wheat and oats, the sky an azure blue with nary a cloud. Occasionally, dust devils ran along the dried bed of a rivulet. Cattle tethered under trees, some contentedly chewing cud. Herds of goats were standing on hind legs and stretching to reach the leaves on thorn bushes. Towns and cities were only miles from each other but mostly the same in architecture and activity. There were people standing in knots, and when a bus slowed and stopped in front of them, they scrambled to climb aboard with no regard for forming a line, just muscling their way in, the tallest and strongest first, the elderly and women last, dragging children behind them. The conductor clambered up the ladder and dropped the suitcases or bundles into waiting arms on the side.

Helene had read some about India and its history, and what she read mostly emphasized the spirituality, which was not evident in the hurly burly of life she had seen so far. It seemed no place for the weak-hearted or the spiritual except for the saffron flags fluttering above white spires of temples all over the countryside. Karam had warned her about the lack of facilities and the poverty of infrastructure, and when she spied the odd bare buttocks pointed towards the road as the owner of the repelling pair looked away in modesty, she understood and sympathized. (And she was suitably horrified, looking away quickly.) Once in a while, she met the watchful gaze of Karam, quiet and contemplative today: lost in thought. Those brown eyes set and were slow to blink as he studied the landscape of India speeding by.

They stopped to eat at the rest house in Karnal, the waiter rushing them into a smaller, less crowded room to the side. Some white people dug into the food on their *thalis*. Others were rougher looking with long hair, wearing white Indian *kurtas* over sturdy and dusty jeans, feet in sandals or moccasins. Some wore *tikkas* of saffron and white like pilgrims to holy places, searching for enlightenment or adventure. These people gazed at them with open curiosity, having picked up the one Indian habit that unnerved her: people gazing unblinkingly at her like she used to look at an animal in the zoo. "You will get used to it," Karam had said reassuringly, hugging her at the guest house her first full day in New Delhi, "They are absolutely harmless and just curious."

But it was unnerving nonetheless.

She dozed off after lunch and must have slept for hours because Karam was trying to wake her up as the car slowed to a stop at a better looking hotel. "Wake up, honey," he whispered. "We are less than an hour away, now."

They all piled out and headed for the washrooms, and she brushed her teeth, washed her face, combed her hair, and applied some make-up, trying to make herself more presentable to her potential future in-laws.

* * *

"They are coming, they are coming!" The shout went up as soon as the youth scrambled from the roof of the *haveli*, seeing the cloud of dust lifting behind the black outline of a car as it turned from the main road onto the one to Noorian. The crowd of gaily dressed family and friends, all eager to see the white woman accompanying Karam, rushed for the closed gate as Punna stood her ground.

"Behave," she ordered. "We are going to follow tradition and greet them ritually."

Outside the gates, a crowd of the higher castes had already assembled, ready to witness the arrival of the award-winning boy from the village with a white woman on his arm. All kinds of rumor and speculation were rife among the villagers, perpetuated by idle chatter around their hearths in the dog days of the spring and awaiting the start of the busy season of harvesting. She was already his wife, some said. She was coming to inspect his family; some smiled and snickered at the thought of a *Mem-Sahib* wanting the now corpulent village watchman and his busybody wife. Of course she was going to absolutely respect his hangman of a grandfather. "I will bet that she takes flight as soon as she sees Bola," boasted a lout-turned-head-of-a-family now of the *Jats*, once having had his shorts dirtied by the mere growl of the fearsome *Chura*.

The car came around the curve, slowly, ethereally, and coasted soundlessly to a stop a few feet from the gate. The expert driver already aware of the gravity of the occasion was suitably impressed by the knot of onlookers standing along the ring road, some dangling from the branches of trees to get a better view. He stepped out and opened the rear right door to let Karam out, and Jaswant Singh did the same for Helene; a gasp rose from the crowd for what emerged was no *Mem-Sahib* of their imaginations wearing a frock but a vision in a demure Punjabi suit, her head suitably covered with the *choli* wrapped expertly around her neck and its long folds falling in front and back. Her hair was in a severe bun, her face half-hid behind the dark glasses. She came around to the front of the car and stood a foot behind and to the side of Karam.

The gates swung open, and Punna stood in the middle of the welcoming party, carrying a small bottle of oil that she poured on either column supporting the gates. She handed the bottle to one of her daughters and opened her arms as she cried out to her son. Karam moved forward, first to touch her feet, then his grandfather's and father's, and he fell into the embraces of his sisters. Helene repeated his actions exactly, folding her hands and bowing to receive the traditional blessing of the elders, who placed their right hands on her head in benediction. Karam talked in staccato English, introducing the family until the crowd parted and allowed him to guide his guest into the courtyard.

Behind them, Bola, expressionless but bursting with pride and joy, slammed the gates shut, depriving the highborn the thrill of witnessing the activities within the celebrating courtyard.

Chapter 15

The Gaylord Hotel in Ludhiana had the elegant facade of a Mogul palace and sat in an extensive and beautiful garden set back from the Jagraon Road. The suites, some still recalling its initial purpose as the manor of a minor royal, and the extensive renovations by the new owners had added the modern conveniences of flush toilets, cast-iron tubs, and running water, both hot and cold. The hotel was patronized by the cream of society and foreign visitors or tourists passing through on their way to Kashmir. English-speaking staff and liveried waiters tended the guests. Karam and Helene had the largest suite with a separate bedroom featuring a canopied bed and the necessary mosquito netting; a big, marbled bathroom; and a large seating area furnished in colonial style with cane furniture covered with pillows. The balcony had latticed walls, allowing it to be airy, sunny, and private.

Helene sat on a chez-lounge and read while Karam slept past noon. The days since leaving Toronto had been hectic and full, and the jet lag had taken its toll. They had decided to have the day free of visits and visitors. She had quite a fright watching a couple of large lizards chase each other in and out of the holes of the latticed walls. Having been raised on a farm, she was not easily alarmed by the rustlings of nature, but she blamed her frayed nerves now on fatigue and lassitude.

They dressed and came down the curved staircase to the

lobby where Jaswant Singh sat reading a newspaper. He spoke to Karam for a moment and nodded pleasantly to Helene, then went back to the paper. They proceeded to the dining hall. She ordered eggs and toast—no sausages or bacon here. The orange juice freshly squeezed over ice and served in a crystal glass. The coffee was potent and fragrant. Karam indulged in *parathas* and yogurt, and he politely and wistfully turned away the strong pickles and the onion salad.

"That was some welcome," she remarked, still in a daze at the colorful and noisy evening spent at the village. She was sometimes unnerved by the unblinking staring of most of his clan, but she was complimented by the smiles of welcome and the attention! "Your older sister and you are so alike. You guys look like your mum."

"You mean good looking," he mumbled through a mouthful, and she gave him a kick under the table.

"Narcissist."

* * *

After having been taken such good care of by Jaswant Singh, Helene could not help but think of him as Punjab, Daddy Warbuck's turbaned butler and bodyguard in the comic Annie. The man was alert to every wish and responded efficiently with such an economy of effort and grace that he reminded her of a cat or a cougar. Tall, lean, and still athletic, he was of indeterminate age. An old army or policeman, Karam had guessed, having never delved too much into the man's background. Karam just knew that he was a top recommendation from the Essential Services Agency. Helene felt safe and secure in his presence, and keeping them that way was the man's job. It had been his job for over two decades: guarding the rich and the powerful, training yearly in updated techniques by agents sent from Pinkerton. The last one had been a retired Mossad trainer.

He and his colleagues were now much in demand because of the ongoing, small-scale insurgencies all over India. It seemed each province was threatening to secede. It made sense that the subcontinent at one time had five hundred different states and statelets, all with their own sovereign rulers. The British had succeeded in putting them all under one central authority, and now the modern rulers of India and Pakistan coped with these tensions.

There were some worrisome trends in India these days, particularly for the wealthy, even the ordinary rich. Some of the groups operating as insurgents were beginning to raise money by simply showing up fully armed and threatening mayhem at the manors and mansions in cities and at the *havelis* and courtyards of the wealthy. Because safety deposit boxes were yet to become popular, most people kept their cash and jewelry in strong boxes at their residences, and police response was hours away due to a lack of phones both in homes and police stations. As a result, very bold raids had resulted in huge caches, and sometimes in deaths or injuries of the unfortunate targets and victims. Every week there were newspaper and radio reports of the revenge killings now extended to innocent family members of high police and politicians. Essential Services had seen a surge in demands for protection by the sophisticated. Others took precautions by hiring ex-army sentries or guards, buying police-trained Alsatian dogs, or keeping a low profile. Jaswant Singh had a long talk with Karam's grandfather, knowing that the reputation of an elderly hangman, while sufficient to deter local louts, was no match for the trained expertise of some of the committed insurgents. They were quick to kill for profit or to instill fear, attracting to their cause more of the educated but oppressed because of caste or creed injustices.

Karam and his family posed a conundrum. As *Shudras*, rising above their expected rank and role, would they be immune to the revolutionary zeal of the *Naxalites*, recently active in the Punjab? Formed to resist untold abuses in a village called Naxalbari in Eastern India, these Maoist guerrillas operated fearlessly now. Their leaders were drawn from educated men and sometimes women, fearless and cold-blooded. The police had responded in kind. Rather than capturing and jailing and putting them through proper court trials, they simply executed them in so-called "encounters." This spawned shootouts to the death, and the very committed and hardened elements operated under the cover of darkness and with the surprise of stealth. Jaswant Singh took precautions to prevent just such a tragic event visiting upon his charges when they were hosting a foreign guest.

As such, he was not alone on sentry. Unseen and plain-clothed, six others had been pressed into service, one or two dressed as beggars and mendicants, carrying more than the alms they received under their robes. Able to insert themselves into any advantageous position or spot, these masters of disguise practiced ancient techniques of the thugs and the use of modern devices of observation and defense, including binoculars, side arms, and training in hand-to-hand combat. Alert like the cobras in the country and just as quick to strike, they had put more urban guerrillas out of commission than most of the police agencies combined.

Thus protected and blissfully unaware, the guest couple from Canada staying at the Gaylord Hotel spent a leisurely afternoon in the comfort of the huge bed in their suite, exploring each other and their erotic zones. The book *Kama Sutra* was their new and indulgent guide.

* * *

Over the following week, Helene and Karam visited the CMC to meet the often-discussed Dr. Muriel King for whom Karam had named the business. Dr. King took the two of them on a tour of the now more expanded hospital, a five-story new building almost complete. It would house the private section and some teaching and office facilities. The centennial celebrations in the fall were awaited with much anticipation as many foreign and local benefactors and alumni were expected to attend what could be a fundraising bonanza. There was always a need for additional funds to support the throngs of suffering humanity that arrived at the CMC's clinics every day, most unable to afford even the most modest of care and medication. Helene registered as a friend of the institution and made her first donation of one hundred dollars. Dr. King presented her with a bible and a brooch with the insignia of CMC.

Then they dined with Dr. Grewal, and the old man was thrilled to host such a beautiful lady as he kept repeating the compliment. He was disappointed that they had chosen the Gaylord over his manor. Karam did not want to burden the now frail man further with the responsibility of hosting a foreign guest. Dr. Grewal presented her with a beautiful set of 22-carat gold ornaments laid out on an exquisite bed of purple satin. The box was made of ivory, itself finely carved with flowers and leaflets. "Belonged to my wife," he explained quietly and sincerely.

When Helene protested, he stopped her, saying, "It could be going to a daughter-in-law I never had."

Karam burst into tears at this gesture by a man he had admired since the day they had met. To be thought of as a son by Dr. Grewal would be one of his life's greatest and fondest memories. Dr. Grewal hugged them both, kissing them on their foreheads. "May God bless you both!"

After spending a day at Noorian, they left on a two-day tour of Chandigarh to visit with the Chief Minister of Punjab in the new Union Territory and the joint capital of the newly divided Punjab, into the Hindi-speaking Haryana State and a much smaller Punjab where Punjabi would be the official state language: overall, a bitter disappointment for many Punjabis. Although eagerly accepted by the *Akali Dal*, the Sikh religious party that now formed the government and tried to hold its fractious sections together with inducements of cabinet positions and other rewards. Corruption ran rampant as power came to those who had never tasted it, and the province was set on a path to ruination, a long but steady path of decline and lack of growth and exclusion from the industrialization that would lift most other states out of poverty and some into world-class destinations for capital and investment.

In the stateroom beside the legislative assembly, the chief minister in the classical blue turban (distinguishing him as an *Akali*) and surrounded by his MLAs, garlanded Karam and handed him a stole to wear around his neck. In a booming voice becoming his true calling as a preacher, he declared him a "Lion of the Punjab" and extolled his largesse to his village and his alma mater, never once mentioning his rise from destitution to the riches he enjoyed today. The minister called upon him to continue his support and double his efforts for those who needed it the most: Punjabis.

That evening, Karam held a small reception for the chief minister and some of his closest confidants, among them a younger man. In flawless English, that younger man urged Karam and Helene to consider investing in the province and to lead the way for the Diasporas of ever-prosperous Punjabi emigrants to consider doing the same. He proposed that Karam accept to heading a committee currently searching for ways to find foreign capital to help Punjab add value to its most plentiful resource: raw grain. "If we could mill, refine, can, package, and process more right here, we could create prosperity," he stated with passion, and Karam promised to do his best.

"Pardesi Sahib," the younger man, Manjit Singh Mangat, also the State Development Officer and a graduate of the Indian Commissioned Services, the highest echelon of administrative, judicial, and executive training for officials both state and central, asked, "would it be possible to meet you alone for a few hours?"

"Of course," Karam replied, and they set up an early morning meeting in the lounge of the beautiful Mountainside Hotel. Helene wouldn't mind sleeping in, and all Karam had to do was go down to the lobby.

The officer showed up with two other men: Ajit Singh and Pyare Lal. Ajit Singh was well-known to Karam. He was in frequent communication with the commissioner who had put Noorian on the map as a Model Gram. Pyare Lal was the budget keeper for Punjab State, and the state was out of money. With little customs duty collected as no airports, seaports, or points of major entry were existent in Punjab, and with little or no sales tax collected, the province squeezed what it could from the tight pockets of the central government: local duties and fees, fines, and estate duties. The treasury was empty. Yet the expectations raised by power-hungry parties at election time had raised public expectations that could not be met in any tangible fashion. The spin doctors were out in full force, diverting attention away from poor governance and paucity of policy by a ruling party full of semi-educated louts now seated as MIAs in Chandigarh; blaming the people in New Delhi for stealing the waters that had enriched the Punjab by building dams higher up in the Himalayas to produce electricity for themselves and pumping the water out via canals to turn the desert of Rajasthan green; and looting the verdant lands of their breadbasket. Bereft of intelligent, long-term planning, it was left to whatever senior bureaucrat still uncorrupted to find solutions.

"Sir," Pyare Lal asked once all were seated in a quiet corner and tea had been served, "what is your annual top line?"

Just like that and typically Indian, curiosity was their trait. In an expansive mood, Karam decided to be frank. "Just over $10 million annually."

The three visitors gasped, suddenly sitting up and contemplating his casual and obviously truthful answer. It was a figure pretty close to the total income generated by the state government. Karam was a true giant of a man, only thirty years old and barely nine years out of India. He had accomplished what an entire province had not. Pyare Lal, trying to remain as tight-lipped as an accountant can be, could only say, "Congratulations, sir. Sincerely. Very, very sincerely."

"Thank you," Karam replied.

"Sir," M. S. Mangat, as he liked to be known, started, "Sir, we have formed an informal kind of group to try and do something for Punjab. It is our fair land, and we love it deeply, and we feel that you too are a true son of the soil. Can we count on you to help us somehow increase the profile of our state in foreign countries, particularly where a lot of our brethren have emigrated?"

"How?"

They told him of their plans and asked for his opinion. Suddenly Karam was confronted with his own reality. He had simply been a beneficiary of being at the right place at the right time, and some fortuitous relationships innocently developed. He had always been a beneficiary of the guidance and direction of men greater than himself in intellect, education, and achievement. He still had accomplished little. As far as he was concerned, the little he had put into his own great fortune was studying, burning some midnight oil. The rest had been *kismet*.

Seeing that he was falling into a pensive mood, they tried to cheer him up. "Pardesiji," Ajit Singh explained, "all three of us here are *Shudras* just like you. We have had to go through similarly hard work as you, but we chose to stay here and work in government, inside the government, to try and make real changes. The politicians are like blunderbusses, firing off in different directions. It is we, the civil servants, who manage to maintain an even keel and deliver what we can control to benefit the people, particularly the Scheduled Caste and Backward Classes provisions in the laws. The more of us there are now making the climb, the more we break the old ways and introduce modernity, albeit in small doses."

"Our culture is based on the feudal system, and it will take time for the average Indian to truly appreciate the benefits of democracy."

"It is our task to take them to that point, to educate them and show the tangible results." Pyare Lal added.

"We can already see the change." M. S. Mangat stepped in. "The green revolution is having a trickledown effect: free education and some primary health initiatives. We are almost eradicating some diseases like polio. We already are rid of small pox."

Karam could see the fire in their bellies, the determination in the set of their mouths. He felt better rewarded by this meeting than either award he had received. He passed his card around and wrote his home number behind it because of the time differences and told them to reverse charges. Fortified by a sense of fraternity, he watched them leave.

* * *

Ruldu gave an accounting of the family assets built in the last nine years: a *haveli* and outbuildings over an acre of land; twenty-five minus two acres for the Sant Baba *Samadhi* of arable land now share-cropped by Piara Singh; an electric motor to irrigate these fields; another fifty or so acres under mortgage to them from *Jats* in the village, mostly with daughters to marry; a $50,000 Fixed Deposit certificate at the Punjab National Bank in Samrala and a few thousand rupees in an open account; several IOUs from families in the village bearing an interest rate of 10 percent given to landless ones to help tide them over accentuating circumstance; a herd of almost ten cattle; an old army jeep purchased from a government auction and now used as the family's mode of transport, his fifteen-year-old nephew the driver (obviously no license required); a motorcycle for his younger brother-in-law Ramu, now subdued and respectful after seeing his older brother cast out of the family fold.

"They call him Seth now," Punna told Karam. "The moneylender! Imagine that."

Bola laughed, adding, "They call him a couple of other names, too," and he poked his son-in-law in the gut. This caused the clan gathered together a lot of mirth, and Ruldu glared at them to no effect.

"Let me show you what I have collected." Punna opened a small, metal suitcase and started taking out jewelry cases full of 22-carat gold sets of bracelets, earrings, lockets, necklaces, and rings studded with precious stones.

"That is a lot of jewelry to be keeping in the home," Karam frowned.

Punna looked knowingly at Helene, who was staring at the glittering display, and Karam grinned. "It's yours if you accept her offer."

"What offer?" Helene asked tentatively.

"To live here as her personal maid."

"Go away," Helene made a face.

"It is her collection for my wife-to-be," Karam said lamely. They had not spoken of marriage in any concrete way, and he had not formally proposed to her.

Helene smiled at Punna.

* * *

The Comrade, the headman, and Punna walked them through the village. Karam was amazed by the changes. There were no more muddy lanes with potholes filled with fetid water. The streets were cobbled with bricks, wide with drains running on either side. The mosquito infested cesspools had been drained and filled, and after the earth had settled and hardened, they became common property to build future facilities and to serve as mini parks or playgrounds. The schools were painted and finished with new desks and lights, with fans on the classroom ceilings; the library was airy and bright and just beginning to take shape. The ring road and the main were both metal, on raised beds with ditches on either side for proper drainage, pipes laid under pathways to fields and connecting gates of courtyards.

The Sant Baba Samadhi, almost unrecognizable with the two acres of trees growing around it, had a widened pathway leading to its enclosure within a low-walled square, its floor laid with brick. The Samadhi itself had been whitewashed and garlanded with drying and fresh flowers from devotees. Behind it, the substantial, reed-covered hut of the current Baba sat with a smaller lean-to for his disciples. They received the visitors with folded hands and voiced a litany of benedictions and offered *prasad* from a *thali* covered with latticed cloth. Punna, the lead devotee, spoke her wish. "Karam, we should really have an annual function to honor the Sant Baba and serve *langar* and hold a three-day vigil culminating in a fire ceremony."

He nodded his head. "Then it will be so," his mother told the Baba. Another loud string of benedictions followed. Helene was fascinated by the goings on, and Karam promised to tell her all about the place and its role in his life.

The next day they returned to New Delhi to embark on a tour of Agra and the Taj Mahal that would also take them through much of the fabled palace cities of the desert province of Rajasthan, which was becoming a must-see for any tourist.

Chapter 16

Ben gave him a day to catch up and get back to business from what sounded like an eventful visit to India. It always amazed him that Indians tanned. Just like Europeans, they got darker with exposure to the sun. In fact, after Karam had spent a hot, sunny day by the pool without his shirt on, he had spent the next two days in agony from the sunburn, which had left everyone astounded, and he had peeled for days. So Karam was darker and had a jump start on what would be an eventful summer for Ben and him and their business, King Laboratories.

After the lawyers, auditors, and Tim sat down, Ben turned to Karam and said, "I have serious news." His tone was grave and barely hiding the tension within him.

"Good, I hope." Karam's stomach clenched. He had escaped the embarrassment of Delhi Belly in India, and surprisingly, so had Helene.

"Better than good," Tim interjected, and he pushed a two-page document toward Karam. Everyone held their breath as Karam slowly read the letter, his eyes widening and narrowing as he went through its five paragraphs.

"So what do you think?" Ben asked, leaning forward with fingers entwined, nostrils flaring and eyes unblinking.

"I don't know what to say." Karam sat back, closed his eyes, and took a deep breath, allowing himself time to think. It was too much, too soon.

Sensing his dilemma, Tim decided to take charge. "Let

us just discuss it and hash it out. It is their first offer and obviously well-presented."

"Yes," Ben sat back, and he and Karam locked gazes. Then Karam let out a small smile, and it grew into a grin, followed by the banging of a fist on the thick table. It made the rest in the room jump, and Ben jumped up to hug his partner. "I told you! I told you!"

"Good job, Ben," Tim interjected. "That bridge financing was a brilliant move."

"Even more brilliant announcing it in the form of a tombstone in the *Globe and Mail*." Ben couldn't stop grinning and sat back to receive the kudos. "It gave them the shits!"

"It sure did," Tim concurred, although a little miffed that his mandate so far had not included obtaining financing from outside of Canada. He had missed a bit of commission on it: quite a bit. But now he was determined to get his due if things came to pass according to the terms proposed in the Letter of Intent. After all, it had come through him, their investment advisor.

The upshot of it all was a good one: twenty million dollars paid half in cash and half in warrants to be exercised once the merged group went public. The warrants were priced fairly and could result in yet another windfall. A paid, two-year directorship on the board of the company for both Karam and Ben would essentially replace their current wages. A non-compete clause would ban them from starting something in Canada for five years. The agreement was to be concluded in as favorable a way as possible from a taxation viewpoint.

"You net ten million plus the two years' wages, practically tax free, Karam." The senior auditor salivated at the amount of fees to be earned in this, his biggest such deal to date.

They discussed the logistics of how the deal should proceed and particularly Karam's natural concern for his staff. The Letter of Intent promised to retain all staff at current wages going forward and maintain seniority and benefits while keeping the current facility in Hamilton; in fact, the intent was to enlarge the facility, adding more services and staff. Karam wanted some thought and weight given to his employees' contributions in making him a very rich man, and they decided to seek a one-time bonus as part of the deal. He wanted to tell them himself of the merger buyout.

"Very ethical of you," Tim stated.

Karam wanted the confidentiality maintained until the deal was finalized and no word leaking out resulting in panic or speculation. That, too, went into the books. At the end of the meeting, the jet lag taking its toll, Karam took his leave and walked to his penthouse, poured himself a large scotch on the rocks, and sat down to contemplate his new world and anaesthetize himself for a refreshing sleep. He needed rest. He couldn't tell Helene until things were final, so he spoke for only a few moments on the phone with her. She was also hitting the sack early at her place in Toronto.

* * *

"So where do we go from here?" he asked Ben the next morning as they read the draft of their proposal back to the bidder.

"All goes well, now," Ben stated. "To the United States of America where opportunity never stops growing or mutating into better opportunities."

Karam hated that kind of reply and asked for more elaboration. He was not yet convinced about America, and he was worried if Helene would want to live there due to the crime rates and racism.

When he expressed those concerns to Ben, his partner dropped the proposal on the desk and took a long look at him. Disconcertingly long. "So, what's wrong with what I said?" Karam asked.

"Let me tell you a bit about crime, Karam," Ben began. "It is in every society, every country, and every town; however, not as blatant in some as in others. Not as well reported as in some. Also not as well used by media to demonize a people, I admit, as in America. I do not worry about that because guess what: where you and I are going to live, visit, and work, those places are well-policed and virtually crime free. There you have to worry about the nice man seated at the table with you trying to steal opportunity from under you: a different kind of looting and perdition. Civilized pocket picking, my father-in-law calls it." Ben paused to catch his breath.

"Racism is another story. As a Jew even here in Canada, I have come across enough of it: subtle but there nonetheless. Thirty years ago, they would not let my people fleeing injustice and death in Europe into Canada. Millions died because the doors were closed to us. And look at you and India. What you have known as 'untouchability' is a vicious form of racism as far as I am concerned. You have been at the point of the spear, so to speak, yourself—your family and your kin. And yes, there is racism, and it's rampant in America, but only in certain regions. But there is an awakening, and just like it is taking Jews two thousand years to get there, it is taking time for racism as a practice and a way of life to be confronted and defeated. I would rather be in America helping with the fight against it than here in quiet Canada, hiding. Imagine how much good you could do with the kind of Midas touch you have for making money there."

Karam pondered Ben's remarks: the ugly truths, but

truths nonetheless. As Tim and his advisors had told him, he had gotten the best of the situation. Many of the early sellers had sold at a pittance of what he got, and the man who guided him to this level of prosperity was not taking his chips and moving to gamble at another table. Ben was sticking with him, wanted to stick with him and go to places neither had gone yet. The very nature of the deal allowed him to gamble a little on America. The warrants needed at least a year to be exercised and maybe longer. However, he had been assured that they were better than cash and could grow in value a lot more than money in the bank. There was not a lot of diversity in the stock market in Canada. The Toronto Stock Exchange was loaded with companies that bespoke of the land: mining and minerals, grain and timber. Throw in a bit of oil and gas. Not much more. A healthcare group would attract a lot of interest from a public dying to diversify its holdings.

"Partners?"

"Partners!" Ben shook his hand and hugged him.

"Let's go do it," Karam stated, his voice a lot more certain, even steely.

They finalized and refined their counter offer and had Tim pick it up for personal delivery to the Canadian Health Services Group's President. Within hours it had been signed, awaiting his and Ben's signature for finalization. They did it together, in the presence of their advisors, and Tim opened a bottle of Champagne after carefully putting the valuable document in his case. A lot of salutes were made, a lot of congratulating done, and it was dark before they left the building, climbed into their cars, and went home to tell their wives about the great occasion. Karam walked home and phoned Helene.

* * *

The harvesting had not gone well in Noorian, all due to a lack of labor, which had been reliable for centuries. Most of the stronger and younger landless day laborers from the village had taken jobs in construction building the schools and the community center, clearing the ponds, digging drainage ditches, and helping lay the gravel and tarmac on the ring road and connection to the main one. After that, they had begun building their families' abodes. Because the work had been continuous and more certain and wages were paid on time, most felt they were above common field labor and began to seek jobs in towns and cities. Unburdened somewhat from the responsibility of paying for their children's education—now guaranteed wholly by Karam Pardesi, his kin, and his father Ruldu, who was willing and able to spot them a loan to tide them over—they were in no mood to labor long and hard for unreliable and seasonal work in the fields. This had left the *Jats* scrambling and furious, some vowing revenge as they could lose crops uncollected and still in the fields by the monsoons. The Comrade, predicting these results, had traveled to Uttar Pradesh and hired a whole band of migrant laborers, which he brought by train to Noorian, and thus eased the pressure.

"Punna," complained the women of the landed class, as she still continued to massage their abdomens to relieve them of the terrible pelvic pains of middle age and help in delivering their babies, the new clinic yet to be staffed. "Our men folk are grumbling about your son's actions."

"You mean his actions' effects," Punna countered.

"He should know …"

"His place?" she asked menacingly, stopping the calming movement of her hands.

"Oh, Punna, do not be angry, but your people need to

know their place."

"They do know it," Punna agreed, "and now they want to change it."

Gathered in the evenings around their hearths, the landed families of Noorian could only talk badly about Karam. Even though they benefited the most from the new tarmac of the transportation routes, the elimination of the cesspool ponds, the upgrading of the schools, and their teens now saving two hours a day of travel time to towns or the city for higher education from the buses they could catch at their doorstep. They complained about the attitudes, the arrogance of the *Churas* and *Chamars*. Some were stinging from the humiliation of having to mortgage their lands to Ruldu (through no fault of the watchman), others from having to knock on his gates during times of crisis, knowing that he or Punna would help. This did not seem to matter. What rankled were the facts, the main one being that they had all been outdone by a *Chura*. By now Karam should have been sweeping and carrying off the dung from their courtyards, his wife probably soothing some lout's animal urges. The more Karam did to help his village, the more some resented his generosity, urged on particularly by the few who were in no need of it. They either had enough income from their fields or from sons in foreign lands sending money home. For those who had neither, Karam and his family were a necessary evil.

* * *

"Wow" was all Helene could muster. Karam had just finished telling her the details of the deal. It was to be announced tomorrow at a news conference arranged at the Toronto headquarters of the Canadian Health Services Group its publicity-seeking and aggressive president more suited, Karam felt, to handle the media. He was still shy and did not come across all that great on camera.

They sat on the sofa for a while in silence. It was a lot to take in, to understand. Helene felt overwhelmed by the suddenness of it all. They had just returned from India barely two months ago, and she had yet to distribute all the gifts to her many relatives and friends. Already the earth was shifting under her feet. Karam was no longer going to be in charge of her largest account, and she knew that the boys at CHSG were bastards to deal with. How was she going to explain it to Mr. Jones, her boss, who had bitched and complained but let her have the month off to go to India? And Karam planned on moving to the States just when things were falling into place for her here in Canada! She had put so much trust and faith in this relationship, and now it was changing too quickly for her.

Karam, sensitive to her feelings, said, "I could have told you earlier, I had to respect the confidentiality clause."

What?! He did not trust her to keep mum about his business, she thought. He did not trust her enough to confide in her while all the hot and heavy negotiations were going on. Used as she was to corporate culture at her worldwide company, this was peanuts. She felt doubly let down. She had trusted him enough to travel to India with him, go where he wanted her to, sat where he asked her to, ate what was put before her. She dutifully followed his lead. She must have earned at least his confidence, his trust. When he tried to put his arm around her, she moved away, pulled back. Tears of anger welled up in her eyes.

Seeing her reaction, he tried to move closer, almost aggressively, and in that state of mind, she was in no mood to be cuddled or to celebrate his good fortune. And how did he expect to celebrate? Having a few and mounting her? What was she to him, an object? Oh, how could he not trust her, not involve her, include her, and seek her council, her advice? He was too affected, she thought, by the Jew, Ben Roman, and his sister, Ella, always watching her, eyes refusing to meet, averting, evaluating. After sitting in silence and letting her emotions roil, she stood up and picked up her purse. She had come to invite him to visit the farm again, her hockey-playing brothers there now that the season was over. Let him open up, relax in their company, and perhaps propose to her during a long walk on the country road.

"Where are you going?" Karam stood up, trying to block her from leaving.

"Sorry, Karam." She opened the door and walked out. By the time she was on the highway speeding toward Toronto, her anger had dissipated and settled into a resignation of missed opportunities. She refused to compromise her principles. She could not love a man who could not trust her.

The next morning, she walked into her boss' office and asked for a transfer to Montreal. Mr. Jones sat back in his wine-colored, thickly upholstered leather chair and pondered the request before asking, "Why?"

She kept her composure and did not mention the imminent sale of King Labs to CHSG or the fact that she was getting away from Karam. "Personal reasons, I am sure they can use a fluently bilingual marketing specialist there."

"No doubt," Mr. Jones concurred. "I will look into it. Hate to lose you though."

Helene stayed in her office, going through files that needed to be studied and updated. There was correspondence to catch up, and the annual performance evaluations were due. She tried hard to concentrate and complete her tasks. She had worked hard to get to this level, and no man—Karam, or the one before him, the philandering bastard, Jean-Luc— could get in the way. Jean-Luc had won the scoring title in the NHL yet again. Every time she saw his picture in the papers grinning through the toothless gap after scoring yet another highlight goal from an impossible angle, she thought of the broken promises, her total surrender, and then the ultimate humiliation of reading about his engagement to a girl in Detroit. An American one, too—a hussy, she was sure. And now Karam could go there and find himself one as well!

Before the end of the day, Mr. Jones knocked on her office door and came in. He sat down, and looking at her with concern in his eyes, he asked, "You going to be fine?"

She nodded.

"Well, you probably knew that CHSG has bought out King," Then noticing the tightness around her mouth, he told her softly, "They can use you in Montreal. In fact, they need you there."

* * *

Karam was surprised by the publicity that the sale of King Laboratories attracted. It was front-page news in the Hamilton Spectator. The business page had a special section devoted to its analysis, the positive impact on Hamilton, and a biography of the original owners, with Karam's and Ben's pictures taken last year on another visit by the paper's photographer. The Globe and Mail called it the keystone acquisition, absolutely needed to complete the puzzle that would catapult the CHSG into the national limelight and its ambitions to expand its operations nationally, into every Canadian province and territory. Their analyst had used words like windfall to describe the profits Karam stood to make and printed a portrait-like picture of him. CHCH TV came in to interview Karam, and once again, he was on the 6 and 11 p.m. news, but this time via feed on CBC and CTV as well. The upstart CITY TV in Toronto, given to covering the accomplishments within ethnic communities, did a much longer interview with him and Ben and aired it the following Sunday as a special. Reuters and CP picked up the story and put it out on their international wire services.

It was front page news in the Tribune, with the boastful headline Indian-born Entrepreneur Cashes Twenty Million Dollars. One of the inside pages was once again covered with his history of rising up from an untouchable from the remote village of Noorian. It then speculated about how India could benefit from this example of education and enterprise. Sure enough, the national and local dailies could not have enough of this karmic fortune making and sent a wave of correspondents, photographers in tow, to lay siege at his parents' courtyard and to come back with "specials," the more exclusive the better.

In reality, his family had no idea of his real business, how much he had become worth, the mechanics of the sale, or even knowledge of the sale, as he had felt it not to be important to tell them, that it would unnecessarily worry them, make them concerned as to the why, what, and ifs of it all. As a dutiful son, Karam had shared as much as he felt they could absorb. In fact he had given more to Noorian, his village and his alma mater, the CMC, than he had his family. What he had given them, they had used in the fashion that suited them and they considered of value: a huge *haveli* in an acre-large courtyard, a herd of excellent cattle, and a sizeable acreage. They had money in their savings to lend out. They had earned prestige and were now living above their rank in the local order of things, better than those born higher in caste to them. Karam had added to his and their karma with good deeds. It was in this milieu that the correspondents and photographers found them blissfully unaware, as it was only four days since the news came out in Canada and a day after the article in the Tribune; the news had yet to be filtered down to the village. Dr. Grewal had read it in Ludhiana, as it was delivered early in the morning each day to his door. The Comrade would get his copy in a day or two.

Bola opened the gate to the cries of an early arrival from the city.

The family gathered around the bespectacled young man with a notebook and the photographer and learned the earth-shaking news. At first in shock and instinctive alarm, Punna started one of her rote prayers out loud, folded her hands, and almost passed out until shaken violently by her father, who had understood with his usual calm what the man had to tell. She fell quiet and let her father repeat the news to her in a way that she comprehended. It was not bad news, but good. Very, very good! The whole country seemed to be celebrating her son's achievement and status. Now in a bit of delirium, she started the rote again, but silently this time. The young man got to work with questions he had carefully crafted and was interrupted in the middle as a competitor's representative arrived, gushing forth his congratulations. Within two hours of a confusing and sometimes acrimonious exchange, the senior man from a venerable daily suggested they try to do it as a news conference.

Thus seated on a cot, the grandfather, the mother, the father, and Karam's two sisters gave their account of their lives and Karam's growing up, his achievements, his generosity, and their prayers for his continued success. "May Sant Baba, seated beside the gods and goddesses, keep him in his good graces." Punna finished most answers with that statement.

When asked if they understood, or comprehended how much wealth $20 million represented, they stared back, clueless.

"It simply means that your son, Karam, can now buy not only every inch and stick of Noorian, but fifty villages like it," the Comrade spoke up. He had arrived to watch the commotion caused by the invasion of Ruldu's courtyard by the newspaper people. A huge gasp went up among the rest of the villagers and idle attendees who had snuck in behind him.

"Like a prince, a rajah," someone in the crowd responded.

From that day, to the press, he was the *Shudra* Prince. To the commoners and their more colloquially cruel language, he was the Raja of the *Churas,* or the *Chura Badshaw*!

Chapter 17

It became an eventful year. The visit to India and touring its historical cities and monuments had been memorable. The sale of King Laboratory at an unexpected and highly profitable price created a well head of wrenching emotions, like the sudden and unexplained breakup with Helene and her immediate move to Montreal, leaving no forwarding address or phone number. The rush of publicity and the resultant letters, so many and from so many people, to reply to left his hand aching for days. He wrote in long hand and in four different scripts: Punjabi, Hindi, Urdu, and English. Most were full of praise and pride and some pleading and platitudes. To all who asked, he arranged help through his parents, feeling that giving money to fellow villagers or relatives behind his parents' back might not be fruitful in the long run. His sisters wanted him to start thinking about their children's futures. His oldest niece was attending college in Ludhiana, and his two nephews were waiting their turn for next year.

He felt old: thirty-one and unmarried. Yes, very rich and accomplished, but not yet sophisticated in the true subtleties of finance, business, or relationships. He confessed as much to Ben and Ella. Ben suggested starting a correspondence course in investment planning. Ella suggested he see a psychologist. When he raised his brows, she said, "You have a lot of repressed emotions, Karam. Just talking about them to a real professional will help." She recommended an uncle, a clinical psychologist with a discreet practice from his home and a public teaching job at McMaster University.

Karam thought, "Why not?" He enrolled in a course offered by the Carnegie Institute and started to visit Dr. Caplan. It filled in the days since he had vacated his president's office and duties at King Laboratories, waiting for everything to get sorted out by the accountants and the lawyers. He had insisted on a six-month hiatus from the States, but Ben could run around and find the best opportunities and argue their merits. He needed time to collect his thoughts, to find his bearings. He did control that much now. He was going to go with the flow. This time, he would wait for the opportunities and then select one, not just take the most apparent option (although doing so had been very fortunate and fruitful so far). He felt adventurous. Dr. Caplan was helping but in ways he had never known. Dr. Caplan was freeing him in a way, slowly cutting away some of the shackles of inferiority, of withdrawal, of letting others take control, of deference to caste and culture, and taking out the poisons and lancing old festering wounds in his conscious. Dr. Caplan had actually hypnotized him several times, and always he had woken up feeling lighter, refreshed, and strangely full of energy. It felt like waking from a deep and satisfying sleep. Time was of no concern.

Ella had stayed with the new employers. They were happy to have her because she had developed a lot of inside knowledge of the inner workings of King Laboratories and was helpful in the transition from an entrepreneur-led organization to a corporate culture that was new and sometimes difficult for some employees. She bridged the gaps and even got promoted to Human Resources, suddenly discovering her calling. She became the orientation coordinator for new employees and counseled and arranged ongoing education and certifications for the current employees. She was thriving. Although she now only saw Karam two or three times a week, they fell into a form of dating, and before long, they started sleeping together. He always made sure she got home to the Bergers' every evening and before midnight. She thought it strange but tolerated his behavior and thought it kind of cute, old-fashioned, and even respectful. She was complimented. Her all-knowing mother and her sister kept their peace, but she could sense their stress. When her mother said something about it to her husband, the old man rolled his eyes. "Cross the bridge when you come to it," he said, rolled onto his side, and fell asleep.

Ben was just too busy to notice or care. He was out scouting an opportunity closer to home and just across the border in Niagara Falls, New York. A small hospital was quietly up for sale for a grand total of $7 million. They could buy it in cash and get a toe-hold in America. Heck, they could still live in Hamilton and commute there.

They drove down the Queen Elizabeth Way and had lunch with the three principals of the Niagara Falls Hospital and Clinic; they met on the Canadian side at the private lunch room in the Falls Sheraton Hotel. All doctors, it became quickly apparent that the ownership group had such a disparity in personalities and inflated egos that they were not and could not become successful as a functioning partnership. The hospital did well, though, because there was quite an industrial base, and being a border town with a large municipal, state, and federal employee concentration, they had a well-insured patient pool. Competition from the big boys like the Mayo Clinic and the Humana Group was nonexistent; the town was too small for them to bother with. They were sheltered from the big city groups. After they signed the confidentiality agreements in the presence of their lawyers, Karam and company received the last three years of financial statements. Ben immediately began to study his copy, and Dr. Hopkins, the chairman of the board, said, "Boys, why don't we eat and get on with the day? You have ten days to respond to our terms. Take your time."

The doctor was scheduled to perform surgery and had three cases to deal with in the afternoon. Ben reluctantly put the document into his briefcase, and they ordered lunch, finishing it with small talk. Before they parted, Dr. Hopkins asked Karam, "Got good contacts with some medical schools in India?"

"He is a big donor to the CMC," Ben piped in.

The doctor was familiar with that school; in fact, he practiced some of the techniques developed there primarily involving hand and foot surgery. "We have a problem attracting good doctors here. If you can do that in India and bring them over, you can really thrive in the States."

In the car driving back, Ben remarked, "See, there will be something other than managing the lab you can do."

"And my trips to India become tax deductible."

"Wow," Ben exclaimed, "aren't we picking up fast?"

Joking thus, they drove to a small strip club on Lundy's Lane and wasted the afternoon in watching eye candy and plotting their foray into America.

* * *

Ajit Singh took his superiors—the governor, the chief minister, the local member of parliament, and the Minister of Agriculture for the center, Chandu Das—on a tour of Noorian to inspect the completed projects in his Model Gram. It became apparent as soon as they turned onto the mile-long piece connecting it to the Ludhiana-Chandigarh artery that he had not allowed any shortcuts to be taken.

The road was now almost six months old and yet to be rutted and run down as most rural roads were within that time span. Instead of 10 percent for this minister and 5 percent for that official, the contractor had spent the entire allocation on materials and labor. With an eight-inch sand base, a four-inch stone base, and properly graded tarmac with the proper mix of ingredients, the road shone like new. The ditches running on either side were open and tended to, lined by two-year-old hardwoods already reaching seven feet in height. The ring road was similarly sturdy. While the contractor could not force the residents to remove the manure piles, they somehow looked neater, less in your face. As they passed the gleaming gates of Ruldu's courtyard, they could already see the shimmer of the village pond, its beach raked and half of it covered in floating plants, their huge leafs like miniature floats and large, white flowers, fully in bloom. "We will introduce the fry this fall," he stated, referring to the aquaculture of fish in the pond.

The high school stood testimony to a dedicated makeover, as did the primary school, now joined to the elementary school and expanded. The two vast plots gained from draining the cesspools sported patches of grass and soccer nets at each end, looking like and being used as playgrounds. The community center was completed, furnished, and staffed with an MD, an RN, and a dispenser overseeing a proper pharmacy. A large, well-lit hall with six ceiling fans sat empty and awaiting furnishings for whatever purposes the village *panchayat* chose to use it, its substantial courtyard already blooming with long beds of flowers, its walkways lined with gravel.

The governor, a resident of West Bengal and a career civil servant, congratulated Ajit Singh on his initiative, as did the chief minister and the honorable Chandu Das.

After a session of tea and speech making, Chandu Das asked them to visit the street on which Karam was born. Now, instead of a muddy lane with the untouchable courtyards built of crumbling mud brick, it was cobbled with drains clear of detritus and lined with brick and mortar abodes, their occupants smiling and greeting the dignitaries with shouts of "*Jai Ho.*" Told that this was a *chamari*, as these sections of rural villages were commonly known, the governor was speechless. "He paid for every cent. Built his entire community new homes," Chandu Das told him with a great measure of pride in his voice.

A week later, the governor requested that the central government provide funding for at least one Model Gram in each of the province's districts. He also requested that the state add to the effort and instructed all district commissioners to set up immediate and urgent visits to Noorian. They had something of great import to learn. He also raised Ajit Singh's pay scale by an increment as a reward.

* * *

The CHSG became a public company, posting one of the highest initial public offerings and stock prices, benefiting the brokers and the warrant holders. Karam had been issued warrants at a dollar each, and the shares opened at twice that, within days threatening to double again. The ten million warrants they held were now worth at least thirty million if fully exercised, which they did on the enthusiastic advice of their broker. They had now fully invested in the Niagara Falls Hospital and Clinic, with another war chest growing that could be liquidated at leisure. When a significant opportunity arose, the partners decided to play a waiting game. Their new investment, while needing ongoing capital investment in building updates, expansion, and equipment purchases, virtually financed itself. They had agreed to flow the excess profits right back into the institution and focus on growing the company's top line by recruiting doctors, signing agreements to provide services to the fifty or so insurance plans, and lobbying Medicare for increased payments and the local state and federal politicians for grants to introduce new services and guarantee the ongoing subcontract for veterans' care. They were in a new milieu, and it was a free for all. In Canada, they had become accustomed to only worrying about the competition. Here they had a whole multitude of issues to worry about but also more opportunities to develop and exploit. To do that, they hired the best public relations officer they could find and added a much more aggressive chief financial officer and investor relations officer to ready them for growth in the American style. It was much easier to raise cheap money as long as you could afford the expertise and were willing to pay the fees—much, much easier than in conservative and cautious Canada! Now a lot more informed and knowledgeable of high finance and the use of money—particularly other people's money—Karam was a lot more agreeable to taking risks and making bold moves. Already they boasted the most updated Radiotherapy and Radiology departments within a hundred miles, having ensnared a CMC-trained specialist and meeting his demands. They began reaping the rewards, their top line already up 30 percent. Then they discovered income-producing asset-leasing programs, and anytime they were asked by their doctors to include a new technology, they called New York, and the leasing company gave approval over the phone for up to $250,000. They felt like kids in a candy store.

Ben's analysis showed a remarkable and eye-popping figure. For every doctor they recruited to work in their system, their top line grew by almost a $500,000. This sum included the fees charged by the doctor, the fees for tests and X-rays ordered, and the prices paid for the hospital care of the doctor's patients. They now had forty doctors, only twenty-five full-time. They could fit in at least ten or fifteen more. Ben begged Karam to consider traveling to India at least twice a year to recruit doctors there. They would start as interns, rising to residents and drawing relatively low wages while awaiting full licensure by the state of New York. In the meantime, The Niagara Falls Hospital and Clinic could bill for their services almost as much as a licensed physician and pocket the difference. It would be a bonus if, after their licensing, they stayed. Karam prepared for a trip to India—this one for business—and accompanying him would be the chief of staff, Dr. Hopkins. The orthopedic surgeon had stayed on after the sale, grateful that his foray into hospital ownership had not cost him his lovely home or his Florida seafront bungalow or his hunting lodge in Temagami, in northern Ontario.

Ella wanted to tag along, but Karam did not want to raise his mother's expectation only to disappoint her; Ella just was not the marrying kind. He felt that she was waiting for an excuse to make a permanent move to Israel; her heart was there. But she was a great lover and taught him some things in bed he could not have imagined, and now he fancied himself as someone just this side of Casanova. Besides, he wanted the freedom to sleep under the roof of his father's *haveli* and eat the home-cooked meals at his mother's hearth. Too much had happened and continued to happen, and he needed a bit of a time-out to relax, to be an Indian, to loll on a cot under the shade of a mulberry tree and feel the breeze of a Punjabi afternoon on his face.

The plan was to visit and recruit subtly. It was still

forbidden for Indian medical graduates to write the ECFMG examinations in India to qualify for foreign employment. Several traveled to Iran to write the exam and then were able to leave under the guise of higher education and training. Few returned home, preferring to stay and work in foreign lands and earn an income in the top percentile of that country, enjoying a lifestyle that could only be dreamed about in India.

Karam's heart and soul was pathology: the study of disease and the measurement of variances in various body fluids from the norm, the examination of tissue under the microscope, the growing and identification of bacterial cultures. Pathology was a much bigger and expanding science. Aided by research and emerging technologies, it was the one component of medical science that established and confirmed diagnosis and provided normative to abnormal data for comparative analysis. In litigious America, it was an important part of self-defense by doctors. To protect themselves from lawsuits alleging malpractice, physicians had started ordering more tests and X-rays and referrals to specialists. All this was needed to be able to mount a realistic defense against liability or loss of licensure. These added necessities increased the cost of health care in general and greatly benefited the owners of hospitals, medical laboratories, diagnostic testing centers. Karam had already invested heavily into improving the medical testing facilities at NFHC—including the pathology section—but he felt there was more to do. One of his aims was to recruit not just doctors, but more medical technologists and technicians. As the owner of a hospital, he could offer jobs, leading to visas and eventual citizenship in the United States.

What better institution than the CMC to attract these people from? He could get introductions, receive reviews, get recommendations, and obtain records of academic achievements. He could influence these people financially.

Ben came up with a series of plausible tools to try in recruiting and Karam, along with Dr. Hopkins, received training from their public relations specialist and human resource management. They developed a brochure about the hospital. The municipality and state provided additional sales brochures about the city and the attractions of the region of Northern New York. Thus fortified and well-armed with material, they flew from New York to Frankfurt, a growing international air hub, and on to New Delhi and its still-decrepit airport. Thankfully, Jaswant Singh was there to make their arrival painless, and he had them ensconced at the Oberoi International Hotel, New Delhi's finest such establishment. They rested there for a day, then drove to Ludhiana. After checking Dr. Hopkins into the Gaylord Hotel, Karam headed for Noorian.

By nightfall, Karam had met every member of his family and clan and given away the gifts he had brought. He was just finishing dinner, sitting on a *pirrhi* by the hearth, when a small delegation of *Shudra* elders arrived to visit. Retiring to the large and airy refuge of the sitting room with its ceiling fans churning, keeping the mosquitoes that still haunted the nights away, they got to the point as tea was served. "We want to build our own *gurudwara*," an uncle stated forthrightly.

"We have a *gurudwara* in Noorian," Karam stated, although he had barely ever stepped into it, his mother preferring the Sant Baba samadhi. Also, the untouchables usually sat outside the main hall of the Sikh temple under the veranda on gunny sacks laid on the cement floor for their comfort. Only the higher born sat inside for worship. However, he noticed that more and more *Shurdas* now wore long beards, long hair, and turbans; some had been baptized and wore the five signs of Sikhism with pride. Some matriculates had chosen to become *ragis* and *granthis* and even performed wedding ceremonies for the *Jats*, held in their courtyards under canopies.

"None of us sits on the committee. The priest does not visit us in our homes. They remain unsanctified because we built them, and we still sit outside shivering on cold mornings," the older man complained. "We have waited for them to change, Karam, and they are too hidebound, although Baba Nanak has decreed all as equal."

Other than the Sant Baba amulet, Karam wore no outward sign of faith. His shorn hair and shaved face pronounced him a Hindu or *Musselman*, perhaps even a Christian. He had received little in formal education in any faith. His caste had not been welcomed by any of the major faiths except perhaps the Christians. He had been so grateful to be associated to the CMC because any form of religious discrimination was frowned upon there. "Maybe if I ..."

"Stop there," his mother said from the doorway. She had planted herself just outside in deference to the male elders. "As it is, they are jealous of your accomplishments, constantly complaining and laughing behind our backs. I do not want you to come under more of their attention or scrutiny. I am fed up." A lump rose in her throat. Karam did not miss it.

"All right," he agreed, "give me the estimate." He then cautioned them not to be pretentious, saying, "Remember, Baba Nanak also preached humility."

They got his point and started discussing the planned building, scaling back its planned ostentations, particularly the plan to build the main dome larger than the current, *Jat*-dominated temple's. Theirs would be more modest in appearance but more substantial in space and would contain a kitchen and a hall for *langar*. They added some rooms as a *serai* for *Shudras* passing through Noorian and a walled front and backcourt. Promising to have the budget for him before he left for Canada, they took their leave. After seeing them off and locking the gates after them and releasing the two huge Alsatians from their tethers to guard the night, Bola said, "Do no more after this for the village because then you will cause division and acrimony. Our family cannot be getting in the middle of these inter-caste affairs. But be fair to all deserving of your help, and I mean all. Misery visits every caste in this village."

It was the best advice Karam had received, and he would follow it to the letter in honor of his grandfather. Karam rose and bent to touch the feet of the aged man. "May you live long," his grandfather intoned, and he placed both hands in benediction over Karam's head.

* * *

Karam picked up Dr. Hopkins at the hotel early in the morning and drove him over to the CMC, where a public relations representative was awaiting them. They were surprised to find that an attractive, tall woman would be taking them on a tour of the vast institution, some of it still under construction. They walked through all the outpatient clinics, the pharmacy, the medical labs, the radiology and radiotherapy and limb-making shop, then through all the wards on three upper floors: the surgical and recovery rooms, the auditorium, and Physical Therapy and Occupational Therapy Departments. Finally, they visited the spinal cord injury section and the leprosy area, which was separated by a huge hall reserved for rehabilitation. After a quick lunch with Dr. King and the hospital director, they visited the medical school, which was laid out in older buildings and spread over a well-manicured area. After visiting the farther flung women's wards and delivery sections, Karam wanted Dr. Hopkins to see where he had lived in the quarter at the Civic Hospital, which was starting to take on a more decrepit look under the new civic surgeon and his extremely frugal budgets. The difference between the two institutions was startling to say the least. Dr. Hopkins politely kept his peace.

The PR lady had quietly started flirting in Punjabi with Karam and taken his corporate card before saying goodbye and extracting a promise to visit her again at her small office on the main floor. As Karam watched Sushila Masih sway her sari-clad hips away, along with the long, braided hair, he suddenly realized that he had never been with an Indian woman. Noting his interest, Dr. Hopkins, himself a known skirt chaser at the NFHC, whispered, "Down boy, down." He grinned evilly. They were both expressionless as they entered the office of the medical director to begin exploring possibilities of cooperation. The director, Dr. Green, was a humorous Englishman who remembered Karam from his student days. This long-serving man greeted them warmly and heard them out before cautioning, "Our mandate is to train the doctors, nurses, and ancillary professions."

"And whose job is it to retain them in India?" Dr. Hopkins asked rather innocently.

"Those in charge of it are outside our gates," Dr. Green replied. "However, a lot of graduates drift off shore, being that the CMC is a commonwealth-wide recognized institution."

"How do we capture some of this outflow?'

"Well, you could try the old Indian trick of reward or bribery," Dr. Green smiled then, raising his hands into the air and adding, "I never mentioned that."

They talked for an hour. Karam left a dozen packages for Dr. Green to pass around. "What I urgently need is a pathologist."

"Talk to Muriel, then," Dr. Green said, referring to Dr. King.

"We have dinner with her tonight."

"Good." He stood up to see them out. However, before leaving Karam gave him a check for $10,000 as a friend of the CMC. This one was from the NFHC and fully tax deductible.

Karam and Dr. Hopkins met Dr. King for dinner that night. She recommended Dr. Thomas Varghese, a recent graduate in pathology and one of her better protégés. Even better, his wife had just finished her housemanship in obstetrics and was eager to go abroad. "You should sponsor some trips to America for some of the guys in order for them to attend international conferences in their specialties," she added. Dr. Hopkins thought that to be a capital idea.

The next day over lunch, Dr. Grewal, their guest in the elegant dining room of the Gaylord Hotel, was even more helpful. First, he recommended two nephews who were already finishing their specializations in England, one in orthopedics—lighting up Dr. Hopkins eyes—and the other in cardiology. "They are adventurous boys, very close to each other. I will phone them myself and get you the details."

Karam and Dr. Hopkins learned that to really succeed, they needed to obtain the services of Ludhiana's most successful travel agency owner, who was also a cousin of Dr. Grewal. He would arrange the obtaining of passports, exit documents, and visas for travel to Iran; he would also arrange for the ECFMG exams and the visas for America. This way, they could agree to pay these costs of their recruits and fast track the supply of doctors. The travel agent suggested, "Not just CMC graduates, Karam; go after the ones coming out of Amritsar and Patiala, and especially from the All-India Institute of Medical Sciences in New Delhi."

Feeling his job done in Ludhiana, Dr. Hopkins wanted to spend the remaining days touring the sights, and Jaswant Singh made the necessary arrangements. Karam retired to the village after having a meal with Dr. Varghese, a thin and introverted man, and his wife. Both were excited at the prospect of going to Niagara Falls. "My dream," Mrs. Varghese gushed.

* * *

Karam spent a day with the Comrade to get his advice on how to establish a long-term scholarship for the matriculates of the village. "I want it for everyone, irrespective of caste or faith."

The Comrade suggested forming a committee of locals, a kind of competition to qualify asking applicants to write an essay to describe their aspirations and ambitions and knowledge as well as demonstrate their understanding of their chosen fields of pursuit. The applicants would need to meet an academic threshold to even be considered. "Gets rid of the chaff," he stated flatly. He agreed to be the chairman for the next ten years. On the subject of another *gurudwara* in Noorian, the secularist said, "There are about fifty Muslim families in our immediate area and no mosque. Now that would be a nice way of showing your true intentions."

He also recommended a gas-fired crematorium and a walled enclosure to render dead animals: a sanitation measure popularly lauded by everyone.

Finally, Karam visited the priest at the *gurudwara*, and in the presence of their committee, he assured the assembled

Jats of his support for a *langar* hall for their *gurudwara*. That evening, a delegation of *marasis* and *gujjar* elders came to the courtyard and presented him with a prayer rug, imported from Afghanistan and exquisite in its detail. They sang a song of *Sufi* benediction to him and his family and left clapping their hands and dancing on the ring road, most of them gifted in music and movement. Then Karam settled in for a long, restful sleep on his favorite cot in his favorite room of the *haveli*: his parents' room.

In the morning, after he had bathed and changed, his mother gave him a substantial breakfast, then set upon him with wails and cries of "I am going to die without ever seeing a grandson."

Bola watched his daughter pester Karam, who tried every possible means to calm his agitated mother. "Almost a *boke* (an aging male goat) now," she moaned. That did it for the grandfather, and he intervened with a shout, silencing the courtyard. Turning to Karam, he asked, "What about the Mem-Sahib?"

"She left for her province," he replied lamely.

"We get offers of marriage, substantial ones from educated girls from good *Shudra* families," Bola said, smiling as he recalled one from a *Jat* family who had arrived after reading his latest coverage in the newspapers. "They swore that they were *Churas* now dwelling in the city, even brought the girl along ... and a pretty one, too."

His nieces and sisters snickered. "But she gave herself away when she slurped her tea."

With that, Punna burst out in laughter. "Seriously," Karam said, "there may be a candidate."

Everyone perked up, and he mentioned the PR lady at the CMC. He had found himself thinking of her. She could be amenable to marry into his caste, he thought. His sisters asked to go see her. One even offered to limp, pretending to need medical assistance. That would be their excuse to run into her at the hospital. His grandfather shook his large head still full of wavy, white hair and left for his walk, letting the womenfolk indulge in their fantasies. He wondered if Karam was now past the stage of marriage, and the thought worried him immensely. Who would inherit his wealth, his nephews? Neither of the boys had an ounce of demonstrable intelligence, he felt. They were already lazy from the spoon-feeding their mothers and grandmother indulged them in. When he reached his favorite spot to sit and rest, he prayed for the first time in a long while.

Chapter 18

Since childhood, Sushila Masih had watched her father, Padri Masih, rise early each morning and leave on his rickety bicycle for the Brown Memorial Hospital, where he worked as a pastor. Ordained by the Church of Northern India, in their lay ministries, he spent the day praying at the bedsides of the sick, the dying, and the destitute. He brought the message of hope and salvation through Jesus Christ to each and everyone who listened or did not object to his presence. Occasionally, he went to proselyte in the villages of the district, especially accompanying the many rural camps the institution held, such as eye camps. There he mingled, bible in hand, and dispensed hope. He was the son of a convert to Christianity from their village, a *Shudra* fed up with his ox-like existence in life. After conversion, he was hired to tend the hospital's gardens and saw his son finish high school and then the course in theology in Phillaur, the seat of the Bishop and a major Christian community.

The pastor had enjoyed good relations with the bishop, and that had led to college scholarships for his three children. The two boys went on to become teachers in convent schools in the hills of Himachal Pradesh, and his daughter finished graduate school to complete a Master's in English, landing a job as a public relations officer in the hospital, where her primary task was to guide foreign visitors and dignitaries on tours of the institution. She had been particularly thrilled to meet a famous alumnus of the CMC, Karam Pardesi.

The pastor remembered him from Karam's student days and the fact that Karam lived with his grandfather, the former hangman at the civic hospital. In fact, the boy had attended two or three of his bible classes but never shown an inclination toward conversion.

A few days later, Sushila came home to the quarter she now occupied on the campus with her parents with a strange request. Karam Pardesi had asked her permission to visit her father.

The pastor pondered this and remembered the shine in his daughter's eyes the first time she had told them of him. Now she was downright demure. A man of the world and a believer in Jesus Christ, the pastor pondered the request long into the night. It could only mean one thing: Karam was going to ask for his daughter's hand in marriage. The proposal usually went the other way: a woman's parents approached those appropriate for their daughters. But Karam was no ordinary man; he was now known throughout India as the Prince of the *Shudras*. Even though the padri's father had converted, his fellow villagers in *Gilhaan* looked upon him as a *Chura*, too. The conversion had not cleansed him of that, but Christianity had elevated them into an educated environ. The foreign churches spent millions making sure that Christian children in India received an education and provided support in the form of jobs or loans to uplift the families. The CMC was a great source of jobs for them, nearly three thousand or more. Bright young men and women got preferential treatment for foreign visas to Christian lands to study or work. Padri Masih had prayed plentifully that his children would be thus blessed.

In the morning, he informed his daughter that he would travel to Noorian alone to pay a visit to Karam Pardesi's family, for that was the proper way.

The bus to Noorian passed close to their home, and Sushila watched her father climb aboard, carrying a newer satchel with a box of *ladoos* as a gift—a traditional and festive one for the Pardesi family. She walked on to her day at the CMC and thought back to yesterday as Karam, unannounced, had walked into her office and asked her to join him for a cup of tea in a small restaurant across from the Hospital gates. A little flustered, she accepted, and her boss had watched them leave with interest. She was surprised to see both his mother and two sisters already seated at a table, and after introductions, he ordered tea and biscuits for her. She had been through several such meetings as any educated Indian girl of the time would until the right and acceptable match was made. Being in the PR business, meeting and interacting with strangers had turned her from a shy person to a more outgoing and talkative, one but this time it was different. The caliber of the prospective mate was intimidating, his wealth and fame needing no terms of reference. She saw that his mother and sisters were obviously enjoying his largesse as they were dressed in the finest fabrics and wore understated but expensive jewelry. She could only dream of their shoes and watches, obvious gifts from abroad, and their purses! All three had "city" teeth, clean and white.

Then Karam had asked to meet her father. "Very straightforward and to the point, this man," she thought, and she liked his take-charge and bold personality, unlike most Indian men she met or worked with. She also liked that he looked into her eyes in an inquiring yet honest way, holding her gaze.

* * *

Padri Masih stood before the massive, shiny, handcrafted steel gates of the huge, walled courtyard and said a silent prayer before calling out. After a bit of a wait, the grandfather, Bola, now stiff in the joints but obviously aging well, opened the gate, and Padri Masih introduced himself. The grandfather immediately brightened, flung out his arms to embrace the guest, and welcomed him to the *haveli*, shouting to his daughter, "Punna, oh, Punna, Padri Sahib is here."

Karam heard the cry and started to dress. He did not expect a visit from Sushila's father this soon and this early in the day, unannounced, but it was the way in India. No telephones meant no need to make prior appointments. People just showed up unannounced, taking the chance that it would be a successful visit. By the time he came out of his room, Padri Masih was already seated in the living room in the midst of his anxious family. Karam entered and bent down to touch his feet and received a benediction. "You remember me, Karam," he asked.

"Yes, yes," Karam nodded and smiled.

"You have done well, and for your parents," the Padri, still stunned by the opulence of the *haveli*, said. He had not been in a courtyard such as this in his entire lifetime. Not even the Bishop had such quarters in Phillaur.

Punna served tea with savories and sweetmeats, and they indulged in small talk. After a sufficient period had elapsed, the grandfather started, "Padri Sahib, it is my grandson's wish to ask you for the hand of your daughter."

Padri Masih looked at the floor and contemplated the statement from the elder. Taking a deep breath, he said, "We are Christians now. Sushila is the third generation of the faith. It poses a problem."

"I have no intention of converting myself or asking her to renounce her faith," Karam stated firmly.

"I respect your view." The Padri nodded. "What about the children?"

"They will be born and raised in America, a Christian country, and it will be up to Sushila to bring them up," Karam replied.

"That pleases me." The Padri reached into his satchel and gave Karam the box of *ladoos*, signifying his assent for the union. Punna's eyes welled up as her son accepted the gift and touched the Padri's feet again, this time receiving a bear hug. Then all the men shook hands and congratulated each other and Punna. Ruldu excused himself to gather the elders from his clan to bear witness, and they started another round of tea before taking Padri Masih on a tour of the courtyard. Later, after the elders had gathered, Punna brought out one of the jewelry sets and opened it to "oohs" and "aahs" and she added a suit of clothing for each of the bride-to-be's parents and brothers and a heavily embroidered suit for her. After letting the gifts be examined and praised by those present, she put them in a small, new suitcase she had bought and was holding in storage for the occasion. She added one silver coin and handed the gifts to the padri. He accepted with a small speech, obviously overwhelmed by the quality of the offerings, and he invited the family for a formal visit to his humble home in Ludhiana before he asked to leave. They pressed that he stay longer, but he persisted, and Karam asked for the driver to bring the car to drive Padri Sahib back to Ludhiana.

Later, Padri Masih alighted from the large, black, chauffeured American car in front of his home to the utter delight of his wife and the entire neighborhood.

In the evening, after the neighbors had left, Sushila and her parents sat in the two-room quarter and surveyed their wealth; Padri Masih was suddenly struck by their poverty. All they had been able to accumulate thus far for a life of preaching was a few pieces of furniture and his paltry pension, now supplemented by his daughter's salary. His sons, already married, lived with their families in similar circumstances, and today, in a fit of insanity, he had promised his daughter to the richest *Shudra* in the world. There had been no discussion of dowry. His wife, watching his distant eyes, spoke first. "All we can offer is our beautiful daughter. I do not think they will be expecting much of us."

Sushila looked up from the jewelry box she had been studying, and it suddenly hit her: what if they were expecting more? What then? "Oh, God," she thought. What a humiliation if that was a reason for his parents to withdraw from the promise.

The padri looked at his daughter's alarmed face. Then he said quietly, "I have faith in my Lord. All will be well. Besides, his grandfather Bola is known for keeping his word. In our lot, that is the most precious of our qualities. We may be poorer than the rest, but we are a people of our promise."

He proved to be right. The next day, when Punna and her daughters came for the formal tea, served by Sushila, they proclaimed, "We are ecstatic about our bride-to-be. Our son has chosen well. Please do not bother with a dowry of any kind."

"Why," started the mother, "we will not be sending our daughter empty-handed."

"Sister," Punna stated in a calm voice, "you are already giving us the finest jewel in your possession. What more can we expect? We do not want anything, not even a reception. Karam will discuss with Sushila, and they will decide. We will all go along with their wishes, but we want a formal engagement to be held at our home. Please come in two days, Padriji, just with a *thali* of sweets and four or five of your kinsmen, and formalize the promise."

"Can we wait another day," the padri asked, needing

to send word to his sons who lived a day's bus ride away but were available via phone. Turning to Sushila, he asked, "Can you call them from the hospital today and tell them to arrive tomorrow?"

* * *

Ruldu went all out for his son's engagement. He hired the top singing duo in the province, balladeers and *bajigars*, dancers and jugglers, and a loudspeaker that would blast music nonstop for the day. He called for a truckload of canopies, folding tables, and chairs; a city caterer; and crates of whiskey and rum and the rotgut that the riffraff drank. He sent messengers to all his kin and had a drum beaten through the village streets, inviting all to join him in celebrations. Punna and the girls were busy preparing the *haveli*, the nephews helping when asked. Their local kin ran in and out of the courtyard on errands big and small.

Karam took Sushila and her brothers to the dining room of the Gaylord Hotel for dinner and got to know his betrothed. They talked about themselves, their schooling, work, likes and dislikes. The brothers sat in silence, still not believing that their brother-in-law to be was the Prince of the *Shudras*, being attended to like a maharaja by the waiters in the liveried best. They had glasses of the best whiskey in India and plates of the tastiest morsels. They looked at their sister, all aglow in the attention of Karam, and felt uniquely blessed.

Karam had to leave two days after the engagement for business reasons. He had a request: "Let us have a civil wedding here in Ludhiana and hold a proper reception and then have a Christian wedding in the big cathedral in Hamilton, in Canada."

She had no choice but to agree. It would also avoid the issue of the dowry. He promised to return in three months and in the meantime work on her visa to Canada. He was confident that Mr. Grewal would be of great help.

The engagement party set a standard that would not be copied for a decade in Noorian. The engagement ceremony was better attended than the weddings of the richest *Jat's* and well-organized by an experienced caterer from the city. The caterer arrived with a truck full of pots and pans, cutlery and crockery, and ingredients of all kinds for the cooking to be done in brass pots large enough to be lifted by two men. The night before was lit by the gaslights in the courtyard, and the neighbors were kept awake by the din of clanging metal and cursing cooks. At dawn, the canopies went up and were festooned with multihued flags and balloons. Strings of light bulbs were strung all over the *haveli*. Coconut-fiber flooring stretched across the ground, and tables and chairs stood ready for five hundred guests. They built a stage for the entertainers, speakers strategically placed on the roof to reach the entire village plus the countryside for a mile. Brightly dressed women guests gathered in groups to sing festive ditties, and their men folk bathed and shaved and dressed in *kurtas* and balloonous *chadras*, curved moccasins on their feet. They sat in knots smoking *hookas* and *biris*, partaking of the ample snacks put out with the soda; there was no liquor. Jaswant Singh, already a nervous wreck from the suddenness of the occasion, had wisely advised the crowd-control measures. Alcohol would be on the menu after the ceremony.

The padri and his party of five arrived to be greeted by the village elders at the gates. Thus received and honored, they took their seats on a dais built especially for the ceremony. Karam dressed in a silk *kurta/pyjama* and wore a red turban festooned with a peacock feather and fake pearls. Barefoot but with a ceremonial sword, he appeared in the company of his sisters and female cousins and was led by the singing escorts to the dais, where he sat facing the Padri. Watched by the guests, his future father-in-law intoned a Christian prayer in Punjabi, blessed those congregated there, and placed a piece of a *ladoo* in Karam's mouth. Then he ceremoniously took out his wallet and dropped a silver rupee into the fold of the shawl Karam held. He was followed by all the elders, who dropped a coin or a note into his lap, put their hand on his turban, and intoned a blessing before moving on. It took almost an hour. The women sang songs of joy and ceremony and blessings, ancient poems passed on in an oral tradition from generation to generation. As the last man left his side, Karam rose, touched the feet of his elders, and was guided back into the *haveli* by his female escorts, now eager to loot his substantial gift of money. Such was customary, much enjoyed, and performed in jest. The photographer hired for the occasion, a dyspeptic hunchback, shouted above the din for a clear focus.

The festivities began in earnest, but as custom dictated, the Padri and his kinsmen took their leave immediately to let Karam's family get on with their song and dance. Most others stayed to watch the singers and performers. The higher born were seated and entertained in a section reserved for them, and they were attended by men brought in from the city. They were served the best foods and whiskey most had ever tasted. Some, caught up in the moment, got up and performed a group *bhangra* and received a loud standing ovation from the *Shudras* and loud appreciative clucking from the women and kin of Karam's caste. Fortunately, no untoward incidents occurred in this rather frenzied, mixed affair of the castes and creeds; Jaswant Singh and his trusted assistants delicately removed the ones demonstrating any signs of inebriation or hostility.

It was midnight before the last of the guests left, and the family sat down to discuss and dissect the event. Ruldu and Bola both blissfully passed out on their cots. It was an occasion to celebrate, and they did so mightily, consuming as much whiskey as they could before their heads spun.

Among the guests, a young man, nondescript, sat at the very edge of the crowd, his face in shadow, and he studied the courtyard and the family. He took sips of water from a glass and ate sparingly of the treats. He was from Noorian, the son of a well-to-do family of *Jats*, and he was studying at the Khalsa College in Ludhiana. He was in his fourth year of political science with ambitions of becoming a lawyer and serving the poor and dispossessed. He read heavily of Marx and Lenin and the exploits and thoughts of his true hero, Mao Tse-tung, the communist leader and liberator of China. Democracy, with its attendant corruption, ineptitudes, and familial loyalties gnawed at him. He felt that India needed a period of dictatorship or communism—he was still unsure which—to cleanse itself of the British ideals of nobility, inheritance, and entitlement. He fantasized about the Congress and communal leaders all in their cloaks of *desh-bhaghati, sewa,* and sacrifice, actually toiling in gulags, digging ditches. It would do them so much good to dirty their hands with the soil rather than fold them in vulpine *Namastejis.* His new friends, men who had appeared out of nowhere, had talked incessantly and repeatedly of the need for revolution and the means to bring it about. The cause needed money, and it could be had from the rich and the corrupt.

He knew the watchman had lots of it, and the old midwife kept jewelry in anticipation for just the occasion he was now witnessing. He should speak of this opportunity with his comrades. Lost in his thoughts and observation, he missed the eyes watching him.

Jaswant Singh had observed the tell-tale signs of an anarchist. Idealistic sons of well-to-do *Jats* sometimes turned to radical parties promoting dangerous agendas. The Communists recruited heavily on university and college campuses, as did the communal parties, like the Akalis for Sikh nationalism and the Rashtriya Satya Sangh, the same Hindu extremists that killed Mahatma Gandhi; their political arm, the Jan Sangh, chased Hindu boys and men. The communists, though, had multiple branches, ranging from the milder CPI-M to the Maoist Naxalites. Most college-going young men of Noorian now numbering in the thirties had at one time or another been their targets. Some were registered members of various political stripes, and the rare one sat on the extreme fringe. This youth, Pratap Singh, had been noticed in the company of a suspected murderer, a Naxalite. Jaswant Singh signaled to one of his men posing as a waiter and gave him instructions to follow the youth, as he suspected trouble brewing with his presence and behavior. Was he scouting the courtyard for a raid at a later date? There were too many people for a typical Naxalite attack; they liked theirs carried out late in the night on sleeping victims.

Sure enough, Jaswant was right. Pratap Singh was seen leaving the village later that night on his bicycle. The speculation was that he left to report to his handlers.

* * *

Karam left for New Delhi. He was a little sad to leave, but he was looking forward to returning in three months. He had really started to like Sushila, and she had warmed to him and was inconsolable upon his departure. Punna had everyone going mad with her demands for this and that, and her daughters finally had to sit her down and calm her a bit.

The padri spent more time in prayer. Karam had quietly pushed a large envelope of money into the hands of Sushila's eldest brother, shushing his protestations and telling him that from now on, they were his family and thus must enjoy his good fortune and share in it. The proud man had accepted it upon that assertion. In New Delhi, he hooked up with a tanned and unusually happy Dr. Hopkins. The next day, their plane took off for Frankfurt, and they caught the connecting TWA flight to New York.

.

Chapter 19

"*Che cosa?*"

"*Scusi, Dottore, Signor Karam al telefono.*"

"*Un momento.*" Stefano excused himself and wiggled himself out of the cubbyhole of an examination room to take the call at the desk in the front of his cramped office in Civitavecchia, a short distance from Rome.

"Stefano," Karam's voice sailed over the line, clear as crystal.

"Why you shout?"

"I am going to get married, and you are going to be my best man."

"Best man? Why, *mamma mia*, Karam, you crazy, no?"

"It is for real, and you better come, Stefano," Karam said, now pleading.

"Sure, sure, your *matrimonio*, for sure," Stefano replied, still not believing the news. He and Karam had remained in touch updating each other through letters and phone calls and counted each other as close friends.

"I am marrying an Indian beauty," Karam boasted. "You have to see her, Stefano; you will faint."

"Have you seen my wife lately?" he wanted to ask, but this was Karam's moment, and he did not want to spoil it with his complaints about his wife who had put on a few kilos after having four kids, one after the other. But he would have it no other way. "When is the *matrimonio*, Karam?"

"In a few months."

"Si, si, no big rush, then." Stefano was already calculating the cost of going to Canada, particularly if his wife insisted on coming along with the bambini. "Mamma mia," he thought.

"You better be bringing Anna and the kids," Karam said, "and it'll be first class. I am making the arrangements."

"No, no, no," Stefano protested, but in vain.

"Remember your own rules, my friend. You wouldn't let me spend a penny in Rome. The same rules apply here."

Stefano, knowing that his friend, Karam, the *Indiano*, had done so well, could not protest, and he gave in. "OK, Karam, you win."

Karam had made a list. It was only a page long of names: names of people he wanted to share one of the most important moments of his life with. He had started with Ella, telling her in his calm, collected way that somehow, facing reality, he had decided to do what was probably the best for him at his age. He definitely could not let the most suitable candidate for marriage slip through his fingers. He had had an epiphany, an awakening, a visceral urge, and Ella had taken it in stride. "We will always be friends," she said, kissing him on the mouth a final time, holding back the tears. She was torn. Dark clouds of threats and aggression were threatening her beloved Israel, and she wanted to be back there. This development provided the cover, and both Mr. and Mrs. Berger gave their blessings; Ella resigned her position with CHCG, giving and honoring the proper notice before leaving for Israel.

"See," Mr. Berger told his wife on the way back from the airport, "you did not have to cross the bridge."

"Yes," Mrs. Berger conceded, "but I worry."

She received an assuring tap on her knee from her husband.

* * *

Sushila was allowed to get on the phone and spend the allotted five minutes each day at work talking to Karam. She knew about the envelope he had given her brother and just how much it had helped ease the burden of custom and ritual and their attendant expenses, saving her father the embarrassment of trying to borrow money from local moneylenders at exorbitant rates just to keep face. Despite the fact that they were Christian and not expected to follow or respect the ancient and ingrained traditions on their culture and caste, it was difficult to escape the expectations of family, friends, and the community at large. Since she had been engaged to such a rich and powerful man, even their frugal neighbors, Christians themselves, expected much in ways of sweetmeats, treats, and involvement in every step and stop in custom. The five thousand rupees was a godsend. It was more money than the family had ever had, and the day her brother had given the envelope to her father, who had opened it with shaking hands and counted it on the cot, they all stood around watching the pile accumulate to a mind-blowing number. She had begun to believe in her good fortune, and she promised to make the best of it.

As the daughter of a padri, essentially dependant on the goodwill of the bishop and having to kowtow to his substantial kin, all employed at the various institutions around Punjab run by or in association with the Church of Northern India, she had felt a burden of obligation to the hierarchy of her church. She had worked, studied, and lived up to her obligations, never missing a bible class, studying by the light of an oil lamp for examinations, wearing the same clothes for six months at a time, and eating every morsel of food and every grain of rice on her *thali* in the residences far away from the comfort of her mother's hearth. She had accepted every growl or frown by her supposed elders in a system totally dependent on foreign charity, but such was better than the fate of her kin in the village of Gilhaan who had not converted, but remained *Chura* and sentenced to a life of sweeping dung and feces.

She was so proud, just so proud. She would gaze at the color portrait of Karam she had demanded and received. She kept it for herself, even sleeping with it held to her breast.

Pratap Singh slipped quietly out of his father's courtyard and wrapped a woolen shawl around his head and upper body in an effort to conceal his identity. He whistled softly, immediately answered by a muffled cough: the signal that all was clear. The cold metal of the pistol against his spine, held there by the *pyjama* string, emphasized the gravity of his undertaking. They were going to raid the courtyard of Ruldu, a *Chura* once oppressed but now a bourgeois and a hated member of society, and rich enough in cash and jewels to finance the activities of his cell for a long time. He felt the presence of his comrades as they stepped out of the shadows and walked just outside the ring road toward the only lit gate in the village. They would first toss strychnine-laced meat over its walls to kill and disable the guard dogs, and then they clamber over the walls to surprise the occupants. His comrades, confident from having done this before, gave him courage simply by their single-minded striding toward their target.

Once beside the outer wall and still out of the circle of lights at the gate, Joga, the leader of the group, gave another muffled cough. They could hear the dogs scratching against the wall. Joga tossed the meat over the walls, and the dogs attacked the treat with gusto. Waiting until it was quiet, one of them clambered over the wall and scrambled to the gates and let the others in. They moved silently past the dogs, now lying on their sides, and moved in a line along the inner walls of the *haveli*, searching for the right door. Finding it, they paused, pulled out their weapons and kicked mightily to break the fragile locks and fell upon the startled grandfather, Bola. Joga shot the old man right through the forehead, the sound and the force knocking the dead man back onto his cot and bringing the occupants awake. As lights were turned on and noises emanated from adjoining rooms, they assailants rushed in and pulled the frightened victims out of their cots and bundled them into the sitting room, quickly closing the door after them.

The watchman, whom Jaswant Singh had warned against just such an occurrence, kept his cool and followed to the letter the instructions of the masked robbers. He opened the strong box, and while his white-faced family watched, handed over a bundle of notes and its remaining contents of jewelry and documents. The robbers, after tying them up, turned off the lights and left through the gates, slipping into the fields.

Punna startled her family into action when she, finding a hole in Bola's forehead, sprawled across his cot and gave out a painful wail. Turning on the lights and raising the alarm, Ruldu ran from one end of the courtyard to another while his neighbors poured into the property brandishing swords, axes, and sticks. As they begun to gather around the distraught mistress of the *haveli*, the enormity of the raid began to take hold, and soon it was as if the entire village now heeded their cries for help. By daylight, the village was crawling with police, trackers, and dogs. Already the escape routes had been retraced. Sentries armed with .303 rifles were posted around the courtyard.

By midmorning, the senior superintendant of police was seated in the sitting room and receiving reports from subordinates while Ruldu's kin and elders of the village comforted the violated. Punna had screamed herself hoarse over her father's inert body, and the Comrade eased her by injecting her with a shot of morphine. Soon she was passed out on a cot, watched over by her teary daughters as her granddaughters served tea and biscuits to the officials while her son-in-law, Ramu, and the two boys sat with the elders and comforted Ruldu. Members of the caste took the day off from cleaning and hauling the village's dung and detritus. The body of the hangman was wrapped in a sheet and placed on a police jeep to be taken to the Civic Hospital to be autopsied by the chief surgeon and then placed on ice in the morgue he once supervised.

The news of Bola's murder and the looting of Ruldu's *haveli* spread like wildfire. Sushila's boss rushed into her cubicle-sized office to tell her what happened. He suggested that she call Karam immediately and told her that the CMC would absorb the charges for the call. She sat shaking for a while, having never really met the dead man. She did not want to be the bearer of terrible news, still an instinctive believer in superstition. Watching her shake in silence, her boss asked for the number and dialed the operator himself. Karam was fast asleep when woken up by the incessant ringing.

He thanked the caller and hung up. The information had been sketchy, just that a terrible thing had happened resulting in his grandfather's death. Unable to call home as there still was no phone line to the village, he got up and dialed Dr. Grewal's number in Ludhiana and got the details from him. As the soothing voice of the elder consoled and condoled, Karam wept.

"It will be thoroughly investigated and the perpetrators brought to justice," Dr. Grewal promised. "I will personally see to it. Don't think about jumping on a plane and coming here; if you are needed, I will call you. Karam, be brave, and accept the will of God Almighty and pray for the peace of your grandfather's soul."

With these words the conversation ended. Karam began pacing the living room torn with emotion. He had loved his grandfather so much, and the elder had given him so much, done so much, sacrificed so much. But he did have the satisfaction that his grandfather had lived to see his accomplishments and enjoy his success, including celebrating his engagement. As a medical man, he was grateful that death had been instantaneous and without suffering. And no one else in the family had been harmed. The dogs were killed, and he was also saddened by that. He wondered how his mother was coping, and came close to booking a flight, no matter the inconvenience. Taking a deep breath, he dialed Essential Services in New Delhi and asked for Jaswant Singh. The agent came on the phone. He had already received a call from the police station in Ludhiana and was aware of the circumstances.

"I believe it is someone from Noorian," Jaswant Singh stated emphatically. "I regret that they acted so fast. Typically these people wait months to strike. I have already given the suspect's name to the SSP Sahib, and they are following up on it."

"Can you tell me who you think it is?"

"Sahib, do not worry. The truth will soon come out."

"I want protection for my family." Karam was emphatic.

"Right now they will receive a police guard until the suspects have been dealt with, but if you wish, I can travel to Noorian and make sure they are taken care of."

"That would be my preference."

After putting the phone down, Karam sat and drafted a

long telegram of condolence and phoned it in. That was all he could do for the moment.

* * *

Bola was cremated two days after his death, his funerary procession led by a band and the *arthi* followed by hundreds who had come to pay their respects: villagers, kinsmen, old mates from the district jail and the civic hospital, even the district commissioner and superintendent of police, as well as officials from the *Tehsil* and Block. He was carried on the shoulders of his son-in-law, grandson-in-law, and strapping great-grandsons. His pier was soaked in clarified butter to burn it hot and fragrant, the older grandson chosen to crack the skull as the fire was lit. The following day, the family sifted through the ashes, collected the charred remains, and placed them in a clay urn. Instead of spreading his ashes over a body of water, Punna buried the urn beside the Sant Baba samadhi. She declared her father a martyr, a *shaheed* who had died defending his family. "Why else would they have shot him," she argued. She commissioned a knee-high tomb to be built over the burial site. Thus preserving the memory of Bola, the hangman and morgue attendant, to be visited and worshiped, bowed to and beseeched by the many *Shudras* who frequented the site: to perform ablutions, fire ceremonies, and prayers and ask for miracles and cures and the birth of sons.

* * *

A week after the cremation of his victim, Partap Singh, carrying on his normal routine and confident that no one had recognized him, was apprehended while attending a class at the Khalsa College. He was brought to the main police station and asked politely a number of questions about the events of the fateful night in Noorian. Pretending innocence, he arrogantly asked that his father be called and informed of the insolence of the constables; the subinspector conducting the investigation leaned across the table and slapped the youth hard, again and again. Once he was on the ground cowering from the stinging and painful blows, two more plainclothes men joined in the kicking and hitting. It continued for a while, and finally unable to bear the pain of their skilled punishment, Partap Singh cried out, "Stop, oh stop! I will tell you all!"

The interrogation lasted into the night. Once they were satisfied that they had extracted every bit of information they needed, they threw him in a cell.

The next morning, his body was discovered shot full of holes. The superintendent of police issued a press release that the youth, Pratap Singh from the village of Noorian and a suspect in the murder of Bola and a member of the Naxalites, had been killed during an armed encounter with the Punjab Armed Police.

What the press release failed to mention was that everyone of the band, including the leader Joga, had been traced and individually apprehended. Their fate, similar to Pratap Singh's, awaited the completion of interrogations that might lead to further information. The Punjab Armed Police, a robust force not to be trifled, with had been given secret approval to execute the Naxalites, rather than parade them through the interminable delays of the court system. It also sent a message to the insurgents that at least in the province of Punjab, they were not welcome anymore. The movement went underground and inactive, its surviving members fleeing to safer havens.

The violent raid on the haveli had other consequences. After receiving a security and needs analysis, Karam read the report carefully. It stated:

Dear Karam Pardesi Sahib,

As per your instructions, I have completed my analysis of the immediate needs of your family, paying particular attention to their need for safety. Obviously your many and lauded accomplishments and acts of generosity have benefited many, particularly the village of Noorian, its surrounding communities, your alma mater, and your caste and kinsmen. Your scholarship foundation will continue to benefit the deserving students of your birthplace.

However, all of this attracted the attention of insurgent elements, resulting in violence being brought upon your innocent family members, the loss of your grandfather, and substantial material loss of money and gold. I have thoroughly interviewed each and every member of your family individually and collectively, going as far as to interview your fiancé and her parents since soon, by the grace of God Almighty, they will be joining ranks.

Your mother and father wish to continue to live in Noorian, as does your younger sister and her husband. They will from now on adopt a lower profile and put certain precautions into effect such as not keeping money and valuables in a large quantity at their residence. They will bank any excess cash from your remittances as well as the substantial income from the land and interest from loans outstanding to about sixty individuals and families. Your father has officially retired from his position as *chowkidar* of the village and your mother as an elected *panch*. Now that proper medical care is available for most women in the village, she has also retired from midwifery. All this will remove the constant contact and exposure to people coming in and out of the courtyard. They are also halving their herd and will only keep two grown and *milch* buffaloes and their young calves. This task of looking after the cattle can be handled by one of your kinsmen. They will no longer be selling milk either.

I have brought them a pair of properly trained guard dogs, and these animals will only accept food or drink from one designated master: your mother. It will be impossible to poison them.

After consultations with your elder sister and your three nieces and two nephews as well as Padri Sahib and Miss Sushila Masih, I propose the following: that you consider purchasing a home in one of the better sectors in Chandigarh. Your sister will move there and watch over the younger ones while they attend college or other training centers. If you purchase a duplex, Padri Sahib and his wife can also live there, providing companionship and presence for your sister. I really do not recommend that the younger members be taking buses to Ludhiana alone and thus pose a problem of future kidnapping and so on.

I can help make arrangements, including recommending a well-respected estate agent in Chandigarh to help find a suitable location for purchase.

Yours sincerely,
Jaswant Singh

Karam read it a few times more and asked for Sushila's opinion on the phone. "It is the best course of action, Karamji," she stated, still shaken up by the violent events.

* * *

Having heard from everyone concerned, Karam bought—through the recommendation of the better estate agency in Chandigarh—an understated but large *kothi*. It had two stories with a total of seven bedrooms and three washrooms, two full kitchens, and two big reception rooms doubling both as sitting and dining rooms. It had a front courtyard with a redbrick wall, an iron gate for a car to enter, and a side gate for pedestrians, bicycles, and scooters. The back courtyard contained two other rooms that could serve as a summer kitchen and storage. Fully walled and brick floored, it had huge, concrete planters to bring some planted relief of color.

His elder sister and her son, Satwant Singh, and daughters, Preetam and Pooran, were joined by the younger sister's son, Tara Singh, and daughter, Ranjit Kaur. The upper section would house Padri Masih and his wife with one bedroom furnished and kept for Karam and Sushila's exclusive use. However, it was opened for the comfort of his parents only when they chose to visit. The nieces and nephews were ensconced in good colleges and schools and provided with scooters for transportation.

With her immigration documents in hand, Sushila boarded a plane for Canada and was seen off at Palam Airport by her now substantial and well-off clan from Ludhiana, Noorian, Chandigarh, and Simla. She had wept inconsolably upon parting from her family, but once in the air, she began to look optimistically forward to her new life with Karam. They had decided upon a civil marriage in Toronto and a reception for his closest associates in Niagara Falls.

Chapter 20

What if Niagara Falls had been in Europe, Stefano had often wondered and asked Karam several times as they had taken cheap bus tours on weekends to one of the seven wonders of the modern world. Karam loved the majesty that nature projected with the falls themselves, the churning foam at the bottom and the force of the water flow so powerful and thunderous at the reversing falls where the Niagara River bent upon itself after meeting the granite wall of the Niagara Escarpment to flow into Lake Ontario. In his early and wonder years in Canada, he had been too happy to witness this overpowering sight and paid scant attention to his friend's thoughtful question.

What if the Falls were in Europe?

Would they have the gaudy look of the Canadian side with wax museums, tourists' shops selling trinkets, prostitutes and drug addicts ruling the sidewalks, and seedy motel and strip clubs lining its main street? As much as the parks service had done a fair job of building reasonable and utilitarian gardens and tourist areas, making the viewing of the Falls in all their glory pleasant, the narrow approaches caused horrendous traffic snarls on busy days, and the whole town of Niagara Falls had a hard-up bordertown look of rundown clapboard buildings and some industry. It was much nicer along the Niagara River and the town of Niagara on the Lake: picturesque gardens, grand and gated estates, budding vineyards, massive clumps of woods, horse-buggy rides, inns hosting royalty, and the central and quaint treat of the town on the Lake now enjoying a seasonal theater of Shakespearean plays.

Niagara Falls, New York, was the poorer and less-endowed cousin and neighbor. A town built on the cheap energy from running water, it hosted industries that for decades had few regulators and controls and produced cheap goods that supplied the United States. While the Canadian side tried to maintain a tourist orientation, the American side, lacking attractions, took advantage of cheap electricity and cheaper storage of waste in the form of chemicals, effluents, and other nasty byproducts of its chemical industries.

This was the beginning of the fall of 1970, and after a quiet civil wedding; Karam had booked the Canadian Falls Hilton to host his reception to be attended by just 100 of his closest friends and associates. The bride had only one family member in either Canada or America, and she could not afford to travel there, having only emigrated six months earlier and still struggling to get settled in California. Her cousin Pushpa Masih, a nurse, spent that day mostly in happy tears because she was well aware of Sushila's good fortune. If any member of her family could be in North America, she wanted it to be Sushila.

The Bergers had hosted her and stood in for her parents at the civil ceremony. Anna and Rebecca were the maids of honor, and Stefano was the best man, backed by Ben. It was pleasant and quick, conducted by a judge of the district court, a very pleasant and fatherly man who had given a small lecture to the couple about the sanctity of the occasion and their responsibilities to each other. They had dressed typically: Karam in his best suit and Sushila in a stunning red sari and the finest set of gold jewelry her mother-in-law had given her for the occasion. Mr. Berger was teary-eyed, having given away such an exotic bride that he insisted on getting a dozen pictures taken of himself with the happy couple, occasionally including some of Stefano's and Ben's broods. Afterward, they had lunch at the private dining room of the downtown Holiday Inn, served by white-gloved waiters. It was a kosher affair.

After the reception, Mr. and Mrs. Berger drove Sushila to her husband's penthouse. The photographer took pictures of all the significant occasions during the day for the albums that would be their memories, copies of which were eagerly awaited by their clans in India.

Finally alone with Karam in her matrimonial home, a fifteenth-floor penthouse apartment, Sushila went suddenly quiet and shy. The wedding party had left after being seen off at the door, Stefano grinning and winking at Karam. Karam led her into the living room, and Sushila, for several days used to the opulence of the Berger residence and the exquisitely furnished home of her new friend Rebecca Roman, Ben's wife, suddenly felt a bit claustrophobic in the clean and neat yet Spartan dwelling of her husband. It looked almost utilitarian, untended, and unadorned. She sat down at the edge of the sofa and awaited his next move. Unguided and unadvised and without the guidance of his parents, clan, and cousins, Karam felt suddenly alone and abandoned. He shook his head, realizing that he was now an officially married man to a woman like Sushila, who now sat quietly and downcast on the edge of the sofa. He took charge.

"Come and see the place," he touched her on the arm and then grabbed her elbow. She rose almost to his height because she was still wearing the high-heeled red shoes that went so well with the rest of her attire. As she gained full height, she leaned slightly into him, and he took her into his arms and they stood there, clinging together for a prolonged moment and breathing into each other's ears.

"Sushila."

She lifted her face, and he kissed her on her full lips, red and moist from the expert application of lipstick by the aesthetician Rebecca had hired to prepare her for the occasion. A slight tremor went through her body; they parted, looked deeply into each other's eyes, and she looked away, promise in her eyes.

He showed her every square inch of the two-thousand square feet of deeply carpeted, three-bedroomed, two-bathroomed apartment. The fridge was loaded with anything she could have wanted, and the *ensuite* was chock full of soft towels, soaps, shampoos, shaving creams, and colognes. "This cupboard is yours," he said opening a mirrored one. Then realizing that they were still in their finery he asked, "Do you want to change?" emphasizing it by starting to remove his tie. A sudden look of panic flashed across her face, so he busied himself with bringing in her luggage and helping her sort it out.

"Could you get out, please," she whispered, eyes lowered. He crept out of the bedroom and ran into the guest room to relieve himself of his formal clothes and put on a silk pyjama/*kurta* he had bought for this very occasion. In the living room, he turned on the television only to find the cackle of a game show. He tried fiddling with the radio and the tape recorder but to no avail and instead uncorked a bottle of white wine and poured himself a glass.

She was in no hurry. He heard water running for at least twenty minutes. By then he was halfway into the bottle. She called out for him to come in.

He opened the door to find her sitting up against the

headboard with pillows piled up high, her long tresses flowing over her shoulders and not a trace of lipstick or makeup on her radiant face. He put the glass on the chest of drawers and slipped into the bed and under the sheets. Twenty minutes later, as he pulled off of her, he realized that at age thirty-two, he had finally slept with a virgin: his wife!

It was perhaps not the honeymoon either had imagined. They had come together as husband and wife on the afternoon of their civil wedding. Used to custom and tradition, Sushila more recently than Karam, they had done what comes naturally after a marriage ceremony. A sudden tenderness gripped Karam. He ran the bath for her and helped dry her long tresses with the hairdryer even as it got oppressively hot and humid in the windowless washroom, its exhaust fan running. As she stood before him in unadorned and undressed fullness, he felt rushes of passion and pride he had never had with a woman before and a sense of protection, of possession. He watched her slip on a gown and look at him with a questioning glance. He averted his eyes, giving his acquiescence to a normal activity, and she led him into the living room and then the kitchen, where she looked in the fridge.

"I do not know how to cook," she admitted in a tiny voice.

"Neither do I," he added in support.

"You are a man!" she protested. "My mother did it all. She just told me to study."

"Good advice," he pressed against her from behind. "You hungry?"

"No, just thirsty."

He pulled out a bottle of Coca-Cola, twisted off the cap, and poured the fizzing soda into a tall glass. She drank it in sips, watching him with those large, brown eyes with the long lashes. She had a tall, lean, and hard body, a wide, generous mouth, a snub nose, and a long neck that tapered onto a broad-shouldered chest and a pair of mango-shaped breasts. Her stomach was flat, the belly button small, and her hips wide with a narrow pelvis. Her legs were perfect, the feet small with toenails painted a brilliant red.

Her arms were skinny, the hands long with fingers decorated with henna and a ring on each. "My mother's doing," he thought.

She muffled a burp from the quick intake of the soda, and the expression of her hand over her mouth, nostrils flaring and eyes wide open, got his juices flowing, his hormones pumping. He grabbed her free hand to guide her back to the bedroom. "No," she pleaded, the look sincere and vulnerable.

And Karam was in love. As long as he lived, he would treasure and hold that moment.

The wedding reception was on Saturday, two days away. He suggested that they drive to Niagara Falls. She came out wearing a red turtleneck over a pair of flared jeans, her hair in a ponytail tied with a red ribbon. She looked so different and attractive. He had never seen her in western clothing before. Rebecca had obviously taken Sushila shopping. With a light jacket over her arm and a black purse, she could have passed for a student. She was eight years younger than him; closer to nine, and just that morning he had already pulled out the first gray hair he had discovered on his head!

As he sat behind the wheel of his new, silver Cadillac, he noticed her caress the wine colored leather of the seat, a smile of pride on her face. "You like it?" he asked.

"My first car," she replied, simply meeting his gaze.

"We have to get you some driving lessons." And she needed a lot more learning to become comfortable living in Canada.

As they sped down the Queen Elizabeth Way toward the Falls, she rubbed her stomach, complaining, "The speed here makes me queasy."

He too had felt that in the beginning. It was so natural for an Indian. At first, the scenery rushing past was a strange and stomach-churning experience. He slowed a little, the traffic very light. Over the Skyway Bridge, she was glued to the window. "So much water!"

Karam began explaining the geography of the Great Lakes, how Niagara Falls was part of a river connecting two of them. He spoke, she listened. Her eyes were on the scenery outside. "Everything here is big," she observed as they passed huge fields with rows of fruit trees and tall corn. The colors were yet to turn, but there was the hint of fall.

Sushila was thrilled and fascinated all at once. She had seen waterfalls in the Himalayas, but nothing like this. The energy, the vibration under foot, the gentle spray landing on her face made her giddy. Her heart beat loudly in her chest, and she clung to her husband's arm. "You OK?" He smiled, watching her face, enjoying her closeness.

She nodded vigorously, smiling happily; she had made him take a lot of pictures of her standing by the Falls, the flowerbeds, the gigantic oaks and spruces and colorful bushes, and later in front of the wax-museum, but she refused to go in to gaze at the oddities. She bought trinkets, touristy memorabilia, and postcards to mail to friends and family back home. She tried candy-floss, a candied apple, and maple-glazed popcorn. "Almost as good as *mithai*," she declared. She made him ride the Ferris wheel with her. Sushila was like a child let out of school after a long semester. Still unused to cars driving on the right side of the road, she was a danger to herself when crossing from one side of the street to curiously look into another shop. After drinking a coffee at a restaurant, too full of sweet stuff for food, they crossed the bridge, through customs, and drove down Niagara Falls Way to the hospital. Karam wanted her to see his prized possession, now humming with patients and fully staffed with doctors and nurses.

"You own it?" she asked in wonder as they pulled into his reserved spot in the parking lot and read his nameplate and title.

"Yes."

"All of it?" She almost refused to believe it. It was almost as big as the main section of the Brown Memorial Hospital back home, and in the failing light it was lit up like *Diwali*. There were a lot of cars in the parking lot, she thought. There were a lot of cars everywhere she had gone. It was as if people did not walk much. There were no bicycles that she had seen yet and certainly no animal-drawn conveyance. Karam came to her side and helped her out of the car.

"Well, Mrs. Pardesi?" he asked, his arm sweeping the vista of the hospital.

"I am proud of you," she said, and he knew she meant it.

Inside, as he showed her around, the staff and patients greeted him so courteously and with big smiles; even bigger ones for her upon learning her name and title. "You are gorgeous, honey," a large, dark woman with the whitest teeth she had ever seen said as she hugged her. "Thank you," Sushila demurred, grateful for the spontaneous gesture.

"Big Mamma," Karam introduced her to Sushila, "my American mother."

"You done me proud, child," and she hugged him, too.

Big Mamma, Frances Johnson, raised five children by herself. As a single mother from Jamaica, she only got the worst and lowest paying jobs: cleaning and washing from

morning till late in the evening, only taking Sundays off as
the Sabbath was God's command for this pious woman.
Somehow she had lucked out and got a job in the hospital
doing laundry in the industrial sized undertaking in the
basement. It got her benefits and a union membership and
paid overtime. The certain income resulted in obtaining a
three-bedroom tenement, an old rusting Ford, and keeping
the kids in school. All of them made it past high school. Two
went into the Army and did tours of Vietnam, afterward
getting a college education. Her daughters all studied
nursing, and one now worked in the hospital and still
lived with her. Karam had a habit of talking with the staff,
particularly the nonwhite staff. Mrs. Johnson, surprised by
his manners and courtesy, was soon smuggling jerk chicken
and dirty rice in for his lunches. They adopted each other.
He read her file, and noting her seniority, promoted her
to a lighter job and gave her a decent raise. Her relentless
mothering of him got her a better car for her birthday.

"You spoil each other," her daughter complained to
Karam. "She only talks about you now."

"She is my mamma," Karam replied, grinning. "She has
to spoil me,"

And now he was in her grip with Sushila. "I put it in your
office," she told Karam before letting them go. "Should still
be warm."

Then she pushed them away. "Now go along you two.
And behave yourselves."

They found the food where she typically left it: in a
casserole dish on the credenza. Sushila gazed in wonder at
his large, walnut-paneled office, the desk with the massive,
upholstered leather chair, and his parents' picture alongside
his grandfather's in gold-flecked frames. She admired the
seven-piece boardroom beyond his desk, the bookcases filled

with leather-bound volumes, and the lovely vases and other small carvings and collectables. Karam grabbed the dish and began setting a sitting for two with silver cutlery and crystal glasses and bone china. "It is so ... so ... rich," she exclaimed.

"Come and eat this, and then we will talk."

She sat down, cut a piece of the chicken thigh, and put it in her mouth. Her eyes went wide. "It is spicy!"

"The best." Karam chewed his happily. Later, he poured her a glass of red wine. She looked at it. "It is wine, not whiskey," he assured her, and she sniffed it and took a sip, making a face, but she kept at it during the meal.

They had just finished, and just like that, Mrs. Johnson appeared and took away the dishes. "Go home and get into bed, you love birds," she advised coquettishly.

* * *

Three weeks later, Padri Masih signed for the thick, heavy registered mail package in Chandigarh and immediately had other hands helping tear it open. It contained three identical albums of pictures and a long letter from Sushila explaining each one. One album was for Sushila's parents, one was for Karam's elder sister, and one was for his parents. Padri Masih immediately hired a scooter rickshaw to take him to the sector seventeen bus station, and he caught a bus for Noorian, aware that Ruldu and Punna had waited for this day just like he and his wife. He would not have them wait a second longer than it would take for him to get there. He brought Sushila's letter along to read to them.

Seated in their *haveli* and surrounded by half the clan, Karam's family spent the afternoon until nightfall carefully studying, enjoying, and fawning over each 5 × 7 color picture, explained in great detail by Sushila in her letter. The first picture was of their civil wedding. Padri Masih noticed the absence of a cross or Christian vestments and swallowed, praying in silence for his Lord's indulgence. Another picture was of the group gathered in front of the courthouse; another one of sitting down to lunch with their happy-looking and smiling friends. Punna especially looked for Stefano and Ben, and she was proud that her daughter-in-law had dutifully worn her *bari* clothes and jewelry, as was their tradition. There were other pictures of Sushila and Karam posing alone or in groups.

There were five pictures of Sushila alone in a red sweater and blue pants in front of trees, bushes, and flowers beds, and a huge waterfall they called Niagara Falls. She looked just like an American, and very modern, thought Punna with a tinge of worry.

Pictures from the reception followed. Punna had never seen such opulence and array. There was her son and his glittering bride with people who looked rich and powerful, like lords or kings, the women with elaborate hair and gowns. The tables were laden with cutlery and crockery, crystal and silver bowls, and trays filled with steaming foods, bottles of all shapes and sizes, uniformed attendants wearing white gloves, and people raising their glasses in a salute. And in one, her son was kissing Sushila on the lips! That one mortified her and particularly the padri, but Ruldu prevented her from turning the page quickly, and several of the younger men of the clan tittered. Ruldu wore a big smile. "Now they are *Amreekans*," he announced.

"And blessedly married," the padri intoned.

"They look so good, so happy, so radiant," cried the younger sister, her eyes full of happy tears.

"And why not?" Punna asked. Then, folding her hands, she beseeched Sant Baba to keep them that way.

"Are you not going to serve some treats?" Ruldu asked

as he noticed that it was dark outside already and no one had fed or milked the cattle or taken care of the dogs. They had been too absorbed in the pictures. Everyone had a dreamy look in their eyes. Punna got up and, followed by her daughter, began serving *ladoos* and *chai*.

Chapter 21

Karam had to calm Sushila down after she had seen the troops patrolling the streets in Quebec; earlier stories of the Front de Liberation du Quebec kidnappings and killings had frightened her. She locked the apartment after he left and stayed in until he returned back from Niagara Falls, some nights very late. The TV kept her company, and she read a lot. Rebecca dropped in to take her shopping or visit the Bergers, where she was treated as a member of the family and fed all kinds of nice foods. "Eat," Mr. Berger would shout, beaming at her proudly. He had adopted her, in his mind, as a daughter, having given her away at her wedding. He only wished it had been in a house of worship—any house of worship.

Her biggest thrill was seeing snow fall for the first time. She had opened the sliding doors and stood in the balcony on the fifteenth floor, bundled up in one of Karam's old parkas and woolen pants, feet thrust into snow boots. She watched in fascination as the first of the snowflakes, some as big as cotton balls, fell slowly in the light wind, drifting around and landing on her face occasionally and immediately turning to water. She must have stood out in the cold for a couple of hours as the snow fell and covered Hamilton with a white layer. The onset of winter had been swift, the leaves turning first and falling. The nights were cooling considerably as the city turned into a drab, smoky, brownish color. The snowfall made it so nice and shiny white, and yet it was all gone by morning, replaced with a cold, wet drizzle that made her bones ache.

"You should start driving lessons," Karam suggested at breakfast. "It will get you out, and there's no better season to learn to drive in Canada than winter. It will build your skills."

"Ok," she agreed, and she enrolled in a driving program. A nice white man named Joe showed up with a huge car, but despite his repeated encouragements, her first lesson was an hour of terror as she maneuvered the behemoth through the streets. She ran back into the Villa Marie as soon as she had signed the appointment book; she was shaking but excited at the same time.

Karam could tell the difference in her that evening; she was much more animated and energized. She did, after all, have a Master's degree in English; learning excited her. Learning to drive for the first time is a thrilling and terrifying experience, and Karam he recounted his own first time behind the wheel. "But you handle the Caddy so easily," she complimented.

"These American cars drive themselves." Then getting into the mood, he asked, "What car do you like?"

Sushila thought for a moment. "A smaller car, maybe a sports car."

"A Camaro, or a Mustang," he suggested. "Those cars are beasts, very, very fast and powerful!"

"Why not a Volkswagen?" she asked, and Karam almost snorted his drink out his nostrils.

"No," he stated firmly. "Cheap tin can, not worthy of my wife."

"I would have died for one in India," she teased him, happy that he wanted something rich.

"How about a British car, a Triumph or a Mercedes,

even?"

"A Mercedes!"

And it was sealed. She would select a Mercedes-Benz the day after she got her license; she definitely looked forward to her driving lessons now.

* * *

She picked a 280SL Saloon.

When Karam told Ben of Sushila's choice of car, without hesitation Ben stated, "She has class, Karam." Karam did not mind the price of the car after the sincere compliment.

And class she brought to their marriage. Karam had lived the life of a bachelor and only spent money on himself if it enhanced his business prospects or standing. Already Sushila had trimmed her unmanageable tresses to waist length, had her eyebrows done and her facial hair plucked, shaved her legs, and had her toenails and fingernails trimmed and professionally painted. She bought the best in perfumes and understated makeup. Her wardrobe brimmed with Western, contemporary fashions and was a close second to the infamous Imelda Marcos in her collection of shoes, purses, belts, and sundries. Every week, a new piece of art hung from a wall or was carefully placed on a side table. Better bedding, towels, cutlery, crockery, and cooking wear filled the penthouse's drawers and cabinets.

The place soon filled up, and they began discussing buying a plot of land on which to build a home. Karam was getting tired of driving to Niagara Falls and back from an apartment in Hamilton: two hours back and forth daily. He suggested they bring in some sort of expert, and they ended up hiring an architect and interior design firm that the hospital engineer recommended.

Little did they realize the process would be so consuming in time, emotion, money, and work. First, they underwent a long interview process. The architect assigned to the project, a British-trained man with a wicked sense of humor, called it a needs analysis. "It is a bit of psychological profiling." He smiled and proceeded to ask a hundred questions. Realizing that he had a nouveau riche pair on his hands, he gave them a half-dozen architectural and interior design volumes to bone up on. "Understand the nomenclature," he explained.

Sushila took to the task like a bloodhound, educating herself on house styles, sizing, landscaping, materials, layout, and a thousand other descriptions. She recruited Rebecca as a willing conspirator, and they were soon joined by the Bergers and "Big Mamma" Frances Johnson, a woman she had become increasingly fond off. "Just get what you need for today, tomorrow, and the day after," were her wise words. "It is not everyday a woman has a chance to build her dream house."

Sushila had grown up in poverty and cramped quarters until hitting residence in college, where she finally had her own bed and a closet. Before she met Karam, she had a two-room quarter she shared with her parents with three cots, a table, and four chairs and two armoires. Then along came Karam and wealth, a transition so rapid but smoothed by her husband's gentleness and support from his associates. Now her parents had a bedroom and reception room on the second floor of a *kothi* in beautiful Chandigarh, and she had a penthouse apartment in Canada. She also had a Mercedes car, two fur coats, and a trunk full of gold jewelry. Karam's money bought and brought any help she ever needed. Every now and then, she still dreamed of her life in India, but she was always grateful to wake up in her warm, soft bed next to Karam in Canada.

* * *

In the end, they bought five acres of fruit land inside

Niagara-on-the-Lake and built a 5000-square-foot, classical two-story, four-bedroom home with a two-story foyer, a walkout basement, and a wraparound deck. They planted apple, peach, and cherry trees and rows of grapes, and they hired an older Italian living in the area to take care of them. Ross Watson, the architect, did his job in getting the right materials and ensuring the craftsmanship, staying within the budget but letting the money flow when it came to furnishings. He insisted on Quebec maple, which offered an elegant country look; expensive, imported Italian drapery; hand-built sofas and chairs; and cabinetry from true German artisans in Kitchener. They adorned the walls with needlepoints of hunting scenes from Britain. Karam bought the odd pieces of oriental or Indian design and placed them strategically. Sushila felt that she had earned a PhD in architecture and interior design by the time they moved to their new abode. The first day there, too excited to sleep, they christened all the bedrooms by making love in them, properly blessing their home.

Karam even started coming home for lunch, and Sushila began to cross the border more frequently to visit him at the hospital. Ben purposed that she take a part-time job with client relations because she was in public relations in India, and she accepted the position, but the paperwork for a working visa took a month, and that was after pulling strings with the state senator's office in Washington. They were on the senator's radar both for their political contributions and the fact that the hospital was a good spot for glad-handing and photo ops for the wily politician. However, a month after starting her new job, Sushila got pregnant with their first child. Thankfully for her, the Drs. Varghese had arrived, and she came under the welcome care of Dr. Mrs. Varghese, who was now an obstetrics resident. Sushila was so much more comfortable with her, having known her in India. Her husband took to his tasks at the hospital laboratory with passion.

"You should sponsor your parents," Dr. Mrs. Varghese suggested, "and your mother can help you with the baby."

"I have a feeling both of our mothers will want in on this," Karam replied when she brought up the subject.

Hearing that Padri Sahib and his wife had been asked to move to Canada to help raise their unborn grandchild, Ruldu smiled. "After he built the nest, the sparrow laid the egg."

"And you better start packing," Punna laughed, "unless you want to sleep with the buffaloes this winter."

* * *

At that time, proper documents made the task of obtaining immigration a two-month affair, and the two sets of parents landed in Toronto together on a sunny August day. Karam and Sushila met their parents at the airport; Karam drove his parents to the estate in his Cadillac, and Sushila drove hers in her Mercedes. They sped down the Queen Elizabeth Way, both mothers bawling their hearts out in happiness and the fathers snoring in the comfort of air-conditioning and the smooth lulling of the road. They did not sleep the first night as there was so much to talk about, see, and examine, and they sipped *chai* tea into the wee hours of the night, spread out on the deck, oblivious to the odd buzzing of a persistent mosquito. They slept in almost into the early afternoon, unbothered by the racket made by the tractor Mr. Tedesco used to cut the grass on the sprawling grounds, now nicely landscaped with his expert eye and hands. He had left just about this much land in his village in Italy to earn a living in an auto plant in St. Catherines, but an industrial injury had forced early retirement from the robotic bending he had to perform on the line. This job was a godsend. He enjoyed telling his wife, "I do it for nothing, no pay."

"I hope you don't say that to the rich *Indiani*, no!" she cried.

He could hardly wait for the grapevines to mature, and then he was really going to show the art that lay buried in him. He had already managed to have the shed built to his specifications, and he was putting the tools of his trade together. Mr. Pardesi agreed to his every suggestion, and they were going to private label the bottles "Pardesi Wines." The boss was going to give them out as gifts to his staff and the doctors, but he would leave enough for Mr. Tedesco to sip on for a year.

His plan was to start with imported California grapes, and the first few years he would experiment with a bit of mixing and matching varieties, making different batches. This year, he had capacity to make 3,000 liters with imported grapes, and over the next two years, he could build it up to 6,000. Once the fruit trees matured, he would start dabbling in apple, peach, and cherry brandy, and if no one was looking, a little *grappa* for trickling in his coffee. He was on the lookout for more land. He knew this place was special; it just needed the right minds and hearts, and they could produce world class *vino* and *liquori* here. As he turned the tractor toward the house, he saw a turbaned figure wave at him from the balcony and a practically bald-headed man next to him. "Ah," he thought, "the *genitori* are here." He waved back, now eager to see the elders and show off his handiwork. He had known that the boss's father came from a village and owned land and cattle. "Same as me," he thought. Mr. Tedesco's family kept cows, pigs, and chickens, too.

They were in the back, standing on the lawn as he came

by. He shut off the tractor and clambered down. "Good day," he raised a hand and walked up to shake their hands. The turbaned elder was huge, while the one beside him was rail thin. Then he saw Sushila walk out with the two old ladies, and they folded their hands and bowed to him. He waved back. She introduced him, and the foursome smiled and nodded. "They want to take a look?"

"Sure."

He led them through the rows over the four acres he commanded. Sushila translated, and at the mention of wine from grapes and brandy from the fruit, the big man grinned and winked at him, obviously a man who enjoyed a sip. He was amazed to find that her father, the skeletal one, was a priest, and a Christian, one too. "Boy," he thought, "what do you know?" So he led them to his pride and joy, the big aluminum-sided shed with a sloping roof, a concrete floor, insulated walls, and all the paraphernalia of wine making being set-up in there. He asked Padri Masih to bless it and stood with his hands folded and head bowed while the holy man intoned a lengthy prayer in Indian. The only word he really understood was *amen* at the end, and they shook hands all around.

* * *

Ben had hired Tim Davis to analyze all the business proposals and investment opportunities that came his way, and they had taken positions in four categories: pharmaceuticals, rehabilitation services, condominium building in Florida, and oil and gas exploration in Alberta. They had a total of $12 million invested in the Niagara Falls Hospital and Clinic and showed a net pre-tax profit of almost $5 million a year. Their $30 million in ventures returned a healthy 12 percent after tax. They technically banked almost $6 million a year after salaries and bonuses to themselves. Now Ben had started making noises about putting some money in start-ups in Israel and also trying his hand at investing in India.

"Why don't you go and look around," Karam suggested, now starting to sport an obvious belly. A sure sign of wealth and a pregnant wife, Ben mused.

"You want me to?" he asked. Karam nodded, and Ben started making plans.

He was speaking to one of their brokers in New York about their plans to seek good ventures in Israel and India when the man suggested exploring an intriguing opportunity. A pharmaceutical company located near New Delhi, owned by two Indian brothers with the last name Jain, needed American dollars to finance the purchase of capsule-making machines and other capital goods. They were unable to raise the money through normal banking channels, including the Reserve Bank of India. Lack of foreign exchange reserves and other priorities had prevented the main source of foreign capital for most Indian firms from doing business abroad. "You can pretty well ask for the moon here," the broker said. "And it is a good investment for someone who knows India and is willing to be patient."

"How much do they need?" Ben asked.

"Two million."

"And what do you think they are willing to give up?"

"Considering the fact that this will make them India's third-largest drug packager, I would say 35 to 40 percent."

Ben whistled. "Let me talk to Karam."

They studied the proposal, and Karam talked to the Jains in Panipat. They sounded sincere and professional, both brothers with foreign PhDs in pharmaceuticals. Karam asked their auditors to suggest an auditing firm in New Delhi to begin the due diligence and find a commercial law firm there. In short order, they got the green light, and the Jain brothers arrived in America to sign the papers. Realizing that they were giving a partnership to a *Chura*, these highborn men held their noses, accepted the terms, and shook Karam's hand. "We can wash off the stain in the Ganges," they pledged to each other. They politely excused themselves, citing strict dietary requirements, when offered food and drink. Back in India, they kept the deal a secret; they did not tell anyone in their circle that they were now growing with the money of a lowborn. It would not help the matrimonial opportunities of their beloved children.

For Karam, it would turn out to be one of the best investments they would ever make as India was slowly but surely starting to look beyond its borders at the rest of the modern world, having failed in uplifting masses through Nehru's policies of self-sufficiency. The patently corrupt political and bureaucratic system had seen to that.

Neither did the fact that one of the most flush-with-cash Indians in America was a lowborn prevent their Indian auditors and commercial lawyer from spreading the word. Confidentiality prevented them from mentioning the Jains of Panipat Pharma Industries Ltd. Within a month, at least a hundred investment proposals had landed at their door. They recommended five to Karam and Ben, who told them to be patient; they wanted to see the first venture mature some.

* * *

In Israel, Ben could not believe the frenzy of entrepreneurism and innovation the country was going through. It was also a matter of survival. Constantly under threat of war and boycott, Israel had turned inwards and started to create, improve, and improvise. They had a vast pool of highly educated mathematicians, scientists, and thinkers, and they enjoyed a flow of capital from the Jewish Diaspora in America and Britain and what was affluent in Asia, Latin America, and Europe, too. They went to places to gain resources others would not dare. Seeing the struggle of his people and the quiet determination on their faces, Ben gave seed capital to about eight eager men and women and their nascent ideas and notions, but he kept in mind his strict discipline of credibility of principle. They were not in the charity business but did perform it when necessary.

They were in it for the money, and if it could be made in places that few others were thinking about—like in Israel and India—it only gave them a head start and a good feeling.

Ben and Karam had stumbled onto even greener pastures.

Chapter 22

With twenty or so Indian doctors and as many nurses and technologists working at the hospital, Sushila had at first dismissed their reluctance to socialize with the boss as customary Indian deference to authority. However, as she noticed the Christians and lower caste Indians accepting their invitations and returned the favor, it became clearer to her that the higher caste Hindus were deliberately avoiding association, just subtly and politely. Dr. Mrs. Varghese, now a closer friend and frequent fellow shopping buddy, was blunter. "Just like the Brahmins in our village in Kerala," she opined.

Karam was dismissive of Sushila's suspicions. "We cannot worry about those things here in North America," he stated, and he refused to discuss the subject further. He cautioned her against showing animosity or grudges against the offenders. "We recruited them for their skills, not their social dancing. They contribute to our success."

When it came to selecting names for their child just three months from being born, she began to obsess about the child's social status and the harm the caste issue could do to its future. She began thinking about ways to avoid the distinctions of their ancient society. Karam had selected the last name Pardesi; she thought to avoid just such linking. Typically *Churas* were Bhangi or Balmiki or variations of either. Her family, despite the conversion to Christianity, still faced discrimination from the upper castes there. Some

Sikhs had stopped treating fellow devout Sikhs from lesser castes as different, but the rural folks were still very much hidebound in their traditions and customs. To them, the highborn were pure and the lowborn *Churas* and *Chamars* polluted and to be avoided, whether from direct touch, sharing a meal, or accepting food or water from them. Some even avoided their shadow falling upon them. Others viewed them as bad luck if seen first in the morning.

Padri Masih offered a simple solution. "Give your children Western names."

Sushila felt better. They would combine Western first names with the last name Pardesi, as it was not a known caste name; it was just a generic term for an Indian living abroad. She asked Karam's opinion. He wanted to defer to his parents, and both Ruldu and Punna wanted Punjabi names. They suggested Sukhdev, which means giver of comfort, if it was a boy, in honor of Karam, and Sukhjeet, a winner of comfort, for a girl. A debate started. Padri Masih, finally unable to take anymore of the persistent arguing that was marring the happily anticipated occasion, recalled Karam's promise to him, reminding him in front of his parents that Sushila would raise the children in her faith.

"Biblical names, then," they all agreed after much explaining about the bible to Karam's nonplussed parents.

Others now engrossed themselves in helping them. The Bergers came up with a list of five names for a boy and five for a girl. Ben simply wanted a boy named after him and a girl after Rebecca. "Because we are going to be godparents," he argued. "You know that your kids will be raised as Hebrews if anything happens to you guys," he added. Karam wished him luck. Frances Johnson spent hours reading the bible in English with Padri Masih, and she liked the name Mark for a boy and Sarah for a girl.

"Why not Frances?" Karam asked.

"Not biblical enough," Padri Masih stated firmly.

Punna and Ruldu watched and listened in impotent silence, the debate having left them behind. Then she finally suggested, "How about Sant?"

"Or, how about Baba?" Sushila retorted, and she suddenly felt ashamed and apologized profusely when she saw the pained look on her mother-in-law's face. "You will have to forgive her," Karam insisted. "It is her condition, all pregnant and fat now."

For that, he got a tongue lashing later in the bedroom.

"So I am all fat now, eh?" She rolled away from his embrace in bed. Karam could hardly wait for the arguing to end.

"Hey, listen," he whispered, "how about Mark if it's a boy and Sarah if it's a girl?"

"Huh," Sushila snorted, but liking his tone and the way he was massaging her when he had pronounced the names, she filed them as done. She was still upset at his description of her to his mother.

* * *

By the time their son Mark turned five, he had a brother named Benjamin and a sister named Sarah. The family attended the Anglican Church in Niagara-on-the-Lake. He would start school at the private campus of Applewood Academy, an expensive institution, now attracting a number of foreign students in its upper grades. His grandparents had settled into a routine of six months in India and six in Canada, its harsh winters hard on their joints, the Punjab offering a salubrious autumn and winter. His two maternal uncles were now teachers in Toronto. Karam's older sister lived in Hamilton, where her daughter was a nurse at the newly minted McMaster University Medical Center, her son studying engineering. The younger sister and brother-in-law still lived in Noorian, but their children were in colleges in New York State. The Pardesi Estate private labeled wines were starting to make their mark as Mr. Tedesco now lorded over forty acres and a group of twenty seasonal and four full-time employees. The winery occupied its own stone mansion and storage on the new plot just a mile away from the main house.

Karam mourned the passing of Dr. Grewal from old age and Mr. Berger from complications of diabetes and heart problems. Ben stayed away more and more, managing their new investment bank, P&R Capital Partners, which formed from the windfall of their Alberta and Florida investments, part of its capital contributed by the Israeli and Indian investments. Ben and Karam were considering purchasing a seat on the NASDAQ exchange but shied from the scrutiny it would involve. The Niagara Falls Hospital and Clinic now owned three other out-patient medical centers staffed by Indian physicians poached from the CMC and other medical schools in Punjab and New Delhi, as well as Bombay and Vellore. Their net worth now jointly approached $100 million.

Around them, Canada was changing. The cerebral and cosmopolitan prime minister, Pierre Trudeau, after a bad start with the War Measures Act and having survived the Front de Liberation du Quebec crisis in Quebec, had turned on the charm internationally, putting the country on the world's stage. Reacting mightily to the plight of Southeast Asians in Uganda, he saved thousands from the atrocities meted upon them by the vicious dictator Idi Amin, opening Canada's borders and letting the fleeing Ugandans into the country, soon followed by greater immigration from the third world. He also introduced multiculturalism into the lexicon of Canada. In Niagara Falls in Canada, Southeast Asians owned most of the motels and variety stores. Others invested in upstart franchises that needed the manpower of a hardworking and dedicated extended family to survive and thrive. Donut and coffee shops, chicken and burger joints, hardware and lighting stores, and pharmacies; all had brown people running and working in them. An influx of needed medical workers, engineers, technicians, teachers, mechanics, and plain, old laborers supported the service and manufacturing sectors.

An Indian restaurant opened in the town, its take-out meals going to non-Indian homes at a 10 to1 ratio. Hindi, Punjabi, and Urdu could be heard spoken regularly as people posed in front of the Falls each weekend, hordes of them descending on the natural wonder from Toronto and other towns and cities within driving distance. At first quietly and then openly, the white residents, mostly of Anglo stock, began denouncing this "invasion" by the colored folk. As racism had become increasingly open in Britain, the word its skinheads had coined to taunt the immigrants with soon became common in Canada.

Paki!

Paki was often used as a curse word whenever a conflict erupted over a parking spot or minor altercation. The newcomers took over the earlier abuse hurled at the Italians and Eastern European immigrants, its cyclical nature now their inheritance. The word was used without discriminating about the origin of the recipient. Thus Indians, Pakistanis, Bangladeshis, Sri Lankans, Iranians, and even darker Mediterranean people found themselves its target.

"Hey, I am Persian," one would protest at a bar to some snarling racist.

"You all look the same to me, you fucking *Paki*," came

the response, and unless the Persian was well-versed in pounding someone's face in, he swallowed his pride, hung his head down, and waited it out or for some outraged white man to shout the perpetrator down.

Young Asian men started to move around in small groups for protection, sometimes with swords and such hidden in the trunks of their cars.

It really bothered helpless parents when their children arrived home in tears from the taunts and bullying by the kids of the majority. Some went to complain to the teachers and principals; others told their kids to suck it up; a few putting their children in self-defense classes. Sometimes, the bullied got help from the other minorities who had suffered similar episodes. In some towns, the Southeast Asians, particularly angry at a woman having been insulted, hit back with vicious beatings of the perpetrator, or in rare cases, attacks with swords, severely injuring their targets.

All in all, it was an unpleasant and disturbing revelation for some older residents who had experienced racism but not such an in-your-face type of intimidating, naked hatred. For the newcomers, it hit like a brick to the head, particularly for the highborn, accustomed to always being able to bully, harass, and push their lowborn fellow citizens around and enjoy their exalted status in their localities; these confrontations left them shaking and shocked. Many felt a helpless rage. The more aggressive perpetrators were like typical bullies, hunting in the safety of packs, but when challenged, they often shut up and hurried off.

Sushila now sat on the boards of several local charities. As the wife of one of the region's richest men and philanthropists, combined with her looks and manners, she was sought after by any group holding a function or fete to raise funds for a cause. Watching her in silent fury were the ignored wives of the highborn who were neither rich nor generous, but they felt slighted. Therefore, a lot of silly chattering went on behind Sushila's back with some very cutting and hurtful remarks made among some tittering. Not realizing that Canadians were some of the least caste- or class-oriented people in the world, they were disappointed when they tried to not-so-innocently degrade her community standing. Word of a particularly nasty woman talking bad about her reached Sushila's ears. She was the wife of a Brahmin surgeon who had finally been able to afford a big house and a Mercedes, but she always smiled nicely and said hello in such a sweet voice to Sushila.

As her son had recently come home from school supporting a bruised eye and a torn jacket, she spoke up at the mall when she ran into Sushila. "My goodness," she started in Hindi, "they are like uneducated, uncouth animals, these whites. Makes me feel so, so ...."

"Like a *Churi*," Sushila finished for her, looking steadily into her eyes.

"What are you saying?" protested the distraught mother of a bullied son.

"Like I hear you often talk about the lesser castes," Sushila continued in an even, polite tone. "Because you are the keeper of Hindu traditions, now the whites think of us all in the same way."

"Why, why Mrs. Pardesi ..."

"Now we are all equals. At least in Canada," hissed Sushila. "We are all *Pakis*."

Turning on her, Sushila walked off in the opposite direction.

* * *

In the pathology laboratory of the Niagara Falls Hospital and Clinic, Dr. Varghese, a resident pathologist, began to notice some abnormalities in tissue and blood samples sent to him for analysis. Thinking it odd that most of them were concentrated from patients in a particular area of the city, he bought a street map and began to track the results street by street. At that period in history, concerns about chemicals were beginning to be raised in prominent medical journals, and certain organizations and media personalities focused on the environmental degradation caused by sulfur in the fuel resulting from coal-fired power generation plants. People blamed the acid rain for emptying the Great Lakes of certain species of plants and animals. Levels of lead particulate in the air, mercury in the waters, and deadly concoctions in pesticides and herbicides threatened human, animal, and plant life.

The Great Lakes were becoming the cauldrons of a chemical soup rather than a life-sustaining resource so vital to the health of a large number of North Americans living in highly industrialized cities on their shores. These industries fed the economy and the standards of living and made the United States the world's greatest and biggest economy and the most dominant military power. These were troubling times, though; the war in Vietnam and its multiplicity of problems both foreign and domestic, an oil shock of only a year before, a president in the White House under siege, and rampant inflation contributed to the unrest.

None of the other issues were of concern for the scientific mind of Dr. Varghese. He wanted to get to the bottom of the bad results in the laboratory that were forming a pattern. He took it up with the chief of medical services, Dr. Holmans, and got a lukewarm show of interest. He felt he needed to get better data—more consistent and statistically relevant—and went to work.

* * *

Panipat Pharma now had an investment of $10 million from P&R Capital and was essentially controlled by its new principal partner, Karam Pardesi. It was now the second-largest packager of drugs in India, with multimillion dollar contracts with large patent-holding pharmaceutical giants in Europe and the United States. Not only did it make cheaper drugs for the domestic Indian market, but it also exported those drugs to the poor countries in Asia and Africa. A few orders started to go to Latin America, the first signs of an emergent drug manufacturing capacity and capability in India. The Reserve Bank of India loosened the investment rules a bit to allow quiet repatriation of capital and profits in dollars and other currencies by investors in some key industries, like pharmaceuticals. With no local research and development capability, technologies necessary to the country's health and security were particular beneficiaries of an otherwise oppressive "License Raj" that strangled enterprise and innovation and left most of the consumers vulnerable to local oligarchies and monopolies controlled by power families numbering about one dozen, the Tatas and Birlas most prominent among them. Due to their diversified portfolio of investments, P&R could move quickly to take advantage of certain situations in these restrictive environments and began to make huge returns on them. It also helped that Karam maintained a dual citizenship. He was unique in that he was an Indian citizen with millions in foreign exchange to invest. They came to him in droves now, often referred directly by the Reserve Bank and its management. It helped also that the honorable Chandu Das pulled strings when necessary.

Karam's nephew, the engineering student, came to visit for a weekend and brought with him a new-fangled calculator. The hand-sized, battery-operated device did all kinds of mathematical computations within seconds. When Karam asked its cost, the youth replied, "Four hundred and fifty dollars, and mother is still smarting from it."

"What?"

"Yes, Uncleji," he insisted, "and I would not know how to function without it. Every engineering student has to have one."

"That is a great cost though," Karam argued, still amazed at the capabilities of the device.

"You should see what they are starting to come out with. I am changing my major to Electronic Engineering next semester."

"What do you mean?"

"Electronics, Uncleji, is going to be big. You see this calculator; Professor Saini told us that he foresees everyone owning one not too far into the future, and with economies of scale factored in, it could be selling for twenty dollars in just five years."

"That cheap?"

"Yes, and more. There is stuff being developed that will be so, so amazing, and I am very, very excited about it."

Karam mentioned the conversation to Ben on the phone. "Well, you and I are booked to hear a twenty-year-old kid talk about the future just like your nephew talked about it in Albuquerque next month."

"Will life ever stop amazing me?" thought Karam.

"Uncleji, invest in this industry; believe me," his nephew emphasized before leaving, giving Karam some of the best advice a family member had ever given him.

Karam had received approval to sever and build more residential area on his five-acre lot. Padri and Mrs. Masih and his parents soon enjoyed their granny quarters, and the many family members now resident in North America had real beds to sleep on when they came to visit. This allowed Sushila and Karam privacy and the children the unfettered run of the main house. The garage, which was once the old wine shed, stored alternately their winter and summer vehicles, and above it lived the Filipino nanny and a housekeeper. In the spring and summer, they hired a local retiree to drive the old folks around and keep them occupied. But intrusions occurred weekly and unannounced. His elder sister called to visit urgently and arrived the same evening accompanied by her teary-eyed daughter, the nurse.

"Tell us, *Bhenji*," Sushila beseeched as Karam's sister wept into her shawl, his parents looking on with downcast faces as his niece cried, curled into a ball on a chair.

"I am ruined. What can I do?"

"What is ruining you?" Karam asked in a thunderous tone that Punjabis everywhere recognized as familial authority. Even Sushila looked askance at him.

Suddenly sitting up straight and somber, Karam's sister replied, "Ask her. She's ruining the family name." She pointed at her daughter, Karam's niece, who now sat ramrod straight.

"What drama is this?" Karam still had memories of Noorian and the elders who struck the fear of God via their voice.

"He is ... he is," the niece began, gaining a bit of confidence as Sushila moved to her side, "he is a doctor from South Africa, Reza Nathoo. His grandfather knew the Mahatma."

The old world was meeting the new, Karam realized. "And what is going on?"

"He wants to marry me."

"And what is wrong with that?" Karam asked his sister, and she looked at him as if he had gone mad.

"They want a love marriage! Do you not see the shame of it?"

"Shame of what, *Bhenji*?" asked Sushila. "A doctor is asking for your daughter's hand in marriage. Where is the shame in that?"

"We are the cream of our caste and can get the best candidate in India for her," Punna intervened, obviously privy to all the information prior to the visit and having stewed over it. Even Ruldu squared his shoulders.

"We are *Churas*," Karam stated.

There was an instant silence as the gathered looked at him as if he had uttered a blasphemy.

"Let us not forget our past," Karam hissed. The childhood of deprivation and want, of insults and hunger, the ancient fetid courtyard, its smells and dirt! He could taste them, and his nostrils flared, his lips thinned, and his eyes turned a strange red. His family cowered. Sushila looked at him with a mouth wide open in shock and silence.

"Yes, we are," he continued, "but because you have all been spoiled by our good fortune and do not trust it, you want to return to the good old days: the same habits, the same ugly customs."

"No, no, no," Punna moaned, covering her mouth with her shawl.

"Then let her break out," Karam said, pointing to his niece. "Let her be loved and cherished for what she is, a beautiful woman, and a qualified woman. Don't enslave her to the old ways."

They heard him: the plea in his voice, the unuttered threat implicit.

Cling to the old ways and lose.

Chapter 23

Punna and Ruldu returned to Noorian to spend six months walking around, sitting outside, soaking in the sun, and visiting their daughter and son-in-law, who had chosen to remain behind to take care of the cattle, the land, and the *haveli,* as well as the Sant Baba *samadhi.* This time, they disappointed many, as they now had to say no to the many offers of marriage for their granddaughter. She had chosen an unknown for a husband, his being a doctor notwithstanding. Punna had truly looked forward to Karam's wedding that never happened in Noorian. No bands had played, no men danced and drank, no women sang or clapped in her courtyard, and she now pinned "greening" the *haveli* on her grandchildren. They were hoping at least to have their weddings held there. She had become an elder of her clan and the village. Such was the impact of Karam's good deeds on the community that several youth now went to college or trained in technical schools. Most *Chura* children, including the children of other lesser castes, now outshone the highborn children in education. No child grazed cattle, suffered the indignity of indenture, or lacked for nutrition. Her son, Karam, had seen to that.

The village was more prosperous from a number of families now enjoying remittances from sons in foreign lands or employed in city jobs or the army. The new varieties of wheat gave bountiful harvests, and the *Jats* began buying tractors with trolleys attached and other labor-saving devices. Electric motors and diesel engines hummed in fields pumping water, running harvesters and cutting fodder. Several dozen men now traveled from the south to work as itinerant laborers in the fields as the youth of the village turned from tilling to other tasks, leaving a shortage of manpower. Some *Jat* families flush with the cash from remittances and the high income from the land now had men who did not work but sat around the village square and played cards, talked politics, watched the women go by, and later in the afternoon, stumbled home, barely erect from imbibing bottles of alcohol. Several thus idled were now addicts to opium and other narcotics or various concoctions. The moral fabric was adrift. Priests in temples screamed sermons and shouted for reform, and some not yet so affected took to religion as a preventative measure. These men sported long beards, *kirpans* slung from the shoulder, and blue turbans. They frequented the *Gurudwaras* at least once if not twice a day to listen to the recitation of the holy hymns and prayers.

Others were liberated from debt and labor, shorned off their Sikh appearance, and spent time in towns and cities picking up the habit of smoking and the chewing of *paan*. It was as if two parallel cultures were developing among the villagers: the devout and the opposite of devout.

To calm herself, Punna began the long planning for the annual prayers and gathering at the *samadhi*, seeking solace in contemplation. Ruldu, of course played cards under the now massive trees in the courtyard with other clan members looking for a free drink and snacks he was only too pleased to provide. His entourage had grown to at least a dozen. To serve them, at least one *chula* at the hearth was constantly stoked, the fires burning and boiling water for endless rounds of tea. Punna went to the temples and the mosque to tithe in honor of her martyred father, Bola, and she fed a meal to the virgins of her clan, hoping that it would be passed on to her parents in the afterlife. Then she swept the *samadhi* with her own hands and did *prakarma* by walking around it and the monument to her father a total of seven times, stopping to bow with folded hands and whisper prayers beseeching their protection of her family, now scattered around Canada and the United States.

Every house had a radio now, and the occupants had several choices of broadcasters, so music played all day, and the young whiled away their time listening and nodding to the beat. A telephone line had finally been strung to the village, and even the *haveli* had a telephone, but it only rang from calls made from Canada or the United States. She had forbidden its use otherwise as the charges were eye-popping, as were the charges for the electricity Ruldu used. But that she forgave as it was more a matter of security. A well-lit home invited fewer thieveries; the perpetrators preferred the dark. The odd antennae was raised on the roofs of some houses after All India Radio started a TV service for the Punjab, although most people tuned to the Pakistani channel from Lahore, even if it was illegal to do so, preferring its fare to the dull, amateur broadcasts of the upstarts from India.

Family planning now provided free condoms and intrauterine loops, and a kind of underground renaissance started to flower: sexual freedom, freedom from the fear of pregnancy. Many young brides were left behind in the village by the husbands seeking fortunes in the Middle East or the city, even the army, leaving many unsatisfied for months or years on end. Rumors of illicit liaisons were whispered unendingly. Everyone was under suspicion, including the single priests and servers at the temples and *guruji* at the *samadhi* and his flock of youthful disciples; the itinerant workers from the south and the lazy, well-fed louts of the village. Bus stop restaurants and *dhabas* offered discreet booths and cubicles for quick encounters, popular with the college-going gaggles and groups. Buses full of young students left each day only to disgorge them back in the evening. The parents were clueless as to how their kids had spent the day: in a classroom or at the back of a *dhaba*. A number of honor killings took place, still failing to put a dent in the suspected activities.

Punna was grateful before, but now she was fearful. She had visions of her grandchildren exercising the freedom their uncle had decreed and marrying any manner of race or religion. How could they stay a united family if her grandchildren started marrying outside their race? Non-Indians! At least the first to fall had married an Indian from Africa. Who would be next, and who would she do the shopping for, the *bari*? Would it even be accepted or appreciated? She found that she had begun to talk to herself. Who else would understand her fears? Progress was exacting its price, and the price was her future generations.

* * *

The first thing that Padri Masih and his wife did upon arriving at the *kothi* in Chandigarh was air it out, as it was closed during the warm months of April, May, and June and during the hot and humid months of July and August. They arrived in October, and it took opening all of the windows for a day to get rid of the staleness. His wife got help from a couple of ladies in the neighborhood, and they hung out the mattresses, rugs, sheets, and blankets. The charwomen who worked in the neighborhood scrubbed the floors and walls to get rid of the fine dust caking every nook and cranny. It took three days to breathe well and live civilly in the substantial home. They encouraged relatives and friends to visit and stay. Some of Padri Masih's old friends, now retired and surviving on small pensions, were only too happy to spend a week or two luxuriating in Chandigarh and being fed the best dishes the cook hired for the stay could muster. They caught up with the news and always talked of the condition of Christianity and its prospects in India, the CMC and any changes, the Church, and the bishop.

They took a daily bus ride for the fifteen kilometers up into the hills to walk the multi-terraced gardens of Pinjore, and a couple of evenings, they went to sit by the shores of the manmade lake and the stalls around it. It always had a festive atmosphere as people came to perform exercises, ride in the paddle boats, or simply walk along its cobbled edge with a view of Kasauli, 4,000 feet up on the closest mountain. By the time they caught the local bus back, all the lights were on, and it looked like a city in the sky.

The other evenings, they visited the famous Rose Gardens, which now exported flowers by air to the palaces of Middle East royalty. The hundreds of varieties of multihued roses were fragrant in the coolness of the setting sun.

They truly appreciated the thoughtful hospitality of their friend and relative, the padri, who in his newfound prosperity never let them feel uncomfortable; sharing what was his selflessly and humbly. On the way back to their villages or towns, they chattered incessantly of the man's generosity and said prayers for the couple's health, hoping that these sojourns continued far into the future.

* * *

The Comrade sat in his office at the community center and began reviewing the academic reports on the village's scholarship recipients. Under his guidance, the Noorian Education Trust, completely funded by Karam, now provided full fees and residence costs to over thirty of the brightest youth, boys and girls, almost half and half. The boys mostly chose engineering or sciences, and the girls tended to choose humanities and education. Few youth from Noorian tackled nursing or medicine. The first group of scholarship recipients had already received their undergraduate degrees or diplomas, and three had chosen to advance to master's programs, a feat unknown in the Comrade's times, and all were young women forgoing jobs and marriages to undertake another two to three years of advanced studies. The records all reflected one fact: the scholars lived up to their promise and never scored marks under a B in all subjects. The Comrade made sure they got their monies in time. Keeping faith was a two-way street, and Karam had left a substantial reserve with the trust to fulfill that purpose.

The elementary and high schools were the envy of the district, if not the province: regularly maintained, cleanliness a condition, teacher and student attendance exemplary, and the library bursting with newspapers, journals, and magazines, not to mention periodicals and reference books. The community center's adult education part housed the regular section of fiction and fact books for general reading. The playgrounds held regular tournaments in field hockey and *kabbadi*. Volleyball was the rage among the girls. Cricket and football were thinly attended. The school band was exceptional, leading all marches and parades; the scouts and ACC provided another outlet of social learning, values, and patriotism, particularly after the two more recent but victorious wars against Pakistan.

The rural health and the veterinary clinics hummed with activity most mornings, slowing in the afternoon to just the odd emergency walk-ins. The Comrade personally supervised the dried milk quotas for needy families and the extra rations for the school athletes. He also took the time to attend award ceremonies, no matter the distance, for any winners on his scholars list.

Unknown even to his wife, he took trips to Panipat Pharma, where he was the nominee director on behalf of Karam to sit through board meetings, sift through quarterly reports, listen to management plans, and examine their performance. It was a capitalist's task, and he performed it with an avid fascination. Karam had opened a whole new world for him: the world of high finance, technology, innovation, and shareholder value and investment returns. He was listed as Dr. Surjit Singh on the brass nameplate that hung behind his chair in the massive boardroom of the organization, now occupying over ten acres of prime land on the Grand Trunk Road. He was chauffeured from the railway station, kept in the onsite guestroom, and chauffeured back to catch his train, traveling in first class.

Not bad, he would muse, for an earlier and ardent communist, now a Comrade in name only. The moniker had stuck, however, and provided cover for the substantial compensation he received from Panipat Pharma for his quarterly duties. It more than compensated for the time he spent volunteering for the Noorian Education Trust.

* * *

The Model Gram concept had spread into every district of every province and territory of India and stood as a progressive beacon for what the country could be in a few short decades. Ajit Singh continued to receive and accept credit for his idea and its proper execution. He now taught it as a subject as a guest lecturer for both the Indian Administrative Services and the Indian Civil Services academies, which trained the high-value technocrats of the future. He had received several rewards and sat on review committees, boards, and advisory panels, and he was one of the few district commissioners who traveled abroad as part of diplomatic entourages to attend foreign gatherings of like-minded developing and unaligned nations. He hosted other Asian and African interns in regional governance and continued to promote Ludhiana as a center of industrial opportunity in small tools manufacturing and textiles and leather goods. He was proud that the city now had consular offices of several countries resident there. They were more like trade offices manned by a one- or two-man team, but it was an honor nonetheless. He was also proud of the Punjab Agricultural University, two medical schools, an engineering college, and a handful of technical training centers, not to mention the five undergraduate colleges and the dozens of private schools for the children of the affluent and the rising middle class. The numerous small businesses, retail shops, and home-based cottage industries employed tens of thousands. The export of finished and value-added goods to almost every country of the Warsaw Pact and other developing nations—particularly bicycles, batteries, woolen garments and shoes—supplemented the barter system of payment, resulting in the purchase of advanced weapons and industrial technologies by the central government without having to raise hard currency loans in Western Europe or the United States.

He was also one of the several hundred civil servants who worked on the Five-Year Development Plans for the country and could see their slow but tangible fruit in the progress India was making in an industrial capacity, agricultural output, and export development. The defense budget, now consuming almost 50 percent of the country's revenue, cut deeply into its central plans, but the slow loosening of investment rules—particularly for individuals like Karam

Pardesi—was helping uplift the private sector without any support from the public purse.

The biggest enemy of progress for India was its unfettered growth in population, which often wiped out and overwhelmed the snail's pace of growth and progress.

Ajit Singh had been asked in a letter from a senior advisor, a Harvard-trained economist, to analyze and recommend changes to the ministers of industry and finance and help right the wrongs of socialism. He sat down and burned the midnight oil for a week. In the end, his recommendation was that India remove all unnecessary barriers to trade and foreign investment and make the country welcome with open arms and hearts those that could truly raise it to its old glory: that of one of the richest sectors of the world and of barely two centuries ago.

* * *

The Honorable Chandu Das, member of Parliament, Vice-Chairman of the Congress Party, and in line for the presidency of the country, had recently vacated his ministerial post as part of the horse trading that went on in the reign of Prime Minister Indira Gandhi, a surprisingly steely willed woman, quite unlike her consensus-seeking father, Jawahar Lal Nehru, the Uncle of India. Only the Mahatma was the Father of the Nation. Now, the daughter positioned and maneuvered all her MPs and ministers like chess pieces across India's checkerboard of interests. The lesser classes and castes her main bulwark of support counterbalanced the communal and regional parties. She had put an end to dynastic rulers of India by canceling their royal titles, privileges, and positions, turning them into ordinary citizens. She had fought a successful war against Pakistan and thus liberated the new nation of Bangladesh. The bonus was the capture, imprisonment, and humiliation of 125,000

Pakistani troops, the largest POW number since the end of the Second World War. She had defied the West by exploding a nuclear device, thus restoring another measure of national pride and warning China and its territorial ambitions. Her father had watched helplessly the usurpation of Tibet, too weak militarily and pacifistic to intervene, but she had no such qualms.

Ruthless, ambitious, and intolerant of opposition, this pint-sized woman commanded respect as one of the world's first democratically elected rulers.

Chandu Das was honored to be invited and fully advised of her plans at a private lunch alone with the prime minister. He immediately adjusted his periscope for further opportunities and extracted several concessions, all under the guise of public service and patriotism. He would now wield considerably more power behind the scenes, all the while glad-handing and giving out handouts to the miserable and unwashed and unheard of his caste and community. The *Churas*, despite forming with the *Chamars* and other *dalits* a 30 percent voting bloc, thus empowering their own like Chandu Das, remained as the dredges of society, and on a percentage basis, they were the least benefited despite so many constitutional guarantees. Being mostly illiterate, they were not even aware of what a constitution was, much less able to understand its nuances and be able to manipulate them. Some, though, had benefited more by happenstance than circumstance, but they continued to vote for the Congress Party of Gandhi, and Nehru, and now his daughter.

Enriched now beyond his capacity to hide or thrive in his hidden wealth, the politician lived a double if not a triple life: in the light of day, he performed visible acts of service in humility with folded hands; behind closed doors, he hammered out tough deals benefiting his leader; and in the darkness of the night, he indulged his passion for alcohol and debauchery. Although nearly sixty years old, he could still drink much younger men under the table, and he had a particular taste for the small-boned and dark-skinned women of the south. His substantial bungalow in New Delhi, sheltered behind high walls and massive foliage, its gates guarded by armed police, was mostly populated with maids, who were winsome, lithe, and willing.

He had long ago learned that every society—whether communist, socialist, democratic, monarchist, or a dictatorship—paid a price for governance. He termed it *leakage* and pegged the cost to the national gross domestic product at 10 percent. As part of his hard-earned position in the government of the world's second-most populated country, he had earned his part of the leakage and was going to enjoy it to the fullest. As an untouchable, he had no gods or goddesses to fear.

* * *

Dr. Varghese looked into the microscope a third time. Skeptical, he took off and wiped his glasses and looked again. The cellular abnormality could not be possible in a patient yet to exhibit any signs or symptoms of a disease or pathological process. It was consistent in 6 out of 10 samples from patients living in and around the 99th Street School. He had read of people complaining of foul smells and strange spots erupting in their front and backyards. The area had been built over and around the old Love Canal, rumored to have been storage for a chemical plant long gone.

That was back in the early fifties. The company had virtually donated the land to the Niagara Falls Board of Education for a dollar, in return receiving a release from any future liabilities. Two years later, the Board had built a new school on the site. Now a parent was raising concerns. It got some press but went largely ignored, and local health officials and doctors shrugged off the odd affected individual, not putting two and two together. Dr. Varghese was. He even contacted Dr. de Vries in Maastricht, sending him photos of the samples. Dr. de Vries was now a fellow and researcher at the University of Utrecht, studying the effects of industrial effluents on workers in chemical plants. He was noticing cellular degradation at its basest. Some of the chemicals produced chromosomal changes and fragmentation, essentially destroying the cells' functions, cutting off their brains, leading to a fundamental deformity in the building blocks of life. The cells would mutate into strange and alien forms, altering the normalcy of the victims' physiological functions and causing unknown consequences.

The field was new but emerging regardless. There were so many new chemicals with complex formulae being brought to market in an unfettered and unregulated manner. Some of these had been around for decades, just now showing their real nature. This chemical stew was demanding its price. The payment might be something humanity could not afford or comprehend. Dr. de Vries caught a plane to New York and a commuter flight to Niagara Falls Hospital and Clinic to help one of his brightest students decipher his local mystery.

Chapter 24

"Cytotoxicology."

Dr Varghese, along with Karam and old Dr. Murray, the chief pathologist, listened attentively.

"New conditions, new diseases, need fresh ways of diagnosing them," Dr. de Vries, careful to act only as an observer and advisor, continued. "Industry is making very fast progress; there is a new chemical being invented and its use started every day, and no one knows how the chemical will degrade, if it will ever degrade, or how it will react when it comes in contract with other chemicals. What concentrations are safe, what will produce toxicity and damage to human beings?"

They were faced with a spreading disaster: an epidemic, but not in the classical sense; a new plague, yet not a plague, but just as devastating to its victim.

Dr. de Vries had moved in a methodical way. First he had asked for the town map, then a list of present industries, a list of defunct factories, locations of suspected and legal storage, and dumps of industrial effluents and waste. He had Dr. Murray and Dr. Varghese drive him by the depressingly large acreage given to this activity and the proximity to the Niagara River and thus the Great Lakes basin. He collected samples from spots where local residents had pointed out the ooze of foul-smelling muck. Then, in a kind of war room, he put up the city map, using colored pins to put the pieces of the puzzle together. The others, still maintaining a cloak of silence and confidentiality, watched the specialist at work, amazed at the detective techniques he was teaching them in the new phenomenon of chemical poisoning, or as he termed it, a *manmade disaster*.

The evidence was now convincing and alarming, but not much could happen without valid scientific testing demonstrating the ugly results and ongoing damage if things did not change and the government did not move forcefully against the Wild West of enterprise and its reckless attitude. He had two folding tables set up and covered with color-coded files: one table of collected and analyzed scientific results, the other of citizen complaints, the odd media story, personal stories, pictures, and other evidence. It was powerful stuff in the hands of those who could move, shake, and shock the authorities into action. Dr. Murray, a lifelong resident of the town and county who knew all of the players and stakeholders, was charged with the duty of strategic planning. "Identify the friends we will need and the enemies we will face," Dr. de Vries told him. Dr. De Vries was well aware of the power of money and lobbyists.

They were going to need a lot of powerful friends and very quickly.

Dr. Murray had a large family on both his parents' side, including his wife's extended family and the in-laws of his five children. "Damn it," he thought. He had kin going to the 99th Street School and kin that had graduated from there. It was built over the cesspool of toxic waste now finding its natural way to the surface. He imagined all kinds of bad science scenarios.

Sitting beside him, Karam thought of Stefano and his remark. "What if Niagara Falls had been in Europe?" He wondered if it would have been all that different. The Germans were destroying the once lush and stately Black

Forest, now marred and browned by their acid rain. There were other horror stories emerging from behind the Iron Curtain. In India, one drive through the city of Gobindgarh was enough to choke lungs full of soot and turn them black. It was the epicenter of pollution in the Punjab thanks to its coal-using foundries. Even the city of Ropar at the foothills and just miles from the largest source of electricity in India, the Bakhra-Nangal project and dam, now spewed a host of poisons from its coal-fired generating station and its new fertilizer and agro plants, all in the name of progress and profit. What about Burlington Bay, filled with the effluents from the Dofasco and Stelco steel mills? Karam had stopped wearing a white shirt as the collars turned black by midday and the soot never washed off. He had gladly moved to Niagara-on-the-Lake. No big smokestacks in sight. The air was crisp. Or was it? What was happening to the tender, growing bodies of his children? His jaws tightened.

* * *

Dr. de Vries was a devout man. He had volunteered to spend the prime years of his life teaching pathology to students in India. His Christian Orthodox faith sustained him, and now he had devoted his life to stopping and studying the new threats that doctors would be dealing with. Western science and technology had done much to end or lessen the suffering from naturally occurring diseases. Now it was creating a whole new category of sickness and suffering and had not bothered to develop the tools to deal with it. He felt it was his mission to do just that, to be at the forefront. He looked fondly at his two students from India, men he had never dreamed would become his allies in this new war: Varghese, the serious, cerebral scientist, and Karam, the reluctant Midas; it seemed that everything he touched turned to gold.

The wine was good—rather good. Mrs. Pardesi, the beautiful woman, had cooked the tastiest chicken curry and rice and fresh *roti*, just as Dr. de Vries had requested. Sitting in the dining room of Karam's estate, he marveled at the size of the dwelling: the opulence of its furnishings, the lovely furniture. Karam had traveled so far in such a short time. It was mind-boggling for him to contemplate. Karam did all this without becoming a doctor. Dr. de Vries was convinced that Karam would have made a good doctor but maybe was doing better as a businessman. He also marveled at the humility his student still exhibited, almost apologetic about his wealth and unwilling to show off.

This was a true sign of good character and upbringing. He had forgotten that Karam was an untouchable to his own people. Dr. de Vries had moved on in his opinion of his student. His pride in him overrode the past and its values. Plus, he had never really paid much heed to Indian caste and customs; only to India's needs and those of his students.

Later, he spent an hour in the brisk air of the vineyard, wearing a parka loaned to him by Sushila, who offered to join him for the walk. As they passed through a row of leafless vines, he noticed they were still heavy with unpicked grapes. "Why are you wasting these fruits?" he asked.

"We are not wasting the grapes. They are being left on to freeze and later turned into ice wine."

"Ice wine!"

"Yes, Dr. de Vries, you will be served it with dessert and coffee."

Thus he was one of the very first Europeans to taste the soon-to-be world-famous Canadian twist to the elixir of the mighty grape, a unique product of Niagara Falls and its now verdant vineyards and fruit farms.

Before he left for his hotel room, he told Karam to have

his well water tested, "Just as a precaution."

Karam wasted no time in calling the Ministry of Health, and a representative showed up to be met by three highly qualified doctors. He in turn called his supervisor, who called his supervisor, as the request was not for a bacterial count but for benzene, chloroform, lindane, and the deadliest of them all, dioxin. Dr. de Vries had already confirmed the presence of these toxic chemicals from the soil samples he had collected from people's basements and backyards around Love Canal and the 99th Street School in Niagara Falls, New York.

* * *

Dr Murray agonized over the decision, not because he was unsure who to call, but because of whom he couldn't. This would become a major story in America, and careers would be made and destroyed over it. It was too visceral, unforgivable, and would not be soon forgotten. He was afraid of alerting the wrong individuals and causing a panic. He needed the competent, the strong, the discrete, and the dedicated. His first call was to a woman pathologist he had the privilege to have supervised as a resident a long time ago, now a professor at a state university. His second call went to a journalist he trusted, a local with deep roots in the community with a lot of kin to protect, just like himself. The third call was to a man he thought he could trust: the state's attorney-general. He wanted the perpetrators punished, pursued, and prosecuted. He wanted a tight net with no holes to wiggle through. He had seen and understood the evidence; it was unforgivable.

* * *

Dr. De Vries left before the story became public and began to gain traction in the media and the conscious of Americans. He felt he had done his job. He wanted no part of the glory or recognition. He had set the standards, educated the players, and started the process, and it was now their responsibility. It was their land and community. They were now the stakeholders. Their children would be their judges. But it had been nice to visit, work, and watch his protégés. He was amazed at the hand of God, how it guided him to India to teach these two men who would now play a role in saving the lives of countless innocents in a fast-growing world, unaware still of the price of progress and the unforgiving laws of nature. You could tinker with it only to a point, but you could never be its masters, as the scions of industry believed they could. They were about to have their bells rung. As the plane lifted from the single runway of the Niagara Falls, New York, airport and banked to point its nose toward Kennedy International, he marveled at the vista a couple of thousand feet below him: the Falls with mists rising, the greenery of the Niagara escarpment, and the smokestacks of Hamilton in the distance. The plane straightened, and he opened a novel to read. Reading made him relax, and he loved westerns. He read his share of cowboy and Indian novels; that was what really defined America for him.

* * *

The young man took the commuter train from Khanna to Ludhiana and back each day for a week. As it approached Jogpore, he would, without fail, see Sajjan, now grey-bearded, leaning on his staff and watching over his flock of pigs as they grazed in the ditches along the railway track. The train, pulled by a smaller, coal-fired engine, slowed enough as it passed Sajjan for the youth to identify him well and correctly. There could be no mistake. This was the man who had stolen the life of his older sister in her prime. Married to Dial Singh's son in the village of Noorian, she had fallen under the spell of the *Chura*, and once discovered, her fate had been sealed. Brought in disgrace to her ancestral home after having been beaten badly, the mother-in-law had demanded that justice be done, the stain of shame washed with her blood. He watched his own father, shaking with rage, strangle her. At only six years of age, he had vowed revenge, and now, as a fully grown, six-feet strapping and strong man, he had come up with a plan.

The days were shortening, and yet the herdsman of the pigs kept his flock out in the dying light.

On the eighth day, the youth, accompanied by two husky cousins and armed with knives strapped to their waists under their heavy jackets, alighted at the Jogpore station about 500 yards north of the quarry. In the failing light, they spread out on either side of the tracks, and one walked along the narrow path below the elevated beam supporting the track and surprised the dozing Sajjan, who had swallowed a big roll of opium and was feeling its effects. He barely felt the knife slice his throat, and the attacker bent him forward to contain the rush of blood from the severed arteries. His companions suddenly fell upon the body, slicing and dicing the still tremulous and warm Sajjan into pieces. The herd, smelling the blood and flesh, gathered around the action, hidden from the view of any passerby by the reeds. Soundlessly they finished the task and began distributing the remains to the eager pigs, which immediately went to work tearing morsels, snorting loudly in satisfaction.

The trio walked south in silence and coming to a farmer's well, washed off any stains and blood off their weapons, hands and clothes. Satisfied, they walked through the darkened fields to a village two miles away and knocked on the gates of a cousin's courtyard. Seeing them, the man immediately smiled in satisfaction. Revenge had been had.

He pulled them inside and set about feeding the trio and slaking their thirst with homebrewed rum. They talked late into the night.

Sajjan's elderly parents raised the alarm after midnight as the pigs began arriving at their pen with no master in sight. Men of the clan grabbed lanterns and flashlights and set down the gulley to search for their missing kin and soon found the bloodied reeds and soil in different locations. Well aware of the deed that had occurred but unable to trace the perpetrators, they returned to the colony and waited for sunlight. A brisk, unexpected winter shower washed away whatever evidence they had found, and in the daylight and with policemen searching fruitlessly, they gave up the effort, blaming it on his many misdeeds and enemies. The events of Noorian had long been forgotten.

The youth made his way home to his family and informed his dying mother that her daughter had been avenged.

* * *

Sushila got the call from Punna, a first for her mother-in-law. Informed of the circumstances, she immediately phoned Karam just as he was entering a meeting at the hospital. He asked her to phone his sister in Hamilton and console her. He would do his duty later after attending to urgent business. They were going to meet with the state's attorney-general and local prosecutors, who now smelled blood and political advantage. Because these were elected offices, each was now more eager than the other to be in the forefront. This was after weeks of vacillation until the professor at the state university released her definitive report. Love Canal was causing severe chromosomal damage to its victims, and there was no denying the facts. Politicians and officials who had at first denied the evidence as speculation and conjecture now found themselves eating crow. Karam, at the center of a gathering storm, was disconcerted by the news of Sajjan's death, but it was of less importance to him than the current goings on. He was heavily invested in the issue of the chemical leak. His hospital and its excellent pathology department had done their work in providing the cement to show concrete evidence of culpability by the industries that had used Niagara Falls, New York, as a chemical toilet.

The meeting and the subsequent press conference where the attorney-general of the state of New York announced the upcoming prosecution of the offenders of this catastrophe and called upon the federal authorities to intervene and own up to their silent acquiesce of the situation made the national news; the next day, the international news. By then, Karam was too involved in his duties as a brother-in-law and uncle to an aggrieved family. When his mother demanded that he come home to personally attend the mass and prayers for the departed soul, he exploded. Frustrated by the interference of Sajjan's untimely death in one of the most important events in his life, he basically told her to take a walk. He defied her for the first time in his life and told her of his fatigue in carrying the weight of custom and commitment. Thus spurned, Punna suddenly felt the ground shifting beneath her feet. Her son wrestled with far greater issues than the murder of a wayward brother-in-law. She had to look at the younger brother of Sajjan and deny his demands: that Karam, the Prince of *Churas*, be present for his murdered brother's memorial ceremonies and put him in his place.

"How much can we ask of him?" Ruldu growled.

Punna looked at him askance. She felt her authority slipping, her son drifting away. She went to seek comfort at the Sant Baba *samadhi* and asked *Guruji's* opinion. The sage, now wizened to the questions and enquiries of his flock, understanding that mostly worldly concerns were caused by fragile egos and ethos, stated, "Sajjan met a just fate. Karam has no culpability; he is not to be bothered."

Punna accepted that as the divine word.

* * *

Ben the lawyer had an epiphany. The Love Canal tragedy was a precursor, he thought. What more lay buried across communities in America waiting to emerge? How many Love Canals were out there, and what opportunity did they hold for the bold?

"Considerable," replied the accountant in him. He began plotting a new course for P&R Capital. First, he set up an environmental diagnostics corporation. It would provide an immediate response team, collect and collate the damage, gather enough to entice a tort law firm to sue the perpetrators in a class action suit and thus benefit from its newfound expertise. Bringing Karam onside, he made the now well-quoted Dr. Varghese as its nominal CEO and brought in a highly skilled operations man to provide the actual management muscle. He subsequently hired a high-profile public relations firm to promote the service, which had an immediate impact. Within weeks of garnering extra publicity through expert work by the agency, they landed a number of possibly huge contracts, surprisingly from both the victims and those standing to be accused. Karam had to shake his head in admiration.

* * *

Padri Masih had been horrified when he and his wife traveled to Jogpore to pay their respects to Sajjan's parents. The hovel they lived in and the relentless crying from grieving their son had further damaged their clouded eyes. It became apparent to him that somehow they had not benefited at all from Karam's generosity. Punna confessed to him that she had quietly given money to Sajjan all these years, and the reckless man had spent it satisfying his anger-fueled addictions and had reverted to his role as a breeder of pigs. He took considerable pride in his flock that ultimately had feasted on him. But he had totally ignored his parents, primarily because they had become a querulous couple in their old age, eyes dimmed by cataracts, and they tottered around the colony complaining about him. He had found solace in staying out as late as possible, arriving home only to pen his prized flock after starting to feel the numbing effects of his last indulgence of the day: the sizeable marble of black and tarry opium.

He had been suitably mourned by his family and clan, his younger brother returning to the luxury of Noorian, leaving the elders with sufficient rations and fuel, the pigs long slaughtered and sold.

The padri called Karam, in Canada, who called his mother in Noorian, who talked to the younger son, who went to fetch his parents to reside in the relative comfort of a well-appointed room in the *haveli*, thus assuring respite in their final days. Unfortunately, this good deed only inflamed the passions of Sajjan's clan in Jogpore. "Where is justice?" they asked. The rich Prince had not done enough for his dead brother-in-law, and they began to speak ill of him at every opportunity. They had nothing to lose; they had yet to benefit from his largesse. And this, after having offered their best and most beautiful girl to him in marriage! They had been spurned in favor of a Christian woman from the big city. They complained louder to the honorable Chandu Das. He did what he could and had all the senior police officers in Jogpore transferred to unfriendly outposts. The clan felt a measure of satisfaction.

Chapter 25

President Carter had a tumultuous presidency: high inflation, energy concerns, the Soviet invasion of Afghanistan, the troubling relations with Iran, and Love Canal. But as a decent man dedicated to improving America and its citizens, he made a lot of positive contributions to good governance, albeit ignored by the citizenry whose expectations exceeded his capacity to deliver. His shining moment was the Camp David agreement, taking a huge step in making peace in the Middle East. A conciliator and consensus builder who was much troubled by the Love Canal issue, he invited a delegation from the area to hold a discussion about possible solutions. The delegation, at the insistence of his chief of staff, included Dr. Varghese and Karam. After the meeting, Karam and Dr. Varghese had their picture taken shaking the president's hand. The PR agency immediately crafted a press release and sent it via wire to all national and international news services, and Karam found himself on the front pages of all Indian newspapers and on the inside page standing by his newly acquired private jet that had flown the delegation to Washington, DC.

That got a lot of attention, as most Indians took pride in two of their own being so honored by the most powerful leader of the free world, unusually popular with them after the clumsiness of Nixon and the disdain shown for India by Kissinger. The photo went a long way in healing perceived insults from the world's richest democracy to its largest. The honorable Chandu Das immediately urged the government to award Karam the *Padma Shree*, a national acknowledgement and one of the highest honors. Approved by the Privy Council, the recipient was immediately informed.

It was by now a well-known secret that Karam Pardesi had invested millions of his dollars helping emergent private companies achieve great size and market share. By one wag's account, his investments had led to direct employment of over ten thousand people and helped staunch the brain drain from the country. Business articles were written about the extent of his achievements, from wine making to pharmaceuticals, engineering ventures to hospitals, on four continents of the globe. Now dubbed the Global Indian, Karam much preferred the new moniker to Prince of the *Churas*; he looked forward to receiving the award. He would, however, travel commercially to India. The new jet would stay in America and be of use to his constantly traveling partner, whom he had dubbed the traveling salesman, for Ben sold the virtues of P&R Capital wherever he went. He raised money in tens of millions for the tons of investments they had in start-ups to steady-dividend–issuing established cash cows. They easily exceeded in sheer volume any private fund in Canada and were in the top one hundred in America.

Padri Masih read many newspapers a week, papers published in Punjabi, Hindi, and Urdu. He also read periodicals and magazines. On his walks in parks or Pinjore Gardens, he struck up conversations with other men of similar age now whiling away their days in retirement. Most were civil servants and educated with minds still clear and curious, opinionated with impressions ingrained of long experiences. He found these revealing and sometimes regaling. However, a lot of them—99 percent of them—were men of higher castes. When he offered to buy a round of tea or snacks, they shied from the offer, politely and courteously, citing health or other vague reasons for not accepting food even if cooked and served by waiters or stall owners or pushcart-*wallahs*. He would accept their excuses with a smile, adding, "Perhaps another time."

Looking around, he watched the exponential growth of the city. New sectors were mapped out each year and lots sold by the authorities via lottery. Some were reserved for retirees from the civil service or military officers. The character of the architecture was meticulously maintained as close to the original view of Le Corbusier, the famous French planner, as possible. But he rarely met men of his own caste in idle chatter, dressed in clean clothes and relaxing under the warming sunshine on cool, breezy days, seated on benches or on a cloth spread on the grass of huge open parks. Instead, he saw them dressed in tattered rags, pushing carts loaded with refuse they had swept with huge brooms.

On visits to his home village, now almost a part of the sprawling city of Ludhiana, or friends and relatives in other towns and villages, they remained geographically separated in their own colonies or crowded courtyards. He did note with some hopefulness that at least the younger generation was emerging as an educated and informed class, taking advantage of some of the many programs the politicians had promised and put into play but which remained underfunded. It still took bribery or a push from a powerful individual to get them to receive these entitlements. Some youth were opting for police or military service, joining the burgeoning class of municipal, state, and central paramilitary forces. Some had attained greater positions, mostly in the civil service. Some showed enterprise by moving away and adopting a different name, one that sounded more like a higher born, and they thrived.

Karam was a role model and often quoted but could not be copied yet in India. Too many barriers remained, mostly in attitudes. Some in the lower castes failed due to their own self-defeating acceptance of their karma. It turned into self-fulfilling prophecies, and they lived as they had for centuries: scratching the grounds, the floors, the roads with their brooms and clearing the clogged drains of streets. They took away the soiling from the latrines to be dumped in municipal dumps overrun by every kind of rodent or scavenging animal or bird.

As a learned man, he knew that in the ancient Vedas and texts, some thousands of years old and forming the underpinnings of the world's oldest religion, Hinduism (or Arya Dharma, as it was called then), there was no cut-and-dried caste system, either written of or promoted. There were just states of men in four distinct occupations that could be achieved by anyone in their lifetimes. Thus one could rise from a *Shudra* to a *Brahmin* or fall from a *Brahmin* to a *Shudra*. Only in the last few centuries had these so-called castes become entrenched. It was stated that the Ramayana was originally quoted verbatim by a *Chura*, Balmik his name, thus the term *Balmiki* ascribed to the caste. How could a *Shudra* have recited the Ramayana? The word caste came from Spain or Portugal, describing the geographic separation of occupations existing within a city's walls, each category of occupation having its own street or a portion of one, not a birthright that should follow one like a curse or an entitlement. Was a mentally unstable and cruel Brahmin better than a clean-living and virtuous *Chura*?

No, thought Padri Masih, he was glad that his ancestors had the foresight to let him escape that occupation and its misery, even though the prejudices lingered.

* * *

Punna and Ruldu rued the fact that few of the highborn had come or even bothered to commiserate the death of Sajjan. They probably still supported and smarted from the stain the man had caused on Dial Singh's family and its ignominious exile to places far away. The move was self-imposed and well-compensated, but it was a stain and exile of a kin nonetheless. Not even those that owed them money or had children benefiting daily from their son's largesse came to pay respects, the debts ignored and forgotten.

Punna stewed in these thoughts, shutting herself from the village. Where every day she left the *haveli* to visit old clients of her midwifery days, the children she had delivered now grown, the women older, some grandmothers like herself. When visiting the *Jat* courtyards, she carried her own cup to accept the offer of tea. They would also offer a *pirri*, the low, cot-like seat much favored by women around hearths. When she went to the street she had lived on, she was dismayed that only a few years after getting brand new housing, the abodes were already starting to look rundown and dirty. The occupants were more concerned with their day-to-day struggles to make ends meet. Here she came face to face with the rural misery of the landless laborers so dependent on the seasonal work in the fields or the odd few days of employment in construction or clearing. A bout with untimely sickness could result in real difficulty in putting food into the bowls of the children. Wives of afflicted men lent themselves out to the *Jats* and thumped cow patties for fuel, scraped grass off pathways and *nullahs* to bundle and sell as fodder, washed clothes, did any task available, and accepted a bowl of grain or flour, a measure of buttermilk, a kilo of *jaggery* . In the evening, they begged to pick enough greens from a field of mustard or a plot of vegetables to make a side dish in which to soak the rough *rotis* of mixed grains. If attractive and desirable, she might accept discreet offers of indulgence resulting in a handful of coins, a bag of grain, a bundle of cotton, or access to the vegetable patch for her pick of rutabaga, carrots, onions, or squash.

Whenever asked or approached, Punna gave charity. She relieved the stress apparent in their faces and received unending prayers for her family. Blessings! She was virtually the sole support of three families where the breadwinner had died or suffered a stroke or an injury severe enough to disable. There was no social safety net, as she had learned in Canada. No government schemes of baby bonuses, old-age security check or life- and dignity-sustaining welfare. It was the wait, sometimes agonizing, for relief in the form of charity from a kind hand or abuse from a lecher. Interest rates on loans could cripple or indenture a person into slavery, the release totally in the hands of the lender. However, even within the community of *Shudras*, there were some families now with sons in steady posts in the army and civil service or working as factory labor in the cities, sending money home. Not a lot, but enough to keep their families from the clutches of fate uncertain. Some had even gone to work abroad in Dubai. These came back after two or three years flush with cash in amounts unimaginable before. But they suffered the heat and long hours of extreme labor all in the cause of uplifting their families somehow. Untrusting of the *Jat*s, fewer and fewer now stayed to work the land as hired hands. The older generation and the very young still carried on cleaning and carrying.

In the evening, she hosted the discrete, faced with the task of raising a dowry for a daughter of age and in a hurry lest her eyes wander. Quietly and without fuss, Karam had allowed her to give a sufficient amount for an acceptable dowry; it

saved the poorer folks from indenture. Since he had begun
sending money from Canada, he had been responsible for
twenty or more weddings that left no debts for the burdened
parents. Punna thought this, the marriage of *kanyan devis*,
virgins in the community, to be one of the greatest charitable
acts. And she was proud and grateful when she had the
pleasure to perform one. The brides always stopped by the
haveli for years afterwards when visiting their kin, often to
show off their babies or the husband particularly if he had
gotten a better job with higher pay and now rode a shiny
new bicycle.

But Ruldu did not miss the undercurrents of agitation that
were taking hold in the Punjab. The Sikhs were promised so
much by the British for their service and loyalty to the Empire
and then by Gandhi and Nehru, only to see what was once
their empire, the greater Punjab, sliced into a Muslim part of
Pakistan and a Hindu-majority Indian one. Their language,
a binding force and mother tongue, was soon threatened by
the imposition of Hindi as a national language, which was
voted as the mother tongue by the majority Hindus. After a
lengthy but largely peaceful struggle, they ended up finally
in a majority in a much smaller rump of the greater Punjab:
just eleven districts and a divided capital in Chandigarh to
be shared by the newly carved province of Hindu majority
Haryana. Slowly, the central government took over their
water rights, too. The waters of the Punjab's three rivers,
Sutlej, Beas and Jhelum, were dammed and diverted to
feed the needs of arid Rajasthan and rapidly industrializing
Delhi and its surrounding cities. The *Jats*, all Sikhs, felt
their agrarian fortunes threatened by falling water tables
and an insidiously encroaching central government of Indira
Gandhi. Led by their religious political party and its semi-
literate leadership, they indulged in more protests, sit-ins,

and demonstrations. To feed the frustration of the most productive province of India, geographically the country's neck, neighbor Pakistan stoked the flames by supplying arms and training to a militant wing that soon morphed into an insurgency.

Soon, some Sikhs fell under the influence of a charismatic holy man. He appealed to their martial roots. A lot of the rural sons of the soil began to follow his dictum.

Danger reared its ugly head in the prosperous and productive province, the breadbasket of a recently self-sufficient India, now a net exporter of food.

* * *

The events of Love Canal had brought Karam to national and international prominence. But it had reduced the long-term prospects of the Niagara Falls Hospital and Clinic. Some of the doctors decided to move their families to cleaner environments as they could foresee the decade or two it would take to rehabilitate large swaths of the township. The population count began to fall as industries were forced to close because of their very nature or the enforcement of more rigorous environmental regulations. Niagara Falls, New York, was not seen as a good place to either live in or raise a family, although Niagara Falls, Ontario, for some inexplicable reason, began to thrive. There were scant opportunities in health care investment for P&R Capital in Canada, and Ben recommended that they consider selling their hospital holdings. The consulting company was generating a better Earnings Before Interest Taxes Depreciation and Amortization (EBITDA). Within weeks they found a buyer, a publically traded health services company, and got their money out and into better returning investments.

"I hope it does not mean we have to move, daddy." his

daughter Sarah said. She was popular with her classmates because of "Castle Pardesi." Most of them showed up at one time or another to take advantage of its huge size and big yards.

Sushila watched him put down his knife and fork and finish chewing before replying. It had taken her a decade to teach him not to talk with his mouth full. "No honey, we will not be moving."

He had already made that clear to Ben, who still lived in the same home in Burlington. The private jet was going to get used more and could fly out of the Niagara Airport on the Canadian side, even easier for Ben to get to.

Before long, they purchased a company that had been started by a visionary doctor but was soon available because of a lack of growth capital. He did not want partners. "Never had one, and I ain't going to now," was his laconic comment. It had been started to handle clinical trials for a plethora of pharmaceutical giants and start-ups to conduct independent clinical drug trials. The FDA had strict criteria for drug testing as consumer watchdogs harassed the once-porous agency, forcing it to be more transparent in its dealings with big pharmaceuticals. Independent drug-testing companies were more trusted, ostensibly for being independent, and earned large and lucrative contracts. It meant recruiting participating physicians, collecting and collating the data, and verifying its veracity. They already had sufficient expertise in data management thanks to their environmental services investment. New computers and programs made the task easier. They were ecstatic about their investment in Microsoft. The synergies between their varied investments started to payoff in ways they could not have imagined. Karam became the CEO of P&R Pharma Services and was charged with its growth. In three months, he had a roster of fifty hospitals and five hundred physicians enrolled with him to conduct clinical trials on new drugs seeking FDA approval for sale in America, the world's most lucrative pill market.

The company was incorporated in Las Vegas for its nonexistent state taxes.

* * *

His parents and in-laws returned from India with news of a changing-for-the-worse Punjab before he was to leave to receive his *Padma Shree* from the Indian government. He and Sushila listened to their sometimes dramatic descriptions of events unfolding in the province. Padri Masih had his ears closer to the ground in Chandigarh.

"Do not even go to the village," Punna urged, looking worryingly at her son. "I do not want anything to happen to you."

"Mother!" Sushila cried.

"It is not safe nowadays," Padri Masih confirmed and illustrated with some of the reported incidents.

"It is bad," Ruldu, hands folded with a look of sadness, whispered. "Noorian is not the Noorian of old. No one trusts anyone. You do not know who is who now. The nice, young man smiling at you could be a spy for the police or the others."

"Really?" Karam had studied the Vietnam War, a local insurgency that had cost billions in money and hundreds of thousands in lives and had left a generation scarred.

"This could be bad," Ruldu continued, "really bad."

"And you and the children are no longer going to India," her mother interjected, having already warned her sons and their spouses.

"So what happens to our *haveli*, our land?" Karam asked.

"Sit it out," Ruldu advised. "I want your younger sister and brother-in-law pulled out of there. The land will not walk away by itself. The *haveli* can be locked up, the cattle sold, and our clan will keep an eye on it."

"What about India?" Karam was worried about his extensive holdings there, although he had none in the Punjab outside of his village.

"It will grow and progress. Only the Punjab and the Punjabis will suffer," Padri Masih replied. Used to self-inflicted wounds, he thought.

Using the pretext of his upcoming and very public visit to India, he phoned for Jaswant Singh's opinion. The old hand at watching over and providing security to the rich and famous and the powerful was blunt. "Karam Sahib," he stated emphatically, "I will not permit a visit to the Punjab unless of course you have government protection. Even then I would not trust it. The loyalties are suspect and shifting."

Karam read between the lines and wondered if he should decline the honor.

Chapter 26

*K*aram talked more to Jaswant Singh at Essential Services and was convinced that a trip to New Delhi to receive his Padma Shree honor would pose no danger. Despite the fact that it would be foolish to travel to Noorian in these troubled times in the Punjab, he resolved to try once there. It was fortunate that quarterly board meetings were due at three of the companies in and around New Delhi that P&R Capital had invested in. Ben felt that it was time Karam took an interest and see for himself the places millions of his dollars now resided; Ben had already been to visit in the private jet. In fact, he now had use of this indulgence 90 percent of the time. Karam was content running the clinical trials and diagnostics divisions, his core competency. Their partnership worked so well because he let Ben take care of the corporate structuring, staffing, tax planning, and evaluation. They had devices, a single-page system to analyze the performance of the twenty or so companies they had effective control of as well as the fifty or more they had sufficient shareholdings to warrant a seat on the board of directors. They never put their money where they could not have a say in forming corporate policy at the board level or the power to appoint at least the chief financial officer, the man with the power to say no to idiotic financial decisions.

Investing in convertible debt that often resulted in significant common stock, they were able to exit companies and pay minimal possible taxes on profits because capital gains were taxed at a lower rate than income. There, rolling stock alone in cold hard cash was in excess of $25 million, not including cash available from the plethora of limited partnerships and other instruments they had been able to form to raise tons of cash at short notice, giving them a distinct advantage to take advantageous positions in companies experiencing cash flow problems and growing pains.

Karam spent four out of the seven evenings a week at home. Sushila, the mother of three very active and involved children, was like a dervish, constantly on the move. As her children grew older and their demands of her time multiplied, she withdrew from a lot of her community and volunteer work. She was a typical mother and housewife despite having the help of a full-time nanny and housekeeper. The vineyard was her pride. Never having owned land before she arrived in Canada, she discovered the joys of planting and watching the fruit trees and vines grow and become heavy with their bounty. The picking of fruit and taking down the grapes were her happiest and most fulfilling days, almost comparable to Sarah's first piano recital at four years of age, Benjamin's first goal in a hockey game, and Mark's scoring a three-pointer in a basketball game. During those times, she had screamed herself hoarse. She dragged the grandparents to events whether they appreciated the event or not. They surely enjoyed watching their grandchildren perform and play and collect trophies to be proudly displayed in the huge recreation room in the basement, its stone fireplace a centerpiece of their juvenile accomplishments.

She was used to owning a company today and selling it tomorrow, all in the name of capitalism. Ben and Karam, although living in Canada, were largely invested in America and somewhat globally. They had the swagger of success, worked hard for their money, and protected it jealously.

The year-end statements that she saw took her breath away because she still had a habit of multiplying their increasing fortune into Indian rupees and working out what it meant in India. A lot, she calculated. She had not visited India even once since leaving it more than a decade ago. All her family—the ones that mattered to her most—were here, and Karam gave her and Padri Masih tremendous leeway to help those left behind and desperate. For that, she was proud of him. Still, her heart remained in India. But her duties were in Canada now, and she took her status as a Canadian citizen seriously. She gave her children every advantage of being Canadians and did not burden them with teaching them Punjabi or Hindi, languages she knew they had little interest in learning. She only made them speak a few common words to please their grandparents, who tried hard and relentlessly to run interference and give them Indian values. As far as she was concerned, she had escaped the ignorance and the bad things inherent in the Indian culture and wanted to retain, in her mind, a better, kinder, and gentler India, the one the Westerners now flocked to discover: the spiritual India.

In his travels, Karam started to run more and more into other Indians in airports, hotels, and seminars who were starting to prosper in America and become somewhat like him: nomadic investors not afraid to take risks, assert themselves, and assume significant executive powers. He found them to be intelligent, intuitive, and complimentary. Most had known about him and were genuinely happy to meet him and try to interest him in co-investing in their enterprises. These he referred to Ben for follow-up. He avoided the odd one sent over by indulgent and filthy rich parents in India to cut his teeth in America. He could not bear the arrogance, the boasting, and the complaints of having to drive their own cars or do their own laundry. He actually had to shut a particularly obnoxious whiner up by saying, "Sorry, Bhai Sahib, but you are stealing my karma with your negativity." And Karam walked away as the young man looked askance at those sitting near them.

He had no patience with time wasters, time being money. Time was better spent doing something positive than listening to the bellyaching of a spoiled brat. Each evening, he called home and spoke to Sushila, but before he could get a sentence out, the phone would be besieged by Sarah or Ben. Mark he had to ask for. Their boy was cerebral and quite taciturn but obviously proud of his father, and that was the reward Karam appreciated the most: his eldest son's respect.

His parents and in-laws only talked about the little ones. With both his sisters and all his brother-in-laws in Canada now, he had just kin and clan left in India, and he received letters from the Comrade only on a weekly basis, replying to them each month. Talking on the phone was more economical. Letters took a long time to write, send, and arrive, and they were old news by the time he opened them.

"You are getting a belly, Uncleji," his niece complained during a recent visit.

"He is looking prosperous, and why should he not," his mother objected.

"He has to watch his weight. Indians are more prone to heart problems and such."

"Oh, Sant Baba!" Punna intoned. "What will people think of his wealth if he shows up all skin and bones for his award ceremony?"

"That he takes care of himself!"

It was a new phenomenon. Having a belly, no matter how modest, was no longer in vogue. Fitness clubs like Vic Tanny's were barely open and had crowds lined up for blocks to sign up as members.

* * *

The room at the Oberoi International was overstuffed and chilly. Karam escaped to the lobby and walked through its boutiques served by eager, English-speaking young people. It had not changed much since the last time: the same decor, the same commercial outlets, and the same overpriced service while just outside its gates a pushcart-*wallah* could feed you for 5 percent of what they charged with food that would be fresher and tastier. He walked through the lobby dressed in his *kurta/pyjama* and moccasins. The Rolex on his wrist, his western haircut and the way he walked gave him away as an NRI, a *non-resident Indian*, a term beginning to catch on in some places. He could see the antennae rising, sizing him up. Gathering his courage, a young man approached him only to be shoved aside by Jaswant Singh.

"Pardesi, Sahib, Ram Gupta, from the *Hindustan Times*," the youth shouted, trying to get around the still agile security agent.

Karam waved him on and Jaswant Singh let him approach, watchful for any false move, his hand in position to draw the pistol under his belt concealed by the vest.

"Sahib," the reporter continued, "I am hoping for an interview, one on one."

He looked so eager, desperate. He was dressed in a bush shirt and pants but wearing dusty, worn-out sandals and carrying only a notebook and a pen, his hair held by the pomade he had generously applied.

"Sure," Karam smiled, and he sat down in one of the many armchairs spread across the huge marble lobby. The young man immediately sat at the edge of the one next to it and started to say something. Karam silenced him with one hand and waved a hovering waiter over with the other. "What will you have?" he asked, and he saw the hesitation in the eyes of the *Kushatriya* immediately change to eager acceptance; this being the Oberoi Hotel, after all.

"Sahib," he confessed, "I do not know what to say," meaning he did not know what to order.

The haughty waiter with majestically grown sideburns merging into his beard, a white and gold stitched turban on his head, looked with raised eyebrows at the nervous youth, then politely at Karam, bowing. "Vegetarian or nonvegetarian, sir?"

"Vegetarian," piped up the youth.

"As you please." The waiter handed him a single plasticized sheet of a menu. Karam watched the skinny young man's Adam's apple rise and fall as he read the obviously tasty offerings, finally deciding on a plate of potato dumplings with mango chutney and a cup of tea.

"Nothing refreshing?" asked the intimidating *Rajput*, now a waiter in New Delhi.

The refreshments served and consumed, thanks received and humbly waved away, they got down to business and spoke for two hours. The young reporter was surprisingly a very good interviewer: in depth, patient, and not judgmental. Not pushy. He allowed Karam, suddenly interested in answering his intelligent and probing questions, time to reflect before answering the difficult questions asked in a most humble but insistent politeness: disarming and complimentary.

To the question of if he had lobbied or somehow asked for the honor, Karam had burst out laughing. "I at first wanted to decline it."

"But Pardesiji, it is being speculated that the *Dalit* block wants these rewards to go proportionately to *Dalits*."

Dalit or *Shudra* were one and the same. Karam replied, "If I have earned my reward on that basis, I will decline it right now."

Ram Gupta looked steadily at him, trusted the answer, and moved on. "What makes you want to invest in India?"

"I am from India. It's my motherland. I have an obvious interest in seeing this country progress, its people lifted out of poverty; given opportunity, a hand up."

"Not for pure profit then?"

"One only invests for profit," Karam replied. "And profit can be defined in so many ways: monetary, a form of service, or a devotion to a cause accomplished."

"Right, sir, you are so right. India can use all the help it can get."

Karam nodded. "But it also has to allow the help to be given. Make it easier. Make it accountable. Make it possible."

"As a *Shudra*," the Adam's apple bobbed a few times, "how do you perceive the lot of your people to have changed, in view of the fact that India has now been independent for almost thirty-five years?"

Karam thought of that for a long moment. "In my village of Noorian, for my clan, not much has changed, except for what I as a clansman have done for them. Too little! I see the same prejudices, the same divisions, and the same walls. Not much has changed, here, I feel." He tapped his head for emphasis.

Ram Gupta held his gaze, then lowered his eyes. "I am sorry, *Sahib*," he started, "and must apologize for hesitating to accept your offer of refreshments."

"That is precisely what I mean about no change for the *Shudras*, or *Dalits*, as you call them now," Karam said, in a calm voice. "I truly wonder when that time will come."

"I hope soon," Ram Gupta agreed. Then letting his journalistic mask slip, he added "This accursed country needs it. Or it will destroy itself."

* * *

Even before the ceremony, Karam had made it to the front page of the preeminent newspaper in the country. His candid interview sold so many copies so soon that by midmorning, as he arrived at the Rajbhavan as the only recipient without an entourage, the newspaper was sold out and the Parliamentary *Dalit* block out in full force to witness the honor to be bestowed on their man. The honorable Chandu Das, dressed in his full regalia of hand-woven glory, lead the delegation to take its place, the visitors' gallery chock full of the giddy fans of a famous Bollywood actress also being honored. They called Karam's name first. Karam was introduced as a true son of the nation, a real hero of the people, for he had risen against all adversity to attain such heights of success in business and international fame. It bestowed honor on his nation of India and particularly on his caste, uplifting them as a whole!

In his speech he simply thanked his benefactors, starting with the Sant Baba, the Comrade, headmaster Mansa Ram, Sardar Pardesi (whose name he had adopted to honor his selflessness), his teachers in Noorian, Dr Grewal, his grandfather, his parents, the CMC, Dr. de Vries, and Dr. King. Then he spoke of the great country of Canada and the generosity of its citizens, the enterprise of America, and the chances it gave to everyone, anyone to succeed; and his hope and prayer that India and its majority of citizens, the Hindus, revert to the true teachings of Arya Dharma, its true faith, and give up its caste system.

The applause was deafening. Tears flowed down the cheeks of the *Dalit* dignitaries seated in their British-era embroidered chairs of beige-colored wood with lines of gold, emphasizing the royal ownership, now inherited by the impoverished country whose riches had been looted for their manufacture.

* * *

The Comrade rode to Noorian in the nondescript car provided by Jaswant Singh. He sat in the backseat of the old Ambassador as it coughed its way up the Grand Trunk Road. A couple of outriders on motorcycles kept a watchful eye out for trouble. When Karam asked, the Comrade explained in a flat and unemotional voice of someone defeated in the cause of nation building. "It is getting bad, particularly in the villages. The *Jats* now fully believe that the center means to impoverish them by stealing their water and electricity and flooding the Punjab with Hindu migrants meaning to raise it back to a Hindu majority state, crushing the Sikh cause once and for all. The fundamentalists are calling it the final war leading to a 'Sikh Raj' as promised by the tenth Guru Sahib."

Karam watched the countryside roll by, its greenery stretching for miles.

Then the Comrade asked for the favor he had been holding back all these years. "Can you get my family out to Canada or America? I am worried for my three sons, that they might come under the influence of the religious zealots by becoming martyrs, fodder for their cause."

Karam could not bear the pain in the Comrade's eyes. The Comrade had shrunk into half the man he remembered, and Karam promised to do his best.

In Noorian, he circumambulated the *samadhi* and kissed his grandfather's marker. He toured the *haveli*, hugged his kin, and pressed notes into their claw-like hands. Then, sighing deeply and wrapped in a cotton *parna*, he climbed back into the Ambassador and tolerated its puttering back to New Delhi. After a day's rest at the Oberoi, he boarded a BOAC flight to Heathrow in London.

* * *

Karam cut an impressive figure, now more fleshed out into his six-foot frame, the Italian cut and tailored suit fitting his profile enhanced by the mane of thick wavy hair just beginning to show a touch of grey. Few first class passengers were on board, giving him ample room to stretch out. He found Heathrow airport more interesting as a number of Indians and Pakistanis worked there as porters, cleaners, waiters, ticket clerks, and security guards. The London Constabulary boasted turbaned policemen, and he would see the odd one, regal in the uniform, patrol the massive terminals. Speaking in flawless British accents, they were the second generation, British-born or raised there from an earlier age. He marveled at the number of colored people employed there, happily conversing, joking, and joshing with their white peers. The other European airports were still largely uniracial, nonintegrated. He was grateful Canada was on its way to a multicultural hue, and America had always celebrated itself as a melting pot. The Civil Rights Act was giving chances to the African-Americans and the ever-growing immigrant numbers from Asia and Latin America. In this milieu, he faded into the scenery; less obvious and observed.

This time the lounge was less crowded, the management taking advantage by marshalling a large number of cleaners to wipe the floors, clean the toilets and sinks, and wipe down the chairs and sofas and remove the stale ashtrays. They were mostly Indians with a few Rastafarian dreadlocked Jamaicans, all in blue coveralls and distinctly assigned tasks to make the job quick and efficient. He was quickly attracting glances, especially form the Indians and a particular turbaned fellow pushing a mop in semiconcentric swipes, as the only colored guest, the rest being all white. Either new at the job, nervous, or whatever, the white supervisor kept asking him to go over a spot here or a missed spot there. And every time he would give Karam a nervous glance.

Feeling the man's discomfiture, Karam smiled

encouragingly and nodded, getting an immediate flash of white teeth under the black moustache, the face framed by a tidily bound beard in the proper fashion of observant Sikhs.

Thus encouraged, the man rotated around about the floor, managing to come within conversing distance of Karam. Realizing that the supervisor had left the lounge, he rested his swiping and folded his hands. "*Sat Sri Akal Ji.*"

Karam returned the gesture.

"*Sahib*, where are you from?"

"Canada."

"Oh, but I mean back home," he spoke in Punjabi, well-crafted and accented. He was obviously educated.

"Ludhiana, and yourself?"

"Then we are *bhais* from the same city. I am from Ghillan."

"Oh," Karam said, "and what brought you to England?"

"My parents found me a match, *Virji*. I am so glad. I was unemployed for three years after obtaining an engineering degree."

"So how come this?" Karam innocently pointed to the broom.

Crestfallen and now embarrassed, the man, finding a sympathetic ear, continued. "There are no jobs like that for Indian graduates *Virji*. Here there are only jobs like this one. Imagine me, a *Jat*, pushing a mop like a *Chura*, in England. I am ashamed."

The sympathy for the man that had started in Karam was now blown out by the remark's poison and replaced by a cold rage. To untighten his jaw, Karam took a few deep breaths, blinked his eyes, and stilled the rage. He thought of all things as equal and gave the man the only explanation for his miserable condition he could think of.

"Kismet."

Chapter 27

1938

The herbs, potent and bitter, had kept the pain in check, but now it had broken through, wracking his body in a paroxysm of exquisitely searing spasms. His throat was too raw and dry to emit the screams that welled in his ravaged lungs. The senior monk worked the mortar in the pestle, crushing a stronger *butti*, this one from a dried root found in the higher altitudes of the distant mountains. Mixing the powder with water from the well, he trickled it in drops into Sant Baba's mouth and watched his peer's eyes glaze, the muscles in his face and neck relax, the breathing become slower and steadier. The disciples started wiping down the skin with cooling rags.

The potion took its effect and would hold it for the night. The senior monk put the rest of the powder in a coconut bowl and covered it with a large leaf, placing it in a cranny of the hut's fragile wall, a gourd of water underneath. The senior monk stepped out to announce that the Sant Baba was on his dream quest, perhaps meeting his *avatar* tonight to receive instructions about the journey his soul would soon take.

Sant Baba had been on a journey all his life, even while living beside Noorian in the orchard: a quest for knowledge for twenty-five years ever since his guru had shown him the way. He could transcend the consciousness to enter a higher, more tranquil state but could go no farther, rise no higher, gain not another step. His guru had died before being able to instruct him in the next step to *moksha*: salvation. As a loyal disciple, having attained that much at the feet of his revered teacher, he had sought no one else to replace the one he had lost to the indignities of old age.

He lived the life of a mendicant, seeking alms for sustenance, counseling the troubled, arbitrating worldly disputes, and dispensing relief with his knowledge of ancient herbal remedies, both for humans and their animals. Each season he set out to gather the leaves, flowers, and roots. He arranged them on the smooth floor of his hut on a piece of clean cloth and mixed them in perfect harmonies into piles by measuring with his trained eye their precise portions. It took days to hunt the rare plants and hours to prepare a single dose that could stop a severe attack of the runs or black cough in its tracks, kill the pain, chase the chills from a fever, soothe a severe bite, relax a spasm of the muscle superficial or deep in the guts, relax the birth canal of a cow or a buffalo and deliver a live calf and save one from taking the other's life and its own.

He calmed the urges that pent up and then rose in him: the urges of *Kama*, of *krodhe*. The control of both was so essential to the life of a *sadhu*, a seeker. Lust and anger were the most destructive passions of man!

Born a *Chura* in a village more than a hundred miles north on the border of Punjab and Kashmir, he had grown into a tall, gangly youth and helped his parents clean the courtyards and carry the dung out to the manure piles on the edge of the village. First his father, then mother, struck with consumption, died lingering, painful deaths while he struggled to hold all three souls together, working like a donkey, begging and beseeching, living on the handouts of a people inured to hard times and harder lives. Alone and lonely, he had been called to the local landlord's mansion and informed without ceremony that he had been indentured in the rich man's service for twenty years to retire the debts and obligations of his parents. Their medicines, the opium to salve their pain, the food, the shelter, and the work unperformed now totaled a value of 100 rupees, the interest at 30 percent. All he would receive for his labor was 3 meals, the odd glass of milk, 2 sets of clothing, and the right to keep his cot in the lee of the hovel. He was allowed to keep his plate and a brass mug, a blanket, a *dari*, and a wrap for his head. He was ordered to keep his head down, his eyes on the ground, and his hands busy with tasks, or else.

The "or else" meant beatings from the landlord's supervisor, a *pathan* from the hill tribes to the west, but a hand shorter than he. He did his duty for six months, but when the nights grew intolerably cold with no coals to heat his *chula*, he got up one night, wrapped the blanket over his shoulders, and started jogging until daybreak. He was a hundred miles south and had crossed the river Beas within two days. He joined a group of mendicants and received a saffron robe, rubbed his body grey with ashes, and totally changed his appearance, adopting the familiar name of Sant. He was confident that the landlord would no longer seek him now that he was in the territories controlled by the British and law abiding. He kept a low profile nonetheless until his hair had grown into foot-long dreadlocks, his chin had sprouted a scraggly beard, and he no longer looked like the boy from the north. He could do little about the color of his eyes—hazel—except look down when spoken to, a sign of humility and respect, much appreciated by all. The alms proved to be more nutritious and filling and provided a greater variety of tastes and textures than the leftovers from the landlord's kitchen. It took three years of wandering, but he was finally ensconced as a disciple in the vast orchard on the common lands of the village of Noorian, a mixed community of Sikhs, Muslims, and Hindus living in peace and harmony and generous to the resident mendicant and his tall and humble disciple.

During the three years of wandering, he had walked to the main festivals, celebrations, and ritualistic gatherings of Hindus, Sufi Muslims, and *Mahants*. He had spent time listening to the legends and storytellers late into the night and the teachings of learned Brahmins and charismatic Pirs. He had watched the nightlong, hypnotic dancing and heard the strains of devotional music. He enriched his vocabulary and mind and built his body and exercised it under the instruction of *hatha* yogis and martial *Mahants*. He learned the defensive and offensive moves of *gatka*, the art of fighting with a staff; he suffered long hours of torturous asana, his joints screaming for relief from the agony when he would pass out in blissful unconsciousness. He had inhaled the smoke from all types of concoctions of tobacco mixed with leaves and flowers of the hemp plant, consumed the tarry marbles of opium, and drunk deeply of the *dode*. He attained different and strange levels of conscious and unconscious stages and learned to focus his mind on a single symbol for a full day and a full night, unaware of time or space.

He overcame the fear of the unknown. Adopted as he believed by his own avatar, he was guided in his quest by unseen forces, his fate no longer in his hands. He was no longer of this world while in this world.

He sought the only means to *moksha*: salvation from the repeated cycles of reincarnation. All he needed was a guru to

guide him, and he had found his in the orchard that would
be his home for the remainder of this cycle of existence.

Knowing that unquestioning service and sacrifice for his
guru was the only path, he followed it heart and soul. He
served his master day and night, and absorbing all the subtle
guidance, he learned to see the universe differently, to see the
animals and plants like a parent, avoiding hurt or harm to
his environment. He learned to understand them like living
beings, each recognizable by its unique appearance and
known for the role it played in the endless cosmic game for
the indulgence and the pleasure of the One: the *Paramatma*,
the Ultimate Soul. The taker and breather of life!

The aging guru developed *sokka*, a wasting and
progressive disease that consumed him in a few short
months. Before dying, he anointed Sant to follow him
as the inheritor of his *gadhi*, his seat in the pantheon of
gurus, from his sect of seekers, his lineage. Thus honored,
Sant stayed in the orchard but as an unaccomplished and
incomplete *sadhu*, not fully trained or uplifted. But he was
far better off than his birthright, that of a *Chura*, he thought.
He respected the *Paramatma's* reasons for him being born
so lowly and therefore had no reason to refuse alms from
these poor and oppressed kin of his in caste. He had seen the
seductively beautiful Punna when she first arrived as a bride
in the village and then had saved her from being savaged
by the louts of Noorian. He had cracked a couple of skulls
with the skilful wielding of his gnarled and trusty old staff.
He surprised himself with his own ferocity in coming to her
defense and thus formed a lifelong bond with the woman,
watching over her. Sometimes he scolded her mother-in-law,
that querulous and garrulous woman, constantly talking,
giving him a headache if he got caught in her snares while
in her courtyard. He avoided eye contact with the beautiful

daughter-in-law as she hovered in the background.

* * *

The avatar guided him through the moonscape of colorless landscape until they came upon the tree of wisdom, its silver leaves lit with votive lamps giving out a divine light, soothing in its luminescence. Beside it lay a river of still waters, the surface like granite. It was as shiny as a mirror, and when he gazed into it, he saw the faces of everyone he had known, now no longer of this world, floating by serenely. He saw his parents, grandparents, aunts and uncles, and kin. He saw friends he had chased as a child. He saw his guru and other holy men he had followed and sat at the feet of; he saw men and women of Noorian and its surrounding villages, now dead but alive in this river of eternity. He looked up the river, and in the distance he saw a water head emanate up high in the heavens and fall noiselessly and without turbulence to start the serpentine journey to the Sea of Truth and Enlightenment.

The avatar spoke. Without expression, it uttered, "Choose." The avatar pointed to the river, and Sant saw the women with breasts bursting with milk and bellies extended with fetuses, and he understood. He was to live again, another life. No *moksha*, but another opportunity to improve his karma and get closer to the ultimate goal of oneness with the One, eternal relief from the cycle of life.

He watched the succession of women float before him. There were women of all colors, of all races and regions and creeds.

And then he saw Punna, her arms outstretched as Ruldu rose out of the blackness and beckoned.

Sant entered the river.

* * *